MW01610888

# FAITH

## THE FAITH TRILOGY
### BOOK 1

## NICK NIELSEN

Edited by
LESLIE WATTS

LUMINIS PRESS

# PROLOGUE

Hi.

You …

Yes, you.

It's no accident that you're here. How could it be?

And I need you to listen.

You won't believe what I'm going to tell you. I wouldn't have. Not at the beginning.

You may even forget this message. In fact, it will probably help if you do.

Since it happened, the world's been in shock. All kinds of stories have been told by all kinds of people, all over.

Yet I've refused to speak about it. Because to understand it, you need to live it. Right from the start.

So that's where we'll begin. No matter how ugly, how crazy, or how embarrassing.

It'll move fast, and I need you to be ready.

But of course you are.

Otherwise, you wouldn't be here.

**1**

SUN RISING. Light blinding off the top of the disused factory, the three-storey hulk of a building sitting a mile downriver from London's city centre. Close enough to the water for the familiar rotten smell to be dogging my nostrils.

Tramping across the cracked concrete, I squint into the darkness of the entrance. The outline of several sprawled figures roves into view – crackheads slumped against the walls of the factory, most out cold while some stare vaguely back. And beyond them stand the muscle, two lines of guys with their shooters on display. And they're all six staring at me.

I fix my gaze on the reinforced door between them, stride right up to it, and bash my palm against the corrugated metal side.

A peephole slides open to reveal a set of dark glasses while the sound of distant voices reaches me from beyond the door.

I stare back into the lenses and hear a rough clank. The door's heaved open. The voices grow louder – a cacophony of bickering, chatting, and shouting – as I step through.

"It's a fucking *miracle*," Wynn says, the burn marks on the doorman's cheeks stretching as he gives me a half smile.

I don't reply. Just shift out of the way of the door when he slams it. And by the time he's hoisting the large metal bar back into place, the chatter's already hushing behind me. A tingle climbs my spine as I swivel to face the cavernous factory interior, and the sound dies completely.

Two dozen fellow grunts. All staring at me. Some stand on the wide concrete ground. Others on the upper floors, on the three tiers of scaffolding that Mandem have erected around the edges of the central space.

The muscle are there. The weapon and drug couriers, too. Plus my fellow thieves. And lastly the girls, a group of them leaning over the railing. Some of the grunts' expressions show excitement, but the majority range from resentment to scorn.

Perspiration forms across my back, and I pivot to face Wynn. "What the hell's this?"

"Ain't every day a bonded gets released," the doorman says, turning to his equipment rack.

My heart thumps, and I breathe deeply to calm it. Then lift my wrist toward the doorman. "Not my release," I say. "I need a recharge."

The doorman grabs a paddle-like tool off a hook. "Won't be long, though," he says, his half smile broadening. And some of the muttering starts up again. "And that means you've got a fair few pissed off. Cos soon, they'll be hustling for *you*."

I shake my head as he brings the tool up to the tracking bracelet. With a beep, the bracelet unlocks. And I can't help the sigh of relief as Wynn removes it from my wrist.

*Pay off the bond. Lose the tracker. Raid my security box. Disappear.*

"Jake!"

I spin. Liam's hurrying toward me with those long arms and gangly gait. The kid was pressed into Mandem less than twelve months ago, and he's rake-thin, barely sixteen, and looks five years younger.

"*Not here!*" I hiss under my breath as the kid gambols up.

Most of the grunts are staring again, many now flicking their narrowed eyes between us.

But the kid stops right before me. "Them skills," he says, his hands even miming the damn movements in the air. "I been working, and I reckon I'm ready—"

"*On your own*, Liam," I say and slope away toward Wynn and his sets of charged trackers. They hang from a high railing by different-length ropes, some so long they almost reach the floor.

Liam hurries up to my shoulder.

"You got to do this *on your own*." I keep my voice low and hold my arm up to Wynn, who's got a new tracker off one of the longer ropes. "I'm not gonna be around forever."

Wynn snaps the bracelet around my wrist, and I spot movement over my shoulder – another figure striding toward me. Relaxed gait, easy smile on his crooked features, though his neck muscles remain taut.

I shove Liam away as Max pads up to me.

"New partner?" Max drawls, staring Liam up and down as the kid shuffles off.

"Fuck no," I say. "Never trust anyone. You taught me that. Remember?"

Max continues to smile as I step toward Wynn's hanging bracelets to slip past him. But the grunt darts right in my way.

"You rolled with me once," he says.

Sighing, I lift my eyes toward the far-off ceiling while grabbing one of the hanging ropes below Max's eyeline. I begin tying a scaffold knot with one hand, just like the thousands of times I've practised before.

Max's eyes burn into mine. "You rolled with me, and now I'm due."

I hold his gaze while completing the knot by my thigh and then slip my forearm through the slack loop.

"You're due nothing," I spit.

His entire body tenses. I go to shove past him when his fingers shoot out and grab my wrist. My pulse fires, my stomach constricts, and I fling my other hand across. Clasping the middle of the rope and yanking it sideways hard, I slip the loop down my forearm and onto his wrist as I dart aside.

He leaps toward me. The rope tightens around his arm, and he gets jerked backward.

I spin around him and butt his forehead with my own. "It was an age ago, and when we *did* roll, you fucked *me* over," I say, my heart pounding.

He tries to grab me with his other hand. But I dodge and then swivel away, my gut still tight, and bump straight into a wall-like chest.

My eyes flick upward to find Don staring down at me. He's in his customary designer threads – T-shirt, baggy pants, and a diamond stud, along with a handgun tucked in at the waist. I stumble backward.

From nothing, a wide grin splits his features.

"Jake!" he says. "Last week, is it? You a young'un to have cleared your bond." Don claps me on the shoulder, leaving my ribs aching. "Seven years a grunt, and you're twenty-five. Right?"

Six long bloody years, and I'm twenty-three. Though I keep my trap firmly shut.

His smile lingers, however, and he motions me to follow him up a set of steps. On the first landing, I find two more enforcers waiting for us. Twist doesn't meet my gaze. He's leaning against the plywood wall in a threadbare shirt open over rippling muscle, rotating a flick knife between his fingers. Maddox, however, is dressed in designer jeans and jacket, and he's holding something out with one massive arm.

A suit. Silver grey in colour. A styled cut with almost invisible seams and not a crease on it. A high-end brand, for sure. Much pricier than even enforcers could afford.

Maddox's gold teeth are smiling also as he lifts the suit toward me. Don continues to pad down the passageway.

"Not that we won't be gutted to see you move on," he says. "Best thief and best earner we ever had."

I follow closely behind as we pass one of the side corridors with its endless row of mattresses and cupboards – one pair assigned to every grunt. My gaze stays fixed ahead to avoid glancing up toward my identical cupboard one flight up, the loose section of stud walling at its back with my spare security box key hidden behind that. While my main one's hidden under the insole of my shoe.

*Bond. Tracker. Security box. Disappear.*

Don stops in front of a door at the end of the passageway. "But we'll still be passin' the cream on to the bosses. Won't we?" he says. Then he pushes open the door and motions me through.

I approach the threshold. The room's one of the few they've fashioned at the back of the factory. It's twenty feet by thirty with four plywood walls, a stolen desk in the middle, and a man behind it.

Staring at him, my lungs seize, and I stumble to a halt.

Ryle, one of Mandem's top bosses. He's never seen. Hardly ever in the building, as I've heard it said. And now the guy's perched there in his silk shirt, his neck wider than his head. And he's staring up at me with fierce dark eyes.

Don shoves me in the back, causing me to stagger into the room. Then the enforcer steps in behind me, followed by Maddox and Twist, and they all take up positions around the walls.

I stand between them, my weight shifting, as sweat makes tracks down my back. And still Ryle stares at me with jaw clenched, somehow entirely motionless. The stand-off lasts an eternity.

Finally, Ryle rises to his feet. Stalks around the desk and whispers something in Don's ear. The enforcer nods, his gaze aimed at me the entire time. Then Ryle vanishes from the room.

My eyes track back to Don, who's ambling behind the desk.

"You're *proper* lucky. Y'know that?" he says.

I can hardly speak.

"They were gonna wipe your whole bond credit," he says and dumps himself down in the chair.

"*What?*" I can't help shouting.

His eyes narrow. "You broke the regs," he says. "Earnin' on the side, skimmin' the extra cash."

Every part of me goes cold. I clench my hands to stop them trembling while tensing my neck to avoid glancing up toward my hiding place.

Don drums his fingers on the desk, and I find myself staring at them, waiting for him to produce the familiar steel key. But there's no sign of it.

Don nods. "Smart move not actin' clueless," he says. "Cos we're wise to it. Got an insider sayin' you both did. And now we know you *rolled* together." The grin's back on his lips, and he glances over my shoulder.

The door opens behind me, and my stomach's already dropping. I spin to find Max standing there. The fucker. Maddox motions him into the room.

"That was—" I start.

"An age ago," Don says. "Right. We heard."

Then his grin vanishes, and he bangs his fist on the table. I jump.

"It matters none," he snaps. "*All* your scores are *our* scores. And skimmin' means stealin' from *us!*" He shouts the final word, and the sound's like a slap to the face.

I can only stare back.

Don's voice becomes dangerously low. "The bosses are bloody *livid*. Can't have some grunt breakin' their rules." He tilts his head. "Still, we fought hard for your grunt-ass, bagged you a way out with you nearly an enforcer, and all." He glances between Maddox and Twist. "See, we're permitted side hustles, if small. So the little beer money you been collectin' wouldn't mean much."

I swallow as Twist grabs up a loose bit of board and starts cutting chunks of wood off it with his knife.

"But the bosses gotta know you're *their* guy before that tracker's off," he says, pointing at my wrist. "So, we vouched you'd pull a goodwill job, a deed that proves you're willin' to make things right, something grand," he says with a nod.

My stomach plunges deeper.

"We said you'd be up for taggin' a whale," he says.

For a moment, I just blink back at him. He holds my gaze.

"They're impossible to get near," I stammer out.

"Not on the morrow," he says, his tone singsong and excited. "Launch bash for some posh new train. Moorgate. Gonna be plenty fat marks around, maybe even one or two of the gilded."

Maddox holds the priceless suit toward me again and grins.

"Yeah, because of the protection they'll have," I say, my voice almost a yell. "The place will be *crawling* with pigs. And if I swipe from the rich, you *know* they won't just arrest me. Word is that people like us are disappearing all over the city."

"Don't fall for every rumour you hear," Don says. "And fret not. We'll have your back."

My voice falters, my ribs squeezing. "*You?*"

"Yeah," Don says with a nod. "It's your gig. You plan it, but you'll be needin' a four- to five-man crew, for sure. And with that kind of mark, there'll be a large upside for everyone involved. *Plenty* of spoils to go round."

Each enforcer is smiling now. Even Max, who's bouncing up and down on his toes by the wall.

I shake my head vigorously. "No way. I don't do partners."

Don's smile vanishes. "Course you will," he says. "We stuck our necks out for this." He grits his teeth. "And you got any notion of what the bosses will do to you if you say no?"

They're all staring at me now. All the smiles gone. My heart hammers, my tongue like dust.

"Okay, okay," I relent eventually.

Don leans back. "Course it is," he says.

"But I'll roll with only one other," I say.

He stares back at me like I'm an idiot. "You'll use a two-man crew?"

"And it'll be Liam," I add.

"*What?*" he roars, shooting to his feet. And Maddox steps toward me from the side.

"You'd ice us out?" Don shouts. "With a kid that can barely totter? On *this* job?"

He stomps around the desk in my direction, and I stumble backward. Don reaches his hand out toward my throat. When Twist slams his blade down into the desktop. Everyone turns.

"Peace," he says. "Let him fuck it up. Let him piss off the powers. They'll just slap him with a triple bond before he's free of that thing." He points the tip of his knife at my tracker and stares at me. "We'll *own* you."

My insides squeeze.

Don leans toward me, his eyes burning. "But after all our graft, we'd still be losing this score," he says, indicating himself, then Twist and Maddox. "So, you're gonna square it by boosting some fat cat wallets right off the bat."

I force a nod. And Max fidgets by the wall before stepping toward Don. "But what about me?" he whines. "You said I'd—"

Don's hand shoots to the side, grabs Max's head, and smashes it into the wall behind him. The grunt collapses without a sound, but Don keeps his eyes on me the whole time.

"You'll be where Jake is if he fucks it up, either earnin' triple duty or at the bottom of the fucking river. *No* one steals from Mandem," he growls and then stabs a finger at my chest. "And don't be thinking of cuttin' and runnin'." He clasps my arm with the tracker. "If this stops transmitting for even five fucking seconds, we'll be hunting you down ourselves."

## 2

HIGH-RISE SENTINELS of steel and mirror tower above me as I slink across the concourse and through the chattering crowd.

Several hundred of the coiffed sharks in their extravagant suits and dresses all circle this palatial new train station. Built right in the centre of London's financial district, its glass atrium extends high above, like a giant face mask designed to keep out the stink of the city beyond.

As if.

My shoulders twitch, the early afternoon sun making my back itch through Maddox's fine suit jacket, and I can feel the weight of the three wallets I've already boosted. A few of the crowd eye me haughtily as I pass, their gazes sharp enough to etch glass. Though I make sure to keep moving, not to hunch.

I glance toward my chosen mark, forty feet away. The guy stands at the edge of a group of men, fingering his phone. Sufficiently isolated and sufficiently distracted.

Peering at the phone, I try to make out the model. It's slim enough. With a wrap-around display. *Shit.* Maybe? The crowd's milling by so fast, the parading bodies keep blocking my view.

I go to weave closer but stop, holding the line. Arcing around the mark, I move parallel to the tracks. The sprawling concourse is a hundred yards of sparkling marble tile with the exits along one edge and the tracks along the other. And almost all of it's scanned by movable CCTV, every camera position seared into my brain. I keep my gaze averted and slip around the convergence points.

An announcement booms from a stage before the tracks, and before I know it, I've glanced up at the golden clock face.

*Idiot.* I squeeze my fingernails into my palms and concentrate on the pain. A stopwatch in my brain counts seconds and minutes continuously. I know exactly how long I have left.

Just over eight minutes.

I'm about to squint at the mark's phone again when I notice my gut twist – my early warning system, my internal alarm. I swivel my head.

The police are out in force – at least twenty officers with their guns and uniforms by the exits opposite the tracks, like knots in a blue net ready to be drawn tight. Again, I scan the crowd, searching for those in plain clothes, for any faces I've glimpsed before, for anyone tailing me.

Seven minutes left.

My gut doesn't untwist, and my mind catalogues every risk, every possibility. Maybe the police? Maybe CCTV? And I've been spied boosting the wallets—

And then it hits ... Mandem.

Of course. The enforcers are bound to come, stir stuff up. My forearms tighten as I scan for them in the throng.

No sign. And no other evident concern, no obvious cause for my alarm. So, I close it down, counting the seconds and tensing my stomach muscles. Gradually, my heart slows.

As the tension eases, another announcement booms from the speakers, and I jump.

"Not long now, ladies and gentlemen!"

The crowd's attention shifts to the stage while I slip between them, my gaze straight ahead.

"With the very greatest pleasure, we present to you a

triumph of engineering!" a woman proclaims from the podium, her squawking grating at my ears.

I concentrate on keeping the scorn off my face.

"At three hundred miles an hour, the fastest urban connection train ever built!" the announcer calls out.

"So quick, its loaded passengers won't clock the crumbling burbs they're speeding through," I find myself muttering.

A lady in a ball gown frowns down her nose at me. I return her glare for an instant and then squeeze my shirt cuffs before pushing myself on. I force my gaze back to Liam.

The guy's between me and the tracks, dressed in his shoddier suit and fidgeting in the midst of the glittering crowd, only thirty feet from the mark.

My jaw clenches, and I come to a halt, my doubts starting to jabber. Though standing there, the image comes of Ryle staring at me, the fury in the boss's eyes, and I feel the tracker tightening around my wrist.

I raise a finger to my ear, making the first signal.

Message received. Liam begins the walk, spiralling in toward the mark and getting into position on his opposite side, the tracks beyond.

I can't help glancing at the mark myself. The guy's still toying with his phone, sneaking occasional glances at the shapely legs around him. I risk sidling a few steps closer, my eyes taking it all in …

The guy's shallow breathing, slouched shoulders, sluggish fingers tapping the display. Definitely in finance, not IT. And there's the pallid complexion, badly ironed shirt, and concealed paunch. A wannabe. Still hovering on the edge of the group, his body angled half-toward the other guys, and his gaze flitting between the beautiful creatures nearby as if they're going to eat him.

I peer again at the guy's phone, and my heartbeat quickens. It's the right model. I reach into my pocket for my own and grip it to make the casing all sweaty and familiar.

My internal count continues. Only six minutes till the train's due.

I eye the stage. An engineer joins the announcer at the podium, the big presentation about to begin. It will draw everyone's attention. The perfect moment.

My gaze finds Liam again, and I raise two fingers toward my chin – the second signal – and then stop. My gut's twisting again.

I turn my neck away from the stage and scan the exits. The police are still there. All two dozen of the bastards.

I swivel back to a sudden movement in the crowd ahead, a single file of children led by someone. A nun. Some kind of trip. They push past me, heading toward the tracks, the damn parade blocking my path to the mark.

My back muscles knit, and I clench the phone in my pocket, my mind continuing to count the seconds down.

*296, 295, 294 …*

The children file past me, and the nun steps to my side, raising a shaking arm to shield them from the swarming crowd.

A suited man almost barges into them, his pupils huge. On some kind of stimulant.

The nun glances up at me with a sharp gaze. "Will you help?" she asks, her voice gritty.

My hand goes to my chest. "*Me?*"

She rasps what I think is a yes before swivelling back to her brood. I follow her gaze. They're heading toward a sculpture by the tracks, twenty feet away. The ancient stone cross has a carved monk in prayer, almost completely engulfed by the surrounding crowd.

My eyes flit back to the children. Each one's dressed in a uniform of grey and black. Puritans. Unlike other Christian groups, the movement's not allowed to wear colours or use technology. And suspicion's etched in the little ones' faces as they gaze around at modernity's excess and wickedness.

*273, 272 …*

I focus back on the mark. The children are almost out of the way. The nun swivels to stare up at me again, fixing me with her gaze. This time her brow knits as if she can read our plan in my eyes.

My ribs tighten, and I open my mouth. But no words come, my throat so dry.

She sighs and turns back toward the sculpture, lumbering after her brood. I exhale slowly.

*258, 257 …*

Again, I lift my hand to give the signal, my internal alarm still ringing with no obvious bloody cause. My fingers hover in mid-air and perspiration coats the back of my neck while strange thoughts circle my brain … *Did the nun appear to make me think twice?*

I shake my head at my own bullshit and then scan the concourse one more time.

And there they are.

## 3

BEYOND THE CROWD, in the far corner of the station concourse, twenty yards on from the exits, stand three sizeable guys. Mandem's enforcers. Maddox and Don together, Twist hovering thirty feet further along the wall. All three staring straight at me.

*Shit, shit, shit.*

I peer closer. Don's holding up a small tablet – a GPS monitor – undoubtedly tuned to my tracker. Then he nods and smiles.

My heart pounds, heat rising inside. And I prise my gaze from the enforcers to the mark, taking a quick breath in preparation. Then I pivot back toward the stage, pushing down the tension in my stomach again and easing the alarm. And my eyes scour the crowd for Liam.

But the throng's growing denser around me. I risk going up on my toes, craning my neck. Eventually, I spot him. Twenty feet from the mark. Standing still, gazing blankly around.

My calves tense, and I stare intently at him. Finally, he spots me, and I raise two fingers to my chin. Message received again. Liam begins his approach, lumbering on toward the mark.

I swivel away from the CCTV cameras and then weave even closer to our target, only ten feet away. Me, the mark, and Liam – all in one line – the stage to our side. Liam continues to snake toward us, building up speed.

Fifteen feet from the mark. Ten.

A further announcement booms from the loudspeakers. I shut out the sound.

*244, 243 …*

Five feet. Liam puts his head down.

Collision. Despite Liam's gawkiness, he's definitely getting better, his movements smooth and contained. One second the mark has his phone out, the next it's gone.

"Hey!" the mark exclaims.

I watch him closely. The guy gives an indignant stare but remains rooted to the group. The surrounding men ignore the outburst and continue bantering among themselves. Profiling them, I counted on it.

Liam barrels on toward me, and his shoulder slams into mine. Something clatters to the ground.

"Oi!" I shout, the heat exploding inside – so easy – leaving my fingers tingling. "Watch it!"

I spin toward Liam as he scampers on, my arm raised in a sign of annoyance. Liam disappears into the crowd beyond.

I take a settling breath and pivot back toward the mark. Then I dip my head, narrow my eyes, and peer at whatever dropped before me. Make a show of it.

The mark shuffles his feet. I can feel him watching me from several paces away. Everyone else in the crowd's gaping at the stage.

I stoop leisurely to pick up the phone and turn it over in my hand, trying to look quizzical. The seconds count down in my mind, the train's arrival approaching fast.

*222, 221 …*

The crowd continues to thicken around me, their murmuring intensifying, the air buzzing with a growing sense of anticipation.

I force myself not to glance up at the mark. Yet still, the guy doesn't bloody react, doesn't make another damn sound. I clasp the phone tighter, my mind conjuring images of him having spied my approach, of him searching for the police right now.

I tense my neck and keep my gaze on the electronic display. While the desire grips me to step toward him, I anchor my feet. He's got to leave the safety of his group. It's the only way.

"Hey," the mark says, voice squeaky.

I allow myself a slow exhale and then glance up at the guy, squinting as if I'm looking into a bright light. He's staring down at the phone in my hand. I make a show of following his gaze.

"This yours?" I ask and then almost wince at the harshness in my tone, at how fucking terrible I am at the spiel.

The guy nods, keeping his eyes on it with his mouth shut. But still, he doesn't bloody move.

I hold the phone out.

"Thanks," he says. Then gives an embarrassed nod and eventually shuffles over.

I shrug slightly and hand it to him, trying but failing at a smile.

*195, 194 …*

I turn away from the mark, toward the exits. And wait, scanning the crowd once more. Normally, it takes only three to five seconds. For the really passive, ten to fifteen.

My gaze finds the enforcers. They continue to stare at me from the far side of the concourse, Don and Maddox grinning. Again, the heat rises inside me and memories flash through my mind …

I suddenly see my childhood home. All those years ago. Different gang, same approach. A few enforcers broke my nose in a beating, and they grinned then. My nose was never set properly. I inherited my mother's good looks, but looking good means nothing. And a crooked nose attracts attention.

"Excuse me."

I spin back around. The mark's standing there, gawking at me. Might have been for a while.

"What?" I ask again with that bloody sting in my tone.

I clench my teeth, swallow, and flex my jaw to soften it.

"My phone," he says.

I work my best surprised look – lips parted, eyes blank – and glance down at the screen the guy's offering me. A coloured bar moves slowly across the electronic display.

"What is it?" the guy asks.

I open my eyes wider, furrow my forehead. "A virus probably," I say.

"A *what?*" Somehow, the guy goes even whiter.

*Excellent. Definitely not in IT.*

"A virus," I say.

The guy taps in his code frantically to unlock the phone. I slide my arms behind my back and sign the numbers with my fingers for Liam. I even risk doing it twice with the swelling crowd around me.

The guy jabs more violently at the screen now as the coloured bar continues to creep across it.

"They're stealing your personal details, your browser history," I say, all from the script, though the words sound almost robotic in my mouth. "It gets sent to them and every other person in your contacts."

The guy's hands shake, and sweat sheens on his puffy neck.

Exhilaration sparks in my chest. *Right again. Heavy porn user. Has to be.*

"What do I do?" he says.

"Got virus protection?" I ask, speaking quickly, as the con maxims revolve around my brain … Misdirection, urgency, control the mark's attention.

The guy's eyes bulge.

"Here," I say and reach for the phone.

The guy gives it up. I press a combination of buttons to

call up new browser windows. And the guy's shock becomes obvious in his silence.

"I'm in IT," I say.

The guy nods blankly while the crowd continues to swarm around us, more of them pressing toward the stage to our side as well as the tracks and buffers behind it, the train's arrival getting ever closer.

I raise my head and gaze at him. "Bytedefender okay?" I say.

Another blank face and then a nod.

"Got an account?" I say.

Just a shrug.

I do my best disappointed sigh, and my fingers fly over the phone again. I call up a screen requiring personal information for a new account setup.

"Your details," I say and offer the phone. "So you can get the malware protection."

The guy simply looks at me.

"Be quick or everyone will have your personals," I say.

The guy grabs back the phone and starts inputting the information. He comes to the fields for his bank account details and stops.

*147, 146.*

My shoulders tighten. "There's no time," I say.

The guy stares at me for a moment and then back down at the phone, his fingers poised over the screen. They quiver, begin typing, and then stop once more. And he doesn't fucking move.

My heartbeat speeds up again, and I notice the twisting in my gut. I feel my gaze drawn away from the stage, to the edge of the space.

The crowd clusters thickly around us, the gaps between people shrinking. While, oddly, acres of room still exist toward the outside of the concourse near the exits.

I scan the empty area, searching for the cause. Then shoot

my gaze to the far corner of the space, toward Mandem, looking to them for some kind of clue.

But they're gone. And more of the enforcers' warnings come back to me ... *You'll use a two-man crew? On* this *job?*

The crowd continues to bunch around me. Maybe to get a better look at the new train? It's almost here. And my chance of an easy escape's closing, like the walls of a well pressing in. It's get out soon or be trapped.

# 4

WITH A JAB IN MY BACK, reality dawns. I swivel my head and grasp the phone Liam's pressing into my spine, keeping my body angled away from the CCTV cameras. I hold the unit down at my side.

104 seconds left before the train arrives.

I pivot to face the mark again. "You done yet?" I press, my voice barely calm.

The mark nods frantically as he enters the last of his bank details and offers up the phone.

I nod too and take it with my free hand. The creeping bar's gone – of course it is. It's all fake on my preprogrammed unit. The mark's phone has been with Liam the entire time. He didn't drop it. I dropped my own unit – the same model. And using the screen-lock code that I mimed, Liam will have extracted lots of helpful personal data – pin codes, account logins … everything useful in the world of identity theft.

Not my scene, but for the Mandem bosses, with this kind of mark, the data's priceless.

A lady passes close to my side, and I lean into her. Faking a collision, I grab the mark's arm to steady myself. He glances over, his attention diverted. I swap phones with my other hand and slip the preprogrammed unit into my inside pocket, opposite the three wallets I stole earlier.

The mark gazes back up at me. I return his phone. He blinks, and I force a smile as I turn.

*91, 90.*

Con done. I face the station exit, picturing Liam slipping away as I wait for the customary relief, the relaxation in my chest.

It doesn't come. My insides coil ever tighter.

I glance around. The throng continues to push toward the stage, hemming me in, clustering seriously tightly.

It's fucking weird.

Though the train *is* almost due.

I tense my stomach again, breathe, and focus hard on the descending numbers in my head, working to access the still-ness I've been able to conjure since childhood. I anchor my feet and concentrate, blocking out distractions – thoughts, sensations.

*84, 83, 82 …*

And gradually calm descends. My mind sharpens as the moment expands. But instead of closing down the alarm, I coolly observe the crowd.

The great and the good stand pressed around the stage, staring down the tracks just behind it while chatting in excited voices, every one of them straining to see the marvel of new technology. I crane my neck.

Almost everyone.

A guy right by the tracks – the prime location – is trying to push his way out of the throng. Elderly, unkempt white hair, an archaic-looking suit. He resembles a leper among royalty. A group of extravagantly dressed men have lined up against him, refusing to let him through, as if insulted by his very presence. Surrounded, the old man struggles for every step. He begins scrambling to get around the group, occasionally glancing over his shoulder toward the tracks. Perspiration coats his forehead, his eyes dinner-plate wide, his face chalk-white.

A strange chill prickles the base of my spine. Again, I try to breathe, to dampen my nerves. But fail. Then, barging for the exit, I stop dead an instant later, all too aware that if there *is* a threat, I might be running straight toward it.

I squeeze my fingers. Force my brain back to basics ...

Analyse, plan. Analyse, plan.

The crowd continues to push, walling me in. I swivel my neck. Pore over my surroundings – the excited horde around the stage and tracks, the security services by the side of the concourse, and the weird gap in between, still growing.

I fix my gaze on the edge of the packed crowd between the stage and station exits. And the breath catches in my throat.

Someone's moving ... or some*thing*. Dark shapes shift around the horde's edge. I get just a glimpse. Then it's gone. Some sort of rippling current corralling the crowd toward the stage. I keep blinking at it, my brain trying to compute, as a voice inside starts yelling at me to run.

But the sight's magnetic.

I find myself staring at the edge of the bunching crowd, straining to catch another glimpse of the dark shapes while I count on, mustering every ounce of concentration and holding on to the numbers as if they're floating debris in a shipwreck.

*72, 71.*

I feel the stillness deepen inside me. The moment expands. But the image of whatever's corralling the crowd refuses to resolve itself. My brain starts to ache, unable to comprehend.

The crowd presses in on me from all sides, pushing me further toward the stage. I concentrate on the memory of the fleeting glimpse and try to abandon all reason to still my doubting thoughts. The ache grows into a wild pounding behind my temples, and it feels like my skull might split.

A strange smell, acrid and burning like charred solder

from a circuit board. Like cordite. And a sound too, like a bell in a distant tower. The strange chill crawls up my back.

Again, I grasp for the memory of the dark shapes, focusing even more intently.

"Yes, child."

Low words, distorted, almost unintelligible. Even so, they trample my mind like stampeding animals.

I whirl my head from side to side. But the surrounding people remain oblivious, craning their necks to stare down the tracks.

"Let me help," the voice says again.

And the world explodes around me. A veil's ripped from my senses, as if I've previously been living a hundred feet underwater, staring through murky depths with my eyes and ears confounded by mud and slime. And now I've been catapulted above the surface.

I stare at the people pressing around me, at the glass dome above and the skyscrapers beyond. Everything glimmers. Every angle's impossibly sharp, every feature somehow crammed with detail. The air hums with a solidity that makes me want to reach out and touch it.

My attention falls on a lady pushing forward at my side, on her dress. Simultaneously I'm aware of the fabric's intricate weave plus every minute motion of the dress, of the body that wears it and every body to her every side.

It's transfixing … the movements of the entire crowd. Figures sway, lips move, limbs flex and straighten. A thousand shifts, a million, and each one somehow discernible in my mind. It's like I can feel them all.

I've trained myself to notice everything, but that's nothing compared to the insight that now bombards me. The conman inside me weeps with the possibilities, my normal analysis unnecessary, the computation effortless. The crowd's movements become predictable … as if it's all a giant tapestry before me, itching to be read.

The sound of the pounding bell continues. And realisation

dawns. They're bloody handclaps. And then the voice comes again. No longer distorted.

"You see?" A haunting tone from somewhere to my side.

Cold hands scale my ribs. The clapping stops. And despite my internal alarm blaring louder than ever, I turn my head toward the sound.

A blinding light, a few feet to my right, like gazing into the sun. I tense my legs and fight to avoid stumbling backward. The light dims, the heat diminishes, and the outline of a man emerges amid the crowd, yet with space on all sides. He's of similar size to me and somehow, simultaneously, much taller and broader. And *his face*. I have to avert my gaze, his beauty too painful to behold. I try my usual profiling – clothes, posture, movements – but my thoughts just can't gain purchase. It's like trying to scale a sheer glass wall.

But worse, with every thought, pain arrows behind my temples. I abandon my thinking and relax into the strange stillness. All around me, the shimmering scene remains. The crowd's movements grow more sluggish, as if time's slowing down.

*44.*

*43.*

*Shit.* The obvious occurs. I'm still counting, the numbers automatically descending in my mind.

*42.*

*41.*

And now an aeon stretches between each one. Life has become a set of freeze-frames, advancing ever so gradually.

"Startling, is it not?" The words reverberate around my head. "How feebly your world compares."

The movements on the concourse – so much more visible. I can take in the shifting attention of the police officers, the flows of the pressing crowd. All of it. And yes, the dark shapes again.

They're figures, yet not people, with a strange awfulness to their movements as if they flow rather than walk around the edge of the crowd, more fluid than solid. I can see they're herding the people inward, packing the throng ever more tightly around the stage.

"Yes, yes," the shining figure says. "Impressive, child. And to think you almost perceived them." The voice is like an elder talking to a toddler, with something else underneath – a hint of surprise.

And the words probe at a memory. Even amid the overwhelm, familiarity tickles my mind.

Then the man gives a deep sigh, which rattles my chest like thunder.

"But we can't have you witnessing any more," he says.

I blink. People continue to press forward to my side, and I feel my head being tilted downward, beyond its volition. I try to concentrate, to pull away, to force my chin back up. But it ends up stuck to my chest.

And I can't fucking move, my gaze averted from the shifting crowds, the movements on the stage, the white-haired guy's fretting. Yet the shimmering world remains indelibly printed on my consciousness – the solidity of the air, the detail inherent in each surface, the effortless awareness of every movement.

"Yes, I've been watching you and your schemes." The voice carries a strange amusement now, a lyrical quality. "You do not like your fellow men a great deal. Do you?"

I see images of the wealthy and powerful parading before my mind.

"Why is that?" the voice says.

And then excruciating pain, as if a scalpel's rooting around in my brain. I yank at my hands, trying to grip my head, but they remain glued to my sides.

The man sighs again. "I see," he says, the pain abating. "And so you deceive them."

Now my hand moves involuntarily upward; my heart pounds as it creeps toward my inside pocket. Despite every effort, my fingers remove Mandem's fake phone, and I offer it up to the man.

"Interesting," says the voice.

And with my gaze still fixed on my shoes, I picture him inspecting my phone.

"You know, we have more in common than you think," he goes on.

*Oh god.* A con. A gigantic con. That's what he's doing, what I've stumbled into.

"But you aim too low," the man says.

My fingers open. I can't stop them as they let go of the phone, and it falls, smashing on the ground. I stare at the ruin of my takings, my final payment to Mandem, my freedom. Yet I feel all my fiery rage sublimated. The chill coats me inside and out.

"The arrogant will be humbled," the man says, contempt lacing his tone. His glow shines brighter, and I can sense him staring out across the sparkling crowd. "Unchecked, all they ever produce is hollow, rotten." And then the contempt morphs into feigned levity. "Their wealth will not save them."

My body shakes. Something terrible's about to happen. I know it.

I scrunch my eyes shut and try desperately to restart my brain. Concentrating hard on coaxing each joint into action, each limb, my mind catalogues every minute movement.

Yet with each thought, the pain in my head augments, the scalpel rooting deeper into my mind. The heat intensifies against the side of my neck as I feel the man turning toward me. He barks a laugh like a cymbal crashing, and the invisible bonds around me tighten.

"I'm afraid we can't have you leaving, child," he says. "Your newborn eyes have glimpsed too much."

I strain to open my mouth, but no words come.

"We are not so different, you and I." The voice sounds almost whimsical. "And long ago, things might have been different."

Then the playful tone changes. "But they are not. It would be remiss of me to let you live."

Sweat breaks out across my whole body. Still, I strain desperately to move.

"I have enjoyed this little diversion, however," he says. "And take solace. You're better off facing the end now, given what is coming."

Then the man disappears, the glow to my side vanishes. And I can move again. My head shoots up, relief flooding through me.

The world's as it was. The veil's returned. Objects are one-dimensional. Surfaces no longer shimmer, and time advances at normal speed. A fissure forms in my chest, an ache like nostalgia, while the man's last words whirl around my brain.

And now I'm out of time. The period behind the veil felt like an eternity while my internal clock continued to count down throughout. Only twelve seconds till the miracle train arrives.

*11, 10 …*

The crowd continues to pack around me, pressing ever closer to the stage as they strain to glimpse the tracks to its side, only fifty feet away. While I dig my nails into my palms, the ache in my chest plunges deeper.

The mysterious man. *Clever.* He stole any chance I had of escape.

My eyes find the old guy by his white hair and odd clothes. Only ten feet from me now. And his movements are more desperate, clawing his way against the flow, past excited onlookers but getting nowhere. His face is paler than ever.

A commotion starts on the stage, an argument between the announcer and chief engineer. The announcer peels away from him toward the microphone.

"Our miracle train is not only on time but early!" she says, the pride in her voice tinged with worry.

Sudden whispers of concern break out from the crowd. And my stomach squeezes up my throat.

I peer toward the tracks. Something's in my way – the stone cross. The children stare on nervously from its base, the nun having herded them onto the surrounding steps. Then she swivels in my direction and looks directly at me with piercing eyes.

I avert my gaze. The air thrums as the crowd continues to press around the stage. There's hardly room to move. I blink hard but can't shake the white-haired guy's expression, the terror in his stare.

A scuffle on the stage. The engineer shoves the announcer away from the microphone.

"Ladies and gentlemen," he blurts out, "please make your way to the exits. Swiftly. Calmly."

The whispers diminish. Movement dies around me. A grey blur appears in the distance and hurtles in our direction down the tracks.

"Please!" the engineer says, now yelling. "Run!"

The grey blur grows, a sleek metal bullet careening toward us. Then the screaming starts. Everyone battles to flee.

I'm packed tightly amid the jostling, shoving crowd, everyone going absolutely nowhere. My mind flits, images forming of Liam, hopefully already well away. And I find my eyes fixed by the approaching blur, my pulse hammering behind my ears.

The train shoots into the station and hits the buffers at the back of the stage in a gigantic explosion, like a bomb blast. The shock wave slams into my chest, and I barely keep my feet. The train jumps the tracks and ploughs into the far wall, shattering it like a hammer through plywood. Then comes a ripping sound beyond anything I've ever heard. Metal shears. Glass smashes. People screech.

I glance upward. Debris falls as the atrium above us fractures. A metal girder plummets directly toward me. The children scream.

My mind stops, and my eyes fall. The nun's somehow right at my side, staring up at me again. Automatically, my arms shoot up. My fingers reach for her shoulders, my muscles coiling. And I go to push her out of the way of the falling girder—

But her hands are already on my chest, and she shoves. Her strength feels impossible. I'm thrown backward just as the girder smashes into the ground exactly where I was standing.

# 5

SHAPES FIRST. Moving. Then darkness again. A long corridor. Lights play on the far side of it.

There's a buzzing in my brain. Sound. Movement. Sharp objects shift beneath me.

Thoughts flicker, like embers sparking and dying in the cold of night. I try to roll over, to sit up, but my limbs won't obey.

I open my eyes. Shapes come into rough focus – jagged contours, strewn rubble. I blink, my eyes not working properly, like I've been plunged into fog. Something hovers before my face.

Dust is everywhere. With every breath, more fills my lungs. I cough and choke with a bitter taste on my tongue.

I go to sit up again, and I feel as if a switch has been thrown. Pain surges in on me. My head pounds and needles sting my hands. I shut my eyes, desperate to curl into a ball, but my warning system buzzes on, thoughts yelling *I'm not safe*. And I feel my awareness dragged kicking and screaming to the surface.

I squint. A wasteland, the dust like a barrier on every side. An awful silence presses in on me as my mind stumbles, memories slowly coming. I was at the launch of the new train.

Glancing up, I can just make out the dome above through the haze. Half-destroyed – a gaping hole with contorted metal edges like giant teeth. Shattered stone and twisted metal lie all around. None of it feels real. Images flash of the place before, all majestic architecture, sparkling marble, steel and glass. Now devastation.

I rack my brain. I was working, and the three enforcers came to check on me. They were on the edge of the concourse, far away from the impact. I peer out over the ruin toward the exits but can't make out anyone or anything through the haze.

Then my thoughts flit to Liam. He should have been long gone before the destruction. More memories come – the con, the phone, the mark. I put my hand down to push myself up, touch something warm and wet, and recoil.

Blood.

I stagger to my feet. Flounder. Sway. My mind keeps crashing. I gaze around, searching for signs of other people. Where moments ago were hundreds, I now only see bits of stone and sheared girders.

An enormous piece of twisted metal stands before me, like a tree splintered in a hurricane. An unmoving body lies near its base, and another. The smell of burnt dust is in my nose, plus a sickly sweet odour. It's like some kind of war zone.

I gaze at the girder in disbelief. I was standing just there. *There.* Where the wreck lies embedded in the stone floor. And somehow I'm still alive.

The memory's like a body blow. Her eyes. The nun. She saved my life. The pounding behind my brow becomes stronger, and I raise a hand to squeeze my temples.

The stone cross remains there, to my side, somehow still standing among the ruins. And grouped at its base … the children. Some cry, some hug each other, while most just sit in shock. The nun was right there with them, and she'd undoubtedly still be alive if she hadn't moved to push me out of the way.

I shake my head, and the memory comes of her piercing eyes. I try to blink them away, but the image won't go. Her hands on my chest, so strong. She was tiny, yet somehow she threw me clear. Saved *me* – a nonbeliever, a non-Puritan, a criminal. The heat grows inside, squeezing my ribs and tightening my fingers.

*Why?*

Noises. Distant shouts. They reverberate in the dust, echoing in from remote lands. The images of the bodies linger in my mind. And I try to push them all away.

All of it.

Then I bite my cheek and press my fingers together, focusing on firing up my planning brain to identify the coming threats.

I glance back toward the tracks, the train. Once state-of-the-art, it now resembles a crushed aluminium can lying against the rubble of the station's side wall.

Yes, there have been numerous accidents and breakdowns – power outages, computer failures, equipment breaking. And every time, I've assumed conspiracy. A company designing in a fault they'd be compensated to put right, the government and companies in each other's pockets, multiple cons on a societal level. Yet this feels very different. My eyes take in the broken bits of station around me. A lot of rich people died here.

Again, my thoughts fail. My concentration slips. The pain is yelling at me. I touch my right forearm, and my fingers come away red.

I clench my jaw, take a deep breath, and then try to count, try my focusing technique. But the effort is agony.

The shouts come once more, closer now. The dust is thinning, and I'm able to make out people moving toward me through the debris, checking the wreckage. I spy uniforms, and my shoulders tense. Paramedic crews.

I stumble away from the voices. They'll find the children and usher them to safety. It's incredible they all survived. The

Puritans will undoubtedly call it a miracle. I scrabble over the cracked concrete, past steel rods, where the stage once stood, and toward the shattered side wall. My arm burns with pain, and I shove the sensation away. Something's fighting for my attention – a memory – but it's slippery, just beyond reach.

As I scramble on over the debris, my foot hits something. An arm, a torn tweed jacket, a shock of white hair, a black briefcase – all poking out of the rubble.

I freeze. The memory tries to surface once more, and I see that jacket in my mind.

The paramedics shout again, trying to get someone's attention and describing clothes – *my* clothes.

I keep my eyes on the jacket, the white hair. The tension squeezes my throat like a noose. Still I can't remember. My thoughts spiral faster – the explosion, the panic, the devastation. More memories coming – stalking the location, planning the con.

I glance over my shoulder. The paramedics are only five yards away, picking their way through the wreckage as they head directly for me.

Still I don't move. The memories keep on coming – choosing the mark, selecting the equipment … Mandem's phone. My hand flies to my inside pocket. It's empty.

And something clicks.

Icy fingers squeeze my heart. The mysterious man, his immense power, how he glowed yet remained invisible from the crowd, how he controlled my body like a puppeteer.

I shake my head as if to scatter the insanities like birds into the sky.

A hand on my shoulder. "Sir." A voice in my ear. "Will you come with me?"

I shut my eyes, trying to remember. The mysterious man who ripped the veil from my senses. The shimmering world, the vast insight available. And here, standing among the ruins, the experience seems so far from reach, the strange familiarity ghostlike in its absence.

Thoughts surge, and with each one, pain skewers my brain.

"Can you hear me, sir?" the voice says.

Still I ignore it.

The mysterious man – also a conman – here to humble the arrogant. The slithering shapes herding the crowd around the tracks, packing people together so everyone would die. This was sabotage. My stomach turns inside out. The man's final words—

The hand shakes me. "Sir!"

I spin to face the sound.

"What's your name?" the paramedic says.

I stare into the guy's face, his eyes wide, his mouth tight, his eyebrows squeezed.

"Do you know where you are?" he goes on.

I try to focus on my words, my thoughts still tripping over themselves.

"Your *name*, sir?"

My lips just open. "Jake," I say, the word tumbling out before I can stop myself. I clamp my trap shut and pain sears through my jaw.

"Jake …?" the paramedic says. Then pauses.

I breathe, fighting to find some calm. "Wilson," I lie.

He nods, and I peer over the guy's shoulder. His colleague is searching the rubble to his side while two police officers are clambering toward me, the fuckers only thirty feet away.

"It looks like you've got a nasty cut on your arm, Mr Wilson," the paramedic says, gesturing to his colleague. "We need to take a look."

I keep my gaze fixed on the police and try to kick-start my thinking mind again.

The children and me. The only survivors. And I can still feel the stolen wallets in my inside pocket. I'll get searched. Pinned as a thief. And then blamed for the whole crash. There'll be pressure to find a culprit.

My hands shake, those rumours nagging at my brain, the chance that they'll bloody disappear me.

The two officers continue their approach, their expressions hard, only twenty feet from me now. Despite the pain, I tighten my gut and start the silent count in my head. And in my peripheral vision, I focus on the faces of the officers, waiting till they flick their attention to the side. Then I swoon, grip my cut arm, and rotate my body away from the paramedics as my knees buckle.

The nearer paramedic grabs me under one shoulder while my other hand moves like lightning, flipping the inside pocket and discarding all three wallets onto the ground. They fall among the rubble, my body as a screen, and I allow myself to be lifted back to my feet.

"I'm alright. I'm alright," I say, coughing.

The paramedic shifts around me to get a better grip, his feet about to step on the wallets. I dart my hand to my stomach and retch, stumbling a few feet forward. The paramedic follows, holding my shoulders to steady me.

"You sure?" he says.

I nod.

"But this is most likely concussion. Will need medical attention," the paramedic says, already scanning the area for other survivors. "Go with my colleague. We'll get you taken to hospital, checked out, stitched up."

He turns away. And my body tightens as his paramedic colleague steps to my side. Another damn uniform. He reaches for my arm, but I yank it out of his grasp. My wrist comes into focus. My right wrist. Bare. No tracker.

My heart seizes. I whirl around, scouring the surrounding rubble.

"What is it?" the second paramedic says.

Still I search, the same dire thoughts spiralling in my head … The wallets, the phone, the data, all lost. The tracker no longer transmitting. They'll think I'm trying to run. Don,

Maddox, and Twist all undoubtedly encamped around the ruined station right now.

"Please, sir," the paramedic says. The police officers are eyeing me suspiciously. Only ten feet away now. The paramedic places a hand on my arm.

I grit my teeth, tense my shoulder, and force myself not to pull away.

"Come with me," the paramedic says. And he tugs me gently toward the edge of the devastation.

I take a breath and eventually allow myself to be led away through the haze of dust. We pass the two police officers, their eyes fixed on me. I hunch my shoulders, keeping my gaze trained on the ground. I can hardly breathe as I wait for the command to stop.

The paramedic prattles on about blood loss, shock, nausea. And I tune him out, trying to think amid the growing dizziness while pain knifes my arm with each step.

The white-haired man in the crowd. His panic, his urgency to flee. He must have known what was about to happen. But how? And the mysterious man, his other warning … *It would be remiss of me to let you live.*

I peer through the haze, searching for any sign of him. Because the train crash was an act of sabotage, and I'm the only witness.

# 6

"EMERGENCY'S SENDING TWO MORE UP!" a voice shrieks from the nurses' station, twenty yards down the ward corridor and around a corner. "Burn victims, ten minutes away!"

My jaw clenches, and I grip my ears.

"A botched atheist attack, can you *believe* it?" the nurse prattles on. "All because of the train crash."

I push against a wave of exhaustion and strain to sit up in bed. My vision's hazy from the blood loss, and my stomach churns, my last meal over eight damn hours ago.

The nurse lowers her voice. "It's official now," she says. "Only one adult survivor. This guy, Jake Wilson."

My pulse scampers, and I train my gaze down the corridor, past the tightly packed beds, images forming of the Mandem enforcers coming for me. I try to force my planning brain into action.

But a nurse shuffles into view around the T-junction corner. It's the raven – beady eyes, wrinkled hands, and that awful screeching voice. And she's staring at me, bustling in my direction past the neighbouring bays, a puckered smile on her lips.

I scoot forward in my bed. She reaches the end of my bay and makes a lunge for the suit hanging over my chair. I grab for my jacket, the material all bloody and ripped. She grips a sleeve while my fingers clench the torn collar, pain searing up my forearm.

"Hand it over!" she hollers, her dried face all screwed up. "It's a health risk!"

"Yeah, well I need it!" I wheeze and lever myself up on the bed.

With a hard pull, I tear the tattered jacket from her grasp and then clamp it to my chest, feeling for the security box key I stitched into the lining. The spare is still hidden behind my cupboard in the factory.

The raven clenches her bony hands in mid-air. "I don't have *time* for this," she says. "There's only three of us covering the *whole ward*."

"And?" I say, my eyes ranging over the broken bits of equipment, the grime spawning in the corners like shadows. That's no surprise. Most hospitals are now in private hands, for exclusive use of the privileged. "Didn't make the elite cut?"

The raven stalks to my bedside table, huffing. Then grabs up the untouched pain pills from the paper cup. "You don't take these, you don't get 'em," she snaps.

I ignore her and shove my bundled jacket under the pillow behind me. Again, hunger gnaws at my belly.

"I could do with a bite, though," I say, my voice still raspy.

She tilts back her head and emits a laugh that's half spasm. "What do you think this is, room service?" She snorts.

My ears grate, and I watch her stalk off down the corridor and around the T-junction corner. She doesn't return. No one else does either.

I settle back into the bed and reach for the tongue depressor – a short, flat piece of wood – I stuffed underneath the mattress, and begin twirling it between the fingers of my stitched-up arm again. Pain flares and the stick drops. I clench my fist. Then swap hands. The wood moves faster – appearing, moving, disappearing, all in the blink of an eye. I use it to focus my mind, to distil the problem.

*No Mandem phone. No wallets. No tracker. No clothes. No plan.*
I calm my breathing.

*Yet—*

A homeless guy a few beds down screams abuse again, yelling for morphine. But the sound doesn't needle me. I feel a strange kinship with the guy – a fellow undesirable, an entire society stacked on top. And those fucking rumours. I shake my head. People like us disappearing – criminals, drifters, vagrants – being tortured, turning up dead. My mind flits back to the train crash, trying to find a connection. But the station victims were über-rich. It's totally different. Makes no damn sense.

I force a slow breath and begin the count. Focus on expanding the moment, on clearing my scrambled thoughts.

A new sound pops my concentration. The raven's voice again, irritated.

"Father, how did you get in here?" she says from around the junction corner.

I lean forward, trying to recall the sound of the ward doors clicking open.

"Apologies, my child," someone replies, the voice shaky, just barely intelligible. "There was a sole survivor, I believe, from the accident. Is he here?"

My insides squeeze tighter, and I grip the tongue depressor, my eyes tracking the sound.

An ancient-looking man appears around the corner, the ward doors and lifts behind him. It's a bloody priest, stooped, wearing a long habit, its neck and cuffs frayed to pieces. The guy's leaning heavily on a walking stick. Looks barely able to keep himself upright.

"Well ... yes," the raven says. "We shouldn't really, but ..."

She hesitates. I dig my fingers into the mattress. And she swivels in my direction, staring right at me.

"*Bitch*," I mutter and grip the sheet to thrust it off me, my core tensing to scramble out of my bay. Then stop.

The guy's squinting vaguely toward me as if he can't see properly. He overshoots the nurse's gaze and ends up staring much further down the corridor.

My muscles relax, and I shrink down in the bed, forcing my breathing to slow. I go completely still, ready for him to shamble right past me.

"Thank you, Sister," the priest mumbles.

The nurse heads back toward her station while the priest hobbles up the corridor in my direction. He taps the end of his stick against the floor as well as each of the beds he passes.

And with my breathing calming, I force my planning brain into action again, vain notions sparking of raiding my security box for Mandem. But they'd want to know where that much cash came from, far more than fucking beer money. My pulse quickens once more, and I tense my neck to avoid shaking my head.

The old man trundles on, and I find my gaze drawn to him. His grey hair is wild and dishevelled, tufts sticking out in several directions. His mouth gapes open, and both his eyes are dull, his gaze roaming over the wall above the bays. I hold my breath. The priest goes to pass my bay. Then stops, right at the end of my bed, and turns.

I blink.

The guy says nothing. Simply stands there, both hands held tightly around his stick. He stares at me for what feels like a fucking age. My throat goes dry. My back and legs itch. And I suppress the urge to move.

I hear a click from the doors to the ward. And like an idiot, I swivel my head.

Raised voices sound at the nurses' station.

"This is God's work, Sister," says one voice from around the corner.

"We have met the children and simply *must* see the man," says another.

I grit my teeth so hard it's like they might break.

Two more priests appear around the junction. They glimpse their older colleague by my bed and stride straight toward my bay in their newer habits, large crucifixes hanging around their necks. I bang the back of my head against the frame behind me.

The homeless man calls out to them. But they march past, chins high, shoulders back. Their near-blind colleague shuffles out of the way.

One priest steps right to my side, his bald head almost blinding under the working strip lights. His bearded colleague picks up the chart from the end of my bed with his fingertips.

"Jake Wilson," he reads and then drops the scientific readings as if they might contaminate him.

Puritans. My hands grip the sheets.

He raises his eyes and smiles expectantly at me. Then he opens his mouth. I jab a finger back down the corridor. The bearded priest's smile morphs into a frown. Still, he holds my gaze.

"Not buying," I say. "Not interested."

"How can you say that?" he asks, genuine surprise in his voice. "It's evident God is interested in you."

I scoff, and pain stabs at my ribs.

The bald priest at my side leans in, his eyes wide. He resembles an egg. "He delivered you from the heart of darkness, my son," he says. "For a sacred purpose."

"That's your angle?" I mutter and glance away. "There's always a fucking angle."

"Surely you feel gratitude?" the bearded priest presses.

"And the hundreds dead?" I say, swivelling back.

The man straightens, chest out. "Modernity is an illness, replete with gluttony and pride," he says. "These failures are not accidents. They are symbols, warnings …"

I stare back into the priest's gleaming eyes, his smile wide. There's total surety in his expression. And I imagine all modernity's recent failings scrolling through his mind – smart energy grids failing and killing scores of the infirm in winter; driverless cars inexplicably colliding on motorways; the continual increase in plane crashes; train derailments. All signs of God for the growing Puritan movement. More people turning away from technology every day.

I shake my head. "There was no miracle. I told you. I'm not buying."

The raven bustles forward to the priest's side. "Father, please," she says and forces a sinewy arm across him. "Patients are being sent up. We've no time for visitors right now."

She moves to escort both priests back down the corridor. And I glance past them, searching for their older colleague, the partially blind guy.

There's no sign of him.

The bald priest allows himself to be led toward the T-junction but then stops and swivels on the spot.

"Be careful. Judgement is coming," he says, his pompous voice and single digit raised to all. "Society has become a dwelling for every unclean spirit, every unclean mind. It must be purged. *Will* be purged!"

The raven continues to shove as he prattles on. I grab up the tongue depressor again and start twirling it between my fingers. The Puritan's voice ebbs around the corner.

Another click sounds, and I sit up straight, my heart pounding. There's the sound of trolleys rattling past the nurses' station and then numerous yelling voices, both the priests' and a couple of new ones. After a while, the shouts grow loud enough for me to make out the words.

"Atheist barbarians!" the bearded Puritan seethes. "Modernity's failings—"

"Are pure chance!" an atheist calls, his voice trembling with rage. "And we will prove it!"

"By attacking religious sites?" the bald priest yells.

"By demonstrating there's no bigoted god!" a second atheist calls out. "No divine hatred of progress ..."

The argument continues, both pairs bellowing louder, while the raven screeches in the middle of it all, desperately trying to keep them apart.

I close my eyes and let my head fall back onto the pillow. The crazy things people believe. Manipulation on all sides.

## 7

LATE AFTERNOON. The hospital ward's quieter, my bed's soft, and the heat's like a physical weight on my eyelids. My eyes droop, and the tongue depressor falls from my fingers to hit the floor.

I sit bolt upright and blink wide. No one around. I lean down to pick up the wood. Squeeze it. And try to drive my mind onto Mandem. Yet for the hundredth time, my thoughts circle back to the station, to the war zone it became ...

Who the hell sabotaged the train? A rival company? The government? Then there was the mysterious man. A shiver runs through me at his final words ... *You're better off facing the end now, given what is coming.*

My ribs tighten, the strangest thoughts circling my brain. Should I go to the authorities, the police? I shake my head and rub my eyes with my palms. No one would believe a word of it. Him controlling my body, the shimmering world, the white-haired guy's panic before the crash, the dark shapes, the nun saving me. Not a fucking word.

Another shriek sounds from the nurses' station. "Concussion patient, he's refusing pain relief!" the raven calls. "Demanding things like we're some sort of hotel."

The muscles in my legs and arms tense. The new stitches pull. The pain builds.

"Just call the orderlies if he gives you problems," the raven prattles on.

One more tyrant on the march.

I pull the sheet up over my paper-thin gown. And in that instant, I'm back in my mother's house, hiding from the gang. Eight years old, folded up on a cupboard shelf. Waiting, eyes screwed shut. I grip my head to try and clear it.

The nurses step into view around the corner, my mind already picturing the next specimen – a baboon, a hippo, a vulture ...

No.

She's younger, not cast adrift in middle age. Early or mid-twenties, her figure slim and tall. Her immaculately starched white uniform lacks even a single crease with an identity badge pinned flat on her lapel. Her long brown hair's tied up behind her head, every strand in place.

She pads toward me as the raven blusters away down the corridor.

"Mr Wilson?" she says, stopping at the foot of my bed. "Jake? How are you feeling?"

I focus on the sound, noticing a slight accent at the end of the sentence, like she's trying to hide it. Polish? She's looking at me, her eyes fixed, as if she's genuinely waiting for an answer.

My pulse quickens. And I scan her for clues of her game. She's beautiful, no doubt – heart-shaped face, prominent cheekbones, and large hazel eyes. But she wears no make-up, no jewellery either. Just a simple chain with a crucifix around her neck.

Puritan? My jaw tightens.

"You do not want your medication?" she says, with a nod toward the empty paper cup on my bedside table. Her eyes never leave mine. "That's fine."

I feel myself frowning. She steps toward me alongside the bed. And my hands scoot me backward. Beauty is just another means of manipulation.

"You look pale," she comments, leaning over. "May I take your temperature?"

I find myself nodding. And she gently places a handheld thermometer in my ear. My thoughts jump to my mother. I can't help it. Memories come of her before—

I shut my eyes, and my insides harden.

She removes the thing from my ear, examines it, and nods. "Are you eating?" she inquires.

I shake my head.

Her tone turns disapproving. "You must," she says, sounding so bloody earnest. Her smooth forehead's etched by a single line.

"I can't," I say, my voice barely audible. And I nod in the raven's direction.

This time the younger nurse shakes her head. "I do not care about the time," she says and then smiles. "I will get you something." She busies herself with the chart at the end of my bed. "You have lost blood," she goes on. "You must sleep."

Visions flash of the mysterious man, of Mandem's enforcers. My heart beats faster, my fingers grip the sheet, and before I can stop myself, I'm glancing down the corridor toward the junction and the ward doors beyond.

She follows my gaze. "Are you alright?" she asks and puts down the chart. She swivels back to me. "Is anything wrong?"

I hold her gaze, focusing hard on banishing the images while keeping my mouth firmly shut. She doesn't avert her eyes. Simply holds the silence for a long while.

"No," I say eventually, the word coming out all hoarse.

She fixes me with a doubtful gaze. "Okay," she says. "If you are sure." Then after another moment, she starts back down the corridor, her neck turned. "But I will return to check on you later."

I breathe a sigh of relief and watch her pad away without pretence, either entirely ignorant of her power or giving a fantastic performance.

But which is it?

## 8

IMAGES OF DESTRUCTION. Smashed stone and torn metal. A wasteland. The sky burns red, blood leaching up from the horizon. I'm a small child, walking alone amid ruins. The air sears my skin. Bodies lie strewn among the wreckage – limbs twisted, broken. I can only stumble, my tiny arms wrapped around my middle. A creeping hollowness fills my every pore.

Something's coming. A wall of wind, far off, as tall as the sky. It rages toward me across the landscape, sweeping everything away. Death approaching – somehow, I know it. I hunker down, scrunch my eyes closed, and wait for it to rip me apart.

But then the wind softens and cools. The howling diminishes, and a new sound begins, gentle and soothing. My muscles relax. My arms fall to my side. I open my eyes and blink.

An image forms, unfocused – long hair over one shoulder, the warmth of a smile. A tender touch on the back of my hand. A fresh scent's in my nose. And that face – I've not seen it for years, for lifetimes.

I scramble to maintain the vision, to prolong the dream.

Her hair's tied up. Strange. She normally wears it loose,

like strands of silken gold. She's staring at me, a soft light in her eyes. All her attention on me, just as I remember. It feels like nectar, like sunlight. Love itself. And I curl up under her shining gaze, the knots at the heart of me loosening, all concerns dissolving in an endless moment.

I blink again and glimpse a plastic band on my wrist. The soothing sound still echoes in my ears. A shushing.

Reality slams into me. I'm lying in a foetal position, on a hospital mattress, and someone's touching my hand. My head shoots up. The young nurse is sitting on the side of my damn bed.

"It is okay, Jake," she says. "It was only a dream."

The shock's like a jolt of electricity. My cheeks flush hot, and I jerk the sheet up over me.

"You talked in your sleep," she says.

I shut my eyes and force a slow breath, trying to calm my racing heart. But the vision of my mother returns – so damn vivid – like she was sitting right there. And I feel again the exquisite joy of her presence along with the stabbing pain of her loss.

I blink and see the nurse once more. Focus on her image. Try to order my thoughts. Mandem, money, escape …

But memories keep cascading through my mind. Lazy mornings, lying in bed, my mother and I telling each other stories, the sense of time suspended. I played with her hair, and she called me angel. I never knew my father. She was my everything. But tragically, she couldn't stay. The dark moods would take her. I'd try everything to help, but nothing did. She was powerless. Terrified. Then despairing. And so she took drugs. Then more. They stole her away.

I open my eyes. The nurse is still there.

"It's okay," she says again.

She reaches for my hand. I yank it away, heat rising in my chest. My legs are damp with sweat as I take a sharp breath, beginning the count to shut down my thoughts.

"You were calling to someone. May I contact them for you?" she asks.

I glance away and shake my head. The shame cramps my ribs, squeezes tears to my eyes. My throat feels like barbed wire has raked it.

"Water," I croak, my hands clenching the sheet.

She reaches for the jug on my bedside table. My fingers tremble as I take the cup from her and lift it to my lips. My insides burn. And despite every attempt to empty my mind, the memories keep coming …

The gang that preyed on my mother. Initially, they came just to deal. Then they experienced her presence and stayed, no matter how hard I tried to make them leave. They kept feeding her drugs. Deepened her addiction. As a kid, I received more beatings than I could count.

The memory comes of the final time I saw her. The image still flays me. Fourteen years old. She was stoned, standing in the hallway of our home, her eyes like glass. She didn't even notice as I waited in the doorway, my bag packed over my shoulder. She stared at me – her angel – blinked and turned away. And I left.

I sip from the cup, my hands still shaking. The fucking gangs. Of course, leaving home, I stumbled straight into their webs, eventually to Mandem. My entire body tightens. They'll know I'm alive by now. Might already be in the bloody building. I shrink into the mattress.

The young nurse leans toward me. "The accident, what happened?" she asks, her voice almost a whisper. "Do you feel you're in danger? Tell me. I want to help."

Once more, the mysterious man's words ring inside my head … *It would be remiss of me to let you live.* The nurse gazes intently at me as if reading my mind, that single line creasing her forehead.

"Except for the children, you alone survived. Just you," she says. "And you have almost no injuries. What are the chances of that?" Still she stares at me, and I can't look away.

Again, her image morphs into my mother. And I feel my mouth open, words poised on the tip of my tongue.

"People are calling it a miracle," she says. "What did you see?"

The nurse swims back into view. My chest constricts, my throat tightens, and I feel myself shutting down.

She takes a deep breath and smooths down her uniform. "That's fine," she says, straightening up. "No pressure, no more questions."

She gazes down. And I manage to avert my eyes.

"If you want to talk, I am here," she says and pops a few pain meds into the paper cup on my side table. "Just in case ... to help you sleep."

I simply nod.

"I will see you shortly," she says and then begins padding away.

The air trickles out of my tight chest. I glance from her to the tablets but then leave them be, stretching my arms instead.

Time to get out of here.

# 9

THE NURSES' screeching voices echo down the corridor as I scoot to the end of my hospital bed. Night's taken hold. The curtains are pulled shut around the bays, and only a few of the lights are still on, the shadows deeper along the edges of walls and floor.

I peer out of my bay. A set of double doors stands in one direction, the junction to the nurses' station in the other, twenty yards away. Beyond the junction, the corridor continues straight for another forty yards to a further set of double doors, beds lining each wall. I've gone to piss a few times. Got lost till I learned the layout of the entire floor.

I lean out a little further into the corridor. There they are. The raven and another nurse, her face more fish than bird, resembling one of those deep-sea creatures. Their ward round's almost over, and they're busy distributing the final medicines from their cabinet.

Serious riches inside – a way to placate Mandem. *If* I can get the drugs without the nurses noticing they're gone. Then get clothes, get out of the hospital, and get the medicine to the Mandem bosses. All before the enforcers find me. Or they'll just steal the drugs and say I had nothing.

I clench my jaw and bring my thoughts back to the plan,

to the location of the nurses and their cabinet. Just before the junction, with four more patients to visit. I pull back into the bay and lick my lips.

I'm fed, watered. The young nurse watched me the whole time before heading off on her break, as if checking I'd take proper care of myself. So fucking weird. A shudder runs through me. Still the image keeps coming of my mother.

I squeeze my fingers together and listen hard. The voices grow louder. Two more patients. I've mapped the nurses' movements all day. The timing needs to be bloody perfect.

I do a last check of the plastic bag tucked into the hem of my underwear. Heavy coin. Shard of glass. Length of string. All my scavenged items inside. Then I slip out of bed and shove the pillows under my sheet, creating a man-shaped mound in the low light. The cooler air nips at my calves.

My feet take me to the far side of the bay. Aside from the sparring nurses, the corridor's still empty. Everything's quiet. Just the faint sounds of patients snoring, along with my pulse thumping behind my ears.

I smile, finally active again, the familiar adrenaline kicking in.

Sounds reach me of keys jangling, of the first drawer opening. I ready myself, picturing them finishing their ward round, counting the drugs in the medicine cabinet.

The second drawer opens. And I step into the corridor, swivel away from the voices, and begin the timer in my head. Then I pace toward the double doors, keeping to the shadows, all too aware of the nurses twenty yards behind me down the passageway. Absolutely no cover in between.

I force a steady stride, the rubber floor pulling at my bare feet. And the seconds count down in my mind.

*Fifty-eight, fifty-seven …*

The double doors approach, the remaining half of this corridor on the other side. I check each bay I pass. Most people are dozing or fully asleep already. No one gives me a second look. I push through the double doors, keeping my feet light.

*Forty-four, forty-three.*

I hurry along the empty corridor, out of sight of the nurses. Past more bays – a woman out cold, a man sitting up reading in bed. I reach the toilets at the end of the corridor and allow myself a glance over my shoulder. Still no one.

I slink inside the far cubicle and pull the door closed behind me. Twenty-five seconds left. And here, the pace changes. My hands fly.

I slip one end of the string onto the plastic knob at the end of the emergency alarm cord, the loop prepared beforehand. One yank and it's tight. The other end of the string goes over the inside door handle, right at the end for maximum leverage. And my fingers tie a quick fastening knot.

*Five, four …*

I dart out of the far cubicle and yank the door closed while giving the string one last pull, fastening the loop around the inside handle and tightening the string between handle and alarm cord within. The glass cuts the excess string. And with the coin, I work at locking the door to the far cubicle from the outside.

It doesn't fit the groove. The coin, too thin, keeps slipping.

Sweat prickles my scalp, and I barely stop myself from scrambling back up the corridor before forcing a calming breath.

I dash inside the nearest toilet cubicle, grab some toilet paper, and moisten it with my mouth. Then I stuff it into the outside of the far cubicle lock before shoving the coin into the groove. After a few tries, it triggers the mechanism, locking the door from the outside.

My heart beats faster. I'm ten seconds behind schedule.

I dump the coin and paper into the plastic bag, leap back into the near cubicle, and yank the emergency cord. The high-pitched screeching is like a dozen crows in my head.

I bolt back out of the toilet and sprint up the corridor

toward the double doors. Just before them, I slide to a stop and listen …

There. The beat of hurrying footsteps from the other side. I grab at a curtain and scamper inside the nearest bay, tugging the thin material around me.

The woman in bed is still unconscious, a drip connected to her arm. I hear the double doors swish open beyond the curtain, the annoyed muttering of the raven, her heavy steps passing by.

I start my internal countdown again. Run through my calculations once more, the time the diversion will buy me. At least ninety seconds.

One alarm screaming and an empty corridor means the nurses will try the other cubicle, which I've locked with a coin. And as soon as they pull the outside handle, they'll tighten the string I've attached to its inside counterpart, triggering the second alarm. So they'll think the offender's inside. With no easy way of turning off the alarm without security, there'll probably be lots of shouting and banging on the door first.

That's the plan.

With the raven already past, I slip out of the bay and step up to the double doors. I peer through the porthole to the corridor on the far side, my shoulders tightening. It's empty.

I dart through the doors and hurtle up the corridor toward my bed. When I'm within five bays of it, barked words sound from the nurses' station up ahead, followed by a phone being slammed into its cradle. I stumble to a halt.

The other nurse – the fish – has alerted security.

Then her shuffling footsteps approach from around the junction corner, and I dive into the next bay without looking. I spin to face the bed, breath held.

The guy in the bed's sleeping.

Same approximate size as me – average height, strong shoulders, wiry build. Plus, a nice-looking watch sits on the bedside table, a satchel on the floor. My fingers tap my lips.

The fish hobbles past. I glance again at the guy's stuff before pulling my gaze away. The double doors swish closed, both nurses soon at the toilets. I dash back into the corridor and barrel past my bay.

Finally, the medicine cabinet comes into view, a few feet before the junction to the nurses' station with the ward doors and lifts beyond. I skid to a stop beside the cabinet and scan my surroundings. Corridors still empty on both sides. No sign of stirring patients. The toilet alarms only just audible through the double doors.

I drop to my knees, heartbeat thumping, and fix my eyes on the cupboard door. Closed. Which means they've finished the medicine count. I check the mechanism and my exhilaration spikes.

Closed but not locked.

I fling open the door and end up staring at boxes upon boxes of pain meds – oxycodone and diamorphine, the pharma companies making a fucking mint. It's not compensation for losing Mandem's phone, but it's something. And despite my injury, my hands move like a hummingbird's wings. Bigger packets first. I tip their contents into the plastic bag, close and replace them, my ears still trained on the surrounding corridors while my thoughts start to flit to what's next.

Drugs. Back to bed. Then work out the rest. With the cabinet door closed, the count having been finished, the nurses won't spot the missing drugs for hours.

Twenty-five seconds to go. I shove the last of the large packets back into place and I'm reaching for the first smaller one when the main ward doors click open behind me, just around the corner of the junction.

My hands go still, and I listen for clomping boots, for the telltale sign of security guards. But it doesn't come. Along with a sudden cold against the back of my neck, a strange sound emanates, more slide than step. Then the scent of burning metal.

## 10

I shove the cabinet closed, leaving the smaller boxes of medication, and leap to my feet, my plastic bag in hand and my internal alarm ringing loudly.

Still no footsteps.

The nurses' station lies just around the corner behind me, and my mind conjures images of dark forms sliding quietly past it.

I sprint back toward my bed, my thoughts darting to the nurses. Undoubtedly still at the toilets, banging on a locked door, half a bloody ward away.

Careening past a table in the corridor, I grab a bottle of hand sanitiser and swivel toward the homeless guy. He's finally sleeping peacefully in his bay, the air around him empty of his ranting.

After a moment's hesitation, I lift the bottle and toss it at him as my feet scrabble past, a weight forming in my chest. It arcs down, hits him in the stomach, and bounces onto the floor.

The obscenities start as I jump beyond the curtains into my bay. I grab my bloody jacket from underneath my pillow and begin ripping at the stitching, my fingers shaking in the growing chill. The key comes free. No damn pockets. I throw it into the plastic bag, along with the medicine.

The double doors further down the corridor finally swish open, and both nurses hurry past my bay. My hands stop, visions forming of them finding whoever's entered the ward, confronting them …

"Can I help you?" the raven says.

I listen hard. There's an edge in her voice. And there's no charming response from Don, no veiled threat from Twist.

No reply at all.

The chill descends my spine.

"It's pretty irregular, pretty late to visit, no?" the raven goes on, her tone tentative, lacking its normal bluster. The homeless guy's also gone silent.

Bag in hand, I slip to the edge of my bay and into the corridor, in full view of the intruders. I keep to the shadow of the curtains and hurry four bays along, breath held.

No one shouts.

I steal into the bay with the nice watch. The guy's still asleep. I open the cupboard as quietly as I can and pull out a set of clothes – trousers, shirt – and start to dress.

"What are you here for?" The raven's voice again. Louder. Tone just as taut.

I rotate my head, trying to pick out some kind of response while gooseflesh forms across my shoulders.

Still absolutely nothing.

Trousers on, I stop dressing to throw the plastic bag into the guy's satchel, grab up his shirt and shoes, and creep to the end of the bay. I peer around the curtain.

Two guys stand in front of the medicine cabinet. Uniforms. Badges. I force myself to breathe.

Police.

The officers are ignoring the nurses' protests and slinking down the corridor in my direction. While my mind yells at me to hide, I risk another half step forward for a better look.

There's something else.

Their clothes. The uniforms are spotless, the shoes shine. Odd for beat police. And their movements ... They hold their upper bodies too still, their motions more of a glide than a walk. In the dim light, I find my gaze drawn to their shadows. They don't make sense. It's like they're separate creatures, misshapen animals clinging to their heels.

The sight's mesmerising. Cold needles prick my whole back, and my head starts to pound, a part of my brain whispering vain prayers at them to keep on walking ... Past my bay, past me, and on down the corridor.

But both officers halt right at the end of my bed, swivel toward it, and disappear behind my curtains, poised to discover nothing but pillows under the sheets.

My heart thrums as every muscle tightens. I take a quick breath, begin the count, and try desperately to find some calm, to expand the moment, to be able to fucking *think*. But my thoughts die so quickly, memories taking their place – the shimmering world, the mysterious man appearing, controlling my body ...

I banish them and end up whirling around, staring at the inside of the guy's bay, focusing on nothing.

"Where the devil?" the raven's voice sounds, and the nurses' footsteps clatter to the other side of my bed.

My lungs seize, and I stumble out into the corridor, my hands full. A great urge grips me to spin around, to glance behind me. And I tense my neck, keeping my gaze fixed forward.

The double doors. More corridor. The toilets. Then another exit on the far side. Then the memory hits me of the electronic lock I spied there earlier, one that needs a fucking security pass to get through.

I hear the scraping sound of my bay curtain being yanked back.

I risk blanking my mind again, my heart stampeding. And before images of the mysterious man can press in, I follow my first instinct and ram the double doors with my shoulder, slamming them against the walls. The noise explodes in the silence. Then I wheel back around and dart behind the curtain of a bay on the nearside of the doors with doubts shrieking in my head.

I fling on the rest of the clothes – shirt, jacket, shoes. No socks. No time. My injured arm burns with the effort.

Feeling eyes on my back, I spin. An older woman's sitting up in bed at the end of the bay, her gaze narrowed. A simple cross stands on her bedside table. No equipment around her.

A Puritan.

I sense her judgement, and it sparks the heat in my chest. My eyes narrow in return, and her face turns white as she hunkers back down under the sheets.

The uniformed men speed past with that strange sliding sound, their heavy boots making hardly any noise. And I find myself staring through the tiny gap in the curtain, my eyes gripped by their shadows. They're like sticky tar pooling behind their heels, spreading toward me as I watch.

A growing numbness grips my body, and it takes every effort to avert my gaze, to rip my head around.

The figures push through the double doors, the raven and the fish right behind them. I wait one second. Two. Then throw myself back into the corridor and bolt the other way.

I sprint beyond my bay, reach the junction, and dash around the corner, scrambling past the nurses' station. Then I skid to a halt and swivel back to lean over the desk.

Three handbags – two large, one smaller. Got to be hers, the young nurse's. It's sitting perfectly upright, the strap wound neatly. Everything in place. I peer closer. Her spare security pass sits inside the zip, a phone and wallet visible underneath.

I scoop up the bag and grab a stethoscope that's beside it on the desk. Then swivel my head and listen.

No sound from beyond the junction.

I leap toward the ward doors and slam the release button at the end. A foyer beyond. Two lifts – the far one ascending from below, the other already at my level. I jab the call button and, an instant later, the nearer doors open. Then I jump inside and hit the button for the ground floor, before diving back out of the closing doors.

Stairwell.

I bound through the stair doors and, pushing against every instinct, leap up the steps, not down. My mind conjures up the hospital architecture. This stairwell in the middle of the building, a long reception area on the ground floor, and an exit to the street at each end.

I reach the empty foyer of the floor above, the entrance to two more wards. Both doors locked. The stolen security pass turns the electronic lock green. I pause on the threshold and glance down at the card.

Natasha. That's her name.

I grab out her phone, thrust her handbag into the satchel, and sling it over my shoulder. Then I shove the stethoscope around my neck and smooth down the front of my stolen shirt. And after a quick breath, I wrench the door open and dash through.

A nurse stands up from behind her station. She stares at me, her eyes bleary and mouth open.

"Drugs. They've been lifted," I almost yell, the moronic words simply tumbling out. "I'm trying to find security."

The nurse closes her mouth and says nothing.

I rush past her and dart around the corner. The corridor stretches forward and back. The exact same as the floor below. All the bay curtains are pulled, and a set of double doors lies ahead.

A chair screeches behind me, and I can feel the nurse peering around the corner, staring at my back, a hotline to security right beside her.

I keep moving. Feeling the satchel with the drugs against my hip, I force my attention onto the phone in my hand, onto getting a message to the Mandem bosses.

Pushing through the double doors, I turn the phone to and

fro under the dimmed lights, hunting for the fingerprints, the smudges of grease.

But of course, the screen's immaculate. No telltale streaks. No code to decipher. I grip the phone and squeeze, images flashing of Natasha, fucking spotless in her uniform. My fingers shove the phone back into the satchel.

At the end of the corridor, I shoot through the door into another foyer and then into one of the far stairwells.

I go still.

No sound from above or below.

Creeping downward, I listen intently. Third floor. Second. First. And then ground level. I step lightly toward the door and peer through the porthole window, my gaze landing on the hospital exit. Freedom. Only fifty feet away.

My heart beats faster, and I scan the lobby in between. It's late at night, but the space is still packed. Patients. Families. Some people sit, others lie on the floor asleep. Everyone's undoubtedly desperate to see a doctor.

Dropping the stethoscope, I feel the pressure of the satchel across my shoulder and notice a strange sensation, a weight in my stomach accompanied by a thickness in my throat. Guilt?

I grip the nurse's bag, prepared to dump it at the bottom of the stairs. But my gut suddenly twists, my internal alarm.

I press my nose to the porthole glass, searching the slice of lobby I can see. There's no sign of the police, of the strange figures. But a large sliver of the lobby remains invisible behind the bloody door.

My gut continues to twist as a door swishes open in the stairwell above, only one flight up.

I leave the nurse's bag in the satchel and jab the release button before shoving the door open. I stumble through, just waiting for the violent pull, the hands around my neck.

They don't come.

With my head down, I shuffle across the lobby, the exit only forty feet away. My eyes pinpoint the obstacles – people standing in groups, lying on the ground – and I plot a path to weave between them.

New scents play in my nose. Antiseptic. Stale sweat. Plus another smell underneath that's vaguely familiar – a burnt metal. Cordite.

Something pulls my attention from behind and almost causes me to turn my head. Then the officers' mesmerising shadows flash through my mind, and I lumber forward more quickly.

Shouting sounds from the entrance ahead. I glance up. Two orderlies are pushing a trolley in through the hospital doors, a gaggle of grey-robed Puritans following behind. They're chanting biblical quotes, stuff about an Armageddon. And the onlookers staring at the passing trolley utter gasps of shock.

I find myself gaping at the trolley also, and it takes me a while to work out what I'm seeing.

A dead body, no doubt. Blanket pulled over its head. But the limbs have been folded at strange angles underneath. One arm extends out, its surface covered in burn marks, like puckered craters. The skin's a mottling of pale white and dark sections, black with blood. And the smell – vomit and piss. Another homeless victim.

And the Puritans continue to chant.

"The end is coming!"

"The damned will be cast into a lake of fire!"

I try to tear my gaze away from the body but can't. The strange chills climb my limbs, dark spots creeping into the corners of my vision, and my thoughts start to spin, my feet slowing.

Something grabs my satchel, causing me to whirl around, my fingers tightening to yank it back. I recognise a fresh scent. A figure before me comes into focus.

The nurse. Natasha. The grip belongs to a guard standing at her side, his hand clenching the strap of my satchel. He has a solid build, a leathery face, and stern eyes. Natasha's gaze is much fiercer. She stands staring at me with a furrowed brow and folded arms.

"Going somewhere?" she asks, her Eastern European accent more pronounced. "Got everything you need?"

She doesn't even glance at the satchel. The guard, however, is looking directly at it. I hunch further down, keeping my head below the level of those around me. The metallic scent's strengthening, and the force pulling at my attention from behind is growing stronger. My eyes find the exit over the guard's shoulder. Only ten feet away.

My feet twitch.

Natasha raises a hand, palm up. "Just give it over," she says.

The guard pulls the strap off my shoulder, but I jerk it back. The guy yanks back harder, which puts us into a tug of war, more of the surrounding crowd glancing over.

My heart pounds, and I drop the satchel strap. The guard pulls it clear.

Then revelation hits. My stomach plunges. "No!" I exclaim and try to bite off the cry.

I dive for the satchel. The guard spins it away behind his back.

"I believe for now, our friend Ethan will keep it," says Natasha.

The guard nods.

"You can't," I say, spinning to face Natasha, my throat tight. "It's *mine*."

Natasha grips her hips. "*Yours?*" she says, eyes wide. "Medication that people need?"

"It's not that ..." I splutter, the words dying on my tongue.

Natasha narrows her eyes.

I swallow. "There's something inside I need." My stomach heaves with every pathetic word. "Can I explain?"

She simply stares at me, hands still on her hips, her fingers tight. The strange chill continues to climb my spine, the dark shapes growing at the edges of my vision. Again, I force myself not to turn, to search for the officers, as Ethan roots around in the satchel.

My heel bounces up and down. The wait lasts an eternity.

"Very well," she says and folds her arms across her chest again. "I am on a break. I will hear you out."

Ethan lifts the open satchel toward her, and her features tighten as she grabs out her bag. I shuffle backward half a step.

Natasha leans in close, her crucifix necklace hanging down from her neck. "This better be good," she says.

## 11

Amid the trickle of patients, Ethan turns for the hospital doors with my satchel. I find myself stretching for it, but he walks away, slinging it across his front and out of reach. My fingers curl.

Natasha's still staring at me, her face stern. "Shall we?" she says and spins away as well before striding for the exit.

My shoulders tighten like rocks. I fix my gaze on the back of her head as if somehow I can read her mind, can work out what she wants, what her game is.

Because everyone's got one.

She passes through the doors, and I lumber after her, keeping close to the patients trudging around me. They're an exhausted bunch with sunken eyes and unsteady gaits.

I glance beyond them and my vision's assaulted by several bright billboards across the road from the hospital exit. Posters advertise health insurance plans and glitzy drugs for heart disease, a new cancer treatment, and the ever-popular pain meds.

Crossing the threshold, I spy Ethan striding toward a tiny building that stands beside the entrance – some kind of security booth. My satchel with the drugs and key is still firmly in his hand. With my eyes following the bag, my ribs squeeze more the further away it gets.

I drag my gaze from the satchel and scan my surroundings. The hospital's a rectangular building, its long wall extending along the side of a road. This entrance sits in one of its corners, a crowd milling around the pavement in front.

Natasha's heading straight toward them, and the sound of shouted prayers rings in my ears. I traipse behind her into the crowd, continuing to search for the officers.

No sign.

A dozen people hover by a smokers' room that adjoins the guards' shack. Everyone remains outside as it's still so hot, even at eleven o'clock at night. In fucking April.

Beyond the smokers stands a congregation of forty Puritans along the hospital wall with their candles and biblical verses on bits of card. I peer closer. Then start.

I see the bald priest who visited me, the egghead. He's delivering some kind of sermon to the congregation, his arm lifted and voice raised. Similar shouts sound from somewhere in the throng ahead of me.

I hunch even lower and press forward.

"Repent!" a voice yells in my ear.

I whirl and almost barge into a grey-robed man amid the crowd.

"You've seen the signs!" he goes on, pointing toward the hospital entrance and the tortured body beyond. "Be prepared. Judgement is nigh!"

I try to dart around him. But a Puritan colleague gets right in my face and pushes me back.

My gaze finds Natasha striding away to the side of the billboards, already easily beyond the crazies.

"You must repent, sinner!" the first Puritan yells, spittle peppering my cheeks.

I blink up at him. "Me?" I say.

The guy nods, his eyes burning.

"Why don't you go hassle those guys," I say and raise an

arm to point at the billboards behind them, at the pictures of healthy people smiling, the glitzy names and logos, a flashy microscope and double helix. "The cash they fleece from folks, they're the real sinners."

Both Puritans turn their heads just a fraction. I tense my shoulders and shove my way between them. The first Puritan raises an elbow to block me off, but I'm already through.

I dart across the road. Natasha's thirty feet ahead now, her head turned toward me. Is that a smile on her lips? My insides tighten, heat rising.

She spins away and continues padding in the direction of a concrete lot with a row of tower blocks beyond, and a park off to one side. And I'm forced to trudge along behind like a good little soldier.

A young man exits the park, an open box in his hands. He steps up to Natasha and starts speaking in a low voice, motioning over his shoulder.

I search the grass beyond and clock dozens of huddled forms on cardboard mattresses, the stench of stale sweat and piss heavy in my nose again.

Eventually, I get within earshot.

" … can tell the team. I will get you some more," Natasha says.

The guy nods back at her, his eyes beaming, and that's when I spot the other volunteers in the park. Each has a box and is handing out small packages. Natasha turns back toward the tower blocks.

"If that's your game, it's not going to work," I mutter. "You're not turning me into one of them."

"Sorry?" she says, spinning, her expression hard again.

I grumble without meeting her gaze.

"Well, you can explain that and more," she says. "I cannot wait to hear."

She recommences her march toward the tower blocks. And my gaze flits to the park, to the homeless figures sprawled there, as I traipse behind her. The image keeps coming of the scarred body on the trolley as I lumber along.

What about these rumours? Is the government *really* torturing undesirables? I'd thought it was all bullshit, government propaganda to scare the growing unwanted off the streets.

"Ready?"

I blink.

The nurse has stopped walking. And she's standing by the base of the first tower block in front of a ground-floor apartment. The place has been carved into some sort of diner. Most of the glass front is broken, and only fragments of light escape the layers of security grating. That, plus the smell of frying meat. My stomach growls.

I glance behind me. Still no sign of the strange officers around the hospital. The place is almost directly opposite the entrance, however. Easily visible. I shuffle to the side and peer through the diner grating, searching for some kind of back exit or escape route.

I hear a muffled shout from inside, and a figure crashes through the diner door, propelling it toward me. I dart to the side, hands raised, but the wooden edge still bangs into my shoulder.

I stumble backward, pain flaring down my injured arm. Then spin around to face the entrance, my fingers tight.

A man stands on the threshold, hands on his hips. A filthy apron covers his lean torso while brawny arms protrude from narrow shoulders.

"Fucking bum!" he shouts at the figure sprawled on the ground.

The prone guy is spindly, aged, and reeks of dirt and sweat.

I pivot to face the diner owner, who's now turned his accusing eyes on me. The heat continues to grow in my chest. My arms tense as I stalk toward him.

Natasha darts in between us. "Are you still open?" she asks with a smile.

The guy turns toward her and stares at her as if she's some kind of apparition.

"May we get something to eat?" she continues.

He blinks and then takes a step back.

"Thanks," she says and ducks past him into the diner.

The owner's blank look disappears, and he tracks her movement with hungry eyes.

I step toward him, and he edges only a foot to the side, still half blocking the door. I go to bump his arm out of the way when Natasha swivels and fixes her stern gaze on me. My shoulders tighten, and I clench my jaw. Then I step around his sneering face and trail her inside.

The diner walls are exposed brick, the tables made from breeze blocks and wooden boards, and the place has an odd assortment of chairs. I scan the corners. No cameras.

A single bulb dimly illuminates the other customers. And my eyes range over them – a few pairs, mostly loners. A television on the far wall spouts commentary about the train crash, but none of the customers seem to care.

For the poor, the happenings in the islands of privilege occur in a different world.

Natasha heads toward an empty table in the corner. I halt in the middle of the space, stare past the counter into the kitchen. No obvious rear bloody exit.

The owner passes me. He heaves a large change bag from behind the counter onto a nearby table and begins scooping up a pile of scattered coins into it. Small denominations. Undoubtedly from the *bum*.

Natasha seats herself at the table. I slump down opposite and swivel to ensure I've got a view of the entrance.

Eventually, the owner walks over. He's sweating – a lot – excreting oil from every pore. Could probably use it to cook with. Probably does.

The guy licks his fingers and brings out a pen and paper. "So …" he says, eyeing Natasha.

She turns to me. "What will you have?"

An itching discomfort climbs my back. I grab a plastic sauce bottle and begin spinning it between my fingers.

Natasha continues to stare.

"Nothing," I mumble. "Not hungry."

My stomach growls again an instant later, and heat blooms in my cheeks. The owner's sneer broadens.

Natasha leans toward me. "Come on. You should eat," she says.

I angle my head at her. "*Got no money*," I mouth.

"Sorry?" she says.

"*No money*," I say, heat flaring. I spin the bottle faster.

"That's fine," Natasha says. "I will pay."

I stare back at her, the sauce bottle gripped in my hand as well-worn suspicions run through my brain. *What* is *her game?* I shake my head.

The owner grins, revealing browned points that might once have been teeth. "No food, no table," he says, angling his pen toward the door.

Natasha smiles at me, and I glimpse the same warmth I saw in the hospital. It seems strangely effortless.

"Accept it," she says. "It won't kill you."

I avert my gaze from both of them and simply stare straight ahead.

Natasha glances up at the owner. "We will both take a sandwich," she says. "How much for two?"

"For both?" the guy says and his eyes crawl up the length of her body. "Let's see …"

Natasha blushes and lowers her gaze, shifting in her seat. All assuredness flees the diner like a waft of fresh air.

"Fifty," he says, drawing out each syllable.

My hand slams the sauce bottle down on the table. "*What?*" I say. "For two *subs?*"

Natasha fumbles for her bag, her cheeks still red and breathing elevated.

"That's okay," she says. "I will pay."

My scalp tightens. *No fucking way.* The prospect of more indebtedness feels almost painful in my chest.

The creep's still staring hungrily at Natasha, his pupils dilated from tiredness or fumes. Probably both. My eyes find the change bag on the counter, an idea coalescing at the back of my mind.

Natasha pulls her wallet from the handbag. I quickly lean over and grab it out of her hand.

"Hey!" she says.

I open the wallet, glancing inside. A hundred-pound note. Various smaller ones – a twenty, a fifty. I yank out the hundred and hand it over to the guy. The owner looks down at it and sighs before moving away to grab his change bag.

Natasha hisses in my ear, "What are you *doing?*" she says.

"Paying my way," I mutter, riffling through the wallet. I find the fifty.

The guy returns with change. He counts out fifty pounds in five-pound coins. I wait till the last coin hits the table.

"Sorry." I try a sheepish grin. "I found a fifty," I say. And then with one hand I give the guy the fresh note while I scoop up all the coins with the other.

The guy frowns and takes the fifty.

I palm two of the coins and then offer the remaining eight to the guy in a loose pile. "Can I get the hundred back?" I say.

The guy frowns again. Stares at the fifty he's holding in one hand, the coins sitting on top. He hands me the hundred.

Natasha leans forward. "Wait," she says.

My chest squeezes. I glance at her.

"Can you count your money?" she says to the owner. "Make sure we have it correct?" Then she turns steely eyes on me.

The owner glances down at the pile in his hand and nods.

He counts them out, discovers the missing coins. "Hey!" he says and slams the change bag down on the table.

"I am so sorry," Natasha says, smiling, palms raised. "How much do we owe you?"

"Ten," he says, staring at her. Already he's calming, his breathing slowing down. It's like he wants to be angry but doesn't know how.

She nods and snatches the wallet back off me before finding some coins and passing them over. The owner grunts and shuffles away.

"Why did you?" I say and slap my palm on the table. "The guy's a bastard. Deserves—"

"*That is not the point,*" Natasha snaps, staring back at me. "You think everyone is selfish, so you are selfish first." She raises a hand. "You rob, you steal, and so everyone becomes selfish, too."

I just sit there, my thoughts spluttering. It's like she lives in a dreamland.

"People can be generous, but you will *never* experience it," she says as her hand falls back onto the tabletop.

My ribs tighten, and I look away, my fingers spinning the stolen coins under the table. I stash them in my pocket. Then I glance back at Natasha. She's sitting there, staring off to the side, her nostrils flared and face even sterner than before. My mind conjures images of my security box key, still stuck with her bloody friend in that bloody security shack. As far away as ever.

## 12

THE FOOD ARRIVES. The diner owner dumps it down on our table, and I just stare at my plate. It's all the same shit in this kind of place – cheap meat, old veg, and sauce with as much flavour as anyone can create. Diners like this are springing up in reaction to the drab Puritan canteens. There, taste isn't permitted. All enjoyment purged.

Natasha picks up a fork, contemplates her food for a while, and then stabs a chip. The etched line across her forehead has smoothed some, but not completely.

My hand hovers over my sandwich. The mingled scents, so hard to ignore. My mouth's already watering.

"I told you," she says and raises the chip to her lips. "It will not kill you."

I grunt and stare down at the sandwich for a moment longer, the cramp of indebtedness still there in my chest. Eventually, my stomach wins, and I tuck in, licking sauce off my cheek.

After a while, Natasha puts down her fork. "So," she says, folding her arms, "you wanted to talk?"

I shrug and finish a mouthful. Then I gaze around the cramped space of the diner – the handful of customers, the single exit. I pick at a burnt chip and put it in my mouth. Chew. Swallow.

"Who are you?" she says.

"I need that satchel back," I say.

"You stole medication," she says, the bite back in her voice.

I gesture vaguely toward the diner door. "Lot of sick people out there."

She scoffs. "Those were opioids," she says. "With a high street value. I know this, and I am sure you do, too."

My legs squirm, images of the satchel spinning, probably locked in some kind of safe in the guards' shack. The heat rises inside me again.

I dump the remains of my sandwich on my plate and meet her gaze. But her expression doesn't soften at all. The stolen shirt feels so tight across my chest. I swallow and squeeze my fingers together. Still, she holds the silence.

"I've got to pay some people off," I say eventually.

"You're a thief," she says.

My jaw clenches. "You don't know shit about me," I spit.

She lowers her voice. "I know you need to make better choices."

I snort. "Like you?"

Natasha reaches up and fingers the crucifix around her neck. "I know who I am," she says.

I raise an eyebrow. "Someone who's going crooked, hanging out with a criminal?"

And there's her smile again, the warmth in her eyes. "Not a very good one," she says, playfulness in her tone.

My stomach tightens. I force my gaze away and stare at the muted television on the diner wall.

Her words soften. "What is this thing you want?" she asks.

I glare back at her.

"In the bag," she says.

I sigh and close my eyes for a moment. "A key," I say

eventually. "To a deposit box. My *own* box," I add quickly. "Stocked up with all my things, savings I've been putting away for years, and unless I can get it, I'll be trapped ..."

I trail off.

I've never raided my box before, and my insides convulse at the idea. It's my ticket to freedom, to leaving Mandem far behind. Because even with the bond paid off and the tracker gone, they'd still hunt me down. I'm too good an earner. But with enough cash and enough time, I can forge a new identity, a new life. Escape the fuckers forever.

Natasha's still staring at me. "You only have one key?"

"No, I've got two," I snap back. "The other's still in the factory."

"The *factory*?" she says, a tiny crease above one eyebrow. "It sounds big."

"It's not only mine," I say. "Plenty of others live there."

"People like ... you?" she says.

I grit my teeth and nod. All the bonded ones. My thoughts dart to Liam. He should be back at the factory right now, probably being grilled by the enforcers about what happened.

"And your key remains safe in this factory?" she says.

"Of course I've stashed it," I snap.

One side of her mouth curls up in a smile. "Under the floorboards?" she quips.

I grip the sauce bottle, squeeze hard, and glance away at the diner exit again. The urge seizes me to scramble away from the table, from the diner, from *her*.

I steady my breathing, trying to find some calm.

Natasha leans forward. "Look, I'm sorry," she says, warmth replacing the jest in her tone. She places a hand flat on the table. I stare at it, only a few inches from my own. "I want to help, truly."

I lift my gaze and raise an eyebrow. "Get me the key, then," I say.

She shakes her head. "It is not so simple," she says. "The

accident, the station. What were you really doing in a place like that?"

For an instant, I feel myself lying among the rubble again, bodies strewn around me.

My chest constricts. "I need—"

"You need to tell me the truth, and I will get your key. I promise," she says, nodding. "But it is not just about that. Is it?" She looks expectantly at me with those large hazel eyes. "You must tell me what you are mixed up in. You must tell *someone*."

I avert my gaze, my thoughts spinning back to the police officers coming for me in the hospital, the odd way they moved like the dark shapes in the station.

"Probably better if you don't know," I say eventually.

She inches her hand toward me across the scratched table. A strange warmth grows in my chest.

"If you do not trust people, no one can help you," she says.

I shift in my seat. Sitting there, memories assail me of being that fourteen-year-old kid on the streets again, trying to work with others, trusting them. Every time I did, things went wrong. People got hurt, or they stole from me.

"Jake," she says.

I glance up and realise I've been staring at the table.

"You are obviously worried about something. It *was* the station. Wasn't it? You were the only person who survived," she says. "What *happened?*"

She stares directly at me. I feel naked under her gaze, like I'm back in the hospital bed, the image of my mother sitting in her place and the crushing ache of vulnerability in my chest. I force another deep breath and find my fingers drumming on the tabletop.

She doesn't let up her stare, eyeing me for an age.

I sigh. "It's confusing." My gaze lands back on the table. "The crowd at the train station … they looked like they'd been squeezed together, packed tighter, like it was on purpose, to do the most damage when the train hit." I hear the words coming out of my mouth. It's as if I'm saying them out loud to test my sanity.

"How?" she says.

I see the dark shapes again. Remember the shimmering world exploding my perception.

"I'm not sure," I say. "But I'm pretty certain it was no accident."

I describe the terrified white-haired guy pushing against the crowd, trying to get out; the strange police officers that came for me in the hospital. It feels oddly calming, a weight lightening with every word that passes my lips. But I leave out the mysterious man. The shimmering world. The guy's final warning that something worse is coming.

Raising my gaze, I search her face for any sign of judgement. But there's nothing.

"How did you survive?" she says.

Again, the memory's like a punch to the sternum. I take a breath. "This nun saved me."

Her eyes widen.

I nod. "Crazy, right?"

"Maybe not," she says.

I feel myself frowning across at her.

"You should go to the police," she says.

My head shifts backward. "D'you catch what I said about the people who came for me, their uniforms?" I ask, trying to keep my voice low. "Whoever this lot are, they're connected. Knew the exact hospital I was holed up in."

"What about the press?" she says.

"*The press?*" I ask incredulously. "They'd never believe me."

Natasha sits straighter. "You cannot just look away," she says. "If what you say is true about the crash, about a conspiracy, and they are after you, it makes it doubly important that you do something."

My chest constricts. The sweat builds again up my back.

And my throat's so dry. "Whatever's happening has nothing to do with me," I say.

Natasha presses a single finger down on the tabletop. "You're the only one who survived. You *must* tell someone," she insists. "Because, if you do not, who will?"

She opens her palms like it's the simplest question in the world.

I shake my head. *No fucking way.* I'd end up in the loony bin, or in jail … or worse. I find myself on my feet, my own palm extended out toward her.

"I've said my piece," I say. "Key, please."

She sighs and closes her eyes for a moment. Then she stands as well, giving a curt nod. "Fine," she says, her voice dipping with disappointment. "We will go and see Ethan."

# 13

Natasha pushes away from the diner table and stomps toward the exit. The owner pauses his work at the counter to watch her go. A few of the male customers do, too. She remains entirely oblivious, however. And I follow behind.

She reaches the door and is moving to push it open when I rest a hand on her arm.

"Hold up," I say.

Natasha tenses under my touch and spins to face me while I'm already shifting across to the security grating. I stare out across the open space in front of the diner.

"What is it?" she says, a bite in her tone.

I ignore her and continue scanning the space, peering carefully at the park, the road before the hospital, and the buildings to the side of the entrance, for any sign of the officers. But there's still absolutely none, as if I invented the whole fucking thing.

"Look … I'm tired," Natasha says, motioning toward the diner door. "I must get back. My next shift begins soon—"

"Your mobile. Can I have it, quick?" I extend my hand while keeping my gaze fixed on the world outside.

She keeps quiet. I swivel back to face her.

Her smooth brow's creased in annoyance. "You cannot be—"

"I'll be done in a sec," I say, my hand still extended. "Need to buzz someone."

"Who?" she says.

I return her stare, my lips parted. "Someone," I say, images forming again of Liam, back at the factory.

She raises an eyebrow. "A friend?" she says. "You have one of those?"

I shrug. "Kind of."

She continues to stare.

I wet my lips. "I've got to tell my bosses I'm bringing them something," I say, and my insides clench. "From my security box. Otherwise, I'll never be free."

I keep my gaze on her, trying to form some kind of smile. Finally, she gives an exasperated sigh, pulls out her phone, thumbs in the code, and dumps it in my hand.

"Only one call," she snaps and shoves past me through the door.

I dart out of the diner in her wake, and we head out across the concrete lot toward the hospital.

My eyes take in the guards' shack and the adjoining smokers' hut. They're actually a single rectangular windowless structure, fifty feet long and much thinner, made from what looks like plasterboard, with a dividing join in the middle. A light glows through the top of the guards' shack door while the crowd beside the smokers' hut is as big as ever – an easy target for the Puritan congregation's angry glances.

We continue on toward them, past the park. And I keep to the cover of the trees. Upon reaching the far pavement, my gut starts to twist.

I dart my gaze around, staring in both directions down the road. Most of the streetlights are broken, and aside from the occasional car, it's deserted. No one visible. No one hiding in the shadows. And still, no obvious sign of the officers anywhere.

I bite my cheek and dial Liam's number. I glance around again, peering more intently through the hospital entrance and down the alleyway to its side.

Liam's phone rings in my ear, and some of the tension eases from my chest. He left it hidden in the factory, so he's been back to turn it on.

But oddly, the phone keeps ringing. There's no answer. Despite the fact that he'd be waiting to hear from me, wanting his cut.

We approach the guards' shack. I jab redial as Natasha steps up to the door. The phone rings again.

She calls out, "Hello, Ethan!"

The bottom half of the shack's door is closed, the light spilling out the top, and a radio's audible through the gap. Still no response from inside. And no other windows to see in.

The monotone ringing in my ear suddenly stops. The call connects and a voice barks, "What?"

Automatically, I hold the phone away from me, the voice all too bloody familiar. Natasha's still standing poised outside the door, her hands on her hips.

Reluctantly, I press the phone back to my ear. "Where's Liam?" I say.

"Who the hell's this?" Don retorts through the phone.

My throat narrows. I open my mouth and then close it, for my internal alarm's clamouring now.

I glance in both directions. Several people trail out of the hospital entrance. The crowd beyond the smokers' hut to my other side ebbs and flows. Again, no obvious threat. However, along with my alarm, the strange chill grows at the base of my spine – a sensation that's all too familiar from the ward, the officers.

I sniff the air for the strange metallic smell while voices at the back of my brain yell at me to run. But my eyes find the shack's door once more, my security box key just on the other side.

"I said, who the hell's this?" Don says again.

My brain's jabbering warnings at me now. Yet I take a slow breath. "It's Jake."

Don gives a low chuckle. "Well, well, well," he says, shifting from a bark to a purr. "Where *you* been?"

Natasha remains on the threshold, her hands still on her hips. "It's weird. The door is open. Ethan *should* be here," she says.

I swivel away from her, try to focus on the conversation with the enforcer.

"And where's our phone?" Don demands.

I swallow.

"And where's Liam? What you two playing at?"

I feel my brow furrowing. "He's not there?" I ask. "You're on his phone."

"Ethan?" Natasha calls out again.

I glance back at her. She tentatively pushes the bottom half of the door open, steps inside, and peers around the corner of the doorway.

"Course he's not here!" Don's voice snarls in my ear.

"Oh, wow," Natasha says from within.

And while the prickling chill climbs my back, I find myself following her into the shack.

Without a window, the place looks even smaller than it did from the outside. Probably only fifteen feet wide and just over half as deep, with most of it taken up by an L-shaped desk. Natasha's staring down at the pile of clipboards that litter the floor, a register with a pencil on a string.

"Has he been robbed?" Natasha says.

My eyes scour the shack. Fire extinguisher in the far corner, crumpled clothing and communication equipment on a set of low shelves against a side wall – all seemingly untouched. A tall cupboard stands across from the door, still closed. I peer over the desk. No sign of a safe or my satchel.

I bring the phone closer to my ear. "Did Liam leave word?"

"There's nothing here, you dipshit," Don says. "Look, you need to come in. Chat with the bosses. They're fuming now. You fucked up …"

Don continues, but I tune him out, my eyes drawn to the base of the cupboard. Something's on the floor … a drop of blood.

I picture my landing in the factory, the mattresses assigned to Liam and me, the places we stash our stuff.

"My cupboard," I say, interrupting the rant on the phone.

"What?" Don barks. "Liam's not touched your shit—"

"Just head to my cupboard," I say, my ribs tight. "Open it."

I find my hand moving toward the handle of the cupboard in front of me. My fingers hover above it.

There's a pause on the other end of the line and then a grunt. "You're in some deep crap …" Don says. Then there's the sound of footsteps. More cursing. And I picture the enforcer stomping to my cupboard.

Natasha swivels toward me. Stares at my shaking hand. "What is it?" she says.

I grip the cupboard handle and pull. The door swings open easily.

Bile climbs my throat and bites at the back of my mouth. I almost retch.

"Oh god …" Don's voice becomes a horrified whisper, the sound distant in my ears.

My gaze remains fixed on the body before me.

It's Ethan, the guard. Somehow they've folded him in half. Bent his legs back over his head. Stuffed him between the cupboard's narrow shelves. His face just visible. Strange scratch marks around his eyes.

## 14

NATASHA STUMBLES to my side and stares into Ethan's cupboard. Her hands go to her mouth. "Oh god, no," she says.

"What have you done?" Don says through the phone in my ear, his voice shaky.

I can only stare at Ethan's body, wedged between the cupboard shelves, while my mind conjures images of Liam, dead and stuffed inside my cupboard in the factory.

Don speaks again, his tone rising to a shout. "How the *fuck* did you know?"

The acrid scent's stronger in my nose now, like burning solder. And the phone slips from my hand.

Natasha says, "Who would—"

"It's the ones behind the crash, has to be," I say. "They tailed my friend from the station. Killed him too. And now they're here to shut me up."

The mysterious man's words … *It would be remiss of me to let you live.*

My body spins, and I stare through the open door of the cramped building. And while every logical part of my brain's yelling at me to bolt, my attention latches on to the strange chill, nestling deeper in the small of my back. I tense all the muscles in my legs and end up wobbling on the spot.

"Jake?" Natasha says from behind.

I grip my temples, my thoughts scrabbling for purchase. The radio prattles on from the far side of the shack. I force a steadying breath. Start the count. And try to calm my mind, to bloody *think*.

Natasha's staring at Ethan's body again, her face pale. And I shove the cupboard closed with trembling hands.

"Why would they have done this?" she asks.

I search the rectangular space again for my satchel. No sign.

"Might be a trap," I say.

Natasha spins to face me, her mouth open, and I push past her toward the shack's door.

"They clocked I'd come here, that I'd want that satchel back," I say. "And maybe they want us to panic, to bolt, to do something stupid."

Then I grab the two halves of the door, snap them together, and slam the door shut in front of me. Though it's got no fucking lock.

Natasha stares at the closed door with a gaping mouth. "Is that not pretty stupid?" she asks, pointing at it.

I squeeze past her, scanning the cramped space. There's hardly anything here. Only the curved desk. A chair sprawled to the side of it. A taped-up ventilation grate. The low shelves stacked with clothes and communication equipment. Plus the small fire extinguisher in the far corner.

"I guarantee they're watching us, right now," I say and grab at the desk. I try to haul it toward the door to block it, but the thing's too damn heavy.

Natasha puts her hands on her hips. "*What?*" she says.

"I told you, these people are connected," I say, my eyes taking in the door closer – the arm and hinge that slow its shutting. "They found my bay in the hospital easily enough and then tracked Ethan bringing the satchel here before swiping it. Must be tapped into CCTV or something. They always know where I am."

Natasha's staring at me again.

I spin and nod toward the clothes on the shelves beyond the desk. "Grab me a spare belt," I say and reach for the office chair to start hauling it toward the door.

"You want to block a door with a belt and a chair?"

She says it like I'm insane.

"No!" I snap and leap up onto the swivel chair. It spins, almost causing me to fall off, and I grip the door closer to steady myself. "I mean, yeah!" And I thrust my other hand out toward her. "Throw it to me. Quick!"

"This is ridiculous," she mutters, shaking her head, and slips behind the desk. She fishes a belt out of the pile of clothing and tosses it to me.

I catch it, fasten it into a loop, and wrap it around the arms of the door closer to jam it shut before jumping down.

"Now what?" she asks with derision. She makes a show of looking around the cramped building, at the lack of other doors and windows. "Do we teleport out of here?"

I ignore her and pivot to face the side wall, the join toward the smokers' room. I lift a hand and rip a large piece of silver tape off the plasterboard to reveal the ventilation grate underneath.

"Smokers' room's next door," I say. "If we can make it through, there's crowds on the far side to hide in. Smokers, Puritans …" And my mind forms images of the road and housing estate beyond. A maze to find anyone in.

"*We?*" She sounds incredulous.

I drag the set of low shelves away from the side wall. "They killed my partner, too, maybe because he saw the sabotage, maybe as a warning to me," I say, raising my leg. "And they'll have spotted us together, will guess we've been talking about the train crash. You reckon they'll let you live?"

I kick out at the wall underneath the ventilation grate. The plasterboard dents but otherwise holds firm. Another kick. Another dent. Still, the wall doesn't break.

"Brilliant!" Natasha deadpans, her voice dripping with scorn. She turns from me with hands raised, as if addressing an imaginary audience. "What *will* he think of next?"

I close my eyes, my mind cataloguing everything I've seen in the shack … An instant later, I jab my finger over her shoulder. "Fire extinguisher, now!"

With a grumble, she heads behind the desk, rips the tiny thing from its holder on the wall, and throws it to me.

"You think I will go with you?" she says. "That I won't stay right here?"

I spin away to face the opposite wall. "God, that's fucking tempting," I mutter under my breath. Then I raise the fire extinguisher and go to ram the grate with the metal end.

"Look, you can't just …" she says, her tone exasperated, like she's talking to a child. "If someone is out there, they are bound to hear—"

"The radio!" I yell. "Crank it up!"

"Ex … cuse me?" she says.

"To the max!" I say.

She shrugs and does as I ask. And with the music blaring out, I smash the extinguisher into the wall, timing the impacts with the drumbeat. The dents become a hole, which grows gradually larger. I dump the extinguisher.

"Okay," I say and thread one leg into the hole. Then I squeeze the rest of my body through till I'm standing in the smokers' hut – a thirty-foot oblong shell with benches against both long walls and an open door at the end. Potential escape beyond.

While every instinct shouts at me to bolt, my mind flashes through all the things I've told her … about my security box, the spare key I hide in the factory. They'd be able to extract the information all too easily. My ticket to freedom … gone.

With gritted teeth, I swivel and reach back through the

hole. Offer my hand. She stares at it like it's a tentacle or something.

"Coming?" I say.

She lifts her gaze to my face, lips pursed, expression defiant.

I keep my arm extended and breathe. Work to maintain an even tone. "Look, you really fancy strolling out of that door?" I say. "Running into whoever's lying in wait? You feeling that confident?"

Her expression softens a fraction. Doubt shows in her eyes.

"They wasted Ethan, maybe just to get my satchel," I say, cocking my head toward the cupboard. "And the last person I was spied with wound up dead right after we split. You really want to be next?"

I edge my hand toward her. Lips pursed, she takes it. And I haul her through.

## 15

Natasha stumbles into the smokers' hut at my side, the air a haze around us. The rectangular space remains empty, benches bare. Everyone is outside because of the heat. I step carefully toward the doorway opposite our smashed hole and peer through the opening.

It looks out along the long wall of the hospital, away from the entrance. A group of fifteen smokers chat in twos and threes. Beyond them, the forty Puritans still huddle in a mass, covering the pavement and some of the road. And across from them ... the labyrinth of tower blocks opposite.

I chew my lip. Thirty feet between the estate and the edge of the crowd. No cover. There's no sign of the officers, though much of my view's blocked, the hospital entrance and security shack hidden behind us.

The strange chill's still nestled at the base of my back. And my fingers dig into my pocket and start revolving the two coins.

"What—" Natasha starts.

"Keep your head down and follow me," I say, swivelling my gaze around to face her.

Her eyes widen.

"Step fast but don't run," I add and dart out in the open.

We begin slipping between the smokers, hurrying toward the Puritans. I keep one eye on the road to my side while glancing occasionally back at Natasha padding behind me, my thoughts yelling that she'll bail at any moment.

The Puritans peer at us with narrowed eyes and raised chins as we approach. I feel a powerful urge to run, to barge past their pompous faces, though I force myself to tread slowly through their midst, my head bowed. They inch back from me with curled lips and bibles clasped to their chests. Still, I keep my progress steady, finally reaching the edge of the group.

My eyes take in the two nearest tower blocks just on the other side of the street and only ten yards away.

I hang back. Natasha stumbles to my side.

"Now *go*," I hiss.

She gazes back at me.

I push her across the road and hurry behind her toward the estate ahead. The first two blocks tower above us, each one square at the base and twenty storeys high.

We approach a pathway between them, and I glance over my shoulder, scanning the space before the hospital.

While there's still no sign of the officers, the strange chill's just as present inside me, starting to edge up my spine.

Natasha follows my gaze as she reaches the pathway. "There is no one—" she starts.

I urge her on, keeping my hand on her back as we hurry under an overhang into the estate itself.

It's like a jungle. Dozens of tower blocks spread out over many acres of sprawling concrete, with walkways connecting the buildings at various floors and sizeable areas of littered ground in between.

The place lies veiled in darkness, only a few of the street-lights working. And we hasten beyond the first tower block into an area used for garages, most of the doors smashed in and hanging open.

"Wait," Natasha utters between breaths.

I hurry onward. Past torched-out flats, piles of strewn rubbish, and turned-over bins. Gang tags dominate every surface – graffitied over crosses, walls, signs, everything. I keep us to the shadows of the building edges, making sure not to run.

Hurrying between another two blocks and out into a large open space, Natasha grabs my arm. "Hold on ... stop," she says, yanking me to a halt.

I pull at her grip. And she wrenches against me, anchoring her feet.

"This is *stupid*," she says.

I glance out across the space. The seventy-yard square with tower blocks on three of the sides is deserted. We're standing by one of them, under the shelter of a few spindly trees still clinging to life. The branches sway in the breeze, casting fingered shadows on the ground.

I blink.

Something's calling for my attention. Shadowed shapes move across the cracked asphalt in front of us. The trees continue to shift in the wind. And my gut twists again – my internal alarm.

"We cannot just keep run—" she says.

I hold up my finger to shush her.

The branch shadows. They seem to be darkening, creeping closer, coalescing into something. But the image won't resolve itself. It's fucking maddening.

Just like in the station.

The strange chill is spreading across my whole back. And realisation hits ...

These guys didn't attack. They happily followed us here, away from the watching crowds. Clever.

"*What is it?*" Natasha asks, her voice tight.

Again, I tune out her voice, keeping my gaze fixed on the moving shadows.

It's like the darkness is rippling, and images circle my mind – the police officers' fluid movements in the hospital, the dark shapes flowing around the crowd in the station. And in the next instant, the smell of cordite bites at my nose.

Every muscle in my back knits up, my heartbeat fires, and I lean forward, straining to see. And still, I can't make out a bloody thing … just the looming buildings to either side, the swaying branches, and the strange shadows pooling ever closer.

Part of my brain screams at me to run while another part scrabbles for understanding, my gang training yelling at me … *Know your threat.*

Natasha squeezes my arm, her hand trembling. "You need to tell me what is happening," she says.

Her words barely register. More memories from the station spin through my mind – the shimmering world erupting around me, suddenly being able to see the dark figures, and how it felt like I was going mad.

Just like my mother did.

A shiver runs down my neck. The shadows continue their approach as the smell of cordite grows ever stronger. I tense my abdomen, beginning the count. My thoughts slow, a window of stillness opening …

And nothing happens. Still, I can see only the deepening gloom. The tree branch shadows reach to touch me, the strange chill climbing my legs and back.

My doubts yell louder, my calves tense to bolt, and I stop myself. I root my feet and concentrate more fiercely on the escalating numbers. Then, instead of thinking or planning, I breathe into the stillness and try to remember the enormous shift of experience from the station, the exploding of each of my senses. I train all my focus on the memory.

The world lurches, everything shimmers, time slows, and a fraction of the veil drops away.

And I see them.

# 16

BEYOND THE VEIL, I find myself staring at two men and a woman. They're already two-thirds of the way across the concrete square, only thirty feet away. It's like I've been slapped. I take a faltering step backward.

"What?" Natasha says and wheels on me.

Their movements. Impossible. My mouth falls open. The way they slip between the swaying shadows, swimming through the gloom. Bloody mesmerising. And getting ever closer. I find my eyes drawn to the woman's neck, to a black shape shifting beneath her skin.

My vision hazes, my knees weaken, and cold pours into my nose and mouth.

"*What is it?*" Natasha yells.

"There!" I shout and jab my finger at the figures.

The woman wears a pencil skirt and blouse. One guy's in a preppy sports jacket, and the second's in a golfing top and trousers. All the clothes look new, and all of it fucking weird, as if I'm being hypnotised, or already going crazy. And with the growing thoughts, the shimmering world dissipates, and the veil reasserts itself. But the figures remain. Only twenty feet away.

Natasha narrows her eyes, following my gaze. "Where?"

she asks.

"*Can't you see them?*" I yell.

Natasha swivels back to face me. "Jake, we do not have time for—"

I grasp her by the wrist and start pulling her to the side.

"Hey!" she protests.

"We have to get away!" I say, the chill deepening, like wings of ice unfurling inside my ribs.

She spins around to face the open space again, peering into the darkness. "*From what?*"

"Fuck!" I dive into my pocket and grab one of the stolen coins. "Watch this," I say, measuring their approach. I pause for a beat … and then throw.

The coin hits one of the men in the shoulder. He stumbles for a millisecond.

Natasha's body tightens. "What the …?" she says and edges backward, her eyes out on stalks.

Our pursuers give up on their fluid movements and run toward us. The woman's only ten feet away. Her dark eyes stare into mine, and I feel the numbness growing in my limbs, my gaze increasingly trapped.

I tense my neck and wrench my gaze away. "Come on!" I yell and seize Natasha by the arm again. I yank her out of the way of the woman, throwing myself to the side.

And I end up colliding with a tree.

Pain flares up my arm while Natasha's already bolting along the edge of the tower block. I scramble behind, my arm throbbing.

We get within ten feet of the corner when I spy ripples in the shadows just beyond, all too familiar now. A spike of icy cold grips me.

"Wait!" I say, skidding to a halt.

Natasha draws up a few feet in front, and I shove her away from the corner. I sprint at her side, and beyond the edge of the building, I can't help turning my head.

There he is. Another damn figure, in a police uniform this

time, just like in the hospital. Our eyes lock for a moment before he sets off in pursuit.

Natasha turns to stare, slowing her steps. I grasp her arm again and haul her onward.

"That was a—" she says.

I drag her toward the next tower block while scanning its neighbouring buildings, my eyes flitting between the walkways that connect them.

We head into a narrow passageway, and I sprint for the entrance to the block. I jerk the door open and thrust Natasha through.

A lobby area. Everything a dull green, lit by emergency bulbs embedded in the ceiling. Doors are on all sides with a stairwell behind one and bright corridors beyond the others. I yank Natasha toward the nearest door.

"Wait!" She grabs at my wrist. "What if that was the real police?" she says. "We cannot run—"

I swing back to face her, my throat tight. "You hear them yelling?"

"What?" she asks.

"D'you hear them yelling at us to stop?" I repeat.

She opens her mouth, closes it, and then shakes her head.

"What policeman does that?" I snap. "Chases you in silence?"

The conviction dies in her eyes, her face paling. Her gaze flicks over my shoulder.

Again, I pull her toward the nearest corridor and try the door. Locked. I kick it hard. The frame bursts inward and slams into the wall behind. Natasha heads toward it, but I drag her away from the broken doors, through the fire door, and up the stairwell in a quick diversion.

We climb two levels, piling through fire doors at each one. The place is mostly deserted, the Puritans undoubtedly encamped at home in the dark. We reach the third floor and the door to another locked corridor. I kick it in, and Natasha sprints through.

"No," I say and haul her back.

She whirls on me. "But … it is the same trick again," she says, tugging me toward the broken opening.

"That's right," I say. "People don't expect it."

She just stares back at me, her face as white as before. "But you're the one saying they're not normal!"

I feel my own doubts clamouring, but I shove them down, taking a quick breath. "They run. They chase. They're normal enough," I spit out. "We've just got to get ahead of them, get across to the next block. This place is a maze. They'll be searching forever."

And with that, she lets me pull her toward the stairs. We reach the next floor, three storeys up, and I spot an open walkway connecting our tower block to a neighbouring one. A large concrete space underneath has a wheeled bin on the ground between the buildings.

I shuffle out onto the walkway. It's fifty yards long with concrete sides that reach my chest. I keep my head down, making sure Natasha does the same. We make it halfway before the door on the opposite block opens, and a figure steps out into the night.

The concrete suddenly feels like ice under my feet.

Police uniform. The guy's almost as wide as the walkway, and he's staring directly at us, no surprise on his face. In fact, no emotion at all.

He slips steadily toward us, his gaze searching mine as the strange numbness climbs my legs. I tense my shoulders and whirl my head around. I'm picturing more pursuers in the building behind us, making their way up through the floors.

"Quick!" I yell and usher Natasha toward the edge of the walkway, a thirty-foot drop to the ground. "Jump!"

I try to lift her over the railing, my injured arm shaking.

"What?" she says, shoving frantically at my hands. "No!"

"Trust me!" I grab hold of her waist. "There's something down there!"

The guy glides faster toward us along the walkway. And

Natasha glances over the edge. She sees the wheeled bin, a mattress lying on top.

"It's for getaways, for dealers!" I say, still struggling to push her over the side.

The guy's only twenty feet away now and has started to run. I glimpse the same black shadow cross his neck and shove harder at Natasha. Finally, she allows me to lift her up. She swings her leg over as I clamber to follow. The guy throws himself at me and bumps into my shoulder just as my legs scissor over the side.

The contact burns cold, and I grit my teeth against the pain. I begin to fall, my balance tipping from the hit. Natasha plummets only a couple of feet in front.

The drop feels timeless as the wind rushes past my ears. She hits the mattress with her feet, and I land on my back, the impact squashing the air from my lungs.

I scramble off behind her and drop to my knees, barely able to breathe. Then I throw myself at the bottom of the wheeled bin and begin shoving it away from under the walkway, my whole upper body quivering.

We both look up. Our pursuer is already lifting his leg over. About to jump. With nothing but hard concrete below.

Natasha puts her hand to her mouth. "No ..." she says.

I find myself backing further away. The guy lets himself fall and hits the ground. There's no exclamation of pain, just an awful crunching sound.

Natasha gasps, and my stomach heaves.

The guy struggles to push himself back up and begins lurching after us.

I don't move. I can only stare, eyes wide, mouth wider as my brain tries and fails to compute.

"Is it drugs?" I find myself stammering.

"Jake!" Natasha's shrill yell explodes in my ears.

I spin. And again, we run.

We sprint around buildings and under walkways, keeping a winding course through the estate. And still our pursuers are always just behind us, always in perfect coordination – one of them peels away one moment to appear at our side from behind a tower block the next – as if they know our movements in advance. Yet they never speak. No obvious communication between them. Plus, we've seen six or seven of these bastards. Three in police uniforms, the rest in the bizarre new clothes. It makes no fucking sense.

And we're slowing down. The air is like cut glass in my lungs now. And Natasha's body trembles as we canter onward while our pursuers draw ever closer.

I force my eyes up from what's in front of me. I risk swivelling my head from side to side, scanning spaces beyond. And my gaze falls on guys hanging around corners, parked cars, and the entrances to the tower blocks. Lots of muscle on display, lots of badly hidden weapons, lots of posturing. A familiar sight.

The rudiments of an idea begin to form.

I know what they're guarding. And while familiar warnings blare in my head, I run straight toward them.

A low building comes into view – an old community centre – with a handful of lookouts idling around it. The remainder of a huge cross hangs from the front, now defaced and disfigured with atheist symbols and more gang tags. Fires glow from inside the broken windows and holes underneath, giving the structure the look of a leering beast. There are large double doors, a chain lock hanging loose. And my mind hollers ever louder about what I'm about to try.

"This way!" I yell, trying to grind more speed from my body.

I sprint toward the building. The spotters gaze at us in shock … No one would dare. No one's that fucking stupid. Still, I smash into the doors with Natasha just behind me.

# 17

I FLY through the community centre doors, slam into someone, and go sprawling to the floor. Pain flares in my wrists, arm, and side. I roll over, push myself up onto my knees, and spin.

Natasha's veered to a stop, her mouth gaping. Thirty guys stand spread out around the large rectangular space. More muscle, more gold. Almost everyone on their feet, staring at us, tense postures, narrowed eyes.

Another gang. Not Mandem. Not their territory.

Throats tighten. Hands reach for guns.

I scramble to my feet, pushing down the burning pain, and hurl Natasha toward the rear of the room. "It's the police, the pigs!" I yell, spittle flying. "They're here!"

With sharp movements to our sides, a number of gang members close in. I barrel on toward a central door in the far wall, one of the multiple exits they always have.

"Three suited!" I shout between strides. "More without!"

Several members swivel to face the entrance behind me as I hit the back door, wincing at the spike of pain in my arm. And an instant later, the front ones bang open.

Exhilaration sparks in my chest, and images flash of our pursuers following us inside.

The yelling and shouting explodes at our backs, the clicks of guns being drawn and readied.

The door slams behind us, and I sprint with Natasha across the estate concourse, around a corner, and toward another apartment block straight ahead. We come to a stop in its shadow and hunker down.

Natasha's got her hands on her knees, her chest heaving, while my own legs quiver, my arm and side throbbing.

I listen hard. No shots, just more distant yelling. And then everything goes quiet.

"We've … got … to … go," I utter, barely able to speak between snatched breaths.

Natasha stares at me with a pained expression.

"But … more carefully now," I add.

Natasha nods, and we lurch along the deeper shadow of the wall, past piles of rubbish. I peer around the building's corner.

A pursuer's standing there, twenty yards away in the middle of a square, so obvious in his front-creased trousers and polo shirt. As we stare at the guy, he starts to swivel toward me.

My heart hammers, and I yank my head back, going completely still, with Natasha gawking at me. The strange chill's still there in my bones, but it's not getting any stronger.

I shake my head at her and search the nearer piles of rubbish. I grab up a piece of glass and hasten to the opposite end of the building before using it to peer around the corner.

No sign of anyone in the reflection.

We move on to the next building and then the next, sometimes spotting the pursuers in their odd clothes, and sometimes the same pursuer having just backtracked to avoid them. So fucking weird. Like they're tracking us with CCTV, or a military spy plane. Yet I still never hear them speak.

We keep going, eventually seeing them less and less. Finally, we reach the edge of the estate.

I breathe a sigh of relief, the pain in my side gradually

fading though my arm is a steady throb. We hurry down a narrow roadway, the far pavement fenced off with razor wire and huge scraggly bushes beyond. I hear the muffled sound of traffic, a motorway somewhere on the other side. Occasional holes line the mesh.

I hasten over to one of the larger gaps, and Natasha stares at the dense tangle of branches beyond.

"Is that wise?" she whispers. "We could get stuck … easily trapped."

"We'll be alright," I say and tug at the mesh, opening the hole for her while my eyes scour the roads behind. "I reckon we lost them."

She purses her lips, eyes me for an instant, and then squeezes through. I scramble behind.

Since I'm bigger, the wire catches on my clothes and bites at my skin. She pulls me after her as we shove through the overgrown vegetation, squeezing under and over branches. The noise of cars grows with every tortured step. Eventually, we break through the undergrowth together, and the roar of engines hits me like a wall.

We stand at the top of a grassy bank, a low barrier lying at the bottom. And beyond, three lanes of cars speed in both directions. I scamper down the bank, Natasha just behind.

"Look!" she shouts, scrabbling to a halt.

I spin. She's pointing but doesn't need to. Another pursuer, the guy who jumped from the walkway. He's staggering wildly along the verge, lumbering toward us on mangled ankles. And my mind keeps replaying his fall, the awful crunch of bone. Yet despite that, he's not uttering a bloody sound, somehow oblivious to the pain.

Who *are* these people?

Natasha reaches the barrier behind me, climbs over, and backs toward the edge of the road.

It's after midnight, and the motorway's still busy – a major road to the north of the country. Cars and vans scream past at sixty, seventy miles an hour, one after another.

Natasha's heels are only a few feet from the hurtling vehicles. The occasional blasts from car horns rattle my brain as I stumble after her.

"This is crazy," she says, her voice shaking. She spins to face the road.

I follow her to the edge of the hard shoulder where I can't help looking behind.

Our pursuer's hobbling on, getting ever closer – thirty feet, twenty-five – the strange dark shapes clinging to his heels. The strange chill creeps up the back of my neck.

I wrench my gaze around. Inch my feet toward the careening cars, breathless, wired, bouncing on my toes. There are hardly any gaps between the vehicles.

The memory comes of the veil pulling back from my senses, of time slowing down. And I try to still my thoughts, to recreate it. But my mind's a wreck.

The car horns grow louder, more frequent. And the strange chill's growing at my core. I can almost feel the pursuer at my back, his hands around my neck.

Natasha readies herself to my other side, her eyes fixed on the road in front of us. I follow her gaze and bend my knees.

"Now!" I yell. And we launch ourselves into a gap. Across one lane. Two. A driver gives us a long blast on their horn. Another car hurtles past.

Natasha makes it to the central barrier. I'm just behind. I spin. The pursuer has reached the first barrier and climbs over it.

"Come on!" Natasha says.

She keeps going. Three more lanes, the traffic lighter on this side of the road. I follow her across. We run. Don't need to stop halfway. I reach the far barrier, grip it hard, and take a breath.

Natasha's fingers clasp my shoulder. "Oh god," she says, her words barely a whisper.

My neck tenses, and while every part of my brain's screaming at me not to look, I find my head turning.

Sure enough, the guy's lurching steadily after us. He makes it to the second lane before cars swerve. He doesn't even glance at them, simply keeps his stare fixed on me, one hand pressed flat to his chest. His lips mumble something over and over, and his expression shines with absolute surety.

My eyes are hooked. I can't look away.

Another car skids. Somehow, the guy makes it to the central barrier and climbs over. The cold seizes my ribs and congeals my insides.

Natasha presses her hands to her ears. "No, no, *no!*" she says.

And still the guy keeps coming. My stomach squeezes up my throat. And still I remain standing there, the chill anchoring my feet to the ground.

The pursuer hobbles into the last lane, hand still pressed to his chest as he mutters on. His eyes lock with mine, and we stare at each other, only feet apart. The guy reaches for me—

The sound of the impact is sickening. The car is heavy and doesn't swerve. Our pursuer flies, limbs flailing. I hold my breath, only able to watch. The heavy car screeches to a halt further up the road while other vehicles brake behind. The guy lands in a heap on the ground, right on the edge of the hard shoulder, fifteen feet away.

"That's not normal. *That's not normal!*" Natasha's screaming now.

I just stare on at the body. Again, my mind unable to compute. Then, as more cars screech to a halt behind me, I run toward the mauled figure.

"What are you *doing?*" Natasha says.

I reach the body, a part of me unwilling to look, not sure what to fucking expect.

Yet nothing's obviously strange. Aside from his broken neck, his face pointing all the way around, and the fact he's still gripping his chest with his hand.

I peer closer and then spring away. A dark vine shifts

beneath the skin of his neck. Then it's gone, a normal body lying before me once more.

I force myself down and start ripping at his jacket, my fingers scouring the suit pockets.

Car doors slam behind me. Raised voices.

"We better go!" Natasha says.

Still, I keep searching, the pain flaring in my arm. But the pockets are all empty. No identity badge. No indication of the organisation we're dealing with. And no sign of any communication equipment. No earpieces. Absolutely fucking nothing.

My fingers clench. And hurried footsteps approach from behind.

"Jake, come on!" Natasha says, her hands yanking at my shoulder.

I go to rise. Then, despite the screaming internal voices, I scoot back down and begin grabbing at the guy's shirt buttons, straining to prise the guy's hand away from his chest.

"Jake, *please*, they might be back, more of them!" Natasha yells, trying to drag me away, her tone more hysterical, her voice shaking. "And remember the diner, you said ... you said this was nothing to do with you!"

Pushing down the pain in my arm, I make one more effort. I manage to tear the shirt open. Then freeze.

A tattoo. Over the guy's heart. The image sears itself into my brain, and needles dance across my back.

Natasha hauls at my arm again. And I let her pull me up and away from the gathering group, several of the onlookers gawking at me.

"Please, we have to go, now!" she stammers, her face as pale as ever.

I don't move, my eyes finding the mark on the guy's chest again.

"What?" she says, glancing down at the tattoo and then at me. "*What is it?*"

I stare back at her. "The symbol, I recognise it."

# 18

I AIM a kick at a steel bollard, close my eyes, and take a deep breath. Then I stare down the street again, at the designer suit shops, champagne bars, and high-end restaurants. The glittering office buildings rise like shards of glass around us, stretching up into the night sky. I scan the visible foyers and reception areas for the symbol, the tattoo on the dead pursuer's chest.

Still nothing.

"Come on, Jake," Natasha says, her voice low and tight. Her shock from the estate has gradually morphed into frustration. "You said it would be quick, but we've been searching for a whole hour."

Heat flashes down my limbs as I press on faster down the street, stalking between two towering office blocks. My feet chafe in the stolen shoes, and I keep to the shadows, checking each junction as I pass.

The financial centre's in lockdown, all because of the train crash. Princes and princesses advised to stay out of their kingdom, private security firms mounting armed patrols.

"Do you really know where you are going?" Natasha says from behind.

The heat continues to rise. And I hurry around the corner

of a building, scanning the reception area for logos, and pass two rushing businessmen in their creaseless suits. They're wide-eyed on stimulants, chattering excitedly about recent market hits, the train crash just another opportunity to exploit. London, the financial speculation and legal money laundering centre of the world.

"Wait!" Natasha calls.

Still, I ignore her. We head under an archway, into a spacious courtyard. Mosaics of gold and fossilised stone decorate the floor, the excess outrageous. The Puritans would hate it.

I scan the limestone-fronted buildings. But still no bloody sign of the symbol on any of them.

"Jake!" she says.

I spin around. *"What?"*

She meets my gaze. "This is not working."

*"Not working?"* I ask.

"It was a tattoo," she says with a sigh. "Could have been anything."

I grip the sleeves of my jacket. "But it wasn't. I've seen it, somewhere around here, for *sure*. And memory is my thing." I jab my chest. "I've trained it my whole life!"

Natasha raises her arms. "So, why have we not found it?" she presses.

The heat rises inside, squeezing my lungs, and I whirl, every instinct yelling at me to get rid of her. Yet the same images form – our pursuers capturing Natasha and with her, my box, and every chance I'd ever have of paying off Mandem, of disappearing.

With ribs tight, I take a quick breath and gaze down the street. I call up a mental map of the financial centre in my head, the few roads we haven't tried.

"Look, *why* do you want to find them?" Natasha asks, softening her tone.

I inhale through gritted teeth. "Because it's the first rule," I say. "Know your threat. Know their game. We've got to find out who they are and what they want. How else are we going to craft a plan to get free?"

Her frowning eyes hold mine, that single line etching her forehead.

"You want to head back to the hospital?" I snap. "Hang around there till they find us? Because they will." I shake my head vigorously. "And I'm not doing that."

"We need to speak to someone, to get help," Natasha says, hands on her hips. "We could go and find the police. The *real* pol—"

"The police?" I make a fist and tighten it till it shakes. *"What would we say?"*

She opens her mouth.

"They'll just laugh!" I say. "Think we're mad. We have no evidence."

"My friend ... your partner—" she says.

"Are dead, yeah," I say, an extra weight dampening the heat for a moment.

"Their bodies—" she starts.

"Will be gone." I slice my hand through the air. "This lot will have sorted it, for sure. They're too well connected. They sabotaged a bloody train and made it look accidental. Created fucking carnage."

Natasha eyes grow distant again. "Who would do that?" she breathes.

"I don't know. That's the thing," I say. "But did you see the guy's tattoo?" I bring the image back to mind. A crucifix with a broken circle at its top, thicker at each side, like shoulders, and the gap at the bottom. A cross with a crescent moon. "Might be Christian."

"How can you be sure?" she says.

"I can't be," I retort and then breathe. "But it's the only thing we've got. All the guy's pockets were empty. Odd for a government agent. Don't you think?" And many of my previous ideas continue to fall away – the train crash as a governmental plan to allow increased powers, our pursuers part of some sick experimental programme. "Could be religious nuts. Willing to sacrifice themselves at a moment's notice."

Natasha clasps her fingers to the crucifix on her necklace. "You think this will stop me. Don't you? Stop me going to the authorities," she says, speaking faster, louder, "just because you say they are religious—"

"We shouldn't go to anyone!" I shout. Then I shut my trap and glance around the wide square.

Still empty.

"These guys have always been a step ahead. Probably wired into databases everywhere." I work to steady my voice. "We speak to the police, and they'll get our details. We'll end up dead. You *and* me, I told you. We've both witnessed them now."

Natasha's frown deepens. "You are attempting to find a location from a tattoo, one you think is religious, but we are standing in the middle of the business world?"

She says it like I'm crazy. And while my mind desperately scrambles for explanations – a mad cult embracing modernity, using technology to create crazed hallucinogenic states – my own doubts plummet like hailstones. I can't speak, can hardly think.

I blow out stale air. Contract my stomach and start the count in my head, focus on the climbing numbers. I begin to calm and the image bubbles up once more – a crescent moon facing down a slim crucifix. The connection *there*, just out of reach. For an instant, I force my mind into action again. But then, I let the image hover. Relax. My thoughts blank, the internal count continuing.

Something pops deep inside my head. And finally, the memory comes … an office building, and one nearby.

Natasha says, "Let's—"

"This way!" I shout and set off like a whirlwind. I sprint toward a narrow avenue, laughing as I run. "How'd I not see it before?"

Natasha hurries behind, her protests eventually ebbing into silence. And after only a few minutes, we reach a pedestrianised street, mirrored glass walls on both sides. I slow my steps and peer ahead into a large courtyard of office buildings.

"This is it," I breathe and inch up to one of the columns that line the rounded edge of the semicircular space.

"Even if you are right," Natasha says at my side, "what will you do?"

"Watch them ... learn," I mutter under my breath and then lick my lips. "Get their address and then research. Resources, contacts, how they operate."

I gaze out at the obsidian-fronted high-rises on the far side of the courtyard, seventy yards away. There's a church too – ancient-looking. Compared to its pristine neighbours, the walls are of dirty pale stone, lower, and ageing. Like some runt child the rest of the family is trying to hide.

"What do you see?" Natasha asks.

I bite my cheek. *Not much.* My skin prickles with doubt, and my gaze darts away from the church to the four modern buildings. They're more impressive, rising like dark statues in the night sky – beautiful, stoic, the chosen ones.

I peer more closely at them, my pulse throbbing in anticipation. But every time I think I glimpse the symbol, the image slips. And with each thought, my temples pound – the same sensation as in the estate, in the station.

The veil. I can sense it. Like a screen hovering over my senses, a curtain ready to be thrown open, almost imperceptible.

Standing there, images bombard me of my mother, going increasingly mad – her eyes scrunched shut, hands knotted in her hair, body trembling. I stretch my arms and swallow, my throat bone dry.

Natasha mutters behind me. And her words fan the heat in my chest, yanking at my attention. I start the count in my head again to clear my mind and let my eyes dance repeat-edly over the buildings.

Fuck all happens.

Natasha fidgets at my side.

I take a breath. And my mind forms snapshots of the veil peeling back before – the station, the estate, how time slowed, the shimmering world. I focus on the memory, and when my thoughts quiet, I move my gaze from one side of the court-yard toward the other. Fourth building … then the third, with its higher top floor … on to the second … and then the first, the tallest.

The connection explodes in my brain. The veil sweeps back from my senses, time slows, and the sight almost knocks me backward …

Everything glows – the stones of the courtyard, the walls of the office buildings, the church. Matter somehow becomes fluid. The edges of the office windows ripple like lapping waves. All impossible. Yet each thought disintegrates as quickly as it arises. The rational mind I rely on feels shattered.

One particular image grabs my attention … The first building. It's suddenly clad in gold and silver, with columns superimposed over its walls. Pedestals line its front with statues of what look like saints and winged angels. The entrance is no longer at ground level but three storeys up – a golden arch with blinding light. The whole thing resembles a cathedral viewed through a kaleidoscope. And so much *more* is visible – every glowing surface, every distance and dimen-sion – all integrated effortlessly into my awareness. Just like in the station.

Breathtaking.

"Jake."

Natasha's voice sounds tight and far away, like she's retreating down a distant corridor.

*There*. I glimpse the symbol. A cross with a downward-facing crescent moon. It sits above the new entrance to the building, in blazing light on a gold background.

I stare at it all – the fluid shapes, the glowing surfaces – a part of my brain unable to fathom the weirdness. My mind starts up again, doubts firing. With another pop in my ears, the veil returns as quickly as it lifted. The office building stands as it was before. Black obsidian walls, grid-like windows, and a darkened reception area. Entirely normal-looking.

"*Jake.*" Natasha's voice trembles. She touches my arm. Fingers ice cold. "Are you okay?" she asks.

I blink.

Was that seconds … hours? I shake my head, trying to kick-start my thinking brain. This is no government agency. The images are religious for sure – angels, arches, statues. And their building is *here*, in the city centre, which means resources and connections, deep roots. Not some new group.

And the shimmering world. *Incredible.* I sniff the air for a hallucinogenic gas, my heart thumping. My gaze finds Natasha—

She's shivering at my side, hugging herself tightly.

My own legs shake. And then it hits me.

The cold.

I suddenly feel it burning my ears, stabbing at my skin, like I've been encased in a coat of ice. I flex my fingers. They're almost frozen. And the bottom falls out of my stomach. It's the same strange chill from the hospital, the estate. Just much stronger.

I spin to face the edge of the courtyard, searching for any sign of our pursuers. But the entire world's dimming, the far streetlights struggling through some kind of smog. I take a step back. It's like being covered by a shroud.

"Something's wrong," Natasha says, squinting forward. "I cannot see."

A sudden smell – burnt metal. It scrapes at the back of my throat, sharper than ever. And all that drive I had to be active, to be predator not prey, now feels like mere sparks engulfed in darkness.

I glance across the courtyard at the building that transformed. The shadows deepen, only its outline visible, like I'm steadily going blind. Then the image comes of Ethan's body folded into the cupboard – the scratch marks around his eyes – and I almost choke.

This is it. We're going to disappear. Just like the tortured body on the trolley. Just like the other undesirables. Just like the rumours.

## 19

THE DARKNESS CONTINUES to press in on me – a strange coalescence of cold and despair, as if all colour from the surrounding courtyard is leaching out. I shiver, the oddest notions arising in my mind … *Just lie down, give up* …

The odour of burnt metal's so strong. I feel Natasha's fingers searching for mine. Random thoughts and memories drift through my brain … the train crash, psychedelic states, tortured and burnt bodies, the crazy rich, society's breakdown, religion on the rise, Puritans foretelling damnation.

And with the thoughts splurging over each other, the counting starts up in my head – my stillness technique, automatic after so many years. The associated space catapults me out of the sinking spiral for a moment.

Just a moment.

I focus in on some of the stinging memories – the mysterious man, our pursuers, Mandem's enforcers, the gang that ensnared my mother and destroyed my home – and heat rises from somewhere deep inside. In the growing dark, I hold fast to the sensation. Little by little, it breaks through the numbness.

I come to and blink out at the wide courtyard ahead as I rub desperately at my eyes.

The gloom remains as profound as ever. I can barely see the buildings straight ahead. My eyes dart to the streets on either side, searching for a way out. Yet the darkness there is just as deep. A new feeling forms in my gut – the sense of being surrounded, of a trap springing shut.

Natasha follows my gaze, her teeth chattering. "Is it them, our pursuers?" she says.

"No," I say, my own voice shaking. "I reckon it's something else."

Natasha's icy hand squeezes mine and tries to get me to move. But I anchor my feet and bring back the sensations from behind the veil, snapshots of the buildings opposite – the glowing walls and fluid surfaces. A vague memory tugs at my mind.

I try to scan the shadowy buildings. Maybe a narrow passageway between, an open door? But the high-rises are almost entirely invisible now. And with each effort to concentrate on the niggling memory, my head aches more, and the image floats further beyond my grasp.

My jaw clenches, and I lean forward to scour the gloom. But the strange chill simply deepens in my bones, my heart pounds louder against my ribs, and the darkness thickens on every side.

And still, that memory needles my mind.

I grip Natasha's fingers and pull. Not toward the exit roads but straight across the courtyard. We lurch into the deepening black.

"Where are we going?" Natasha asks, her voice so weak.

I stumble on, only a few feet visible in front, with only the vaguest notion of escape ahead of me. My legs feel like they've been set in concrete, and the desire to stop is all-consuming. I focus again on the heat in my chest and grit my teeth as we stagger across the hard stone ground. It remains pitch-black on all sides. And *so cold*. My legs tremble, and time stretches into eternity.

Then something appears out of the darkness. Grey stone. Arched windows. I come to a juddering halt.

The church.

Natasha bumps into my shoulder, causing me to stumble forward. The ageing wall is only a few feet in front of us, entirely solid. My head whips from side to side. No door. No way through. And the strange sense of being surrounded is growing, the awful chill increasing.

My arms tense. My fingers curl. And I go to slam my palm into the church wall when the memory finally comes, the insight from behind the veil. I glance up.

The church windows.

They're arch-shaped, about ten feet high, two feet wide at the bottom, and split into two by a horizontal ledge around two-thirds of the way up. A few of the top windows are broken, boarded over with cardboard.

I stare upward, taking in the dimensions, and any spark of hope dies in the growing chill. The top windows are too damn narrow – not much over a foot wide – and ten fucking feet above the ground with only a thin ledge beneath them.

Natasha stares up at me with wide eyes, her hand still tight around mine. I swivel and peer out across the courtyard into the darkness, trying to picture us running for the exit roads. The night wraps itself tighter around me. Frost speckles my breath, and it feels like my body's being submerged in icy water. Whatever's approaching draws nearer with every moment.

I dart my gaze back at the church and take in the layout – the outline of the lower and upper windows, their tiny ledges. To my left, a thin bit of wall borders the neighbouring building, jutting out of the church wall. Despite my mind screaming insanities, I estimate distance and angles.

"Hold tight here." My voice trembles as I disentangle my fingers from Natasha's.

She wraps her arms around herself as I stamp both feet on the ground and take a shuddering breath. I turn to the side from the church to focus on the thin bit of wall fifteen feet away where a drainpipe runs down the middle of it.

I explode into a run, my feet pounding at the ground, the vague outline of the drainpipe getting ever clearer. Three steps, four, five … I jump, my limbs like lead, and grab clumsily for the pipe just above head height, grasping it with both hands.

The plastic tube shakes but holds. I steady myself, feet on the wall, and climb, one frozen hand over the other. My injured arm begins to throb. I reach some anti-climb paint, steal a quick breath, and launch myself backward.

The nearest upper window's an arm's reach behind me – ten feet off the ground. I pictured myself getting an elbow on the ledge, maybe a knee. But I barely manage both sets of fingers.

I grip harder. The pain bites at my wrist. And my hands start to slip while a voice in my head whispers venom at me … *Just relax, fall* ….

I grind my teeth and press a foot onto each side of the lower window. Then, with a grunt, I inch my fingers back onto the upper ledge, one hand at a time.

And I climb, shifting my feet gradually up the sides of the lower window while breathing hard and fast. Twelve feet from the ground and counting.

My arm's pounding now. And finally, I get both forearms on the upper ledge. I push myself up till I'm kneeling on the top window ledge.

Exhaustion tugs me forward, and one of my hands goes through the cardboard covering the top window. I barely manage to grab the window frame to stop my whole body following when the cardboard flaps on its bits of tape, and my eyes glimpse the church floor far below. Dark and empty.

I raise myself up till I'm standing with both feet planted on the ledge of the open top window. Then, swivelling around, I stare back out at the courtyard and almost topple to the ground.

The darkness is like a physical thing, pressing into my eye sockets, into my mouth. I feel it swathing every inch of my body, burying me like frozen earth. Hovering in the blackness, the contours of a face appear, its hollow eyes searching for me.

While a distant thought shouts in my brain …

My gaze shoots downward for Natasha. Only the outline of her slumped form is visible, ten feet down, her arms still around her middle, barely breathing.

*"Here,"* I hiss. "You've got to move!"

She glances vaguely up at me.

"Natasha!" I say.

She blinks once, twice.

The cold pierces my body like sabres. My legs shake so badly I almost fall.

*"Come on!"* I say.

Slowly, she raises herself.

"The bottom window ledge." I point with a trembling hand.

She hoists one foot up.

"Now *push*," I order.

She reaches up with both hands, and I have to squat down to grab her fingers, my arms between my knees.

"Okay." I take a deep breath. "Now walk up!"

I take the strain and pull up as hard as I can. She walks up the bottom window and my shoulders shake with the effort. I almost drop her, twice, almost crash my back into the arch of the top window behind me. But eventually she gets a foot onto the top ledge.

Another pull and we stand together by the upper window.

"I'll … lower … you." I stutter the words between shuddering breaths. "Inside, there's another ledge, halfway down … it's wide. Go quick!"

I rotate around her, our bodies chest to chest. Then, facing away from the courtyard, I grab her hands again. With my feet braced, I lower her through the upper window into the church, toward the sill below. My shoulders ache, and my injured arm's screaming at me.

I count time, concentrating fiercely on my grip.

Finally, her voice drifts upward. "I'm there. You can let go."

I do, then spin as quickly as I can to drop through the window myself. Then I flip the cardboard back into place. My legs find the sill, and I jump down into the church, the impact echoing off the tiled floor.

I take a long breath, the tension easing from my chest and the cold shroud lifting from my skin.

My eyes take in the statues along the rear wall, the outlines of candles, of framed paintings, the shadows thick but unmoving. So different. Features come into focus – crosses, scrolls, memorial stones. And images of the building next door seep into my mind – the gleaming statues of saints and angels.

Our predicament crashes in on me, and my chest seizes. We're in a fucking church. If this *is* a religious conspiracy, could I have found us a worse place?

I spin into a crouch and stare into the surrounding dark. Pews extend away from us, a central space bordered by two rows of columns, the outline of more statues against the far wall, faintly lit.

Then the low light flickers.

My insides tighten further, and I peer forward, my eyes searching for a burning candle. Maybe one in a draught?

Natasha steps to my side. "It's okay," she whispers. "We will be safe here."

"Yeah, right," I mutter and gaze around.

We're standing in a narrow aisle that circles the edge of the church – from the altar at one end to the doors at the other. Another stab in the gut. There's one set of doors, only one way out of this place.

My brain screams again at my idiocy.

I creep toward the church entrance, listening hard, my eyes scanning for a nook to hide in – the pews, the recesses, the columns …

Natasha nods to the side of the church with the altar. "There may be rooms at the back—"

I put a finger to my lips. I hear a sound, a faint tapping, wood on stone. I whirl on Natasha.

"That is not me!" she says.

I stalk on down the side aisle in the direction of the doors, keeping low, my nerves stretching with each step. A large stone column stands a few feet up ahead, a gap in the pews beyond it, and a passageway runs across the middle of the church. I slink toward the pillar.

The tapping sound continues, getting louder and echoing around us. My heartbeat's accelerating, and my head swivels left and right, trying desperately to locate the source. I peer beyond the column.

A figure looms out of the darkness. The shock jolts my body like electricity, jerking my chest and arms. I utter an involuntary sound of surprise.

The outline of a tortured-looking man lurches toward me. Natasha screams at my side but then quickly cuts off the cry, her hand over her mouth. I stumble backward half a step.

The man's voice is low and rasping. "Who's there?"

## 20

I FIND my breath as I regain my footing. The man stands just a couple of feet away in the gloom, a church column at his side. I scan his posture – stooped and off-balance – and lower my centre of gravity to set myself.

"So? *Who's there?*" the man demands again, his voice strangely familiar.

I lean forward, trying to make out the man's features, when a blinding light jabs at my eyes. The flashlight beam is aimed directly at my face. I shrink away and raise a forearm to shield myself.

"*What do you want?*" the man asks.

The beam dances around my head. I strain to see. The man's short and slight. I raise an arm to knock the flashlight away, at the same time Natasha pushes forward at my side.

"*Father,*" she says, such relief in her voice.

"Who is that?" the man says and reaches to the side with his flashlight hand. He presses a switch on the column, and a few pathetic lights flicker to life high above us, bathing the church walls in a dull glow.

I see him fully for the first time – wild grey hair, stooped posture, dishevelled habit, wrinkled face peering dimly at us – a priest.

My insides tighten with the realisation.

"You!" I say.

Natasha swivels to me, her mouth open.

"But who are *you?*" the priest cuts in, his voice trembling. He holds the long walking stick I remember in the other hand and peers at us with the dome of brightness from the flashlight, straining to see.

"You showed up in my ward," I say. *Just before the two Puritan fuckwits.*

"Did I?" the priest asks, lines multiplying across his forehead. His gaze drifts to the side, the flashlight beam following. Its cone of light sweeps along the far wall, the lower church windows undoubtedly visible from outside.

Jaw clenched, I reach out to grab the flashlight from his quavering hand. "Look, just turn off—"

The priest jerks at my movement, rattled. His whole body lurches back toward me, his walking stick spinning with him. It clatters into my shin. And I recoil, pain pulsing up to my knee.

"Father," Natasha says, her tone intimate and expectant, like she's talking to an old friend. "We need your help. Someone out there wishes us harm."

My insides squeeze. "We've got no *time* for this," I mutter through gritted teeth. "We have to get hidden."

The priest gazes in Natasha's direction and then reaches out a spindly hand toward her face. My shoulders tense, and I go to push the guy's arm aside but then stop. The priest's running his fingers over her nose, her cheeks. So gently. His head tilts back, eyes closed. He's *feeling* her.

A prickling chill steals up my back, the smell of cordite strong in my nostrils, and the lights in the church dim. Even the beam from the priest's flashlight flickers. My heart's pounding again, my muscles tightening as I step toward the priest.

He remains entirely oblivious, his fingers continuing to trace downward over Natasha's paling face. And still she stands there, her head tilted back. A forced surrender crosses her features.

My heart beats faster, and I raise a hand to grab her arm. She yanks it away, keeping her upper body still as the priest's fingers move down to find the cross hanging around her neck.

The light grows ever dimmer. I toil to see the recesses in the opposite wall, my vision being eaten away with every second and my chest filling with cold water. The priest's fingers linger on the metal crucifix and then withdraw.

I go to grab Natasha again when she leans toward the old man.

"Please, Father. Help us. Hide us!" she says, straining to keep her voice level.

My fingers stiffen, claw-like. "Natasha, no!" I choke the yell. "He's a bloody geriatric!"

The noise jolts the old man, and he spins around. I swivel my body away, but still the stick hits me on my injured arm.

"*Fuck!*" I hiss.

"*Please,*" Natasha says to the priest.

I shake my head, my jaw tight.

The priest shivers and glances toward Natasha, then toward me, his eyes shining dully under skeletal brows.

Finally, he nods. "So be it," he says and pivots toward the front of the church. "Follow me."

The priest shuffles down the side aisle in the direction of the altar while I stand stock-still.

Natasha spins toward me. "Jake—"

"No way." I shake my head again.

The old man shambles away so slowly, like a set of bones only held together by his shabby habit.

"The man can't hide himself, let alone us," I say and scramble toward the side wall, motioning for Natasha to join me. There I search the stone for crevices or niches big enough to take cover in.

There's fucking nothing.

Natasha remains exactly where she was, standing in the middle of the side aisle. *"This way,"* she mouths and jabs her thumb over her shoulder toward the priest.

I clench my fists. "Don't be—"

The sound of wood scraping over stone snaps my attention around. The large church doors are opening behind us. My spine goes rigid.

Natasha hisses, *"Now."* She darts toward me, yanks my arm, and starts to drag me down the side aisle after the priest.

I hold fast, but she keeps on tugging. Images form of the geriatric feebly trying to hide her, or her vainly trying to hide him.

I squeeze my fingers and let myself be hauled along behind the priest.

The old man hobbles silently down the aisle, the columns blocking our progress from the church entrance. He doesn't tap with his walking stick as he did before, and instead holds it above the ground. Which means we're moving so fucking slowly, barely creeping past the statues and candles.

The urgency tightens my chest like a vice as my eyes scan the walls and pews for places to hide.

Natasha hurries to the priest's side. "Where are we going, Father?" she whispers in his ear.

He points a trembling hand. "The pulpit, just around the bend."

Natasha sprints past a column and toward the large carved wooden structure. The base of the railed pulpit stands six feet above the ground, a set of steps spiralling up to it from the stone floor with solid walls on either side.

I scramble behind her up the start of its curved staircase, keeping my head low. The pulpit's wooden walls feel like a coffin around me. Natasha clambers further up the winding steps. I make room for the priest. Then swivel.

And start.

The old man's shuffling away toward the centre of the church. My mouth opens, my pulse firing now. There's more screeching. The church doors closing again. Then silence.

I hold my breath, staring out of the pulpit. The priest stands in the middle of the church's central aisle, between altar and church doors, like a shield. His gaze is fixed at the entrance, his hands knotted in front.

"Can I help you?" he asks someone, his voice shaking. He tries to stand straighter – a pathetic attempt, his body bent and crooked.

"What can you see?" Natasha whispers over my shoulder.

I shake my head. Hardly anything. Just the priest and a thin slice of church behind him, my view blocked by the pulpit walls.

The old man stands his ground while the light continues to dim around us, the flickering candles painting deep shadows on the domed ceiling as the shapes grow into brooding clouds. I clench my teeth to stop them from chattering.

"This is a house of God, and it is late," the old man says, trembling from head to foot. "We are closed to visitors."

Still no reply.

Though the pulpit blocks my view, I sense an immense blackness facing the priest, a yawning nothingness. A part of me is desperate to shrink away, while another part feels pulled, like coiling fingers are tugging at my limbs and wrenching me from my hiding space. I grab my knees and yank them closer to my chin.

"There is only me." The priest's voice seems tiny, a pitiful sound in the growing expanse. He grips his stick to stand tall once more. "No one else is here."

The silence deepens. The chill grows.

I can only crouch. Frozen. Shaking. Again, the outline of a face forms in my mind. It's skull-like with nose socket, forehead, and jawbone all formed of writhing darkness. The eyes search for me, homing in.

My heart pounds like a jackhammer, far too loudly in my chest. And I keep my gaze fixed on the old man … waiting for a hand to reach out and crush him.

*We're all going to die.*

## 21

THE PRIEST'S BODY SHAKES, yet he remains standing there in the centre of his church, upright and stubborn, like a gnarled old tree confronting a hurricane.

There'll be no warning. Whoever's facing him will tear him apart at any moment.

The old man swallows. "Please … leave," he croaks.

My throat tightens like a cord is wrapped around it, and I picture the church layout in my head. My mind spins images of me sprinting down one aisle, Natasha the other.

My thoughts stumble on, mere pinpricks in a dark vastness. And still I sense black fingers pulling at my body, my mind, enticing me from my hiding place. The light continues to dim, all colour fading, total blindness only moments away.

I try to spark the anger, to force myself into movement, to wrench against the cold despair. But it's so hard. I'm barely able to inch my head around.

Natasha sits crouched on the pulpit stairs behind me, hugging her knees. Her eyes are huge, her skin like frost.

"You go … left," I whisper through chattering teeth. "Back toward … the corridor. I'll go …"

No response. She just stares blankly at me. I reach out with a shaking hand and try to coax her back to life.

Then a sound – a low, rasping exhalation behind me, a sigh of relief.

I turn slowly to stare again at the priest. The old man still faces the doors, but his posture's relaxed a fraction.

I hold my breath, not daring to hope. I grip the stair beneath me without easing a single muscle.

The light, is it brightening? And then there's the scrape of the wooden door on stone again. I count my breaths. More scraping, the doors closing.

And still I wait. Warmth embraces my insides. My vision returns, too. The flickering candles become visible once more on the far side of the church. I gaze around at the altar, the columns, the pews. All evenly lit with recognisable colours. Everything is entirely normal-looking.

I stumble to my feet, my gaze finding the old man. He's shuffling toward us with his tapping stick, his dull eyes fixed somewhere above our heads. His features are tranquil, his head tilted, his thin lips smiling as if nothing out of the ordinary just happened.

Natasha stirs behind me. She's gazing downward, arms still wrapped around her knees.

"My child," the priest says. "Hush now. You're safe here." He turns toward a side door on the opposite side of the church and motions over his shoulder. "Come, I have food … beds."

Natasha climbs shakily to her feet.

"Wait," I say and stumble down the steps of the pulpit. I jab my finger toward the middle of the church floor. "What was that?"

"What?" the priest says, swivelling back to face me. He frowns.

"Yeah, *what?*" I say, the words exploding out of me.

The old man tilts his head. Blinks. The lines in his forehead resemble a landslip, and I feel his vague stare scratching at my skin. Heat climbs my chest.

My eyes shoot to the priest's side door and then back to

Natasha. I lean in and lower my voice. "We need to get out of here."

Natasha passes me down the pulpit steps and crosses the floor toward the priest.

"You can leave any time you want," the old man says, still staring blankly over my shoulder. "But I think you're supposed to be here."

I scoff.

"Despite everything, you still don't believe. Do you?" he says.

Strange images flash through my mind – the shimmering world, the dark figures, the outline of that face in the blackness – and my temples pound.

"You're still trying to package your experiences with your reason," the priest goes on. "To discover a neat little bow that ties them all together." He mimes the action with shaking hands. "It's understandable."

I find myself staring toward the far church wall and the high-rise on the other side of it.

The priest pauses. "The building next door … I think you glimpsed something," he says.

My eyes widen.

The priest's mouth breaks into a broad smile. "You did. Didn't you?"

I shift my gaze away and find Natasha staring at me, too.

"Jake, what *did* you see?" she asks.

Statues of angels and gargoyles, golden domed arches, flaming spears. All fucking crazy. More doubts rain down.

I shake my head.

The priest grasps his walking stick tighter. "Impressive. *Impressive*," he says. "But you don't yet *believe*." He raises a finger and then shrugs. "But it won't be long. You'll soon discover that belief is everything, that miracles are possible." He glances up at the altar, at the large cross hanging above it. "If we only believe in the mundane, that's all we see. Faith is the very fabric of reality."

I swivel to face Natasha. "We don't need this bullshit."

"I think he can help us," she says.

My chest tightens. "Man can't help us," I mutter. "He's *deluded*."

Natasha opens her mouth.

I lean toward her and hiss, "And we've got no idea what his game is."

Natasha's jaw tenses. "Come on, Jake," she snaps. "Not everyone is selfish like you."

"I would advise we retire to the back," the priest says and motions to the side door behind him. "It will be safer."

"Safer?" I say, spinning to face him. "What d'you know? Why d'you show up at my bed in the hospital?"

The priest sighs. "My story will come tomorrow," he says and then attempts some kind of bow. "It's late. You need rest."

I glance across at Natasha, who turns with the priest. She takes his arm, and he pats her hand like she's some kind of long-lost granddaughter. Together they shuffle toward the door.

I clench my teeth, scrunching my eyes shut. And again, the same need grips me to stomp out, to leave her. But the same warnings sound an instant later, that I'd be giving up details of my security box, my life, and how I operate … everything. My insides squeeze so tightly it leaves me shaking.

"I'm Father Thomas," the priest says to Natasha. "And you?"

"Natasha," she says with a smile. Then she nods in my direction. "And this is Jake."

"Natalia … Jacob," Father Thomas says and waves a hand somewhere over our heads in greeting. "Welcome home. A great deal must have happened. You must tell me."

He opens the door for her. And together, they disappear through.

I grip the floor with my toes, the sound of their talking

ebbing away. The old man is undoubtedly spinning all kinds of nonsense, persuading Natasha of God-knows-what.

The church space spreads out around me, and I shiver, an echo of the strange chill in my bones. My eyes find the side door standing ajar. And I can almost taste the promise of food and sleep beyond, my legs quivering.

But my gaze flits away to the end wall, to the office building on the far side, and every drilled caution yells inside my brain … *The threat's too close. Don't trust the guy. I haven't scoped the place. There's only one exit …*

And so I just stand there. Alone. The gloom bites deeper around me.

## 22

I push myself up on the cushions and blink into the darkness. The only light source is a dull glow that filters under the closed door. It illuminates a battered table to my side and an old sofa bed beyond.

Father Thomas's spare room.

My gaze finds Natasha on the sofa bed, curled up under her sheet. Her breathing's soft and deep in my ears, her expression so peaceful lying there, so apparently safe under the priest's sacred roof. I can still see the light in her eyes as she listened to the old man's prattling the night before – faith, miracles. And his bullshit words … *You're supposed to be here*.

My insides heat as I push myself to my feet, grab my clothes from the table, and dress quickly. The pain in my injured arm is almost gone. Then I creep toward the door, edge it open, and step through into the light-filled corridor, the priest's bedroom to one side.

I listen at the closed door. There's quiet beyond.

My lips pull into a smile. "Think you can fool us?" I whisper, picturing the old man sleeping like the dead. He's not far off.

The silence remains as I swivel and pad down the corridor, avoiding each of the creaking floorboards. My breath comes easily, my steps so much lighter. No pounding headache. No faltering vision. And memories form of what happened in the church – the encroaching dark, the strange blindness – my mind already cataloguing potential explanations, ways to prove the priest wrong and persuade Natasha to get the hell out of here.

I stalk faster past the kitchen – empty – on down the corridor, and through the side door.

My lips part. The church interior … so different from last time I saw it. Sunlight shines down through the top windows along the side wall, dust hovering in the slanting beams. The arched ceiling extends high above, the columns bordering the central area free of flickering shadow, and no creeping shroud over my vision either, no death-like chill.

I take a deep breath. The place smells of age. And no one's here. The rows of pews extending to the rear doors are all empty.

Natasha's right. Not a Puritan church, then.

I pace away from the altar, down the central aisle. Then glance toward the light switch on the column the priest used the night before, already visualising what I might see.

And there it is. Large and circular with a ribbed edge – a dimmer switch. My pulse beats faster. Maybe not so hard to simulate darkening vision.

I stride to the middle of the aisle, to the space opposite where the priest faced … whoever it was. Approaching the spot, a frisson of cold makes me shiver. Some kind of draught. I take another step, and my feet scuff on something. I glance down.

Sand.

A layer of it in a small circle between the priest and the doors, ten feet from where the old man was standing. I cast my eyes around. Can't spy any more. And feel myself frowning.

I crouch. The layer of sand lies in a circular depression, four feet wide, like something's etched it from the stone floor.

I reach down to touch it but then stop, my insides tightening as the chill edges up my spine.

I straighten and shake off the sensation. Then I step into a beam of sunlight from the side windows and take a long sigh, my body warming.

The main church doors lie straight ahead, freedom beyond.

So fucking tempting.

I stalk toward them. Light shines through the gap, the lock clearly open.

Impressions come of the office building just around the corner and its strange transformation in the darkness. But with the sun filling the church, it's almost impossible to conjure the images of golden arches and flaming spears. I shake my head at the stupid memory.

Nearer the church doors, my eyes take in the wrought-iron lock, clearly broken, much of the iron ring and metal plate missing. A crowbar or sledgehammer? I peer closer for signs of sheared metal or splintered wood. But there's nothing in the door or on the floor below. In fact, it's as if the area around the lock's been eaten away by something.

I scan the surface of the wood. It's covered in minute holes and parallel ridges between the grain lines, all in regular patterns.

Acid wouldn't do that.

I squeeze my temples, trying to order my thoughts, and a vague idea drifts at the edge of my mind.

As I stare at the lock, the veil's thin before my senses. My thoughts begin to slow, and I let them. Then, before I know it, a fraction of the veil peels back.

Memories of last night rush in. Much clearer now. I remember the encroaching darkness, the hollow eyes, and the sensation of cold as it slinks back between my shoulder blades. I feel a strange sense of death, of the eventual erosion of everything, the inevitable road all things take to nothingness.

An idea comes, and my stomach clenches.

*Age.* The lock, the floor – it's as if they've been aged by hundreds, maybe thousands of years. I swivel to stare at the sand – the circle eroded from the stone underneath. All in a matter of seconds.

I find my gaze drawn back to the remnants of the iron ring handle. Two-thirds of it missing, the rest covered in tiny flakes of rust, the obvious question a splinter in my mind … *What could do this?*

Still behind the veil, I feel a connection to the lock, to the door, and suddenly to a strange presence beyond that pulls at me. My toes inch forward. The chill slithers up the rear of my neck. My internal alarm begins to ring. And I watch as my hand rises, my fingers creeping toward the handle.

"Good morning, Jacob," a hoarse voice says.

I jump. Then spin around from the door, my heartbeat galloping.

"I wouldn't go out right now."

Father Thomas is on a bench, twenty feet down the side wall, gazing blankly across the church. He's entirely still, his walking stick held in both hands. And somehow, I fucking missed him sitting there.

My brain scrambles, and I stumble back half a step.

"The side entrance is safer. It leads behind the building." The priest tilts his head toward the opposite wall at the rear of the church. "If you *do* want to leave." And then he grins his wide, toothy smile.

The door to the priest's rooms at the other end of the church opens. I lift my head. Natasha stands on the threshold, forty yards away, wrapped in her sheet.

"What is it?" Her voice echoes across the church interior.

The chill slides up the back of my head. And the image flashes of the broken lock behind me, somehow eroded by thousands of years.

"Nothing!" I say and dart to the side to block her view of it.

138

"Nothing? Are you sure, Jacob?" the priest says and climbs shakily to his feet. He shuffles between the rows of seats toward the central aisle, his hands gripping the back of the pew in front. "You diminish your discoveries."

Natasha pads across the church floor in our direction, her bare calves visible beneath the held sheet. I remain rooted before the door.

"The real question is, how you were able to glimpse our neighbouring building?" the priest says. "To see it for what it truly is?"

I shift my weight.

"Are you not interested in the reason?" he asks.

My eyes find Natasha. She's gazing straight at Father Thomas now, an intent look on her face.

The old man reaches the central aisle and hobbles toward me. "You see, our faith is the foundation of who we are," he says. "It's manifest in every thought we tell ourselves about the way the world is, what's real and what's not." He taps his stick on the floor with each word. "To be open to new realities, first we must suspend our thinking."

As if my mind wants to make his point, my internal count starts up automatically, my thoughts stilling as they've done so many times before.

This priest smiles again. "This is only the first step, however; that's what's interesting." He shuffles closer, only a few feet away, and I feel his proximity like a growing pressure on my chest. "But I think you know this," he continues.

I clamp my mouth shut, perspiration breaking out across the back of my neck.

"To experience another world, we need a taste of it," the priest says. "It's the foundation on which a new faith can be built." He peers up at me from his stooped posture. "That's what happened to you. Isn't it?"

The memory comes – the station, the veil being ripped from my eyes. And even though I keep my mouth closed, holding my breath, I find myself nodding. I can't help it.

"Aha!" the priest says. "You see?" He waggles his walking stick. "An experience challenged your beliefs to the core. Something new took root."

Gooseflesh breaks out over my arms and back.

"This is what you must understand." The priest strains to stand upright before me. "Without our limiting beliefs, the world is far bigger than people realise, full of incredible richness. Some spend their entire lives in pursuit of these mystical experiences. For others, it's simply gifted."

My palms grow sweaty, memories coming of my mother, of the bliss she experienced, the fullness that poured out of her like liquid joy. I feel the priest gazing up at me, or through me.

"But most of us can't control them," he says. "The experiences come and go, and their absence can be deeply painful. And now you can create them yourself."

I find myself shaking my head this time. The awful chill's growing in my body, the strange images from behind the veil crowding my brain, and it's like my thinking mind's being crushed beneath it all.

"Don't worry," he says and places a hand on my shoulder. "We often fight it at the outset. It's entirely normal." The old man smiles. "But come!" He shuffles around to face Natasha and the church interior. "I promised to tell you what I know of all this." He waves us back to the side door. "Now it's my turn."

## 23

I STUMBLE into the kitchen after Natasha and Father Thomas. The space is cramped and sparse. Damp stains the ceiling and a single bulb hangs down over a wooden table that stands in the middle of the room. The furniture's like the priest, rickety and dilapidated.

The old man feels his way around to the table and lowers himself into a chair, grimacing with the effort.

I remain standing, however, leaning against the wall by the kitchen door. Natasha shuffles over to a seat between us. She's still wrapped in her sheet; her hair – immaculate before – looks riotous. She glances in my direction, and her cheeks colour. Then she angles her body away from me and runs a hand over her hair, trying and failing to smooth it down.

She turns to the priest. "So, Father, what's going on?" she says. "What's happening to us?"

The priest purses his lips, his expression almost sad. "It is not just us, my child, it's the whole of society," he says. "What we're facing goes back to the very beginnings of religion, of faith."

Natasha frowns slightly. And I blow out a long breath.

"Hidden forces have been influencing and manipulating

humankind's beliefs for thousands of years," he continues, his dull eyes sweeping vaguely from Natasha to me. "And they are still controlling us today."

"Here we go," I mutter.

"Father, what are you saying?" Natasha asks, sitting upright. She fingers the cross on her necklace. "Religion inspires. It does not manipulate."

The priest gazes at her with so much compassion it looks as if his heart might break. "But it does, my child," he says. "Man has been at the mercy of this coercion for a very long time. There are wolves out there, and we are the sheep."

Natasha blinks back at him and clears her throat. "You are saying forces are manipulating us, controlling our faith?" she says.

The priest nods.

"Turning many of us to God?" she continues, her pitch rising.

He pauses. Then nods again.

Natasha pulls the sheet tighter around her. "I do not believe it," she says. "That has not been my experience. I was an orphan. A convent took me in." Her eyes shine. "The nuns did not pressure me. They simply did God's work. Selfless service. Despite the powers that be. Their *example* was their teaching. When I had to leave, they gave up *everything* for me."

Tears well in Father Thomas's eyes. "Ah, Natalia, that is the beauty," he says, leaning toward her. "What faith did for you, and what you did with your faith. So beautiful. So precious. It's partly why our effort is so important."

"Hold up," I snap and jerk off the wall. "What effort?"

But the priest ignores me, reaching a hand across the table toward Natasha. She removes one hand from her wrapped sheet, at first tentatively. Then she leans forward and takes Father Thomas's hand.

"We have to remember, where there is the potential to create light, there is also the capacity to create dark," the priest says gently. Then he glances from Natasha to me. "One potency can't exist without the other."

"What dark?" I half shout.

"The manipulation, the deceit," he says. "All these years, all of us deceived. The whole of society."

I shake my head.

The priest raises an eyebrow. "Fantasy, is it?" he says, squinting up at me. "You don't see the battle going on for society? The traditionalists versus the modernists? A version of this has played out since the beginning of civilisation."

"You're talking about the twisting of religion, of society," I say, raising a hand, "and you're a priest!"

The old man nods calmly. "It means I'm close enough to see it," he says. "Strings are being pulled behind the scenes, disasters spawned, miracles sown."

"All these accidents, these technology failures," says Natasha, her eyes wide. "You think they are planned?"

The old man nods again.

"To undermine people's faith in modernity?" she says and her hand goes to her mouth.

"Is it such a stretch?" asks the priest, and his eyes drift from Natasha to me once more. "Natalia told me you saw sabotage at the new train station, Jacob."

I again glimpse the dark shapes squeezing the crowd together, the train smashing into the barriers, the atrium disintegrating above me. And my head starts to spin.

Father Thomas grips his walking stick between his knees. "But I believe it's only the beginning," he says.

My mouth opens, but the protest dies on my tongue. The mysterious man's final warning flashes through my mind … *something worse is coming.*

Natasha fixes me with a stare. I shut my mouth again.

"A long time ago, I stumbled across the building opposite and also saw it as it is," the priest goes on. "Before this …" He motions toward his dull eyes. "I had glimpses of what we are dealing with."

I look the old man up and down and then picture our pursuers, their fluid movements. "*You* tracked people here?" I ask.

"God was my shepherd," says the priest. "He granted me that initial sight, led me to this church." The old man glances toward the side wall, toward the office building behind it. "I've served his mission all these years."

"God told you to come here?" asks Natasha.

"And to wait." The priest nods. He glances from Natasha to me. "Clearly for this moment."

My stomach tightens further, and I bang the back of my head into the wall behind while Natasha's leaning in, staring at Father Thomas, her eyes bright.

"So, this … force we are dealing with," Natasha says. "Who *are* they? What do they want?"

The priest grimaces. "That is the problem, my child. I do not know for sure. I believe they are old … very old." I see a new fervour in his eyes, a glint in the dullness. "That they operate on timescales far longer than we can comprehend. I have tried to learn more."

He draws himself straighter. "Even with my sight failing, I have trailed people from that building. There is always increased activity at the time of these technological break-downs, these accidents. I believe these people to be involved, but have been able to learn precious little more."

He goes quiet with a sigh. Natasha's shoulders slump. I remain entirely still.

"I have become old," the priest says sadly. "I have been waiting for such a long time."

Then he leaps up in his chair, his walking stick held tightly in one hand. I jump.

"But there is one place you could try," he says, speaking quickly now. "Many years ago, when I could still see, I trailed guards from the building next door. On numerous occasions, I followed them to a place but could never gain entrance."

"What place?" I ask. "What are you going on about?"

Again, he ignores me, continuing to stare with wide eyes at the wall between us. "I could not get in, but *you could*," he says. "You could go there and discover more, discover their plan, learn how to stop them!"

"*No!*" I say, the pressure building in my chest, my mind conjuring images of the mysterious man, of our pursuers.

I glance at Natasha, poised for her rebuttal, her refusal. Surely.

It doesn't come. She reaches out to grip the old man's hand across the table, staring into his eyes.

"But—" I say.

"There is no bigger trial facing humanity, no bigger challenge," the priest says, patting Natasha's hand and gazing toward her. "I am sorry for the burden."

Tears well in her eyes. And I imagine her picturing her friend, Ethan, the man folded up on the cupboard shelf in his shack outside the hospital.

"I told you, you're supposed to be here." The priest's hoarse tone strengthens further. "It's why you've come."

After a moment, Natasha nods. And I shake my head vigorously.

"No fucking way," I say. "This is *not* our fight."

The priest blinks back at me, his mouth open. "You think it's an accident that you're both here?" he asks.

"We found a tattoo, tracked a symbol here. I was just trying to find …" I trail off, all too aware of how idiotic my words sound.

Father Thomas continues to stare at me, one eyebrow raised.

I shake my head again. "I never asked for this."

"We rarely do," the priest says softly. Then he gives a rattling sigh. "Yet we're part of God's plans, irrespective."

Natasha continues to stare willingly at the old man while I grip the table, my arms like rock. And my mind automatically plots an escape route – down the corridor, through the side door, up the central aisle, to the main church doors … Then I see the corroded lock and feel again the growing chill, the strange presence beyond. My chest tightens.

I gaze across the table. The priest's staring straight at me.

"You *can* do this," the old man says and slaps his thigh. "Believe it's all intended. There's no going back. See where it takes you!"

My mouth opens and closes, my throat as dry as dust.

"And remember, faith is everything," the priest says, gripping his walking stick. "It impacts not just your perceptions, not just what you experience ... but your abilities, too."

## 24

I PACE THE KITCHEN, hands thrust in my pockets, as Father Thomas prattles on at Natasha.

"It's a club, a gentlemen's club – an extremely exclusive one, I believe," he says, tone excited, his fingers still squeezing hers across the table.

He describes tracking guards there from the building next door and his attempts to get in, as well as pointless details about the club entrance and the clientele. Natasha nods along all the while, lapping it all up.

I grit my teeth, squeezing my fingers together.

"I have the address somewhere!" the priest says and staggers to his feet. "I will find it."

And with that, the old man shuffles from the room.

I lean down toward Natasha. "This is *crazy*."

"What is so crazy about it?" she demands. "Do you have something better to do, somewhere better to go?"

I blink back at her.

She nods. "You said it yourself. They will be tracking both of us. You cannot go back to your factory, and I cannot go back to the hospital." Her jaw's rigid. No tears now. "And there is little chance the police will help. No one would believe us."

"But how can you trust him?" I say and throw an arm toward the kitchen door. "He's yapping on about ancient schemes, where we need facts." I slap the back of my hand into my palm. "Something *real*."

Natasha simply folds her arms in her chair. "Okay, if he's wrong, it comes to nothing. But if he's right, we learn more about who is doing this. Is that not what you wanted?"

I just stare at her.

"We need to know their resources, contacts, organisation ... that's what you said, well this is our chance," she says with a nod, a self-satisfied smile on her lips. "It is a very rich club. Does that not tell you something already?"

I clench my jaw and start to pace again, my mind running through the implications ... Whoever's behind the sabotage has connections. And at the club, we'd find the truly powerful. Those at the top.

"And what if he is right also that we are supposed to be here? What if this *is* God's will?" she says.

The pressure builds in my chest and temples, and I whirl on her. "It's not *my* bloody will."

She sits there, entirely unfazed. "Then I will go by myself."

The heat rises inside me, and I clench my fists so tightly my hands shake, the same images coming of my beloved security box disappearing.

"Father Thomas said you can do this," she says, that damn earnestness in her face again. "I am sure you can. And with the club, all we need is a way in."

My ribs remain tight, and with my mind running, an idea begins to form. I only just manage to suppress the smile that comes with it.

"I'm sure I'll think of something," I say.

———

ALMOST TWELVE HOURS LATER, I'm banging on the door to the priest's spare room. No reply.

I tap my feet and then bang again, more of my smile fading by the second.

Her voice sounds through the door. "Go away."

I fidget, the new suit needling me. I appropriated it from a hotel cleaning service, picked it straight off the rack. The shirt too, stolen from a department store along with cufflinks and socks. My shoulders tighten, and I bring my mouth right to the wood.

"Come on!" I say. "It's gone eleven. Getting in will be trickier with every minute we wait."

Silence again. I scrunch my eyes shut and bang the door with my forehead, memories coming of our conversation hours before. I explained the plan – her a dancer, me her handler. Without serious cash, it'll be our only way into the club. Her face went puce, her eyes like embers, and she stared down at the tiny pile of stolen clothes as if they'd burst into flames.

"Soon," she says through the door.

"Yeah, soon, soon," I mutter and turn on my heels to tramp back in the direction of the kitchen.

The priest steps into the corridor in front of me, and I grunt.

The old man raises his hands. "I'm going. I'm going," he says and shuffles away toward the door to the church interior.

Then he swivels and glances back at me. "Jacob, remember." He raises a bony finger. "Suspend your thoughts, and open your mind to new possibilities … trust me." He smiles. "Take a leap. You're already halfway there."

I open my mouth to speak when a latch clicks behind me. I swivel. The door swings open to reveal Natasha standing in the doorway.

I take a second breath.

Her hair falls freely now, down past her shoulders. She's put on the stolen make-up sparingly, but it doesn't matter.

The dress is low at the back, ending above the knee, and hugs every curve of her body. No comparison with the department store photos I saw it in. She fingers the crucifix necklace still around her neck – totally out of place but unimportant too. She shifts her weight from foot to foot.

I scratch at my nose. "Err …" I feel my neck redden and my insides squirm. The desire grips me to avert my gaze. Nevertheless, I keep facing her.

"That … looks good," I manage to get out.

She doesn't reply, just stares down at her shoes. But she doesn't turn away.

## 25

HAVING CHECKED the streets beyond for a good ten minutes, we leave the church by the side entrance and then head through the city centre toward the club. I insist we backtrack several times, scanning continuously to ensure we're not followed. And Natasha doesn't argue. In fact, she doesn't say anything. Simply stalks beside me, features grim.

As we stride along between the looming high-rises, my stomach begins to sink. With every person we pass, Natasha wraps her jacket ever tighter around herself, ensuring not an inch of the stolen dress is visible.

I force a slow breath and stalk onward as we continue toward the club in silence.

The journey feels like travelling between countries. From the brightened city centre with its incident lighting, towering skyscrapers, and marble pavement, we cross the river into darkness to broken streetlights, open fires, and ramshackle buildings. Rubbish everywhere, filth and soot. Old mattresses lie scattered on corners under makeshift covers, their inhabitants gone. Most seem to hide out of sight. Scared of the rumours perhaps, or of something more sinister.

Almost an hour later, we approach Westminster – another rich part of the city, another border. Private security firms bolster the police presence, keeping out the undesirables, and a glow breaks above the crumbling buildings like some false sun. Before long, we're padding along wide pavement, passing working streetlights, tended trees, and sparkling shop fronts. But Natasha's still walking with her arms tightly around herself, still staring suspiciously at everyone she passes.

Perspiration forms across the base of my back.

Continuing, we approach another gentlemen's club – a posh one too, but not our destination.

The building's granite-fronted with multiple floors, the windows black, and a sizeable crowd pressed around some kind of cordon, a mixture of dark suits and cocktail dresses.

To one side, a group of Puritans stand vigil, candles in hand, their stares bearing down on all decadent sinners. The deluded believers hold placards of their political leader, someone to empower the oppressed.

I scoff and shake my head.

Passing the club, Natasha slinks away to the other side of the pavement. And an idea sparks.

"Come on," I say and begin striding toward the cordon.

Natasha hurries behind. "What are you doing?" she says. "This is the wrong place."

"It's practice," I say, weaving through the crowd and eyeing the bouncers at the front of the VIP line. "We've got to be able to get by them."

Pressing on, a cat-call rings in my ears. I swivel. A couple of guys in the queue have their eyes on Natasha. Sculpted cheekbones, coiffed hair, and shoes pointed like daggers. Both oozing entitlement.

I ignore them and urge Natasha forward. She presses back against my hand.

"Hey, beautiful," one guy calls. "Ditch the lout."

Natasha tightens even further under their gaze. I go to block her with both hands. But she spins and stalks away from the queue.

"Wait!" I call, hurrying to catch up. "We've got to try this!"
But she continues on, quickening her stride.

My fingers clench. The top-end club's only ten minutes away now, and getting in there will be a lot fucking tougher.

I kick a loose stone on the road and then steal a glance at her. She keeps her distance while maintaining her focus on the streets ahead, her arms still folded tightly across her body. My mind runs on about how to draw her out, my thoughts continually scrambling and my mouth bone dry.

We continue down the broad pavement, past wide-fronted houses, the club drawing ever nearer.

I step to her shoulder. Clear my throat. "The clothes ..." I start.

Natasha doesn't look up.

"You don't like them?" I say, my insides squirming. Then I peek up to meet her gaze.

She makes no sign of having heard me.

I keep on. "You don't like looking good—"

"You have only ever lived here. Haven't you?" she says, her gaze still fixed ahead.

My lips clamp shut, my chest gripped by the usual tightness that comes from personal questions. I stare across the wide pavement, scanning the street ahead. Just the occasional pedestrian, with the odd luxury car passing by. Still no obvious threat.

She nods thoughtfully, her arms still wrapped around herself, and lapses back into silence.

I grip the pockets of my stolen suit trousers, my mind automatically jumping ahead and plotting the route to the club again, the few roads in between us. I close my eyes for a moment, take a breath, and force my attention back to Natasha.

"In this city?" I say eventually, working to soften my tone. "Yeah."

"I come from an industrial town. In Poland," she says. "There are some bad people there."

153

"Bad people are all over—"

"Sex gangs," she says, her words a caustic hiss. "These people gather girls, tell them lies about nice jobs in the West." She shakes her head. "I was at school when they found me. They talked to me on my way home, but I did not believe them. I knew I would be made a slave."

She lengthens her stride down the pavement. We pass adverts in a row of shop windows – rotating images of models wearing glittering clothes and shoes – the club getting ever nearer, ever faster.

My heartbeat speeds up. I open my mouth but then shut it again, breathe, and just nod.

"I had to leave everything I had ever known," she continues, her gaze still focused ahead, her eyes welling up. "The convent, the nuns. They were my family."

Then she sighs and goes silent for a while, as if contemplating something. I turn my head toward her as we walk.

"I was seven years old, begging on the streets, when they took me in," she says quietly, her arms relaxing a fraction around her middle. "They found such joy in service. It was like fuel for the harsh winters, the hardest times."

Her tone calms, and finally she slows her steps, falling into a kind of trance-like rhythm as she continues speaking.

"They gave away the little we had to others, went up against companies, mayors, anything they saw was wrong," she says. "Yet they were the happiest souls I have ever known."

She smiles widely and gazes ahead, unfocused, the tears at the corners of her eyes reflecting the glow of the streetlights as she walks.

"I loved to read, and one of the sisters used to find books for me," she continues. "A local benefactor died, and she insisted I use the money for school in a nearby town. No other orphan had that chance."

She goes silent as we pass more ornate shop fronts. And I barely stop myself from shaking my head in disbelief. School was nothing but a torment for me, the beginnings of my life as a thief.

"And that is where the group came," Natasha says, her tone lower, harsher. She glances at me for the first time since we left the church. "You ask me to use my looks?" That etched line forms across her forehead, and I see tension in her jaw. "They have been nothing but trouble for me. Always. The group would not accept no." She shakes her head. More tears come and she stares ahead again.

Still, I keep quiet.

She swallows and tilts her chin up. "I had to hide for weeks," she says. "But this group, they kept on coming, coming … In the end, the sister I spoke of said I had to go. I begged to stay, but she said it was God's will, that there was a reason, I'd been chosen to serve him in another place, and that the path would show itself in time. The nuns raised money to fund my trip across Europe, sacrificed everything to get me away from there."

She grinds her teeth. "Men, men, *men*," she growls and paces even faster.

We leave the shops behind, and I follow her toward a lawn-covered roundabout.

"For so long, I had to fight people off, until finally I made it here, to this country," she says, straightening. "And I have worked all day, studied all night to become a nurse, to help people as the nuns helped me." And then her words soften once more. "It is the least I can do in their memory."

She fingers the cross around her neck again. I stare at it – tiny and silver, on a simple chain.

"She gave you that, the sister. Didn't she?" I say.

Natasha gives a small nod.

"Is that why your religion is so important to you … why you're doing this?" I ask.

She pauses and turns to me, nodding again. "When finally, I had a family, God was its most important part." She shrugs.

"So, I cannot believe something that has so much love is actually manipulating people."

My thoughts dart to the nun in the station, her sacrifice, the same questions running ... *Why would she* do *that?*

I gaze at the ground.

"Well, you did ask," Natasha says and a tiny smile brightens up her face.

I nod, and say, "I did." And then I point to her face, my voice lighter. "And you smudged your make-up."

Natasha lets out a small laugh, like a bird chirruping. She sniffs and runs her finger along the edge of her eye, her arms no longer wrapped tightly around her middle.

"I do not suit it anyway," she says.

I find myself smiling. Strange but true. She doesn't need it. Then my thoughts flit back to the club ahead of us, my smile faltering.

Except for what's coming.

## 26

A FEW MINUTES LATER, we turn the last corner, and my eyes go wide.

The club's nothing like the one we passed. Nothing like anything I've ever seen before. Situated on a small rise, like some sacred site, the building resembles a giant flower with a domed roof and interlocking wood and glass petals around its top. A massive triangle-shaped promenade tapers toward the club's entrance with trees embedded in the pavement alongside trickling streams and winding paths.

A sizeable crowd, maybe a couple hundred strong, flounces around the trees and the streams. The super rich, the beautiful, wearing flowing trains, embroidered gold, and bodices like sculpted art pieces. All served from invisible bars by flawless women, naked but for the jewelled patches that adorn their skin. My lips part. And these are the people *outside* the club, the mere aristocrats of the modern court.

All's merry with the sounds of tinkling laughter, and iridescent cocktails circle them like tropical birds. No sign of the train crash here. Each noble is hungry to exploit any gaps created, to secure a few words with the true royalty within.

I pull us to a stop twenty feet from the edge of the crowd, something niggling the back of my brain.

And then it hits me. There's no security cordon. No obvious bouncers. Yet some of society's wealthiest are freely mingling without any riffraff or protesting Puritans in sight.

My heart accelerates, and I scan the throng. There they are, the guards, deftly hidden among the masses. Each in a different designer suit and almost indistinguishable from the guests – *almost* – aside from their military build and bearing, the earpieces, and the way they knife through the crowd. Two are already homing in on us.

Natasha presses in at my side. "What is the plan?"

"I'm working on it," I hiss back.

And that's when my gut twists, and the strange chill slithers into my bones.

Pulse firing, I scour the crowd for the pursuers, for their strange outfits. But I can see only the guards, fucking dozens of them. Plus, several nearby guests are staring at us with sneering smiles – watching interlopers clearly part of the sport. And my eyes start to dim, dark forms shifting at the edges of my vision.

My insides plunge, and Natasha leans in toward me again.

"It would help if you told me," she says.

I grind my teeth, trying to shut out her voice. And my mind clicks into automatic, searching for memories that would normally be there ... recollections of having scoped the place, scrutinised the security measures.

But I've got absolutely fucking nothing.

Sweat breaks out across my back. The guards breach the edge of the crowd and begin stalking toward us, obvious bulges in both their jacket lapels. A voice in my head screams at me to run while Natasha wraps her arms tightly around her middle again. Ever more of the crowd are gazing at us, and she's eyeing them as if they might eat her alive—

I spin toward her. "Your jacket," I say, reaching a hand out.

She tenses and shakes her head. The condescending looks from the crowd become subtle jibes.

*"Give me your jacket,"* I say and take hold of the collar of Natasha's coat to ease her out of it, revealing her figure to the world.

Every muscle in her body tightens, and she stares daggers at me. I hold my breath and urge her around to face the crowd. The approaching guards stop, and I lead her past them, and then past the glittering guests.

The onlookers simply stand silently, watching as we pass.

One guy steps into our path – perfect features, a shining complexion, and a suit that reflects a myriad of colours in its folds. He looks Natasha up and down, his tongue in his cheek like he's contemplating a new mare for his country estate.

She recoils, pushing backward, and I place my hands on her shoulders. I steer her around the guy and on into the crowd beyond but can sense the guy's gaze on us the entire way.

I drop my arms. And Natasha pulls at her dress, trying to lengthen it.

*"Now what?"* she snaps at me.

My jaw tightens. *"Still working on it,"* I say, my anger rising to meet hers.

I keep us weaving through chattering groups, heading toward the flower-shaped building that rises above us. The area in front narrows as we approach the entrance. It's still thirty yards across and covered with areas of grass and pavement, each one bordered by lines of trees and winding streams.

As the crowd grows ever denser, a group of women glance at Natasha and then at me, taking in my ordinary suit and my ungroomed appearance. Their expressions shift from confused to mocking.

I hurry toward a dense bit of foliage and step between two trees, though I'm still visible from almost every direction. Here, I scan the space for any sign of the tattooed symbol or of our pursuers. There's nothing. But the strange chill continues to grow between my shoulder blades, my internal alarm ringing louder.

"Come on," Natasha snaps and starts toward the entrance, toward the many guards milling around it.

I grab her arm. *"Wait."*

She spins back to face me. "For what?"

I press a finger to my lips. "There's no chance that way," I say, the chill slinking further down my back. "Plus, we can't risk it."

She frowns, and I swivel away, sweeping my gaze over the triangular area for *something*. My eyes take in the central dome, the lower buildings that border the forecourt, and the groups of sparkling guests in between. A few nearby are peering down their noses at me, conversing in derisive tones.

My gaze darts beyond them, and I spot a group of three people striding purposefully toward one of the lower buildings that abuts the central dome. A man and two women, the latter's slinky outfits and toned figures poorly disguised by capes. One woman leers at Natasha and then spins her head away, rippling her hair in a glittering arc, before sauntering off after the man.

I watch them go. They're not holding drinks. Nor are they heading for the front entrance.

"Get behind them," I say to Natasha and dart out from under the branches. We weave between guests and trees in their wake.

"Where are we going?" Natasha asks from my shoulder.

I ignore her and increase my stride to catch up with the group. They're approaching the club's lower building. And I scan the wall for a performers' entrance.

Vertical planes jut straight out of it, my height or taller, perpendicular to the wall and all along it. Some kind of art feature. A guard stands rooted in front of some of the broader ones. He's huge, a designer suit barely covering his muscled frame, an electronic tablet clasped in one massive hand, and he's entirely unmoving.

The women and man halt before the guard, hidden from the main crowd by a line of gnarled trees ten feet at our backs. I herd Natasha behind them. The three all search inside pockets and bags before bringing out identification. Two fucking sets each.

My heart thumps faster. The guard motions the first woman toward him and checks both identifications against his tablet. I fidget in place. The strange chill's pooling at the base of my back, and my mind's conjuring images of our pursuers closing in on us, getting ever bloody closer.

I search the wall for any sign of a door. But there's no lock, no handle, just these damn vertical metal planes, each one between six and nine feet high and a few inches thick. They all jut two to three feet straight out of the wall with a couple of feet between them. It's like staring at a line of massive irregular dominoes.

I keep my head still but let my eyes wander. There's a square box on the inside of one of the vertical planes to the side of the guard. A sensor? My eyes scour the guard for some kind of key card.

He finishes the identification check and ticks the woman off on his tablet before sweeping a handheld metal detector up and down her body.

*Thorough.*

She steps between two of the vertical planes and pads right up to the wall between them. The man lifts his jacket, revealing a security pass, and he pulls it toward the sensor on the opposite side of him from the woman.

I feel my shoulders tensing. The pass is on a retractable cable, directly tied to his belt, and impossible to fucking steal.

A tiny light turns green on the square box, and the woman presses on the thin section of wall in between the two vertical planes. It opens inward, and one of the protruding planes rotates with it.

I blink at it. A revolving door. Brilliantly hidden among the art feature. And it only turns one quarter revolution and locks again with a clunk. Only one allowed through at a time.

*Very fucking thorough.*

Natasha jabs me in the side. *"We are not on any list,"* she snaps in my ear.

Again, I feel the heat rising inside and my shoulders tensing. "We're going to have to be," I mutter through gritted teeth.

I stare at the guard. The muscles beneath his sleeves are as big as boulders.

"And you're getting us in," I say to Natasha.

## 27

NATASHA WHIRLS ON ME. And I grab her hand, yanking her body back around to face the club wall. She tenses under my grip.

The guard scans the second woman, and she saunters toward the wall, toward the revolving door.

"Sweet-talk the guy," I whisper and nod at the guard.

Natasha shakes her head.

"I've *seen* you with people," I say. "You charm without even bloody trying."

"How?" she says, her tone tight.

"Misdirection," I say. "Make up some story about why we need to get in."

She backs away toward the line of trees, toward the chattering crowd behind. "It will not work," she says.

"No con's airtight," I say, holding her arm. "Use intensity. Get in close and make it urgent. Control his attention. Just keep talking. Don't let him think."

The second woman disappears through the revolving door. The guard checks the man's identification. Then glances at Natasha, his expression flint-like.

"I cannot do this," Natasha says.

"I cannot do this, *either*," I retort.

The strange chill continues to crawl up my neck. And I force myself not to glance toward the club's main entrance.

"Remember the priest, *the mission*," I hear myself saying.

The man disappears through the door, following his two female companions inside, and the door clicks back into place and locks. The guard pockets his tools and focuses his hard gaze on us.

Sweat's coating my shoulders now. My pulse gallops behind my ears. I plant my palm on the middle of Natasha's back to urge her forward.

The guard glances from Natasha to me but says nothing. He simply folds his massive arms across his chest, accentuating every muscle.

I clear my throat. "We've been recommended," I say and nod toward Natasha, visualising her acting desirable woman instead of walking corpse. "She's here for an audition. She'll explain."

Natasha remains silent. The guard's jawline tightens. It's like staring up at a bear's maw. And a new smell permeates the air, an acrid burning.

I slide behind Natasha, whispering lines into her hair.

"The management said to come," she eventually parrots to the guard. "Food poisoning. They are a dancer short."

Her tone's completely flat, no charm, no allure. The guard's eyes narrow.

She splutters on, "They said—"

"*Shut it*," the guard growls. "You're not on the roster. Period."

He bares his teeth. And the cordite smell's intensifying, the strange chill spreading across my insides. I edge backward, picturing our pursuers homing in on us from outside the building … from inside … from everywhere.

"Which means you shouldn't be here," the guard says.

He raises his huge arm, and Natasha goes rigid. More voices scream at me to run.

Taking a breath, I link arms with Natasha, drunk-style. "It's alright, love," I slur and my lips form a skewed smile.

I stagger toward the guard, pulling her with me, and then lurch to the side, in front of her and toward the revolving door. I let go of Natasha's arm and reach for its protruding plane with my left hand while keeping much of my weight on the opposite foot.

The guard tenses and thrusts both arms out across the door to block us off. The movement peels away his jacket, revealing his belt and his security key.

I shift my weight, swing back across the guy, and fling my right hand out to grasp the key. Then I drag it across the guard's body in the opposite direction, yanking the cable hard toward the sensor on his other side. This brings my torso only inches from the guard's gargantuan chest. The smell of his aftershave along with his sweat fills my nostrils. And the cable doesn't fucking reach.

The guard's left facing Natasha in front of the revolving door. She squeals, and he freezes for just an instant. Then his head twists. I tense my stomach and thrust myself that bit further away from the revolving door, tugging on the cable, reaching for the sensor …

Finally, the light goes green. Natasha staggers back. And the guard whips his elbow back toward the side of my head.

I duck, letting my knees go, and spin around the guy's waist. He drives his swinging arm downward, and his elbow shoots only an inch above my head.

I dart back in the direction of the revolving door, keeping as close as I can to his body. The guy rotates awkwardly and grabs for my collar as I throw myself between the vertical planes. I shove at the thin section of wall, praying, praying …

His hand bounces off my shoulder. The door revolves with a click. And I careen through.

Into darkness.

I hold my breath. A wide corridor extends away from the door and then disappears around a corner twenty yards away. LEDs at floor level cast an icy blue-white light against shiny black walls. Open cubicles line both sides – one filled with what looks like communication equipment, another with immaculately hanging suits and coats. A guard's standing in one of the niches, unpacking a box. Another's walking away down the passageway toward the corner.

No one clocks me. There's no sign of the pursuers. And the chill ebbs a fraction from my core. I let out a slow breath.

Then my brain kicks back into gear, and I dash around the protruding panel of the revolving door. I shrink back against the wall on its far side and keep quiet, waiting for …

The click of a lock releasing. The pressure of the door against my back vanishes as the protruding panel shoots toward me, the door revolving again with me inside it.

I crane my neck and catch a glimpse of the guard from outside sprinting off down the dark passageway. And then the revolving door spits me back outside the club.

Natasha stands there. Mouth open. "*What?*" She stares at me with wide eyes. "What … what was the point of that?"

"You'll see," I say and dart back around the protruding panel of the door again. I reach for her wrist and pull her to me while scanning the crowd beyond the hanging trees, sniffing the air.

The cordite scent's back. And my vision is starting to dim once more.

"We have to go," Natasha says and grabs the sleeve of my jacket, tugging at my arm.

I hold firm.

"He will know what you've done," she says, spinning to face me, her cheeks pale. "He will be back any second!"

"That's the point," I say and back further into the wall, the panel of the revolving door.

I flex my fingers to barricade out the awful chill. And start the count in my head, my heartbeat a metronome to the escalating numbers.

Again I picture the corridor beyond the revolving door,

the guard sprinting down it, searching and not finding us, and then sprinting back. It'll take ten, maybe fifteen seconds.

"What will you do?" Natasha says.

"Same again," I say and yank her closer behind the protruding panel.

The click of the lock opening sounds again. I concentrate hard and fix my attention on the feeling of the door at my back. It rotates away behind me, and I grab Natasha by both wrists before hauling her backward through the gap, into the building.

Again, I catch a glimpse of the guard rushing back outside the club through the other side of the door as it revolves. Then it locks behind us.

I spin and find myself staring down the darkened corridor once more. It's empty now, the guard no longer visible in the niche.

Natasha grabs my wrist. "He will work it out, surely!"

"Same trick twice?" I say. "No. It's like I told you, people rarely do. He'll assume we're off somewhere else ... probably back in the crowd, getting drunk."

And from nowhere, a few of the priest's dumb words sound in my head ... *Beliefs control reality.* I shove them away and glance back at the door.

"He could easily call it in, though," I say and usher Natasha down the corridor.

She slows her steps. "If you had just let me know your plan before," she says, her voice tense again, "I could have played along."

"Oh, sure," I mutter, memories coming of her rigid pose outside. "You'd have played him like a violin."

She halts in the corridor and whirls on me. "I *could* have helped," she snaps back. "But you—"

A large figure steps out of the niche directly in front of us – the guard I spied unpacking the box. Natasha jumps, and the guy stares from me to her with his brow furrowed. His neck's as big as a tree.

167

For a long while, I simply stare. Then I splutter, "Dancer …" and nod at Natasha.

She doesn't move. Just stands there, pulling at her dress again. The guard rakes his gaze up and down Natasha's body, and the battle rages inside her – tensed arms, pinched shoulders, nails pressing into her palms.

Deep furrows appear across the guard's forehead. I go to step in front of her when she touches my arm. She lifts her chin, stands tall, and then sashays past him, her shoulders back, her eyes focused somewhere above his head. I have to focus hard on not biting my cheek.

The guard raises an eyebrow as she passes but doesn't stop her. I stumble behind, making sure not to hurry my steps. Together, we pad to the end of the corridor and then finally turn the corner.

"*See?*" she says in my ear.

I shake my head and press on faster down the new passageway. We pass recesses with x-ray scanners, weapon racks with enough firepower to put down full-scale fucking riots, and reinforced doors with tiny plexiglass viewing windows – holding cells. My heart's beating harder.

Another corner, and we approach a heavy curtain. Fresh scents, a mixture of exotic spices, pique my nose while a murmuring chorus echoes from beyond. And that strange chill is back, building at my core.

## 28

I slip through the curtain first, the murmuring growing louder, and find myself on a railed pathway that runs around the top edge of a conical auditorium. I stumble to a stop, mouth open, and ogle the room.

It's a hundred yards across at the top and shaped like a massive theatre, a stage far below and off to the right. Everything curves, the layout resembling another gigantic flower. Aisles sweep up from the stage to the top edge where I stand in the outline of enormous arcing petals, rows of secluded booths in between. But the real genius is the lighting. Flames glimmer at ground level, and the dimness has a physicality that hangs over everything like a cloak.

I scan the pathway and nearest aisles – the ones running down toward the stage in front of me. It's so hard to see. I can make out only the outlines of booths and the shadowed figures inside each one while dark shapes shift at the corners of my vision. And the strange chill's growing stronger, already prickling deep under my skin. I sniff the air for cordite, though the aroma of the club's so strong – spices, maybe cloves and cinnamon.

My head spins and begins to throb.

"We must move," Natasha says, stepping to my side.

I squeeze my fingers tighter and try to focus on her voice.

"Down there," she says and indicates the rows of booths set into the sweeping petals that roll toward the stage.

I follow her point but don't move, my mind jabbering familiar warnings about following someone else's plan.

"It will be the best place to hide," she goes on. "Security would not risk searching among the guests."

She starts striding down the carpeted stairs of the nearest aisle. And after several blinks, I scramble to catch up. We pass candled lanterns on the edge of each step, and the flickering light merges with the exotic scents and music. I feel it all swamping my attention.

For the clientele in the booths, though the darkness embraces them, there's just enough light to ensure they sparkle – the twinkle of outrageous jewellery, the shine of celestial suits and dresses. This is the true apex of society, the gilded, the tier that those outside and at the station would do anything to reach. And they sit in the curved booths like rows of diamonds set into a golden crown.

I shake my head and try to focus on controlling my rambling thoughts while placing one foot in front of the other down the aisle.

Natasha slips into an empty booth, and I scoot behind. The sofa moulds to our bodies as a barman appears out of nowhere. Natasha smiles, but I wave him away.

Sitting half-exposed in the booth, I start to swivel and scan the aisles behind us for dark shapes or guards approaching. Then I stop, the obvious striking me. My search will attract attention and single us out. My shoulders tighten, and my heel bounces up and down. We're trapped.

Natasha leans forward on the sofa, scanning the audience.

I take a breath, trying to settle myself, to push away the prickling chill. I risk craning my neck for anyone who'd mobilise an army of pursuers.

It's midnight now, and most of the booths are full. I profile what I can see of the clientele – the cut of the suits, the size of the entourages, the lavishness of the clothes – financiers, celebrities, politicians. A familiar sort, yet none of them look even remotely religious. And oddly, the natural chatter's dying down, more of the gilded staring down at an empty stage.

A deep voice introduces the next act. Several young ladies in ball gowns appear, each carrying a basket, their dresses twenty feet long. They're scattering handfuls of petals onto the stage.

The audience starts to hum with building anticipation as the lights dim. My insides tighten, memories coming of the creeping blindness. But no. I clock nearby candles extinguishing.

I dart my eyes faster over the audience. The room's growing darker … and it's getting increasingly difficult to see. My gaze is skimming over faces and clothes now but picking up almost nothing.

I take another deep breath, tense my stomach, begin the count. Focus on wrestling calm from the storm inside. I try again to scrutinise the guests in the booths, going more slowly now, but faces become just outlines.

A delicate glow emanates from the stage. People sit forward, and Natasha tenses at my side. She touches my arm, and I feel an itch of annoyance.

I shut out the sensation and keep scanning the audience, searching for someone I might recognise from the station. And with the thought, images bombard me of the train crash, the sabotage … the mysterious man.

Gazing into the darkness of a booth opposite, I picture him sitting there, staring straight back at me. My pulse beats faster, and memories come of the way he controlled my body, the madness of the shimmering world he opened.

Natasha's hand remains on my arm, pulling my attention to the stage. I shake it off but still turn. And again, my mouth drops open.

I stare at the stage, my thoughts skipping over each other

and my mind growing increasingly blank. Someone's there. A woman. Moving. Dancing. Though it's as if she's still and the entire world's revolving around her.

A metallic smell burns in my nostrils, though faint. And once more, I sense the veil before me – invisible yet solid, timeless yet momentary. The priest's words about the power of faith ring in my brain. I continue the count and clear my mind entirely. I focus on my experience of the shimmering world, concentrate on believing ...

And again, I feel my world blown apart.

Time slows, and the intensity floods my senses. Every detail becomes visible – the dimensions of the stage, the subtle shifts of a hundred audience members in the booths before me. It's almost as if I can make out their intentions, the recent past and near future visible simultaneously in their movements. And the sound – music, chatter, the clinking of glass on glass – every layer suddenly audible.

But it's all rendered secondary, submerged in the sea of her luminosity. I can't take my eyes off her.

She swirls, her skirts an arc of feathers, then rippling clouds, and then falling snow. Her bodice glimmers first like jewels, then gold, and then burning flame. Her eyes sweep the audience, never resting on any section for more than a moment. And it's as if her gaze is nectar, dropped into open mouths, into hungry hearts. I feel a wave of bliss rippling outward. It brushes aside my remaining thoughts and leaves my chest quaking.

Then our eyes meet. Just an instant. Still she dances, flows, whirls on the stage, but somehow she's also hovering only feet away, a glint in her bright eyes, her head tilted with curiosity.

Suddenly it's overwhelming, all her attention on me. My whole body shakes. My heart feels like it's running over, every old wound a memory. Only she exists for me in that moment, and while a part of my brain screams doubt, it's nothing in the face of her draw. I lean forward, feeling a fierce desire to prostrate myself. To gaze upon her, and to be gazed upon … akin to merging with love itself.

My mother – the sensation of being with her in those early days, the warmth of her attention – so similar. But here it's magnified beyond recognition, like I'm basking in absolute joy, utter completeness.

The audience are on their feet now. On stage, she turns toward them, burning brighter, warmed by their adulation like rays from the sun.

Me, an outsider in this place, yet I feel one with the entire crowd, bonded by mutual devotion. It's like nothing I've ever experienced before. My cheeks are wet.

She raises her arms and prepares to leave. The sense of the coming loss becomes a stabbing ache in my chest.

I sense Natasha's gaze on me. Her hand clasps my shoulder. I shake it off, stumble from my seat, and fall to my knees.

The woman before me. A goddess. My thoughts still absent, my internal count's a background to the eruption of bliss and pain within. Excruciating.

She gazes down at me, and I catch a glimpse into her heart. Such love, yet something else – sadness like a vast ocean, with a depth beyond comprehension. It feels like a forbidden glance. She frowns, withdraws, and then disappears altogether.

I stumble forward onto my hands, vainly searching the stage.

She's gone.

## 29

THE VISION FADES. Noises break through to my awareness – the clink of glasses again, the dull murmur of distant conversations. Then the intoxicating scent – cardamom, cinnamon – no more burning metal. And the stage …

"Jake."

The word barely registers. The young ladies in ball gowns are back, reverently collecting the petals in their baskets. And the woman … she's gone.

"Jake," someone says again.

I turn toward the voice.

"Sit back down," Natasha says. She's crouched at my side, gripping my shoulder and hauling me backward.

I glance at the floor and realise I'm on my hands and knees at the front of the auditorium booth. I blink. Shake my head. Then shrink into the sofa, my chest cramping with shame and my back sweating.

I gaze furtively around while trying to reassemble the fragments of my mind, my judgement, my pride. Questions whirl … my feelings for the woman, so damn powerful, and so unlike me.

"We've got to find her!" The words tumble from my mouth as I go to stand.

Natasha yanks me back down. "Who?" she says. "The woman, the *dancer?*" Her tone's laced with scorn.

"*Did you not feel it?*" I almost shout. "It was incredible … same as with the office building, the station—"

Natasha shoots a hand toward my lips to quieten me.

"I saw her … her," I say, "not as a woman, but as a …"

An unparalleled radiance. An unfathomable love.

Natasha peers at me, one eyebrow raised.

"A …"

"Yes?" she says.

"A …"

*A goddess.*

I clench my jaw.

*Shit.*

"I don't know," I say. My mind's like a sandy cliff face being incessantly pounded by waves.

"*Men,*" Natasha snaps. "So bloody predictable. Always following the beautiful—"

"Where'd she go?" I say.

The single line appears across Natasha's brow. "She disappeared. Through a trapdoor, I think," she says. "You really think we have to find her?"

"Maybe … probably," I say, getting to my feet.

"We will be seen!" Natasha says and reaches up to restrain me.

I slip beyond her grasp. "We've got to find out, get backstage," I say and dart into the aisle. I hasten down the steps toward the stage, my heart beating with some kind of wild fever. The woman – light and love itself. And a great sadness too. The notion of her suffering feels like a steel clamp around my chest.

My eyes scour the bottom of the aisle. A carpeted walkway runs around the curved part of the semicircular stage, a curtained exit at both ends. I fix my gaze on the nearer one and quicken my steps.

The darkness thickens as before, and I search the

approaching stage, expecting the next act. But there's no one this time. Only the gowned ladies collecting petals. And the chill ... Icy fingers pull at my limbs.

A shiver rolls through me, and my internal alarm starts to clamour. A part of my brain shrieks at my madness – hurrying down the aisle in full view of pursuers and guards.

My adrenaline fires, the passion still driving me. I reach the bottom walkway, the raised stage to my left, and lengthen my stride, the curtained exit only twenty feet ahead. The gloom pools around my calves, the chill intensifying under my skin.

"Jake!" Natasha's voice just behind me, urgent and low.

I swivel my head. Follow her point toward the top of the auditorium.

A guard. Dark suit, massive neck – the same guy from the inside corridor – his lips now pulled back over glinting teeth. And he's hastening down another set of aisle steps to cut us off. Not running, not yelling. He simply fixes his gaze on us, and I can feel the burn in his stare.

I spin back and throw myself into a run, the curtain only ten feet away. The guard lands with a thump on the walkway behind us as I stampede toward the velvet folds, thrust them aside, and dart through.

Into a curving passageway. Empty, with the rear of the stage to one side. I barrel along the corridor, glancing periodically through gaps in the wall, the wings. No sign of the woman, the goddess. Only the gowned women, tipping petals into large urns, a few of them glancing back at me.

I bolt past, my ears straining for the guard's footsteps behind. Natasha runs at my back, breathing hard.

"Where now?" she pants.

A vision forms instantly of the goddess, and I sprint faster around the bending corridor. It meets its counterpart – another passageway that arcs around the opposite side of the stage – at a T-junction. And from there, a wider corridor runs away from the stage with what look like dressing room doors on both sides.

They're all closed aside from the second one on the left. I careen toward it, shove it fully open, and stumble through.

Into a massive space full of dressing tables arranged before mirrors and six massage tables lined up in the middle. A dozen dancers at various stages of preparation all glance up at me. I hold my breath as I scan their faces.

No sign of the goddess.

Natasha slips through the door, and I shake myself into action, pushing it closed behind her.

"This is wrong, Jake," she says.

"No shit," I mutter, half of my attention listening for the guard's running footsteps outside.

"Hey!" a performer says, standing up from her dressing table.

I raise my palms. And Natasha swivels to face the door.

"I told you," she says. "The dancer went downward, through the stage."

"So, what's your idea?" I say.

The performer takes a step toward me. "This is out of bounds," she says.

Natasha opens the door. And I go to haul her back, my mind conjuring images of the guard's colleagues hurtling past. Then I stop as her eyes go wide.

"Look," she breathes and points through the gap.

I stare over her shoulder. She's indicating a door on the opposite side of the corridor, nearer the stage. It's ajar.

Strange. It was closed before. I'm sure of it. And through the gap lies a set of descending steps. I feel a shot of warmth at my core.

Pulling open the dressing room door a little further, I peer both ways down the corridor. Empty. Silent. No sign of any guard or his colleagues.

Even stranger.

"You shouldn't be here," the performer says from behind.

I ignore her and step through the door, closing it after Natasha. Then I pad toward the stairwell door, my brain yelling at me to go faster, to get out of sight. Instead, I feel my legs slow, the strange chill growing again, settling inside my stomach, my ribs.

I find my eyes fixed ahead, staring through the slightly open door and trying to work out what I'm seeing …

A hand. Hanging above the steps down, frozen in mid-air, the rest of the body out of sight. My brain tries to compute but fails. I feel myself drawn forward while my heart pounds, and my gut twists further. I push the stairwell door fully open.

And stop dead.

The strangest sight – the figure of a man, just in front of the stairs, totally immobile.

My body goes rigid. It's the guard who chased us. He stands there, a statue, a warding arm raised toward us, those burning eyes now wide in horror. Staring over my shoulder.

## 30

I CAN'T TAKE my eyes off the guard's body. It's as if he's been frozen in mid-movement, stumbling backward away from us, from the doorway, one hand raised. My mind flounders on. It feels like the world's stopped dead, a strange silence stopping my ears.

Natasha pushes past me. She reaches for the guard's neck and takes his pulse.

I find my gaze drawn to the guy's face. Gouge marks line his temples and upper cheeks as if he's been scratching at his eyes.

Just like Ethan, the hospital guard.

My ribs squeeze, and my eyes find the stairwell downward over the guard's shoulder. Images come of the goddess from the stage down there. I try to remember her radiance, her splendour, to feel again the fullness in my heart, but the sensations are so weak. There's just the strange chill in my bones and growing shadows before my eyes, my vision dimming.

The intensity of the club seems so far away, my passion to see her so fucking crazy.

Natasha drops her fingers from the guard's neck and

shakes her head. She stares back at me, her eyes wide. And a part of my brain's plotting the route back through the curtain, out of the club, to safety beyond.

Yet still I don't move.

The smell of burnt metal suddenly stabs at my nostrils, the chill scouring far deeper under my skin. I whirl around.

A woman stands in the doorway to the corridor. Clad in clothes as bizarre as those of the other pursuers – a plaid skirt and patterned cardigan – she mouths something, and her eyes are a fathomless black, like they're absorbing all the surrounding light.

A sudden weight crushes my chest. My vision darkens further, and my arms feel sluggish, already powerless to rise.

*No, no …*

A black vine flashes across her throat, under her skin. And I tense my neck, trying desperately to wrest away my gaze. But it's impossible, the strange numbness growing. I can't bloody move. She sweeps toward me. Such ease of movement, such speed. I feel myself grabbed by the lapel, hauled effortlessly up into the air as she hurls me backward toward the stairwell.

My surroundings wheel. The ceiling flies. Then the floor smashes into me, squashing every ounce of air from my lungs and sending pain shooting down my back. My vision blurs, and I skid to a halt just inches from the steps down.

I lie there, my chest seizing, unable to gasp in breath.

I hear a slapping sound to my side, a scream cut off. I swivel my head and glimpse Natasha collapsing down the wall, her hand holding her cheek.

I grit my teeth and strain against the burning ache of my spasming muscles. Just as I'm about to roll onto my side, I tilt my chin to look—

The woman, already there, towers above me.

I groan, my brain faltering, and yank my legs to my chest in the foetal position. I try to find my breath. Start the count. Focus on expanding the moment.

She reaches for my shoulder while a black shape shifts under her skin – from forearm to hand. My pulse hammers, a torrent behind my ears. I wrench my gaze away, and while every part of my body yearns to writhe out of her grip, I concentrate everything on remaining still.

Instead, I fix my eyes on the woman's shiny black shoes.

She leans over me and grips my lapel. The contact burns cold, and I bite my cheek against the pain, trying desperately not to move. It feels like my skin's blistering off.

The black shoe shifts a fraction, the woman's knee bent slightly. She rolls me over onto my back, my knees still raised, and perspiration coats my sides. The awful chill's burrowing further into my bones as I feel her gaze searching for mine, like talons pulling at my head, my eyelids, wanting me to look …

I concentrate hard on avoiding her gaze and focus instead on her legs, on her incremental movements – the tensing of tendons in her calves, a shift onto one foot. The woman grasps me with two hands, dragging me upward so we're face to face. She leans further over me, and I force myself to wait … right till all her weight's on one leg.

I yell and kick out as hard as I can, putting every ounce of energy into it. My foot smashes into the inside of the woman's knee. I hear a sickening crunch when the joint caves to the side. She lets go of me and goes down heavily without a bloody sound.

The chill ebbs, and my vision floods back. I scramble up.

Natasha sits crouched against the wall, her mouth wide in shock. "Oh god, oh god, oh god," she repeats, her voice so quiet. She fingers the crucifix around her neck. Red marks scar her cheek, the outline of knuckles.

I rush over, grip her hands, and yank her to her feet. The woman's struggling upward, the chill growing again in my core as the darkness encircles us. My eyes find the corridor to her side, my brain yelling even louder to go back the way we came, to get the fuck out of this place.

In that instant, I bring the goddess back to mind, and where I sensed nothing just before, now I feel the faintest echo of the love and light.

The woman's reached her knees and is beginning to climb to her feet, swaying on her ruined knee before us. Natasha grips my arm, and I spin away from the corridor to lurch for the stairwell downward. I jump the steps, two at a time, with Natasha following just behind.

We end up one floor down in darkness. Only a subtle orange glow at ankle level emits from lights embedded in the walls. Nothing else. No dressing performers, no glitz and glamour. Just a large open space, thirty yards across with angled walls to our sides, the far end invisible in the gloom.

"This cannot be right," Natasha says.

I stumble away from the staircase. Then on across the floor till its far edges come into view. The space is massive, almost hexagonally shaped. I probe what I can see of the walls all around.

They're blank. Featureless. No visible doors or corridors. The darkness hangs so heavily before my eyes.

A dull clumping sounds behind me, the female pursuer descending the steps in our wake.

"Nothing's here!" Natasha calls.

And my own doubts scream at me.

I crane my neck and sniff the air. I notice a new scent at the limits of my awareness, acrid and harsh.

"You smell that?" I say, whirling on Natasha.

"*What?*" Natasha says.

The clomping sound draws nearer behind us.

"The burnt metal!" I hiss. "D'you smell it too?"

Eventually, Natasha sniffs the air and nods. "It was the same ..." she starts.

"As?" I say, gripping her arm.

"As in the estate," she says. "And also ... with the woman on stage."

Gooseflesh prickles my back, and I dart a pace forward. The smell intensifies, just a fraction. And before I can stop myself, I'm taking leaping steps across the room, following the scent as if it's some invisible thread in the dark. Natasha hurries behind. We reach the far wall and search it.

"Look at this!" Natasha says.

She's standing by an area of the wall and running her hands over its undulating surface. Strange symbols cover a section, top to bottom, with narrow pillars at either side. All hidden in the darkness till I got only a few steps away.

I blink at it. A door?

"So detailed," says Natasha, leaning right in to examine the glyphs. "Amazing. They are old … very old, maybe Aramaic." Her breathing quickens, and she wears the same eager expression as when she sat in the church kitchen, discussing the mission with the priest. "Maybe this *is* it." She swivels to face me. "What we are here to find."

I examine the floor in front of the door. It's different to the modern tile of the club – polished, uneven, like it's been worn down by the tread of generations.

The clomping has stopped at our backs, and a new sound reaches my ears, a faint dragging noise like something's sliding across the floor toward us. The strange chill pulls at my mind.

I have to tense my waist to stop myself from spinning around.

"If it's a door …" I say, trying to keep my voice level, "it's got to open."

I push on one side of the etched wall and then on the other. Top and bottom. Nothing happens.

"Jake?" she exclaims.

"I'm working on it!" I snap and lean my shoulder into the door, shoving desperately at it.

"Well, that is not going to work," Natasha says, hands on hips.

I grip the stone and squeeze, feeling her burning eyes on my cheek.

"You can do this," she says. "Father Thomas said so. You saw the office building for what it truly is. You must be able to get this open." She raises her arms. "Otherwise, we would not be here!"

Standing in her gaze, I feel like an insect sizzling under a magnifying glass. I step back and examine the surface of the door up and down, feeling for the veil, that subtle screen over my senses …

The dragging sound continues to amplify behind us while the chill continues to grow at my core. Memories come of peeling back the veil, of ending up trapped by the enveloping dark, hunted by the skull-like face.

Natasha shivers and stares back across the room. I've started to swivel when she grabs my arm and forces me back around.

"Come on!" she hisses.

The smell of scorched metal gnaws at the back of my throat. Images flash of the goddess, but then familiar suspicions shout in my head … *This is a trap, a con, I'm the mark …*

Natasha grips my arm ever tighter.

I close my eyes and start the count in my head. I concentrate on the memory of the veil, on how time slowed, how sensation flooded my awareness, how I felt connected to everything in the shimmering world.

But nothing happens.

Natasha yells at me again. The sound explodes in my ear, wrenching at my attention. The chill climbs higher up my body, filling my lungs like icy water.

I clench my jaw and focus hard on shutting everything out and stilling my thoughts. I build my concentration like a fortress.

The image of the goddess comes again. And this time, I shove away the doubt and bring to mind the vision of her dancing, the ache in my heart. I feel it like a bird flying and let it carry me.

With a sudden surge of heat, deep in my chest, my eyes fly open. The strange door's gone. The entire space has vanished. I take a slow and trembling breath.

A dark vertical surface stands before me. I sense the symbols but they're no longer fixed. Instead, they've become water, a rippling sheet plunging downward. I try to move toward it, and the deluge recedes from me. I extend my fingers and still can't reach.

My doubts jabber again, and the image of the water begins to dissolve.

I bite my lip, count louder in my mind, and focus on the water being real. Gradually my thoughts calm, and the image of the cascade stabilises. I pivot my head from side to side. And the water rotates with me. I tilt my chin up and down, and the cascade moves as well. Till there's nothing but the water. Nothing above, below, or to the side.

The cascade roars at me, and I sense its touch to be pulverising, annihilating. Shrill warnings sound in my head.

Again, I recall the goddess floating in front of me, the exquisite joy I felt in my heart. I focus on her hovering somewhere beyond. My body starts to move yet also remains still. The water draws steadily nearer, while the anticipation's like claws around my throat.

Still, I cling onto the memory of her. The water creeps ever closer. The sound huge, like a deluge crashing on rocks, a cacophony in my ears. There I stand, in the midst of it … alone.

*Natasha.*

The thought's like a smack to the head. I shoot my arm out behind me, casting frantically around. And find nothing.

The water keeps coming. I keep searching. And finally touch skin. Natasha's wrist. I grip hard and cling on with everything I have.

The water touches me, envelops me. Sensation every-where – light, sound, touch. Raging and wrathful. Inside and out. My mind flails and starts to shut down. I feel myself moving at great speed.

Then all goes black.

## 31

Darkness. Silence. I'm gripping something while another hand cradles mine.

"It's okay," a voice says.

The hand pulls gently at my fingers and prises them apart.

I swivel, and my vision clears. Someone's next to me.

"Jake, it's me."

I shake my head. Natasha's standing in front of a brown rectangular shape. I blink.

The door.

"You made it open, just like that," she says. "Then you pulled me through."

I glance around me. It feels as if we're in another world. There's the door, a set of stairs leading downward away from it. And aside from that, everything else is absolute blackness. Above, below, to the sides. No features at all.

"Extraordinary …" Natasha says, gazing around us. "Where do you think we are?"

I peer into the darkness. It's somehow deeper than black, a devourer of light, as if I'm staring into a million hungry maws. The only source of illumination is the stairs, which glow faintly a strange dark red … almost blood-like in colour.

I shiver and then spin. The door stands there, this side of it much older-looking, the symbols faded. And I find myself tensing, waiting for the female pursuer to barrel through.

Nothing happens. And with the blackness pressing so tightly around us, the shiver climbs my spine. I stare over my shoulder with the vaguest sense of being watched. Then the mysterious man's words from the station flash through my mind ... *how feebly your world compares.*

"What now?" Natasha says, her voice bringing me back. She's staring down the steps, her eyes gleaming. "It's forward or back, right?"

I shake myself and then drop to check the floor. The stone's obsidian black, with thin red veins that glow. And the steps are ancient, the angles worn steep through what could be centuries of use. I picture the goddess, and the sensation of love and light remains kindled in my chest.

"We've got to try and find her," I breathe. "See what she knows."

Natasha doesn't reply, and I take a step downward. And then another. A cool wind gusts against my cheek, bringing the smell of rain on grass. As if we're outside. I glance up, imagining stars above me, yet still there's only black. My vision swims, my legs wobble, and I totter toward the edge of the steps, stopping just in time to prevent myself toppling over.

More slow breaths. More steps down. The red-veined stairs appear out of the black as we descend. I glance back over Natasha's shoulder. No sign of the door now. It's as if nothing exists in the world but the steps and darkness.

Neither of us speaks. We walk for what could be seconds or hours. The sensation of aloneness, of being lost, becomes a growing tightness around my ribs. My heartbeat quickens, and I force a steady pace downward.

From nowhere, I'm standing on a straight path. The steps continue back up behind me, the blackness still all around. I glance down. The path morphs into white shingle for an instant, and my eyes go wide. Then the image of the red-veined stone returns. I shake my head, the feeling of disorientation immense.

Another change, a faint pool of light up ahead. I peer forward. Creep closer.

A door leads off the path. The door's made from aged wood, with wrought-iron hinges. Its frame hangs in nothingness as if carved from the surrounding black while light spills from underneath the sill.

Suddenly, I find myself standing before it with no memory of whether we came to it or it came to us. Natasha's hand rests on the handle, and I feel a tingling disquiet between my shoulder blades.

"You sure?" I ask.

She shakes her head and pushes it open anyway.

Light flares, and I dart my hands up to shield my eyes. Gradually, shapes appear out of the brightness.

Candles. Thousands of them. Row upon row around the edge of an oval stone room fifty yards wide, the curving walls lined with arched, stained-glass windows and religious statues, all capped by a domed ceiling high above.

Like some kind of chapel.

And in the centre of the room, three rectangular shapes appear against the blazing glow. Stone plinths. And the breath catches in my throat.

A body lies sprawled on each one. Unmoving, yet clearly in agony till their last moments: arms and legs extended at terrible angles, faces bleached white, eyes wide and teeth clenched together with lips pulled back. Each body is semi-naked, their skin covered in hundreds of angry red pustules and craters, the surface horrendously blistered.

My stomach squeezes up my throat, my mind conjuring memories of the identical-looking body on the hospital trolley while my brain rabbits on ... *the rumours, undesirables like me tortured, horrible burns, this is it, our pursuers*—

The smell of cordite bites suddenly at my nose, and shadows dance across the flagstone floor, the candlelight flickering. Yet there's not a breath of wind against my cheeks.

My body stiffens. My heartbeat like a drum as voices inside scream at me to run. My mind automatically plots an escape route, picturing the door and stairs behind, while more thoughts yell that I won't make it – our pursuers, their speed – that I have to hide now.

I breathe and tense my stomach, starting the count to still my mind. And in the burgeoning calm, with my body poised, I let my eyes dance over the room – the grey walls, the plinths, the altar at the far end of the space.

A flash of movement catches my eye, only a couple of feet to my side.

And in the expanded moment, my waist rotates ... and I catch a glimpse of the strike coming.

## 32

A FIST FLIES TOWARD ME, but my body's already spinning. Just in time. And while the strike doesn't take my head off, it still catches me on the shoulder and sends me wheeling into the chapel wall behind.

My side slams into the old stones, and the thwack drives the breath from my chest, forcing me down onto one knee.

My gaze darts toward my attacker, desperately trying to catch a glimpse …

Another flash – glittering like sunlight – in the corner of my eye. My adrenaline flares, and I fling myself along the wall as a foot stamps on the stone floor exactly where I've been squatting. The sound like a thunderclap.

I thump down onto my front, the air like fire in my lungs. My body shakes, and I grip the wall to scramble to my feet.

A faint whooshing sound to one side tells me my attacker is spiralling around. My thoughts splurge again, casting strategies, alternatives … I shove them all from my mind and spin toward the sound while focusing fiercely on the count in my head. I remember the mysterious man from the station, how time stretched out, and I concentrate on the memory of the shimmering world with every fibre of my being.

A strike careens toward me – a long sweeping chop to my

neck – and in the expanded moment, it's as if I'm graced a minute glimpse of the future. My legs collapse into a crouch, my hands down between my knees while the strike flies inches above my head.

And for the first time, I catch sight of my attacker – a flash of dark skin clad in gleaming silver. The figure swivels back to face me several feet away across the stone floor. No peculiar clothes, no strange chill.

Not a pursuer.

Slamming my heel into the wall behind me, I grit my teeth and drive my leg hard against the stone. I explode into a dive, a tackle, reaching out my arms and squaring my shoulders. And I hit my attacker full on in the stomach …

The collision barely makes an impact.

The woman's shoulders and arms are sculpted muscle, and I feel myself simply bounce off. She wears a shining breastplate over half of her chest while silver armour protects the opposite leg. The rest is flawless dark skin, like some kind of Amazon warrior.

She grabs my shoulders, rotates her waist, and throws me easily over her head, like I'm a garbage bag. I sail across the stone floor, ten feet or so, and then crash into the nearest plinth.

Pain blossoms from my crown down my neck. I roll quickly away from the stone foundation. My head pounds, and I push myself back up, doubts squawking against the blank background of my mind.

The Amazon's already darting toward me, only a couple of feet away. She thrusts her hand between my arm and side, and then pulls up, putting me into a shoulder lock. It all happens in a heartbeat. But behind the veil, with time slowed, I glimpsed it coming.

As she yanks my head down, the heat rises in my chest. My jaw clenches, and I shove forward, barging my shoulder into her hip. Then I drive my foot into her bare leg with all my weight, right between her foot and shin.

The Amazon grunts, and the pressure on my arm releases. I whip it out of the lock and strike out at her with my other hand. But I'm still stumbling forward. She rotates nimbly out of the way, grasps me around the torso, and spins me, launching me across the room again, toward the next plinth. With my thoughts slowed, the fall feels timeless.

I hit the floor once more, and my chin slams into the hard stone. Pain radiates from my head to my toes while the heat flares hotter inside me.

I sense the Amazon coming up behind, preparing to toss me again. Memories come of being thrown around by the dealers in my childhood home, the images so fucking vivid.

And while my brain yells warnings at me, the heat's blazing at my core, every thought burned the instant it arises and the veil still pulled back. I search the floor desperately … Candlestick. There, at the foot of the plinth. Thin, pewter. I grab for it and yank it under my body.

A hand grips my collar, hauls me to my feet. My rage becomes a wildfire. A distant sound pricks at my ears, an extended word like a record played at a slow speed. The Amazon spins me around to face her, grabs at my hand, and puts me in another armlock.

I roar and ram the candlestick into her armpit. The impact pushes her back, just a fraction. I kick out at her knees while she darts to my other side. Her elbow flies toward my face—

"*Stop!*" The shouted word resolves itself, its tone insistent. "*Please …*"

The Amazon ceases her swing in mid-air. Blinks. She stares at a figure standing beside her.

Natasha. Her hands are raised, her fingers child-sized around the Amazon's biceps. She pulls the woman's arm down by her side.

"*Please,*" Natasha begs. "We only want to talk."

The Amazon tenses and breaks free of Natasha's grip.

I raise my own arm.

"*Wait.*" Another voice. So different. It rings like a cymbal

193

clash, vibrating with power and anger. And implanted directly into my head.

The Amazon stops dead. Lowers her arms. And retreats several steps.

My adrenaline turns cold. I peer around the room, breathing hard. Windows, plinths, candles ... I can't make out anything.

"What's going on?" Natasha says, pressing into my side, her body tense. "What do you see?"

My thoughts start up, the veil slipping back before my senses. The metal odour burns strongly again, and warnings ring about the mysterious man, our pursuers ...

A new heat prickles my forehead, and I scour the brightness of the flaming candles along the edge of the room. They all flicker in an invisible draught.

*"What do you want?"*

With the veil almost back in place, the barked question's a distant echo in my mind, barely audible.

I still my thoughts. The veil starts to peel away once more, and I feel my gaze drawn toward the far end of the chapel, the altar.

A shape hovers there against the backdrop of the fierce candlelight, the outline of a figure. The sensation of warmth kindles inside. Just like in the club. I find myself teetering forward.

And then, from nowhere, she stands before us.

My heart lurches behind my ribs. White flowing dress, golden bodice – the same outfit from the stage. Her image blazes hot, as if she's burning. The air before me becomes a shimmering haze. The same luminescence as the first time I saw her, so intense. Though now it's tinged with fire.

Her words resound in my head. *"Why have you broken this sanctuary?"*

My mouth opens and closes. I feel lost. The intensity tears at my insides like claws, my heart rent open. It takes everything I have to remain upright, not to prostrate myself in front of this woman.

"Jake, what is it?" Natasha says. Her words seem to echo from somewhere in the distance.

The woman glances at her and speaks again in my head. "*She cannot yet see.*"

I swallow and find myself nodding. The shining woman lifts her hand toward Natasha and extends her finger.

Natasha grips my arm, squeezes, and stares vaguely in her direction. "What is happening?" she asks, a growing tightness in her voice.

Then the woman touches a fingertip to Natasha's forehead, and it's like an explosion. Heat soars across the room. I stumble back a step while Natasha sinks to her knees and chokes out breaths. Her whole body vibrates at the woman's feet, tears streaming down her cheeks.

"Daughter of Eve," the woman says, now out loud.

Still, Natasha cowers on the floor, her shaking hands raised up in prayer toward the woman.

"*Now,* you see," the woman says.

Then she turns to me with burning eyes. I feel her gaze raking my soul, every part of me stripped back, layers of memory, of despair, of fury ripped away. Again, I see my mother and live the unbearable wrench of leaving her. And there, underneath the pain … a sense of brimming love, of completeness … the feeling of *home*.

Cheeks wet, I sink to my knees in front of her.

"So, son of Adam," she says, her radiance blinding. So bright I'm forced to close my eyes. "Why have you come to me?"

# 33

I'M LYING on my side, Natasha prostrate next to me, her eyes squeezed shut. She's mouthing something, her lips silently moving. Over and over.

I shake my head to clear it, my thoughts bubbling and boiling in empty space. I push myself to my knees and stare out across the stone room. The plinths are still there, the candles, the curving walls ... but the woman, the goddess ... gone.

I scramble to my feet, the sense of loss immense, like my insides have been hollowed out. I cast my eyes around the room. The door we entered by has disappeared too. And the back wall's now only darkness. I stagger toward it but then stop.

A single point of light burns in the black, a radiant glow. My heart lurches. The goddess stands fifty feet away, side on, staring back at us.

"Come," she says eventually, her voice trilling like music. Then she turns and pads away into the darkness, her shining dress trailing twenty feet behind her.

The same yearning pulls at my chest, that all-encompassing love. So familiar, yet it feels as if it's been so long.

I reach toward Natasha, clasp her arm, and pull her up

with me. Then we scramble after the woman, into the blackness.

The smell of damp grass returns. Plus animal calls. Birds? Images swirl of the stone room morphing behind us – the candles becoming campfires, the stone plinths with their bodies becoming wooden logs. But when I swivel my head around, darkness lies on every side.

I spin back to face the woman, our only source of light. She continues to glide away from us. And no matter how fast I hurry, she remains the same distance away. I keep my eyes fixed on her glowing form as if, in losing focus, I might lose her forever.

In the next instant, she's no longer gliding away but sitting facing us on a chair that's appeared from nowhere … No, not a chair, a huge throne made of stone. Framed by blackness.

I skid to a stop, her heat so intense. Then I take an involuntary step back, and my calf hits a bench. I sit down, Natasha at my side. The bench is made of the same cold stone. I brush its surface with my fingertips. No, wait … it's wood.

I glance back up. The woman's throne has transformed as well. It now resembles a tree, the seat carved into its trunk while branches snake up around and above her.

My head pounds, threatening to split apart with every thought. I start the count again to still my mind.

Natasha breaks the silence. "Am I—"

"Dreaming?" says the woman. Then she smiles, her eyes distant. "Perhaps …" The branches of the throne tree curl and age before me. "The question is, of course … can any of us wake?"

Then the woman takes a deep breath and draws herself up in her throne. Her glow brightens and the branches rejuvenate, reaching upward in response. I stare at them with eyes wide.

"How is it you are here?" she asks, refocusing on us, a hint of disbelief in her voice. "I am not the first of us you have seen. Am I right?" She looks straight at me.

He appears in my mind – the mysterious man, his unfathomable power. Despite the woman's heat, my insides turn cold. I've not told anyone. And when my mouth opens, I feel a sudden tightness in my chest, so many familiar barriers springing up – doubts, suspicions … I sit on the bench and squirm.

She simply smiles at me, and the sensation of love brims again at my core. My body shakes. It's almost overwhelming, like liquid rapture. I feel every ache in me soothed, every crack filled. I want to bask in it … on and on.

I sense Natasha's eyes on me as well. And the words start to come, to press against the back of my throat.

"An accident …" I say, eventually.

The woman simply nods. Waits.

It all tumbles out, unrefined, like scree falling down a slope. I tell the story backward, from seeing the office building transform to our pursuers at the hospital. The further I go telling her the story, the easier the words come and the louder the animal sounds – twittering birds, shufflings in the undergrowth, chirping crickets. I describe finding Natasha's friend dead, my partner, the tattooed symbol on our dead pursuer. And the narrative ends where it started – the white-haired guy in the station, the dark shapes who seemed to herd the crowd, my suspicion that the accident was sabotage, and the nun who saved me.

Then I glimpse the mysterious man again in my mind – his blinding radiance, a face too beautiful to behold – and a frisson of cold makes me shiver. I close my eyes. With my heart so full, his image keeps slipping. And still the pressure builds in my chest. I swallow and force the words out.

"There was this man. His glow so bright. Impossible to look at …" My words falter, my brain spurting doubts again. I take a breath and focus on calming my thoughts. "He appeared right by me. Was somehow normal size but massive, too. Moved me like a puppet. Said things about humbling the arrogant, about ..."

I open my eyes. Blink. An absolute silence has descended on us. No sound except for the loud thumping of my pulse in my ears.

The woman sits there with a single hand raised. Her throne has become stone again, the branches morphed into blades. A brisk wind gusts and prickles the hairs on my arms.

"No more ..." she breathes, a growing shadow creeping into her light. I sense her withdrawing, the brimming love diminishing from my heart. "You have seen him?" Her voice trembles.

And while my thoughts scream to deny it ... held by her gaze, even the idea of lying feels like a knifing pain. I nod.

She pauses, her glow continuing to shrink. "Spoken with him?" she says.

I nod again, my mouth so dry. And Natasha continues to stare at me, the questions so clear in her face.

Then the woman stands before her throne, the blades raised around her. "You must go," she says, her hands clasped together.

My lips part. And in that moment, I glimpse not the goddess, but a little child, trapped, alone, the blades as bars of a prison.

"I cannot help you," she says.

And I sense the depths of sadness I felt seeing her on stage, so bitter. I swallow.

And then her voice changes, her tone lower, abrupt, and she points behind. "You must ... *go.*"

## 34

THE WOMAN'S throne retreats away from us into the darkness, her glowing form shrinking in size while the blades behind her grow ever taller and sharper. I remain there. Frozen on the stone bench. The sense of warmth draining from my heart and a weight taking its place.

The woman turns her head as she moves away, the black an endless sea around her. And before I know it, I'm on my feet, my arm reaching out toward her.

"Wait!" I call.

She continues to withdraw.

"*Wait … please!*" I shout louder.

Finally, she stops, a cavern of darkness between us. She half turns back.

"Maybe we could … help you?" I say, my chest cramping with each pathetic-sounding word that passes my lips.

The silence deepens.

"I'm afraid there is no help you can give me," the woman says eventually, her voice barely a whisper.

My ribs tighten. "Why not?"

From stillness, she pivots to face us again. Stares at me a long moment before angling her gaze to Natasha. And then in the next instant, she's standing before us once more, her throne at her back. The incredible warmth burns in my heart again, though the weight doesn't vanish.

She reaches her hand toward Natasha's chin. "I was like you once," she says, "but that was a very long time ago."

Natasha sits upright on the bench at my side. "How long?" she says.

The woman settles back down on the throne and lowers her hand to her lap. I sit down as well. The woman says nothing for a moment. Simply shifts her gaze from Natasha to me and back again, as if making a decision.

"Four thousand years," she says, eventually.

I feel my eyes almost pop from my head.

"And I am not the oldest," the woman says.

"How can you be so old?" Natasha blurts out.

"For the very same reason that you can't," she says and then gives a thin smile. "I will see if I can explain. It is about faith … conviction … belief."

Then she looks at me sadly, and the weight of her pain's so heavy in my chest.

She sighs. "You must understand. Back then, the world was far more fluid. A great deal more was possible," she says. "Before humanity became obsessed with science, as you comprehend it, with documenting and fixing every facet of existence."

As she continues speaking, the animal calls resume from the darkness – birds, frogs, insects – and the throne gradually morphs back to wood, the blades to branches.

"Many of the gods that you know of from ancient myths and stories were once men and women of flesh and blood," she goes on. "The early gods were cast in the mould of man, for that is precisely what they were."

"Wait … wait, please," says Natasha, her hands clenched in her lap. "You are saying that the gods were ordinary people?"

The woman turns slowly to face her. "Belief … Belief is a power that lies as a spark within each of us – our most precious gift," she says, her voice strengthening. "It delineates the limits of our acuities, of our abilities, of what we can see and do." Then her expression grows more distant. "But in humanity, this power has been dimmed for millennia. One might say the gift has been stolen."

*Stolen?* The thought resounds in my head, her words so similar to the priest's. The woman stares straight at me.

"Before my time, early man's leaders communed with the spirits of animals and nature, seeking advantage and arcane knowledge," she says. "They honed their ability to listen, to commune, and believed in their own powers. Their tribes augmented this power by placing their faith in these leaders. The greater the belief, the more profound the power."

She raises her hands, and the sweeping branches mirror her movements. "As the tribes grew larger, so too did their reliance on their leaders, their shamans," she says. "In time, *they* became the focus of their communities' beliefs, rather than the spirits they communed with."

The sudden growl of an animal makes me stiffen.

The woman continues. "These were man's early gods, individuals who developed powers that cultivated the belief of their peoples, and this belief enhanced their abilities."

"*That was all?*" Natasha asks, her voice rising and her hands clasped ever more tightly together. "Groups believed in the powers of these normal people, believed they were gods, and that made their powers real? That turned them into *gods?*"

It's like the bell of blasphemy's ringing in her ears.

The woman simply nods. "In part. The more people believe something of you, the more real it becomes."

She raises an eyebrow and nods from me to Natasha, scanning Natasha's body up and down with a licentious smile on her lips. Natasha blushes and dips her gaze.

Then the woman turns back to me. "First, these powers granted the individuals long life. You are familiar with stories of these ancient men in the holy books, I am sure," she says.

I can feel myself frowning.

She leans toward me and whispers, "The Bible possesses more power than you can possibly know."

I tilt back, her heat almost unbearable. Natasha shifts at my side.

"Eventually a threshold was crossed," the woman continues, sitting upright once more. "The magnitude of belief and its corollary power extended their lives, on and on. Tales were woven about them, myths crafted. These people were believed to be immortal in the eyes of others and, eventually, that is what they became." Her palms rest on her thighs. "These stories articulated the powers of these gods, which in turn made them real."

My eyes scrunch shut, my head spinning. And I try desperately to control my flailing mind.

"I understand it is difficult to comprehend," she says. "Faith is akin to power. You believe that your scientific advancements propel you forward, but in many ways, they constrain you. They fix your understanding of the world, limiting your capabilities. They blind you and ..." – she lowers her voice – "worse, they make you sheep in a land of wolves."

An animal barks somewhere in the darkness. My eyes fly open.

"Your gods walk among you," the woman continues. "They shape your world for their own ends, but you have no idea because you do not believe it possible." She shakes her head. "And now, you come to me."

Natasha clears her throat, settling herself on the bench. "You ... you're a ..." she starts.

"*God?*" The woman's voice booms. I jump. And for a moment, she towers higher above us, her throne tree stretching up into the dark. The sounds of nature grow even louder. Then she looks away and laughs – with joy or pain, I can't tell.

"There is no adequate name," she says. "We've been called

the Malakh by some – the messengers between God and man – Ankero ... Angelos—"

"Angels," Natasha breathes.

The woman shrugs. "You might say."

The image comes of the mysterious man again – his radiance, his beauty.

"You're *angels?*" I repeat.

And my thoughts flick to the tattoo on our pursuer, the symbol – a thin crucifix and a crescent moon. And then it hits ... the crescent moon. Downward facing with an indentation at the top. Not a moon, but a set of wings. Angel wings.

The woman pauses and then says again, "You might say."

Once more, I notice my natural doubts firing, my brain in a whirl. And I breathe while stretching my fingers.

"There are many of you?" I ask. "Around the world?"

"Religious beliefs vary," she says. "We derive power from those who believe in us, so ordinarily we are tied to our localities." Her lips form a grim smile. "Different angels graced with different natures by their different peoples."

Natasha takes a deep breath and bites her lip. Then she forces the words out. "So ... what about ... God?" she says.

The angel laughs sourly. "*God?*" she spits. "The God you know is a creation of the scriptures. A concept created to serve a bigger purpose."

Natasha stares at the angel. Her fingers shake as she finds the crucifix around her neck.

The angel gazes back, her features fixed but not stern. "It is the same with Jesus," she says. "He was a human, like you or me, a prophet from the ancient times ... impressive, yet hardly a rival for the angels who reigned. He was much more useful dead. A sublime focus for belief."

Natasha's skin pales, her lips part.

I clear my throat. "These people, these angels," I say. "What do they want?"

"Devotion," the angel says. "The more ardently we believe

in our gods, our angels, the more power they have. They have been siphoning human faith for millennia, since the holy books were written." She smiles wryly. "Do you not see the mastery of it? The scriptures enshrined faith, dictated to people what to believe – God and Jesus on high, supported by an entire pantheon endowed with exceptional powers. The shamans in the old tribes required rituals to garner the devotion of their people, while our holy books accomplish it all on their own."

She edges back on her throne. "And do not presume this to be mere happenstance," she says, her voice lower. "Behind the grandest of creations is a master architect."

She stares at me again. And I find myself shivering.

"But … But angels sit at God's right hand," Natasha says quickly. "They are divine … not manipulative."

The angel raises her chin, and suddenly I glimpse a great tiredness in her eyes. "The naivety of the faithful is simultaneously your finest and most flawed quality," the angel says. "Manipulation is the waters we angels were birthed in, channelling the beliefs of those around us."

The branches behind her gnarl and curl in front of us. And the mysterious man's words from the station revolve around my head … *We are not so different, you and I.* Both of us conmen.

"Not all intervene directly in the world of man," the angel continues. "Most angels live abstractly in realms such as this." She waves her hand around. "But there remain those who do."

Then the angel spreads her hands and glances across at me. "And, of course, there are those of us who have no choice," she says, more quietly.

Her branches shrink again. And I feel the sense of her profound sadness returning, almost unbearable. It drives the heat in my chest. I shake my head. Ball my fists. And a connection sparks.

My eyes flash wide. "You!" I say.

The angel nods, and the surrounding sounds diminish again. "To rule only in darkness," she says.

I sit up straighter. Gooseflesh spreads across my back. "The club," I say.

She closes her eyes. "Qetesh" – the word rings – "is my name. Deity of love, of desire." Her voice climbs. "The pinnacle of material experience. Divinity manifest in flesh and blood!" She burns so brightly her heat is almost unbearable.

The desire to give myself over is overwhelming. Then the image forms of her on stage, dancing night after night for the devotion of all those rich leeches.

The tightness grips my chest like a vice. "I ... can't ..." I splutter.

She glances at me, and her lips form a sad smile. "I was born a long way from here," she says. "In the lands of the desert. For a thousand years, I was worshipped." She pauses. "But epochs shifted, and my significance was supplanted by others. I waned in strength, and finally ..." Her voice falters, and all sound dies around us again. No animal calls, no rustling. Pure silence.

"He came," she says eventually and then glances over my shoulder.

"He?" Natasha asks, a new conviction in her tone. "This man Jake saw in the station? Another angel?"

Qetesh gives a slow nod. "So powerful, he was. Without match. Would I have gone with him if I'd known?" She trails off and her throne stands rigid again, harsh stone, the blades of steel taller and sharper than ever.

"He brought you here," I say.

She nods once more. "I am his." Such despair in her voice. I feel like my heart might break. "Taken from my people, like the others, and forced to eke out scraps of love from the adulation of strangers." She spits the words, her body blazing.

Natasha doesn't flinch in the face of the heat. "He has taken others?"

Qetesh turns toward her. "He has acquired more than just me," she says.

My thoughts spin, and memories come of the skull-face hovering before me, its form made of writhing darkness. I feel an echo of the awful chill in my bones.

Natasha leans forward on the bench, her arms tense and her fingers gripping her crucifix. There's fire in her eyes, the same excited expression as I glimpsed in the church with the priest. She opens her mouth—

"This angel," I say quickly. "He's claimed you and others. He's sabotaging trains." My throat's so dry again. "But what does he *want*?"

Silence descends once more. A cold wind blows in from the darkness, ruffling Qetesh's dress. The bench below us morphs into stone.

The angel stands up again. "Are you certain you wish to go through with this?" she asks, glancing between us. "Up until now, you've had the power of belief on your side. He might dispatch his minions in search of you, presuming you'd run and hide. But the notion that you'd possess the arrogance to actually challenge him would be unthinkable."

She pauses and stands before her bladed throne as she did before, this time as the goddess, tall and radiant. I blink up at her.

"I *will* help you," she says, her voice firm. "But if you proceed, please be clear. You'll unleash a wrath the likes of which you cannot comprehend."

## 35

SILENCE. Qetesh is on her feet in front of her throne of spears. Natasha's beside me on the stone bench. And the angel's words hang between us.

My eyes find Natasha. For a moment, she squeezes her crucifix necklace. Then she stands. It seems like a simple act of acceptance. She was raised by God, apparently delivered from adversity for a reason, some kind of mission. And this is clearly it.

I sit there, the sound of distant thunder in my ears. Then the hospital dream slams into my mind – the wall of wind, rushing closer, ready to destroy us all.

Qetesh stares between us. And before I know it, I find myself on my feet at Natasha's side.

The angel nods. "So be it," she says, and so much flashes across her shining eyes – sadness, anger, fear. She glances from Natasha to me again. And I can only stare back. "If you truly intend to pursue this, follow me."

She steps toward us, and the throne disappears. The white shingle path returns, meandering off behind her. She turns and pads along it. Natasha follows immediately, her posture upright and stride steady. And I remain standing there, my familiar doubts railing at me ... *What the fuck am I doing?*

Qetesh draws further away, her radiance diminishing and causing my heart to ache. And so soon, I'm all alone.

I find my gaze drawn off into the blackness, a tingling sensation climbing my spine.

"*Be as quiet as you can.*" Qetesh's words suddenly resound in my head. "*And try not to stray.*"

I spin and hurry down the shingle path to catch up with her, the ache easing with every step I draw nearer.

"Do all angels live in places like this?" Natasha whispers to Qetesh as I reach them.

We trail the angel in single file, me at the back, the darkness still thick around us. I focus on the goddess and try to listen.

"More realms exist than you can imagine," Qetesh says, her low whispers carrying perfectly to my ears. "While humankind constrained your wanderings with science, angels inhabit the older ones. They traverse your world but dwell in the spaces in between."

I see again the office building, its transformation – the glowing statues and arches – how much more of it became visible behind the veil.

"You said power is based on belief," says Natasha. "But surely angels cannot do whatever they want in our world. Surely, they must stay hidden, otherwise their power will be undermined. Could they not be revealed?"

"Yes and no," Qetesh replies. "If a great many people glimpsed the angels and realised what they were, their devotion would be diminished, yes. But, mostly, belief blinds."

I try to order my thoughts again, but still my mind continues to flit. I think of the Puritans, the atheists, each group blinded by their different beliefs.

A bird calls from the side, and my head whips around. The space seems to be narrowing. Even in the darkness, I get the strange sense of tree branches pressing in, crowding the path.

"Angels move in the world, and most sightings are

ignored," Qetesh continues. "People perceive what they expect to see: a flash of light, a bird … a miracle."

Just like the dark shapes corralling the crowds in the station, so hard to make out. Then memories of the angel crowd my brain. Him appearing before me, ripping away the veil, manipulating my limbs. A shudder rolls right the way up my body.

Suddenly, Qetesh stops walking. I stumble to a halt. The angel stands in front of us on the path and stares off into the distance. Absolute silence reigns again.

"He is different," she whispers so softly. "Always has been. He is among the oldest."

My lips press together. And Natasha says, "Who—"

"His name is Gabriel," Qetesh says, and our surroundings throb with the word.

Natasha stiffens. "The archangel?" she says.

Qetesh glances at her, eyes burning. "You have no idea, little girl," she says. And then her face softens. "You truly don't."

I swallow. "This master architect … that's him?"

Qetesh stares back at me, her jawline tight, and then gives a tiny nod. I take a breath.

Gabriel. The ultimate conman. He wrote the Gospels and ensured they were spread around the world, fostering devotion on tap. So clever. And again, the archangel's final words return to me, a pressure building in my chest.

Qetesh spins and begins walking once more. I follow behind.

"Not all angels endorse his deeds," she says. "Many decry direct involvement. They sit aloft, believing it is their right to rule. It has been an age since they have had to earn the belief of their peoples."

*"But not you,"* I mutter under my breath, images coming of Qetesh in the club, performing for mere crumbs of devotion. And again, I feel an echo of the immense sadness, of her boundless rage.

"Why does Gabriel involve himself?" Natasha says.

"For the most dangerous of reasons," Qetesh says. "Because he believes it is right. He hails from an era when we were more involved in the affairs of man. Angels and demons having direct contact, aiding and thwarting. Engaged in a battle for the belief of humankind."

Qetesh lengthens her stride down the path. "In his mind, humanity should worship the divine above all else, should strive toward sanctity, piousness … all other pursuits being empty," she says. "And naturally, given that this is rarely the pursuit of all people, he believes you're in need of divine help – his help – without which, humanity will always fall short."

Again, I glimpse Gabriel in the station, and remember the contempt he showed for the rich and their hollow efforts. The pressure continues to build inside me.

Qetesh lapses into silence as she meanders on down the path, Natasha just behind. The animal sounds quieten around us. And in the stillness, Gabriel's words press up my throat.

"He said something worse was coming," I say finally.

Natasha spins her head to face me as she walks.

I nod, avoiding her gaze. "Gabriel said so. Told me it'd be better to die now than experience it," I say, keeping my focus on Qetesh instead. "What might that be?"

The angel sighs. And I feel a sudden weight on my shoulders.

"I cannot say," she whispers. "It has perpetually been this way with him … grand schemes since the dawn of time. It is no different from the Dark Ages, to the many times before."

"Wait," Natasha stutters, barely able to speak. "Humanity's Dark Ages … *he* created them?"

Qetesh pauses and then nods. "As great purges, endeavours to rebalance belief," she says. "Without which, he fears secularism would crush the sacred." She lowers her voice further. "Faced with immense hardship, we turn to gods for security, for meaning." She shrugs again. "People always have. These purges are the gifts he believes he brings humanity."

*Gifts.* With her words, images from the train crash swirl through my head – the bodies strewn, the limbs broken and bent, the horrendous carnage. And something nags at my mind … something I've missed.

"Surely someone can stop him," Natasha says.

"The archangels? Other angels?" Qetesh scoffs. "Many may cast aspersions on his actions, but how many would spurn the benefits, the strengthening of devotion, of their rule?" she says. "Be as wise as serpents, it is written … as wise as serpents and as innocent as doves. Gabriel is a brother to them, after all. So, in effect, he can do whatever he wants."

*Whatever he wants.* While Natasha's jaw clenches, I stare off into the darkness, the memory continuing to prod at me …

Then it comes. My heart thumps, and I stop walking.

"The bodies on those stone tables," I say, images flashing of their horrible blisters, their contorted limbs, the agony in their features.

Qetesh stops walking as well and swivels to face me.

"What happened to them?" I stammer. "What are they doing here?"

"The poor souls," she says, her glow fading a fraction. "We find their bodies abandoned, forsaken. And we provide them sanctuary for their transition."

"Are they tied to this in some way?" I ask.

Qetesh holds my gaze. "Perhaps," she says, eventually. "I cannot say for sure."

My visions morph, and I glimpse myself lying on a plinth, limbs splayed out.

"Gabriel …" I say. "Is he above torture?"

Qetesh shakes her head. "No," she says.

"So why—" says Natasha.

"Yes, what *is* his plan?" I say.

"*That*, it appears, is the question," Qetesh says with a nod.

She smiles at me and adds, "And here I take my leave of you."

In the next instant, the angel vanishes and then reappears twenty yards further away, the shining cobbles of the path in between us. With the distance, I feel an enormous wrenching pain in my chest, like my heart's being torn apart, and my legs stagger.

"What must we do?" Natasha says, her chin tilted up.

"You must leap," Qetesh says, her words carrying effortlessly to us. She nods to our side.

Following the tilt of her head, features bloom out of the darkness. I find myself standing with Natasha on top of a cliff that surrounds a pool of water, fifty feet across and twenty feet down. Much of the water's hidden by the branches of trees that stretch out from around its edge. And its unblemished surface shines like pristine glass, reflecting patches of brilliant stars.

Qetesh motions toward the pool. "You must find someone," she says, speaking more quickly. "He is like me, a fellow refugee of ancient times. He knows much. Should anyone be able to tell you more of Gabriel's plans, of your path ahead, it is he."

Her voice grows more distant. And my gaze shoots back.

She's standing a further twenty yards away from us, her form smaller, her glow receding more. My insides squeeze. She could be forty or forty million yards away. The anguish feels overwhelming. It's as if I'm outside my childhood house again, my mother standing on the doorstep, turning away from me. The last time I ever saw her.

I tense my stomach, force a quick breath, and focus on shutting out the pain.

Qetesh appears at my side once more. "Don't," she says and reaches out to touch my chest. Her heat blazes against the entire front of my body. "*Feel* it."

And again the pain sears my insides, like my heart's being held over hot coals. Too fucking much. I pull away.

Qetesh leans in and presses her whole hand to my breast. "You've known great love," she continues. "It *was* true, whether or not you believe it. You're pure of heart, your anger like white fire. It is a *powerful* thing. I can feel it!"

I shake my head. "That's not me," I croak, the words tumbling out. "I'm nothing."

"I do not think so," she says. "And Gabriel clearly does not think so, either. He singled you out in the station. Revealed himself to you … a mere mortal. And you *survived*." Her eyes shine, and her voice rises. "This does not happen. And since then, he is clearly concerned enough to send others after you. Perhaps he sees a little of himself *in* you."

I glance between Natasha and Qetesh. Both of them are staring at me. And the priest's words return about my impending role, about how this is all intended. The pressure builds again in my chest. And I can sense Qetesh's imminent withdrawal, my insides continuing to squeeze.

I lift my hand toward her, fingers shaking.

"Do not worry," she says, smiling. "This has already been decided. It's exactly as it needs to be. It is why we are all here." Then she nods to me and Natasha. "But you must also see it as a choice." She gazes back at me.

"Why … why are you helping us?" I croak out.

"*I told you.*" Again, her words resound in my head. "*It has been decided.*" Her features tighten, and I glimpse the resolve, the anger in her eyes – a rage that burns like oil atop the ocean of her pain. She brings a fist to her chest. "*I sense it and choose it all at once.*"

A cool breeze makes me shiver. And the angel glances over her shoulder. "Hurry, you must be quick," she whispers out loud to both of us. "And be careful, the portals are being watched. None of us can travel without being seen."

I feel myself frowning as she gazes between us.

"It may be why none can accomplish this but you," she says.

Natasha stares down at the pool's surface. It's a long drop, the reflected stars in the pool an eternity away. She steps right to the edge of the cliff.

"*Wait*," I hiss and grip her hand. My eyes find Qetesh again, the stabbing pain still there in my heart, the impending sense of love found and then lost … so precious. I feel the thunder on the horizon once more, the wall of wind careening toward us.

Again, Qetesh speaks the words to me alone. "*It's a leap of faith you must take.*"

She smiles. Doesn't withdraw. Even so, I get a sense of an inevitable ending, just like it was with my mother on the doorstep. The weight of grief crushes me. I bite my cheek to thwart hot tears.

Natasha swivels her head to face me. "You ready?" she asks.

My eyes don't leave Qetesh's.

The goddess's voice pervades my head, "*I will see you again.*"

My heart swells. And before I can stop myself, I grip Natasha's hand tighter, lean over the cliff edge, and throw myself off.

# 36

"*Fuck!*" I scream at the rushing air, the reflected stars, and the shining liquid hurtling toward us.

Natasha's hand tightens around mine, and I close my eyes.

My feet hit the pool's surface. The liquid engulfs my legs, reaches up my torso like fingers, and I lose my grip on Natasha. My body shakes as the pool sucks me down, down, down ... and through.

My eyelids spring open. A deep blue sky full of stars swims *below* me. And I'm falling toward them. I gulp warm air, my limbs flailing.

Suddenly, a dozen stars pop out of the night sky, all clustered together and each a few inches across, all flying up in my direction. I grab for the sparkling teardrops as they pass my face. Their jagged contours bite into my fingers, and I hold on tight. My fall's jerked to a stop.

I glance up and glimpse golden statues, some kind of fountain, and tiled floor around it, the ground somehow twenty feet above my head.

Just the thought shifts the direction of gravity. The world flips and the stars are suddenly above me, the teardrops wrenched from my grip. I start to fall, the floor careening upward toward me, my body held up by the viscous air.

I still land heavily and roll away from the fountain, my heart racing. I push myself up onto my knees and notice Natasha at my side.

I'm in a room … a gigantic room, at least fifty yards square. The ceiling lies over sixty feet above me, a rich blue, almost black, laced with sparkling jewels along its length like a quilt of stars. And from it hang enormous chandeliers, the one I grabbed directly above me.

My gaze tracks downward. The walls are even more luxuriously decorated than the ceiling, lustrous red wallpaper the background to every type of ornate decoration. Gilded wooden panels border pedestals with bronze statues of perfectly formed men and women. Paintings of luscious gardens, rainbows, and other religious imagery flank marble columns, while gilded sofas and throne-like chairs stand in clusters atop lush patterned carpets all around the room.

This place is like a palace – complete with its nobility. The room's full. Well over a hundred lords and ladies stand talking in groups, dressed in attire that must have belonged in some kind of royal court – the ladies in long sweeping dresses with embroidered bodices, the men in knee-length coats and breeches, all in shining silk with golden trim. The opulence is unbelievable.

A faint chill creeps up my spine. It's the visuals, and the sounds, too. Though they're all speaking noisily, the language is impossible to place. It's like some kind of background hum. Plus, each one is chatting and enjoying drinks and titbits, entirely oblivious that we landed or that we're here at all. The chill crawls all the way up my neck.

I stand up slowly, my eyes fixed on the surrounding figures. Still they ignore me as I stare around the room. The veil's palpable before my senses. My gaze falls on a painted fresco, and the image shifts before my eyes – the figures in the rustic image moving, the border of the painting changing shape.

"*What the fuck?*" I breathe, my pulse accelerating, and I pull my gaze away.

But everywhere I rest my attention subtly morphs – the statues, the furniture, the walls – and I can feel every shift inside my chest, as if I'm physically connected to everything around me. It feels as if the entire room might disintegrate before my eyes if I focus on anything for too long.

Natasha pushes past me and steps toward the fountain.

"Where the hell are we?" I say.

Natasha ignores me and gazes over the lip of the fountain with fascination in her eyes. It's circular, ten feet wide, and made of what looks like solid gold, entirely smooth.

"Will you look at that?" she says.

I follow her gaze. The liquid's as still as the pool we leaped into. Yet, instead of reflecting the stars above, I see the outline of a network of tree branches, just like those we jumped through.

My focus slips, and the image of Qetesh forms in my mind. My heart aches with the brimming love ... so much ... almost too much.

And then she left me.

*Of course she bloody did.*

The pain builds so quickly in my chest it's like I'm breathing slivers of glass. I feel my heart closing again, my ribs tightening, and hot anger taking its place.

I spin away from Natasha. "This place is crazy," I spit.

"We will work it out," she says.

"So damn sure, are you?" I say, my voice rising.

"Oh, right," Natasha says, swivelling to face me. "You would have liked to prepare before jumping, to share your thinking, to talk things through?" She digs her fingers into her hips. "When were you going to inform me about the angel in the station, his promise about—"

The room drops into total silence, and I shoot an arm up,

my heart pounding. The figures before us have turned in our direction. From a pleasant warmth, the air has turned cool, winds gusting, pulling at dresses, at jackets. And I feel the familiar strange chill from our pursuers burrowing right inside my bones.

I whirl around, my gaze searching for exits, taking in the doors set into the middle of all four walls, my body tensing to run. And I find every single pair of eyes in the room fixed on us, the nearby bodies growing in size, their skin darkening … and I picture the strange black shapes under the skin of our pursuers.

I crouch down, shut my eyes, and hold my breath, while my brain yells madness. And hunching there, I sense something clawing at my attention, pulling at my eyelids, tilting my chin up … And just like in the priest's pulpit, the skull-like face appears in my mind, its contours formed of dark, writhing shapes.

I feel the strongest urge to open my eyes, to glimpse the threat. While my brain screams louder against it. I grit my teeth, tense my neck, and scrunch my eyes tighter shut.

Eventually, the pressure ebbs, and the surrounding voices begin again. The air warms and the winds die. Slowly, I open my eyes.

The crowd moves exactly as it did before, conversing and circulating around the palace-like room. The waiters do their rounds. Everyone is as unaware of us as they were before.

My gaze finds Natasha. She's staring back at me, her face pale, on her knees as I am. She keeps her mouth shut and angles her head toward one of the doors. I nod. And moving as silently as possible, we stand up, weave between the crowds, reach the doors, and step through.

The next room is almost as full. The same extravagantly dressed people, the same small groups in rapt conversation. With the same lavish decor too, the same doors in the middle of all four walls. We continue through that room as well.

We keep going, moving in a straight line through a seemingly endless corridor of opulent rooms. And eventually, the large crowd diminishes to twos and threes. I can't keep my eyes off them. They're almost stranger, standing in tiny clusters and frolicking together as if they were amid hundreds. Still totally oblivious to us.

I quicken my steps down the corridor. And the faster I walk, the quicker my attention flits over my surroundings, and the less the details shift. I breathe a sigh of relief. The veil is less obvious before my senses, the feeling of being physically connected to everything weaker as well.

Finally, Natasha and I are striding on our own through the endless rooms, all with similar degrees of splendour, in silence.

"Did you see the fountain?" Natasha says.

I start at the sound.

"I think this place is some kind of interchange between realms," she continues, her eyes trained on the corridor ahead. "Looking into the liquid, I saw the forest we came from, the clifftop we jumped off."

Qetesh's words about portals come back to me, and I nod.

"We need to find another fountain," she says and glances to her side down another endless corridor. Each square room with the same four doors, the same corridor of rooms extending beyond each one. "That is what Qetesh must have wanted us to do," Natasha goes on. "To find this refugee."

We walk down the corridor for what seems forever. Occasionally we reach a T-junction, but then the corridor of rooms continues in the same direction we started in. We keep walking, traversing vast galleries, climbing majestic staircases, each floor identical-looking. The palace literally fucking endless.

I plod on, scanning every corridor for the glint of a fountain while half my mind remains on our path back to the first one, back to Qetesh. Longing thoughts revolve around my head.

However, the memory of the route is like the finest of

threads, slowly unravelling. Just like my damn sanity. Natasha strides indomitably through room after extravagant room, no doubt in her expression.

Following her into the thousandth room of painted seascapes, the heat flares inside me. I pass what must be the millionth throne-like chair and find myself striding toward it.

"Jake?" Natasha says.

I ignore her, grip the chair, and haul it to shoulder height. Ready to throw it at a painting, to smash a hole through the bloody wall.

Natasha hisses, "Stop!"

I spin to face her, the chair still held in my hands.

"Those people!" she says, her eyes wide, jabbing her finger through the door we entered by. "What if they heard?"

I blink and then nod, an echo of the strange chill still there beneath my skin. But I don't put the chair down. I simply squeeze it tighter.

"We're fucking trapped," I mutter.

Natasha pads away, and I find my gaze resting on one of the lush rugs, the veil so distinct before my senses. As before, the embroidered scene morphs, an entirely new world of sea creatures created before my eyes. Yet, with the heat still tightening my chest, I clench my jaw and hold my gaze.

The image continues to shift, the sea rolling beyond the boundaries of the woven frame. And again, I *feel* the shift as much as I see it, the physical connection so palpable. Still I continue staring, the water spreading out across the rug, climbing the walls, ready to swallow me whole—

"Hey!" Natasha's voice comes from behind.

I spin my head to face her. She's standing by the far door, peering down the endless corridor of rooms. Then she breaks out into a run.

I dump the chair, jog over to the door, and stare after her.

Something triangular and glinting is barely visible in the distance. I sprint behind her, my adrenaline firing, visions coming of finally getting out of this place.

Natasha slides to a halt in front of it. And my run becomes a jog, then a walk, the disappointment so clear in her slumped shoulders. I reach the fountain rim.

Empty. Only the polished golden surface shining back up at us.

Natasha tests the fountain, even climbs in. Then she sighs and straightens once more as she begins striding toward the next corridor.

"Wait," I say.

She stares back at me.

"We can't just keep wandering," I say.

She narrows her eyes. "You have a better idea?"

I stare over her shoulder, down the corridor of rooms. I can sense the veil again, the palpable connection to the surrounding objects, to the doors in front and behind.

"Maybe," I say.

But my thoughts flit to Qetesh once more and the tattered path back to her. It'd be gone forever.

I take a deep breath and shut my eyes, starting the count to still my thoughts. And instead of shutting out the connection to everything, I focus on it, trying to *feel* the surrounding objects while I bring back the memory of the shimmering world from the station.

Gradually, the veil peels back from my senses. And even with my eyes closed, the physical connection to the furniture, the walls, the ceiling, the floor, is greatly strengthened. It's like I'm invisibly linked by cords that start in my solar plexus. The air buzzes with a strange sense of solidity.

My doubts rally … *I'll go mad like my mother … end up totally lost.*

Again, I push them down, focusing instead on the feeling of the next rooms down the corridor as well as the rooms beyond that. I try to imagine moving without walking, using the connections to pull me along.

Nothing happens.

Natasha's voice splits my concentration. "What are you doing?"

My eyes open. She has her arms folded across her chest.

"Tell me," she says.

I raise an arm toward her. "Give me your hand."

Her frown deepens and her arms remain wrapped around her.

"Your hand," I insist.

She sighs and walks over to join fingers with me.

Again, I close my eyes and bring back the feeling of physical connection to everything.

Gravity. I remember how it shifted as I fell through the pool, how the stars below became jewels in the ceiling above. And I focus on the corridor becoming a well, on it plunging away from us. And for an instant, I feel my balance shifting, my body teetering on some kind of ledge, ready to topple forward.

Then the sensation's gone.

"Well, this is touching," Natasha says.

I grip her hand, keep my eyes shut, and concentrate on blocking out sounds as well as thoughts. And then the memory comes – the priest and his words in the church … *Belief is everything.*

And with that, I don't just focus on the feeling of connection to the surrounding objects, of gravity flipping. I concentrate on *believing* we can move.

Suddenly, the world lurches. My eyes fly open. The corridor goes from straight ahead of us to vertically down, only empty bloody space beneath our feet … and we start to fall.

## 37

WE PLUMMET down through endless rooms, the corridor a lift shaft below us, as if the entire palace has been flipped by ninety degrees. The paintings and sculptures fly past and, while we should be tumbling ever faster, we're buffeted in our fall, the rushing wind like a cradle around us, holding us up.

I scrunch my eyes shut again, squeeze Natasha's fingers, and believe that the gravity's flipped once more, that we've stopped. Almost instantly, the world tilts so the ground's horizontal beneath my feet again, and I sprawl forward onto the marble ground.

I lie there, breathing hard. It feels like my brain's been turned inside out.

Natasha picks herself up and stares around. "Wow," she says. "How did you do that?"

"Not sure," I say, pushing myself up to my knees.

The new room looks the same as a hundred others we've seen – more carved mirrors, scarlet sofas, golden-framed paintings, and hanging chandeliers.

My mind flits back to Qetesh, to the first fountain. I swivel on the spot and stare down four corridors of lavish rooms, each one identical-looking. My heart squeezes. We're even deeper in the labyrinth now. Totally fucking lost.

Natasha holds her hand out to me, her lips turned up in a half smile. "Let's do that again," she says. "And this time, we search for fountains."

And so we do. And with each attempt, I find it easier to shift gravity, to have the rooms barrel past us, to navigate the obstacles we come across – T-junctions and winding staircases.

Finally, I spot the flash of gold from a fountain and bring us to a careening stop. It's empty. We go again and find another … then another … then another. The hours tick by. And each fountain is bloody empty.

After finding the fifth one, Natasha squeezes my fingers, preparing for another jump. I shake my head.

She yanks my hand. "Come on!" she snaps.

"No," I say, anchoring my feet. "This isn't working."

And with each jump, it takes me longer to order my thoughts, as if my brain's being rung like a bell, my madness creeping ever closer.

Natasha leans in. "Qetesh sent us here for a reason," she says, her voice intent. "We *will* find it."

I shake my head again and let the idea that's been knocking form in my mind. "We've got to think—" I start.

"Oh, another plan," she says, all sarcastic. She plants her hands on her hips. "Will you share it this time?"

I sigh through gritted teeth and then take a deep breath. "What if we're totally wrong?" I say.

"About what?" she retorts.

"The people," I say, my mind conjuring images of the strange figures in their sweeping gowns and knee-length coats. An echo of the strange chill sidles under my skin again. "What if we shouldn't be dodging them?"

She opens her mouth, stands there, and it's as if all the bluster spills out of her. "But … you saw what happened," she says.

"Yeah," I say, their laser-like attention coming back to me, their morphing shapes, the awful silence. "Maybe that's the point. That's what they do. They're a warning system for Gabriel, or whoever, that someone's using this realm. If it's an interchange."

Natasha goes quiet, simply staring at me.

"Which means—" I start.

"That we need to find them?" she says, her voice quieter still. She glances over my shoulder, down a corridor.

"Either that or we're stuck roaming this place forever," I say. "If most of the fountains are dry, they could be minding the working ones."

And Qetesh's words come back to me … *None of us can travel without being seen. It may be why none can accomplish this but you.*

Only mortals.

Natasha takes a long breath and stares back at me. "So, how do we do that?"

———

WE MOVE BY BELIEF AGAIN – shifting gravity, plummeting down corridors, the air slowing our fall – and for an age we find nothing but more empty rooms, empty stairwells. Then eventually, I hear something and pull us to a halt.

Distant laughing.

I pad backward to spy atop a balcony fifteen feet up. And there, visible through the railings, stand a man and woman engaged in a rapturous exchange. An echo of the strange chill's there once more in my bones, and I quickly duck out of sight.

They don't clock us and simply continue with their odd-sounding conversation, that weird hum. We check the surrounding rooms. All empty. Then travel by belief again, flying through more palace rooms, this time listening for sounds.

It doesn't take long to find the next couple of strange figures, and then the next. We experiment with moving in different directions, eventually finding larger clusters – threes and fours. We keep going, rooms hurtling past, too fast to see, heading toward the larger groups and hopefully a working fountain at their centre.

Then, passing through a door, I smash into something that tears Natasha's fingers from my grip and sends me sprawling … and *the cold*. It's like my torso's been clamped in ice.

My thoughts jabber, my internal alarm ringing loudly, and the veil slips back into place, gravity righting itself. I find myself skidding across a marble floor on my back. The domed ceiling of another palace-like room swirls into view. The freezing sensation ebbs a fraction from my ribs, blooming pain taking its place. I shake my head and scan the space, my vision clearing.

A balcony. We're on the top of a balcony. It's fifty feet long, half as wide, with a set of carved marble railings bordering its edge, and a downward staircase that begins three-quarters of the way along it. A chill grows against the back of my neck, and I swivel my head.

The only entrance – the door we came through – is in the far corner of the balcony on the same side as the staircase entrance. And three of the extravagantly dressed figures stand poised in front of it, two men and a woman, each one gazing intently at me. Two of them have the same cold unmoving stare while one of the men is stalking in my direction, forty feet away.

The cordite smell bites at my nose, and a hissing sound fills my ears. The light dims around me. And I blink desperately to maintain my vision, my eyes still fixed on the man.

My heart stops. The figure's begun to grow, to darken. Its clothing becomes translucent, and underneath, diffuse shadows coalesce into swarming eel-like shapes. Hundreds of the black tendrils stream through his eyes and mouth as well as between his ribs. Like something's straining to break out of him.

My brain yells at me to move. But the writhing shapes are mesmerising. My mouth opens. And the figure glides closer still. Thirty feet away now. I feel its eyes searching for me, pulling at my gaze, like my awareness is its food. I can sense its craving.

"Jake, move!" Natasha's tight voice from behind me.

I force my head around.

She's scrambling to her feet, ten feet to my side, between me and the railings. She lurches for the staircase down. And the dark figure starts to slink diagonally across the balcony, the steps equidistant between them. It's a head taller than me now, and increasingly oval in shape. The black forms reach and thrash ever further from its edge.

"No, stop!" I stammer back, struggling up and slipping on the slick marble floor.

Natasha halts and gawks back at me, her face chalk-white. She stands there, straining for the staircase down. And while I'm seized by a massive desire to bolt with her, a deeper part of me knows we'd never make it.

The dark figure continues to sweep across the balcony to cut us off. And it's as if I can already feel the black eel-like shapes around my neck, the horrible cold of their touch.

"The railing!" I shout and jab my finger at it over her shoulder.

Natasha stares at me like I'm insane as I barrel toward her, grab her wrist, and pull her toward the edge of the balcony.

I can sense the dark figure getting nearer, only twenty feet to the side, the strange chill slipping deeper under my skin. My hands shake, and I drag Natasha faster, picturing the balconies we've seen before, the fifteen feet between the floors, narrow enough to lower ourselves down.

I reach the marble plinth running atop the railing posts. My cheeks ache with the cold, the dark figure so fucking close. And I focus hard on keeping my gaze forward, on heaving Natasha onto its top. Then I follow behind and peer over the edge—

And almost topple straight over, my eyes hooked by the solid ground so far below. Not twenty feet below the railing but *forty* …

I grip the plinth hard beneath my knees and dart my gaze to the staircase. It's not connected to the floor but to another damn balcony, on the far side of the massive room, the forty-foot drop between them. And the opposing railings are twenty feet down and fifty bloody feet away.

I lick my lips. No way we'll make that jump.

Natasha's fingers clamp down on my own while the hiss grows ever louder from over my shoulder. I can almost see the dark figure right behind us, the black vines reaching for me. The icy cold rakes my back like claws.

I lean over the railing again, and my mind forms images of us leaping for the ground below. And dying. It's far too high to fucking jump. I swallow, my saliva turning to sand.

Then it hits me …

I scramble to my feet on the plinth and haul Natasha up with me.

"What are you *doing?*" Natasha yells.

"Flipping gravity!" I say.

And I begin the count in my head to still my thoughts. My mind calms a fraction, and the veil starts to pull back from my senses. The physical connection grows to every object, and I try to feel the floor so far below, the walls, the ceiling, the air around my body … just like I did before. But the wild hissing's now shrieking in my ear, and Natasha grips my arm.

"As we're *falling?*" she yells yet louder, her voice so high. "We'll never make it. You cannot even see the door to fall through!"

"*I know!*" I'm shouting now.

The strange chill's so intense inside me, like hands of ice are gripping my spine. And memories come of Natasha and me perched on the railing of the estate walkway, the jump thirty feet down to the concrete ground …

With no soft mattress below this time.

My own doubts stampede, and the veil slips back into place.

I squeeze Natasha's fingers tighter, trying to concentrate again. Frozen breath sears my neck – far colder than before – and I glimpse the black eel-like forms in the corner of my eye, thrashing toward my head. I tense every muscle in my body, yank Natasha's hand forward, and haul us off the railing.

We plummet, the staircase a blur to our side, and the air billows around us. Again, I fight to regain my concentration, to control my thoughts, to peel back the veil. But the wooden floor's barrelling up so fast to meet us, and my doubts just howl louder … *We're going to die.*

Still falling, I catch a glimpse of a door on the ground floor, in the middle of the side wall. And this time, I clench Natasha's fingers and focus everything on the belief that I can shift gravity, on how it felt to rotate the palace rooms by ninety degrees, on the memory of achieving it before. I grit my teeth and shove everything else from my mind …

Inches from the ground, the veil snaps away from my senses, and the world lurches as it did before. The wooden floor becomes a wall in front of our faces, and the door's suddenly directly below us.

We tumble through it and down another endless corridor, more rooms flashing past us, with the air buffeting our fall. I'm flailing this time, off-balance, less able to feel what's coming. I hold my concentration for as long as I can, Natasha's hand still gripped in mine, and then I believe we've stopped and gravity rights itself.

I slam into the ground and find myself tumbling across a room full of animal furs. I bang into a wooden drinks cabinet, and a few of the crystal vessels crash to the floor on its far side.

And there I lie, head aching, heart pounding, gazing up at a painted ceiling, a hanging chandelier.

"That was too close," Natasha says, her voice breathy.

I push myself up, the sensation of cold gradually thawing from my bones. She's already in a crouch, staring through the door we came through. The room's just like so many of the others – luxuriously furnished, with a door in each wall, and empty.

She turns to face me. "We will need another way," she says.

## 38

Natasha and I continue to look for the strange figures. We travel more carefully now, still moving by flipping gravity but making shorter jumps and focusing more intently on sounds as the palace rooms rush past us.

Eventually, we find more figures. They don't stare at us immediately. And still we avoid larger groups, pinpointing the smaller clusters instead and keeping our distance. We move laterally for a while to get a sense of where their core might be. And having agreed on its general direction, we proceed on foot as the groups grow thicker. Avoiding eye contact, we pick our way between them as silently as we can.

What feels like hours later, I'm creeping laboriously across yet another packed square room, the clusters of strange figures pressed so tightly together.

We reach the double doors. The next room is the largest we've seen, and by far the fullest. Wall to bloody wall with chatting bodies – couples dancing, long rows of diners, sets of gamblers surrounding card tables, and hundreds of others all moving around each other in a frenzy. I come to a halt, shaking my head.

Natasha places a hand on my arm and points over the figures.

The glint of a gold spire. A fountain sits in the middle of the room, thirty yards away. She's nodding with anticipation.

I lean in. "We've got no idea if the thing's even full," I breathe, and my gaze keeps getting drawn back to the edge of the frolicking crowd and the tiny gaps that vanish as quickly as they appear, images coming of us being so easily trapped.

Natasha nods again and creeps through the doorway. With the faintest sigh, I fall in behind.

Our progress is terrifyingly slow. We dart forward half a step and then stop, the way blocked by sauntering figures. And wait … for forever … to leap into the next gap.

All the while, the strange chill slips deeper under my skin, and the voices grow louder. Such strange sounds. Not even an actual language but a thousand murmurs, one great cacophony, as if they're all part of a single organism.

I have to focus hard on not glancing over my shoulder, on avoiding charting a path out of here. I inch onward, following right behind Natasha and trying to banish images of every figure transforming around us, of black vines bursting out of each one.

We get halfway across the room when Natasha ceases moving entirely. She tries to scoot forward once … twice … but there's no way through. The crowd ahead of us is like a morass, a nest of insects with the bodies crawling around and over each other. All still wholly oblivious to us.

I risk craning my neck. The fountain's just as tightly surrounded on all sides. Impossible to reach.

Standing there, my hands shake. The swarming figures pass only inches from my skin, the chill possessing every bone in my body. I swivel my head, gazing over the crowd in all directions.

To my side, fifteen feet away, is a large gambling table surrounded by seated people, all chattering with each other in that same awful hum. And nearer still – only a few feet away – stands a red silk sofa and two neighbouring cushioned chairs. Figures sit in them for a few moments before moving off, to be replaced by others, on and on. Like some kind of crazed automaton.

Natasha turns in my direction, and I angle my head toward the chairs. She furrows her brow but doesn't say a word.

I take a deep breath and pull my arms tightly against my body. Then I nod to Natasha and start edging through the crowd to my side, my fists pressed against my chest.

Eventually, I reach the chairs and stand there waiting as a man and woman sit perched on the velvet seats, conversing in the strange murmuring sound.

Natasha presses into my back, and I glance down. A low table stands in front of the chairs, a set of marble figurines on the top. I slowly lean over and take three, turning to pass them over. With a quick breath, she takes them all.

I pivot back. The seats are empty, the man and the woman shuffling off while two new female figures are squeezing through the crowd toward them, preparing to sit down.

I grab one of the chairs from the ground just as the two women arrive. I heave it to head height, trying to keep it away from the figures. But its weight makes the chair sway in my hands, and it brushes one of the women's shoulders.

Silence flares around us, and an icy wind pulls at my clothes. The surrounding figures all turn. And I shut my eyes, squeeze the chair, and hold my breath, sweat trickling down by back.

Eventually, the murmuring begins again. I exhale slowly and open my eyes. The women have moved off, and other figures have filled the space where the chair stood. I glance beyond them. The card table's still there, surrounded by seated gamblers.

"*Get ready,*" I mouth to Natasha

Her face blanches, but she nods while my own doubts are screaming.

I set my feet, hoist the chair behind my shoulder, and then hurl it toward the gamblers as hard as I can. It sails between two of them, hits one on the side of the head, and smashes into the card table. The splintering crash detonates into silence.

Natasha leans forward, about to throw herself toward the fountain, but I grip her arm and hold her still.

The crowd around us surges toward the shattered table, the men and women bearing down on it as if it were carrion. The lights dim and cold flares across the room.

I finally let go of Natasha. She leaps forward into the newly opened space in front of us, the figurines pressed to her chest, and sprints toward the golden spire, forty feet away. I fly after her, rubber soles striking the tiled floor, impossible to keep quiet. And I feel the attention of the room switching toward us while the winds come in gusts.

The fountain is still twenty feet away. I concentrate hard on it but feel my focus being drawn to the sides as if the surrounding figures are flinging hooks at me, spearing my attention. I can see them transforming, their dark forms lurching up above my head, the writhing vines erupting from their skin.

My heart hammers as I career on, the chill tearing at my body. Dozens of sets of fingers reach for me as I pass. Natasha hurls a figurine into the crowd to our side and another in the opposite direction. The impacts draw attention, creating new gaps to run through, but they're gone so quickly. Soon there's nothing else to throw.

Darting forward, I lean toward a standing lamp and stretch a hand to push it over. But I overbalance and tip into one of the transforming figures. The contact scorches my arm like acid.

I right myself and stumble to Natasha's side. We only have ten feet to go to the fountain now, the crowd in between so fucking thick. I begin shoving the untransformed figures from our path, my hands and shoulders burning cold with every contact.

Five feet left.

Thrashing forms rise higher on every side as the winds rage around us. I grab Natasha's arm and shove her toward the fountain. The hissing's so loud in my ears, like a million angry snakes. She pushes between the final two bodies. Thrusts them out of the way, and reaches the rim.

I glimpse the glass-like liquid beyond. The fountain. It's full. The nearest figures stretch for her while she spins and grasps my hand, trying to haul me with her.

Something grabs my trailing hand, a grip like manacles around my wrist, a blistering chill. It wrenches me backward, and Natasha's fingers slip from my grasp. With the sudden absence of my pull, she loses her balance, topples away from me, and tumbles backward over the fountain rim.

I see it all in slow motion – her eyes widening in alarm, her body jerking as it hits the liquid, its surface reaching up to cover her. And a moment later, the liquid in the fountain's flat once more.

She's gone.

And still the force tugs me from behind. I yell with the pain, fighting every temptation to turn around and lash out. More hands reach for me, and I feel them clawing at my clothes and my shoulders, the skin on my wrist burning. The swirling winds bring a charred smell to my nostrils, and my thoughts scream.

I start the count and focus on shutting off my mind, straining toward the fountain with all my remaining strength. I reach desperately for the fountain, the liquid. Yet all I can feel is the polished gold rim under my palm, glossy and warm. I'm getting no farther.

The grip pulls harder on my trailing arm, threatening to yank me backward, while my panicked voices shriek. And again I fight to push them down, to concentrate on the escalating numbers. A fraction of the veil peels back, and instead of pulling more strongly toward the fountain, I anchor my feet and try to *feel* its waters.

I get just a sense of the glass-like liquid, a faint physical connection in my solar plexus, and I try to pull it toward me. But the grip yanks my wrist again, and I slip back a few inches.

The panic and pain surge higher, making my head rattle. I scrunch my eyes shut and fix every ounce of focus on feeling that water beneath me. And with the grip pulling ever harder on my arm, I concentrate fiercely on remembering the experience of shifting gravity, on believing I can ...

The world lurches. My eyes fly open. And the fountain's suddenly a few feet below my body, me suspended directly above. And with the aid of gravity, the pull on my wrist weakens, and I inch downward.

The hissing amplifies, the chill searing up my trailing arm now as more hands reach for me. I stretch my other arm as far as I can over the fountain rim and manage to touch the glass-like liquid. In the next instant, I feel my body dragged free of the manacles, my arm almost yanked from its socket. The strange liquid swallows me. Envelops every part of my body – arm, shoulder, torso, waist, thighs, and calves.

The world goes dark. And I'm tumbling through space again.

## 39

---

NOTHINGNESS. Then sky. Black this time. And stars, a million of them. All laid out above me as I plummet downward, the wind whistling in my ears, my wrist burning.

A hard surface smashes into my feet, and suddenly, water's swaddling my entire body, biting down at me like stabbing needles, ice cold. I thrash at it, kick fiercely, and eventually break the surface.

My breath's like fire in my lungs, my chest a bellows. I squint through the water and spy the edge of a lake all around me, grey rocks visible in the darkness beyond.

Movement on the nearest bank draws my attention. Someone's struggling out of the water, hauling themselves onto a narrow ledge twenty feet away.

Natasha.

I thrust out in her direction, my forearm pounding, and barely manage to keep afloat.

Eventually, I reach the rocks and drag myself up onto the ledge. I roll over and pull myself up to sit on it.

The wind gusts, and my wet clothes cling tighter, their icy bite even fiercer against my skin. I shiver and squeeze myself tightly around my waist as pain sears up my arm.

"*Fuck!*" I yell through gritted teeth.

"Let me look," Natasha says from behind me.

I turn. She's standing, one hand around her middle, the other reaching down toward me.

I glance down at my arm, my mind conjuring images of those black vines, of the dark shapes that moved under our pursuers' skin, and a deeper shiver runs through me. Another gust of wind sends my teeth chattering. And I cradle myself more gently.

"Come on," says Natasha, motioning toward my injured arm.

I grunt and peel back my sleeve, forcing myself to look at where my forearm burns. Pale skin, almost bone-white because of the cold, but the stitches from the hospital are still fine. And no sign of dark shapes. I close my eyes and exhale slowly.

"The water was probably good for it," Natasha says.

I yank my sleeve back over my forearm, the pain and freezing cold amplifying each other and merging into a growing ache all over my body. The sparking anger is the only heat inside me.

"Where the hell are we now?" I say, glancing around.

A landscape of jagged rock and grass surrounds the lake, with a starlit sky above. Everything lies still except for the choppy waters and the clumps of grass rippling in the breeze. I gaze in all directions. Barren plains extend beyond the rocky crests. A brilliant moon illuminates one side of the sky, creating both spotlight and shadow, and the rich smell of earth's heavy in my nose.

The real world. Has to be. There was no haze as the scene assembled itself, and the soaking clothes feel all too real against my skin.

Probably the highlands. Some place north.

"It is beautiful," says Natasha. She stands there wet and trembling, still gazing around in wonder.

I push myself to my feet on shaking legs. "Bloody freezing, is what it is," I say. "We've got to find somewhere warm."

"We are here to meet someone," Natasha says.

The words bring back memories of Qetesh, of my intense feelings, of all the things I did because of her – battling guards, pursuers, and Amazons; navigating pools, palaces, and dark forms. And now we're chilled in the middle of nowhere. It all feels so fucking weird.

My insides start to harden, and I shake my head.

Natasha keeps her gaze on me. "This is intended," she says, fingering her crucifix necklace with one hand. "Father Thomas sent us to Qetesh, and Qetesh sent us—"

"That's bullshit," I say.

"Qetesh is divine," Natasha says, standing upright. "An angel—"

"She didn't describe angels," I spit. "She described *schemers*."

Natasha blinks back at me.

"If her story's true, there's no God. Just these angels pulling miracles and accidents," I say, waving my arms about, the sparks intensifying in my chest. "Inciting the believers and rescuing the religious. Just like the Puritan kids in the station." Again, the memory comes of the nun sacrificing herself for me, and I shove it away. "That isn't divine will. That's top-tier cunning," I go on. "They're the best con artists ever."

Natasha tilts her chin up, the belief and resolve still so clear in her eyes. Then her features soften, and her expression morphs into one of pity. She sighs, and suddenly I hear again her words to me in the diner … *You think everyone is selfish, so you are selfish first, and so everyone becomes selfish, too.*

"The train crash. Gabriel's warning. Why did you not tell me?" Natasha asks eventually, her voice soft. "We could have held the burden together."

I turn away and gaze out at the night scene, at the strewn boulders, the scarred crags.

"Whatever Qetesh said, God *is* real, Jake," she says. "You have experienced him. You have felt his presence."

I snort. Yet memories swirl of peeling back the veil, of the shimmering world. Then more images rush in – the black vines, the skeletal face, Gabriel … And I feel my ribs constrict further.

"It is like prayer," Natasha continues, that earnest look back on her face. "You have to *believe*. I *know* you have it in you."

The heat rises, and I spin and begin lumbering off the ledge toward a cleft in the surrounding rocks.

"Wait!" Natasha calls from behind.

I swivel.

She stares, mouth open. "We cannot leave!" she splutters. "This is where we are supposed to be!"

"*Really?*" I call back and make a show of pivoting on the spot, of searching the desolate landscape around us.

Natasha follows my gaze. Nothing happens. No one comes. The wind simply gusts harder, Natasha shivers more violently, and the wet clothes bite at my back and legs, getting colder every second.

"We can't stick around here," I say. "Middle of the night, in the middle of fucking nowhere, and we just dived into a bloody lake. We'll catch our death."

I pivot and stride out between the nearest cleft. Natasha scrambles after me.

"But we have been—" she starts.

"We've been dancing to their merry tune is what we've been doing," I snap, keeping my gaze fixed on the boulder-strewn hillside ahead. "The priest's, our pursuers', Qetesh's."

Again, I feel an echo of the brimming love I experienced with her, and I tense my stomach and pace faster between the clefts. The icy wind gnaws at my skin, my hands trembling more than ever.

"No fucking more, I'm leading now," I mutter, charting my way between boulders and on down the hillside.

Natasha hurries behind me. "And I'm not hanging around here to die," I add.

I peer ahead through two crests, spying for the lowlands, for any sign of habitation. I scramble over a low wedge of rock and continue on past a couple of bluffs.

The shadows cast by the moon are so deep that it's near impossible to see where I'm placing my feet. Twice I almost pitch forward onto my face, and the wet clothes cling ever more tightly.

I reach a large plateau – circular, flat, and lit up by the moonlight. Here I lengthen my stride, craning my neck to scan the planes ahead. Still no twinkling lights, no signs of life. My legs tighten, and I kick out at a few small rocks on the ground, sending them skidding over the stones and grass.

"Wait!" Natasha says, her tone ringing with alarm.

I skid to a halt.

"Look …" Her voice tapers into silence.

I swivel toward her.

She's standing in the centre of the plateau, ten feet behind me, staring around her. I follow her gaze.

Massive stones. Twelve or thirteen, set equidistant from each other around the edge of the plateau. All flat-topped and taller than they are wide, each stretching over eight feet out of the ground.

A stone circle. No doubt.

The wind gusts, and a shiver climbs my spine. I sniff the air for cordite, for that familiar scent. There's the smell of grass, damp earth … and something else.

"This is it!" Natasha says, excitement in her voice, though it trembles.

Gooseflesh breaks out across my back. And I stare at each of the stone surfaces. Some are illuminated in the moonlight, others dark, each a different size. The biggest stands behind Natasha, right at the head of the circle. The moon hovers directly above it, and shadows mask its features.

And then … my body jerks, my fingers spasm, electrified. The largest stone creeps silently toward us.

## 40

"Interesting ... *interesting*." A high-pitched voice emanates out of the darkness.

Natasha whirls toward the sound and chokes off a scream. I grab her arm and stumble backward.

A man stalks toward us out of the circle and into the moonlight, leaving the remaining twelve actual stones around us. His straggly hair and beard frame a face mostly hidden in shadow, except for shining, black eyes. He wears a long coat and a collarless shirt that's open at the neck, filthy, and ancient-looking. He moves with none of Qetesh's grace, none of Gabriel's bearing. Yet he's enormous: part man, part mountain. Over a head taller than me. Plus, there's that scent again – burnt metal. It hovers faintly on the edge of the wind.

I continue to tug Natasha away from the colossus, scattering small pebbles on the ground with our feet. The giant jumps excitedly at the movements of the stones. He ignores us and takes two eager steps forward toward them, peering down. He's like some kind of massive child – sprightly, fascinated, and totally oblivious to his surroundings.

I slow my steps, and Natasha does the same. Then she leans in.

"You found him," she whispers, her tone excited, and

nods toward the standing stones that surround us. "Our refugee must be trapped here."

I find myself shaking my head while the giant pauses and frowns.

"Interesting," he says again, one massive finger tapping his lips, still totally ignoring us. "You have become lost." He nods fervently, as if delivering some great insight.

I stare around, the heat rising among the cold. "Course we're fucking lost," I hiss. Rocks surround us like crumbling towers. A million stars dazzle in the inky black sky above. We're in the middle of nowhere, probably a thousand miles from home.

I blink.

The man's not staring at what's around him. His eyes remain fixed on the ground. "Without bearings, my friends," he continues, this time with genuine compassion in his voice. "I am sorry."

My eyes widen, and I follow his gaze.

The stones. The guy's peering at them, placing his feet nimbly in the gaps between. I step backward toward the edge of the stone circle and scan the flat space. There are hundreds of the tiny pebbles. And staring at them, something niggles my brain, a recollection just out of reach.

Natasha's gazing at the stones as well. "What are they?" she says.

"All of life!" the giant says, glee in his voice.

I lean down. Pick up a stone. They're about an inch high and flat, like stretched coins. A symbol decorates one face, while the other side's blank. Focusing on it, I start combing my memories, systematically moving back through my life, just waiting for the recollection to snap into—

It comes, and my heart thumps. "You're reading them," I say.

Just like the circus acts I studied when learning to con. Diviners who read tarot cards, crystal balls, the position of runes …

I feel a surprising rush of guilt and drop the stone in my hand. It bounces on the rock floor and comes to rest near some others.

"But I kicked some," I say. "Moved where they were."

"Indeed!" the giant exclaims and rubs his hands together. "Exactly as you were supposed to." He doesn't look up at me, simply goes to observe the new formation, stroking his beard in anticipation. "It's why you came!"

"No, no, *no!*" I say, my shoulders tightening and my fingers gripping the air.

"What is it?" Natasha says.

"*This* is who Qetesh sent us to, who's supposed to know Gabriel's plan?" I say, glowering. "The man's a fucking simpleton."

"You do not believe," the giant says. He's still traversing the circle, only a quarter of the way across, his gaze sweeping the ground. He shrugs. "That is understandable." Not a hint of disappointment in his voice.

And then he leans further down, as if contemplating a single stone, and says, "Morning sun."

I feel the words slice my heart like a scalpel. The giant glances up at me, and my vision blurs, the stone circle spinning around us, faster and faster. The giant's dark eyes glint and then the circle dissolves entirely.

I'm suddenly back in my childhood home, lying in bed. Light streams through the window, the sun's rays warming my skin. A hand strokes my hair and I glance up. My mother's sitting on the edge of my bed, smiling down at me. I feel such fullness in her presence, such completeness. And Qetesh's words chime in my head – *You've known great love … You're pure of heart.*

And then the vision disappears. The circle returns – stones, stars, and wind. The giant remains standing there, holding my gaze, while the pain of longing's now like a hole in my insides.

Then the giant shifts his gaze to Natasha. "Bell tower," he says.

And I watch her legs quiver, her mouth open in shock, and her lips tremble. She fingers her cross as tears well in her eyes.

The giant inches from the left side of the circle to the right, staring at individual stones, and continuing to voice words that trigger memories of pleasures and pains, desires and devastations. Like files in the cabinet of my mind, yanked open and laid bare.

And as the giant continues his journey, the memories creep closer to the present. In the middle of the circle, he points at a few stones. "And there you met," he says.

I nod. And when the giant takes a first step into the future, I notice my heels bouncing up and down, my excitement building.

The giant stops, his hands tugging at the strands of his beard again. "Seemingly impossible," he says.

My skin itches. And every part of me is tuned to listen, but the man says nothing more. His huge brow simply furrows, his stare trained on something just to the right of the middle of the circle. I kneel and follow his gaze.

My spine goes rigid. Many of the stones stand on their thin edges. Entirely improbable.

The man's shoulders slump. He shakes his head. "A tough path ahead," he says.

I feel my pulse racing. "But what have we got—"

"You already know what to do," the giant says, turning to me. His eyes glow black in the starlight. "You have already seen your destination."

From nothing, legions of memories crowd my mind – the accident, the hospital, the office building that transformed before my eyes …

The giant glances back down at the stones and cocks his head. "I see a man here, in your future," he says, his voice soft. "A man with white hair?"

And in that moment, I glimpse the guy with crystal clarity – the white-haired guy from before the train crash, the man who first alerted me to the danger, his panicked attempts to struggle out of the crowd.

"He's lying there, dead," says the giant.

"Yeah," I breathe, seeing again the man's broken body in my mind, crushed under tangled steel and stone.

Then the obvious hits me.

I glance from side to side across the stone circle. The giant's to the right of the middle, supposedly reading our *future*. Whereas the white-haired guy's dead body is in my past.

"What about beyond that?" Natasha says.

I avert my gaze, the giant's words echoing on in my mind. They make no sense. The timing is wrong. The analytical side of my brain wants to dismiss it all, to focus on Natasha's question, on the giant's reply. Yet I don't. Something's nagging at me, a connection forming, somewhere in the far depths of my mind. Apprehension prickles at the base of my spine.

The giant inches further across the circle, on into the future, his gigantic frame hunkering down and scanning the ground. I start to pivot away, to focus on the connection, and then stop. The giant's slowed, his energetic movements suddenly heavy, as if burdened by some great weight.

I step toward him and follow his gaze again. The stones are all spread out here and they're all symbol side down. Every single one of them. The giant says nothing, simply shakes his head once more.

"What does it mean?" Natasha says.

"I am so sorry," he says, his voice breaking.

And all I can see is death and devastation. The result of Gabriel's plan. And I hear his words to me in the station again – *You're better off facing the end now, given what is coming.* Will it be dirty bombs, mass sabotage, infrastructure disasters? Maybe a lack of food, medicine, fuel, power? The angels could undermine modernity so easily. Society's already teetering on a knife's edge. It wouldn't take much to push it into chaos.

I glance at Natasha. She says nothing. Simply glances down at the stones, her head lowered.

"Is it for certain?" she says.

The giant averts his gaze from the stones, a subtle twinkle in his eyes. He looks at her kindly. "Nothing is for certain, my child," he says.

She stands straighter, chin up.

My thoughts drift back to the giant's words. They run over in my head ... *A man with white hair. Lying dead. The future not the past.*

And an idea starts to form in my mind. So slim, so flighty ... and still ungraspable. The sense of anticipation taps up my spine. And as before, I focus on the white-haired guy and comb my memories of the train station, moving incrementally from beginning to end, waiting to grasp the idea ...

Nothing comes.

"Is there more?" Natasha asks the giant.

The giant doesn't look back down at his stones. "I'm afraid not," he says. "And there is no more help that I can give." Then he glances meekly around the stone circle, as if showing the limits of his prison.

"So now what?" Natasha says, gazing at the surrounding mountains. "How do we get back?"

The giant turns to her again. "*You* know the answer to that," he says.

She glances up at him, eyebrows raised.

"It says so," the giant continues and points at the stones in the middle of the circle.

Natasha smiles and then shivers in the biting wind. She wraps her arms around herself as she turns to me.

I glance away, driving my mind on down the corridors of my memory, scrutinising everything I remember from the station. And still the idea remains like mist.

"Jake," she says and reaches out her hand for mine.

I don't take it and continue to stare down at the stones instead. The fucking idea won't clarify. The tingling sensation climbs further up my spine. My jaw clenches, and the heat flares inside me.

I take a breath, searching for calm.

The connection continues to hover before me, palpable yet invisible … just like the veil before my senses. And in that instant, I remember those moments that the veil peeled back, the shimmering world appearing, and the boundless insight it brought.

I begin the count in my head, still my mind, and concentrate on the memory of the veil peeling back, on believing I can. I abandon my efforts to analyse, to figure out the idea. And instead, I close my eyes and turn inward, simply bringing the strange sense back to mind, the connection that won't form. I rest my attention lightly on it, staring at the black of my closed eyelids, and try to believe the idea will come.

I feel Natasha take my hand. Palm to palm. Cold and trembling. She pulls me back across the stone circle toward the lake. I don't resist while maintaining the count in my mind, my gentle focus on the idea.

And for just a moment, the veil peels back and the breath catches in my throat …

I glimpse my memories of the station, the white-haired guy in the crowd. And as before, beyond the veil, there's so much more … extra details, new features. The bright pallor of his face, his taloned fingers clawing at people as he tried to get through and out of the crowd. Then Gabriel arrived, the train crashed, and the white-haired guy died, along with a hundred others.

And there's something else. Something that's been nagging me about what happened there. Something so deep in my subconscious, I didn't recognise it before. And dancing between those memories, a strange notion begins to unfurl within. I feel everything I knew about the train crash starting to turn upside down.

I squeeze Natasha's hand and let her lead me back toward the lake, between the boulders, and over the scattered scree. From the dark ledge, Natasha spots an unmoving section of the water. We jump. And fall.

# 41

I FOLLOW Natasha down a busy city street, making sure to hide among the bustle of pedestrians. We're south of the river, in one of the rougher parts of town. Shop owners shout. Horns blare. And from the crush of the crowds, it's got to be late morning already.

Late morning. Which means we spent ten bloody hours beyond that door of water. It feels like we've slept and eaten, our clothes bone dry. From jumping into the lake in the highlands, we appeared in front of the glyph-door in the club, then snuck out, and came directly here.

I glance down the road. "How much far—"

"It is over there," Natasha says and steps into a doorway. She raises a finger.

I sidle in beside her and follow her point. The building stands fifty yards away and on the opposite side of the street. It's rectangular, two storeys high, with the same dirty front as its neighbours, but considerably wider. I scan the pavement before it.

Natasha shivers. "Anything?" she says.

I shake my head. "Still nought." No sign of the odd clothes, of our pursuers hanging about. And half my attention remains on my insides, feeling for the strange chill.

"That does not mean you're wrong," she says.

My eyes find the dirty building again. "Or this is the wrong morgue," I say, the giant's words cycling my head ... *I see a man in your future, a man with white hair ... lying there, dead.*

"It is the closest one to the train crash," Natasha says. "If our man died there, he will be here."

"The guy went from being properly panicked to properly dead, I'm sure of it," I say.

"And that is why we've come? Because this man knew the train crash was about to happen?" Natasha says.

Again, memories of the station seize my mind – surrounded by excited and lavishly dressed people, the white-haired guy was the outlier, in a threadbare suit, agitated, scared, and scrambling to get away.

I take a slow breath, trying to order my thoughts, the revelation that started in the circle of stones.

"These are angels," I say. "They'd be able to keep a sabotage hushed up if they wanted. So why does some guy who's out of place, who knows what's about to happen, end up right in the middle of the crowd with no chance of escape?"

Natasha goes quiet, a stream of pedestrians continuing to hurry past us. "But he is just a human," she says, eventually. "Why would Gabriel want him killed?"

Again, the memories of the station bombard me – the guy struggling to get through the crowd, sweating profusely, with eyes wide and skin so pale it was almost white ... terrified.

I grip my temples. "That's the issue," I say. "I've got no fucking idea. But there's another piece, a vital one, that I've not clocked yet." My eyes scrunch shut. "I can *feel* it."

And the same questions whirl ... what con was Gabriel *really* pulling at the station, and what *is* his ultimate plan?

With my thoughts churning, Natasha takes a deep breath and pats my arm. "Do not worry," she says. "I'll get us in."

My eyes fly open. And she's already pacing across the

pavement and out onto the street. I dart after her, my mind a frothing mess.

A car barrels toward me. I barely dodge around it. And then another. I go to reach out, to drag Natasha back. But again, my eyes search the pavement for any sign of the pursuers. Would they be guarding the body?

I duck my head and shuffle closer to the crossing pedestrians for cover. Then I scan those hurrying down both sides of the street while sniffing the air for cordite. But the stench of rotting food and sweat masks any scent.

I reach the far pavement several paces behind Natasha. She strides straight toward the morgue entrance, and I shamble along the edge of the buildings, keeping to the shadows.

I pass shop fronts, doorways, and billboards. The sound of nearby shouting rises above the general murmur, but I keep my head down and Natasha in the corner of my vision.

An image on a billboard plucks at my attention. My head turns. The same helix logo, the same cancer drug advert as outside the hospital. And this one's been defaced with a large cross scrawled over it. The shouts grow louder just ahead.

My gaze shoots up. A Puritan encampment lies directly in front of me, and I veer around it toward the morgue. But a couple of grey-robed Puritans still berate me as I pass, yelling about the abomination of autopsies, of cutting up bodies for scientific progress. And despite the heat, a shiver runs down the back of my neck, all too reminiscent of the strange chill.

I hurry beyond them and up the morgue steps, Natasha already at the top.

Thick bars run across the entrance, and a guard stares out at her from behind the glass. I dart to her side.

Natasha pulls her hospital pass from her pocket and presses it up to the scratched glass. And the guard holds her gaze, his brow furrowed.

"Come on!" I hiss, tensing my neck to avoid scanning the crowd for our pursuers.

Natasha inches her head toward mine. "*Patience,*" she whispers. Then one side of her mouth edges up in a teasing grin. "*I'm working on it.*"

My insides squeeze as she stands on her tiptoes and smiles openly at the guard.

He inspects her pass, squinting at it through the glass for what feels like an age. My teeth grind. My pulse fires. Finally, he nods, unlocks, and opens the door.

"Thank you," she says, bowing slightly, and steps past the guard.

I dart forward to follow her, but the guard starts to shut the door in my face. I shove my foot into the gap. The guard growls and goes to push harder.

"Wait," Natasha says and puts a hand on his arm. "He's with me."

The guard looks me up and down with suspicious eyes. And my body tenses, still in full view of the street.

"Please," Natasha says with a smile, and I barely manage one as well.

Finally, the guard opens the door with a grunt, and I stumble past him into a dingy reception area. It's got a couple of broken chairs further along one wall and a scuffed desk against the other. A line of security gates lie straight ahead, a lift and a staircase beyond.

The guard shuts the door behind us while keeping his gaze fixed on me. I take a breath and wait for the chill to abate from my body. But it doesn't. Goosebumps prickle along my arms, the air significantly cooler in here.

Natasha pads toward a guy sitting behind the desk in a white shirt with a blue security tag around his neck.

"Hi," she says. "I'm wondering if you can help me. The awful train crash a couple of days ago. Were the bodies taken here?"

The receptionist nods.

"I'm here to investigate a discrepancy with a coroner report," Natasha goes on.

The receptionist hesitates. "They're here," he says. "But every request needs to be made in writing, I'm afraid."

"That was not the situation before," she says.

"New procedure," he says. "We've had fraudulent and forced admissions, you see. Puritans causing trouble, gangs looking for their drug mules, others searching for body parts to be harvested and sold."

The receptionist flashes a glance in my direction. And feeling the guard's gaze on my back, I edge away from the guy. The guard follows, his footsteps stopping just a couple of feet behind me.

I try to kick-start my brain but fail, a part of my mind still dancing around the half-formed revelation while the rest of my attention's on the burgeoning chill. My foot bounces up and down, and I sense my gaze drawn over the security gates, visions coming of freezer cabinets beyond, of the white-haired guy lying in one of them.

The guard behind me taps out a rhythm on the top of his baton. I try to focus on Natasha. She's leaning over the desk and speaking more quickly, as if she's remembered my words in the club, the art of misdirection. She reels off a list of people she works with at the hospital and the reasons she's been sent. I can hear the natural warmth in her tone the entire time.

"Dr Kipps, Dr Ankur …" she says.

The receptionist shakes his head.

"Dr Patani, Dr Beech …" she says.

He continues to reject each name, an apologetic smile on his face.

I feel my fingers clenching, my muscles tightening. There's a metal click – the guard opening his baton cover – just two feet behind my unprotected neck. The small part of my brain that's working goes into autopilot, yelling familiar warnings at me and shouting to take the guy out before he attacks.

I breathe through gritted teeth and focus on Natasha's earlier word … *patience*.

"Dr Jessen, Dr Abbasi …" she says.

The receptionist's head shakes become more pronounced. The sound comes of the guard unsheathing his baton at my back. The warnings continue to scream. And before I know it, I'm swivelling around.

"Dr Barlow?" Natasha says, her voice barely registering at the edge of my awareness.

"Yes!" the receptionist says.

I finish the spin and end up facing the guard with one arm out, my fingers reaching for his weapon. He gazes at me with wide eyes.

"And his colleagues," Natasha continues behind me. "Dr Martinez and Dr Haruna."

"Yes," the receptionist says again. "They're often here. You work with them?"

"I do," Natasha says. "And I am all too familiar with Dr Haruna's biscuit cravings. Does he bring his supply here, also?"

The guard's staring down at my hand, his baton still gripped in his own, his expression hardening further.

"He does," the receptionist says, and I can hear the smile in his voice. "And feel free to check for your report."

And with my thinking brain frazzled, I do the first idiotic thing that occurs to me. I thrust my hand forward to shake. "Thank you," I say and grab the guard's free hand.

He hesitates and then returns my shake. I clumsily withdraw my hand and end up lurching behind Natasha through the gates, my internal voices still shouting at my idiocy.

"The archived reports are downstairs," the receptionist calls after us. "Last room in the corridor."

"Thank you," Natasha says with a wave.

"But please don't enter the storage areas," the receptionist says.

Natasha nods, and I swivel to see the receptionist and guard both staring at us, the guard's gaze as narrow as ever.

I spin back and pace across a corridor. Then on down the stairs with Natasha. A deeper chill nips at my skin.

## 42

I HURRY down the last steps into the morgue's basement, Natasha beside me. A single long corridor extends away from us, faintly lit by washed-out strip lights. Windows line one side, a few doors along the other.

The silence is absolute. My ears buzz with it. And while the cold's intense here, I feel my mind somehow calmer, my thoughts churning far less. I scour the shadows down the length of the corridor. No sign of our pursuers. No sign of anyone.

Yet I don't move. A strange sensation's creeping over me. It's as if the whole building's been vacated, as though we've stepped into some kind of parallel world. I blink at the walls, the floor. The scuffed surfaces seem about as normal as you can get.

I take a breath and bring my focus back to the white-haired guy in the station. And abandoning my analytical brain, I simply rest my attention on the memories of the train crash …

I sense my gaze drawn to the sides, and my eyes rove over the chipped brickwork, the grime-covered walls, the exposed wiring, and the flaking paint.

Natasha follows my gaze. "They are all like this," she says.

"The government is forever making cuts. They have no money."

"Perfect place to stash a murdered body, then," I say. "No funds to investigate, and with the crash looking like another cock-up of modernity, the government would want it under wraps."

Natasha swallows. "Yes, but why did this man need to die?" she says, her arms trembling in the cold. "And what could be so terrible that an archangel would need to cover his tracks?"

The chill prickles the hairs along my arms, and it's as if the entire revelation's hanging in the frosty air, like a faint voice urging me on. Again, I don't force it. Simply breathe. Shake my head. "Still not sure," I say. "But I do know we've got to find his body."

"It will be in one of those," Natasha says, striding up to the first of the wide rectangular windows.

I follow behind. It's a large operating room, twenty yards across and half as deep again. Four surgical tables span its depth, each one neatly laid with shiny implements, spotlights positioned in the ceiling directly above. A trolley is parked in one of the near corners, and square metal doors run along both sides of the theatre, four high and many more wide. The refrigeration units are like filing-cabinet drawers. I scan both side walls. At least a hundred doors on each side.

"It's going to take a bloody age to search them," I say, my calves tensing. "And that guard won't give us long, not for checking some report. And this is just *one* of the storage rooms."

I spin to search the corridor for more of the rectangular windows. And my eyes fall on someone standing in the middle of the passageway, directly in front of us.

I stop dead.

Blue uniform. Mop in hand, bucket by his feet – a janitor. He looks ancient, his dark skin like crinkled paper. And he moved incredibly quietly.

My eyes dart to the opposing wall, scanning for some kind of storage cupboard door, while he gazes back at us, entirely still. Somehow, only he's ten yards away – easily within earshot of our prior conversation. My fingers twitch.

Natasha steps forward. And I shoot out an arm to stop her. The janitor simply holds our gaze, his expression unreadable, his shadowed eyes like deep pools. I feel the strange sense of silence deepen around us.

Natasha leans in. "So, what do we do?" she whispers. "The same technique twice? Try again what we did upstairs?"

I feel myself frowning. "Like I pulled at the club?" I say and then shake my head. "That only works if it's the same person."

She nods and goes silent. And I fidget, the security guard sure to descend at any moment. The janitor still hasn't moved a muscle. I scan his clothes for a radio or some other way of calling security.

"You're right," Natasha says.

My body spins, my mouth opening.

"Excuse me," she says, her voice raised. "We need some help."

Still, the guy stares on, statuesque. I tense my legs, prepared to dart forward to prevent him from yelling.

"There was an accident … at a train station," Natasha goes on. "Some bodies were brought here for autopsy?"

The guy nods. A tiny dip of the head – the first movement I've seen him make. Natasha breathes out, and I feel my insides relax a fraction.

"Do you know … were some still unidentified?" she asks.

Another pause. Then the guy nods again, and something bounces around his neck. I find myself staring at a thin necklace of coloured beads.

"Where?" she says.

A shorter pause this time. The janitor points toward the surgical theatre to our side, toward the far end of the bank of storage units. I give a quick glance over my shoulder but then stop myself.

"And their effects?" she asks.

The janitor motions to a room a couple of doors further up the corridor. He wears beads around his wrist too, some sort of bangle.

"Thank you," says Natasha, pressing both hands together.

The janitor nods and then retreats to one side of the corridor, his mop in one hand and his gaze still on me. I don't move, one part of my brain yelling that it's a trap, another shouting about time ticking down.

Shoving the thoughts aside, I dart past the main theatre windows. I push the corner door open and hurry out across the wide space, Natasha just behind.

My eyes take in the polished metal doors, the storage units. Eighty or so on each side of the room. My mind fires up, starts planning a system. *Work in rows, from one end, the doors at waist height first …*

My thoughts calm on their own, the peculiar stillness taking hold. And in that moment, I see the janitor in the corridor again – his strange dark eyes … and his finger pointing toward this room, toward the doors near the end, maybe three-quarters of the way along the far wall.

My doubts fire in an instant. And then, for some reason, I hear the priest's words in my head … *Faith is everything.*

Without thinking, I scramble toward those storage units and begin checking the doors one by one. No system. No plan.

Seven attempts later, I pull back yet another green sheet and the breath stops in my throat.

There he is … the white-haired guy. I stare down at the lifeless face – grey and covered with bruises – and blank my mind. I wait for more insights to bubble up, for further revelations …

A memory slinks in – this man dead in the station, white hair, torn jacket, and *something else* … lying among the rubble.

I spin back toward Natasha. "Briefcase," I say. "He had a black briefcase."

"The effects," she says and glances down before grabbing a toe tag hanging beneath the edge of the sheet. "C1486," she reads and then lifts her head. "Two doors down the corridor."

I nod and shove the tray back into the storage unit before sprinting behind Natasha toward the door.

We dart into the corridor. It's still empty, aside from the janitor, who's not moved a muscle. He simply stands there, mute, contemplating us.

Still, the familiar thoughts come ... *What's his game?* And the strange sense of tranquillity remains as well, like the entire building's on a break, absolutely no one here.

We hurry past him toward the door he motioned to, and Natasha shoves it open.

The room's tiny and rammed with shelves of cardboard boxes, each one labelled with a code. My heartbeat speeds up, and we rifle through the numbers on the different boxes.

"C1486, C1486, C1486 ..." I mumble.

While my doubts nag at me, deeper down, I notice an odd lightness in my chest, a strange confidence.

Then Natasha gasps. "C1486!" She yanks down a box from the top shelf and drops it on the floor between us.

I rip off the top and peer inside. No clothes – probably shredded in the accident. Just a wallet and, there it is, the black briefcase. Natasha tries to pass it to me.

"No, you check it," I say and grab up the wallet first. "These always tell a story."

I rotate it, examining every angle. It's old, well used, and thin. However, the leather sags as if it's been bigger in the past. Odd. It's normally the other way around. I pull open the wallet and scan its contents. My insides drop. No ID card, no driver's licence, only a single gold credit card. A. Lydon. Could be a fake name. And there's nothing much else. This is a wallet with marks of usage in each of the compartments, but one that's been emptied.

I yank out a mass of papers from where people normally store bank notes. Receipts. Probably collected to make the thing feel bulky. I leaf through a couple of them and then glance up.

Natasha's playing with the lock on the briefcase. A single-number tumbler under a hefty handle. Something stirs in my mind. I slip the wallet into my pocket and study the case.

Natasha's turning it in her hands. It's exceptionally sturdy, well built, with bulky hinges. And also quite ordinary-looking. Fake black leather with dark metal corner protectors. It's barely been affected by the accident, by all that stone landing directly on top of it.

And then familiarity dawns. I've seen one before – a high-security case that's supposed to look anything but. And a high-security case would never have a single-number combination.

I grab the case from Natasha's hands.

"Hey!" she says.

"Sorry," I say, not meeting her eye. I'm peering intently at the three digits of the lock.

Exhilaration sparks. They've hardly been used. No fading of the numbers. No grease from fingers using it. The lock's a dummy.

My grip tightens around the case. Another contradiction. I picture the white-haired guy in his cheap, frayed suit with an almost empty wallet yet carrying a high-security briefcase.

I turn it over in my hands, gooseflesh rising across my shoulders, and my fingers search till they find the indentation. I squeeze. There's a click. And a hidden thumbprint panel appears to the side of the handle. Natasha lets out a brief cry of surprise.

I jump to my feet. "We need the body," I say, hurrying for the door. I yank it open and peer out into the corridor, the briefcase in hand.

Still empty. No technicians, no guards. And no janitor either.

And the strange sense of timelessness … it's gone too. It's as if a working day has started. I notice my thoughts flitting again, and my mind spins images of doctors pushing through the theatre door, the security guard barrelling down the stairs to find us.

Natasha hurries away toward the surgical theatre while I remain still, sniffing the air, trying to smell beyond the reek of formaldehyde. There's no obvious cordite scent. Yet my gut's knotting up – my internal alarm.

At the door to the theatre, Natasha spins back toward me. "Come on!"

I glance down at the briefcase in my hand, at the hidden thumbprint panel, before staring down the corridor toward the stairs at the far end, my mind yelling at me to take the briefcase and get out of there.

But more doubts jabber. It's a high-spec case, undoubtedly top-end. What if we can't get it open? And the memory comes of the giant in his circle of stones, the promise of the revelation … So close now.

My heart races, my fingers sweaty around the handle.

Natasha darts into the surgical theatre. And I sprint after her.

## 43

WE DASH across the surgical theatre, past the tables with their macabre tools. Natasha reaches the refrigerated door first, grasps its steel handle, and pulls. I hasten to her side and yank out the tray with the white-haired guy's body. The chill bites at my skin.

I grab the guy's hand through the green sheet, avoiding direct contact, and still almost recoil from the sensation – icy, heavy, and lifeless. I work the end of his index finger onto the hidden panel and after a few tries, the case clicks open with the hiss of a pressure change.

Natasha seizes the briefcase lid to open it. But I grip it tightly.

"*Wait*," I say, my mind conjuring images of guards marauding down the outside corridor. "Get behind there." I nod toward the surgical table at her back and pass the case over. "Open it out of sight, and I'll get this closed."

Natasha scampers away. And I spin back to the refrigerated unit, my breath clouding in the cold air. The chill of the room's crawling deeper beneath my skin. I clamp my trembling fingers together and then shove the guy's hand back, roll the tray shut, and close the unit door.

I dart for the surgical table and skid to a halt at Natasha's side.

"Find anything?" I say.

She's already scouring the contents. Pens, papers, all mixed up. Nothing else. No arrangement, no order. Everything thrown together in a hurry.

I grab some of the papers. They're mainly computer printouts of graphs … pages and pages of dots and lines. I leaf through them, my mind scrambling to decipher the shapes. But none of it makes any sense.

"I don't get it," Natasha says. Her brow furrows. "It is a list of symptoms."

I stop moving, the graphs still clenched in my hands, an awful foreboding squeezing my stomach, prickling my scalp. This is it … the revelation that's been coalescing in my subconscious.

"Necrosis, haemorrhagic lesions, cratering, oral and rectal bleeding," she continues. "Neurological symptoms, gangrenous regions, muscle contractures …"

In that instant, it all clicks into place … and my mind stills. So many details, from so many memories – Qetesh's realm, the hospital, the train crash … and even before – all connected in my brain at the deepest level, and up to a moment ago, still hidden under my countless assumptions and beliefs.

Natasha's voice grows more distant, and it's as if the chill of the room's seeping into my core like freezing water, my chest so tight.

She lowers the papers and stares at me. "We've seen these before," she says.

I nod, head down. "With Qetesh, in that candled room, on the stone tables," I say. The bodies laid out, the contorted limbs, the gritted teeth. "The tortured—"

"But it's not torture," she says, glancing down at the papers. "It's a disease … a grenade of diseases."

I nod again.

Natasha's mouth gapes. "*You knew?*" she says.

"Eventually … yes," I say, my heart in a clamp.

Images flash of the door to the surgical theatre just behind us, the empty corridor beyond, internal voices again yelling at me to run.

"How?" she says.

I take a deep breath and stand. My arms tighten, my legs tense, every instinct fighting to keep me away from the freezer door. Nevertheless, I hurry back toward it and drag the white-haired guy's tray back out.

"What are you *doing?*" Natasha says behind me.

I reach over and pull the green sheet off entirely, keeping my distance. Natasha gasps. And even though I was prepared, I still stumble back a step.

Blackened craters cover the old man's crushed body, far fewer than on the bodies on the plinths, but still raw and angry.

Natasha drops the papers and walks numbly over. "He was infected—" she starts.

"The paleness in his face," I say, picturing again the old man's ghostly skin in the train station, his streaming sweat. "I got it wrong. I thought he was just scared. Scared and hot under that glass dome."

Natasha stares down at the white-haired man.

"They've been experimenting on drifters, on undesirables," I go on. "Taking them off the streets. Hence the rumours." I nod toward the man. "I think this guy may have known, may have even been in on it." The wool jacket, the atmospheric-controlled briefcase, the printouts inside. "Might have been a scientist who cooked up the disease but then had a change of heart, maybe even infected himself—"

"*Infected himself?*" Natasha says.

"Could be," I say. "To send a message, tell someone about the danger." I shrug. "He brought evidence." I motion to the printouts in the briefcase.

"So they killed him," she says.

"In a way that no one would investigate," I add. "That was key."

"Wait," says Natasha, taking a step forward. She scans the old man's torso and face, her lips pale. Then she darts back to the case, grabs up a pen, and hurries back over to the body.

I go to block her, but she pushes past.

"It's okay," she says. "Look." She inserts the pen between the old man's teeth and forces the jaws apart. "No marks, no blood."

"So?" I say.

She dashes back to the papers on the floor, her fingers rifling through them. She finds the list of symptoms.

"Lung scarring is marked here," she says. Then she grabs up a graph with a quivering hand and thrusts it toward me, her face almost as pale as the corpse's. "*See?*"

I stare down at the page and still see only dots, dashes, and a line that rises before flattening, trying to connect them.

"*What?*" I say.

"It's an epidemiology graph," she says. "Shows reproduction rates of the disease."

I close my eyes, the chill building inside me and out. It feels like my body's been tied to an anchor and thrown overboard, being dragged down into the depths.

"It was not contagious before," she says, her voice strained. "It killed too quickly, all those homeless people, this man." She points at the white-haired guy's body. "But they have created a new strain. It is airborne now. That's what these graphs say."

I hold the freezing breath in my throat.

"They describe the speed of infection," she says, speaking faster. "There is a huge R-nought rate … *huge*. One case would pass to many, many people." She stumbles for a moment. "This would spread around the world in months … weeks. Nothing could stop it," she continues. "It is terrifying. Nowhere would be safe."

There it is. Gabriel's plot.

Natasha's tone hollows out. "It would be better to die now than experience what's coming," she echoes.

My insides congeal with a terrible confluence of terror and fury. The sense of dread I've been carrying since meeting Gabriel – so diffuse before – now comes into sharp, horrible focus.

I glance down at the briefcase on the floor, at the sheets of evidence, brilliantly hidden.

Also there for anyone to find.

My head whips up, and I stare through the row of windows into the corridor, my heart galloping.

Still empty.

I reach for Natasha's arm. "We've got to go," I hiss.

She slips beyond my reach. "But the body," she says and motions to the white-haired guy still lying uncovered on the tray.

"Leave it," I say, my nails digging into my palms.

She stretches down for the briefcase. "We need these," she says and grabs a few of the graphed pages, shoving them into her jacket.

"Okay, *now* we go," I say and thrust her toward the door, my hands shaking.

I run at her side, desperate to get away from the refrigerated room with the awful chill. My gaze fixes on the empty corridor, my mind darting ahead to the security gates upstairs, to the guard, and the locked front door, plans slowly forming.

Reaching the corner of the room, I peer through the rows of windows to the side of the door, toward the stairs. Still no one in the corridor. My fingers grab for the handle, Natasha just behind, and I yank the door open and stare out.

A flash of movement. A wide torso. And an arm like a tree trunk crashes into my chest.

## 44

THE ARM SLAMS into me with the force of a freight train, sending me flying backward away from the door – five feet, ten. I crash down onto the theatre floor before skidding to a stop.

I stare upward, sprawled on my back, straining to draw slivers of air into stinging lungs. My chest feels full of glass. I groan, trying to roll onto my side, while my brain screams at me to move. I clench my jaw and struggle to raise myself, to lift my head.

It's a pursuer – an entire wall bearing down on me. Every one of my muscles tightens. Black suit, white shirt and tie. All new-looking, as if from an undertaker's catalogue. And the way he moves across the floor is mesmerising, like he's gliding, not walking. His eyes bore into me, black, shining, bottomless. And stunned, unprepared, I end up gazing straight into them.

*Fuck.* The memories come – our pursuers in the estate, the club – the strange paralysis I felt. My mind yells warnings. Too late. I'm stuck. I try to rip my gaze away, but my head won't move.

The guy's mumbling something, and the words feel like

physical weights, pressing down heavier on my limbs. I suck wildly at the air as I can barely breathe now.

The awful chill barrels inward toward my core, and my vision dims. The guy's entire form becomes just his face and then only his eyes, like I'm retreating down a long dark tunnel, the world of colour bleeding into greys and blacks.

Time slows, and I glimpse the skull-like face of Death hanging right in front of me – those hollow eyes and gaping mouth formed of writhing snakes cloaked in the deepening black. I sense it summoning me, beckoning. And while I try to fight, to shake off the pressing weights with every fibre of my being … still I can't move.

Sensation continues to fade, everything aside from the razoring cold. It feels like I'm sinking ever deeper into the void, into nothingness.

I'm going to die, and there's nothing I can do about it.

The faintest sound comes, a distant crash. Sensation begins to flow back into me – a rivulet becomes a stream and then a surge. Hazy colour pushes out the darkness. The image of the room forms again, the rows of metal doors to one side, the surgical tables to the other, the windows and door to the corridor straight ahead.

And Natasha. She's fifteen feet away, standing several feet behind a large trolley. She clearly slammed it into the guy from the side, broke his gaze. Now he's staring back at her, leaning over the trolley, hands gripping it.

I shake my head to clear it, then stumble to my feet, my legs wobbling. The pursuer thrusts the trolley back toward Natasha. Such a tiny movement, and still the metal hulk careens across the floor, wheels screeching. Natasha yells and throws herself out of the way. The trolley flies past her and crunches into the side wall, leaving a massive dent in the metal doors.

Natasha rolls onto her back, and I can only watch, stunned. The guy sweeps toward her. She tries to scramble backward as he reaches down with bear-sized hands, preparing to grab her.

Still shaking, I lurch toward him. One step, two. And throw myself at the guy, side on, my elbow aimed at his head. The guy backhands me without even looking. He smashes my chest with his forearm and slams me back into the wall of metal doors.

Sparks dart before my eyes as agony squeezes my ribs. I slump to the ground, my breath stuttering, painfully shallow, while my back screams.

Then the image comes of my own lifeless form on a tray behind me as heat and cold grip my insides, the obvious thoughts coming. The pursuer stalked us here and waited for us to be alone – the perfect way to get rid of two bodies. I grit my teeth to stop them from chattering and haul myself back upright.

The guy's already turning his head to eye me, ten feet away, Natasha forgotten on the floor before him.

I avoid his gaze and glance at the metal doors to my side, scanning the guy in their reflected surfaces. As huge as ever, with a placid expression on his face and not a hint of worry, he swivels his body in my direction.

I back away, the chill taking over my insides and filling me up like floodwaters now. My brain yells and screams … *He's too fucking fast, too fucking strong.* And again, the priest's words come back to me … *Faith is—*

The thought dies. The guy's gliding forward – shoulders broad and arms spread. I take a deep breath and call to mind my confrontations with the pursuer in the club, with Qetesh's Amazon in her candled room. I contract my stomach, start the count to clear my mind, and focus again on peeling back the veil … And try to believe.

The guy lunges, his speed incredible, with a fist like a cannonball. I dodge and throw myself into the mirrored wall. The guy's arm careens past me. It misses my head by inches, the air rippling my cheek. And I bounce off the doors, stumbling further back. The freezing waters inside threaten to drown me.

The guy spins in my direction again, sliding forward while my doubts bellow. I concentrate intently on the count and reach for the space between the numbers, for the aeons that stretch out in the shimmering world, for the enhanced insight beyond the veil. I remember my prior experiences and *believe*. It's fucking gruelling, like my brain's on fire. Finally, time starts to slow …

The guy prepares to strike again – extended tendons in his neck, a subtle shift of balance. I exhale, allowing my breath to flow out, and with all thought suspended, I let my body take over.

The man raises an arm. And, feeling my attention drawn to the storage units to my side, I feint a low blow. He goes to parry it, and I whip my other hand out at head height to grasp the handle of one of the metal doors. I wrench it open with as much force as I can muster, smashing it right into the guy's face.

He grunts and stumbles backward. One step and then another. That's it. The guy barely buckled.

I keep moving and throw open another door at waist height. Then I kick out with all my weight and slam it into the pursuer's stomach. The guy staggers back a few more feet.

I can only stare. He straightens up like nothing's happened, no fucking impact at all.

Natasha's back on her feet. She's grasped the trolley and is trying to ram him again. He swivels on her and grabs the trolley from her hands. He picks the whole bloody thing up – it must weigh half a ton – lifts it a foot off the floor, and sends it crashing down on its side.

Natasha retreats from our pursuer toward me, her entire body shaking. The guy steps across to position himself between us and the door. Again, not a hint of urgency in his movements.

Backing away with Natasha, I stare through the windows into the corridor ... still empty. No one coming to help.

He stalks toward us down one half of the room, the surgical tables on one side and the wall with its metal doors on the other. This forces us closer to the middle of the far wall, and the awful chill is like hooks piercing my gut, pinning my legs.

Shuffling rearward, my gaze darts around the room, my panicked thoughts starting up again. I desperately try to think, to plan: the far door, a hundred feet away, four surgical tables in between, twenty feet of open space on either side of them. But doubts inundate me. Even if I got to the door, Natasha never would. He'd get one of us, for sure.

My legs shake. I take a quick breath and concentrate fiercely on the count once more, reaching for the aeons between the numbers.

*Come on ... believe.*

And gradually, I find a flavour of the expanded world again. The veil peels back a fraction, and time spreads out around me.

Our pursuer approaches steadily, only fifteen feet away now. He positions himself in front of the final surgical table, directly before us, and keeps coming. Ten feet, eight ...

My back hits the wall behind, and Natasha edges in closer at my side. My nerves stretch. The guy angles toward me, raising a hand toward each of us, and I sense my gaze drawn over the guy's shoulder. The tables, the door. A strange compulsion grabs me.

"Run!" The word explodes from my throat, and I shove Natasha away from me along the back wall.

She flings herself into movement. Me, an instant after. Our assailant wheels around, and we dart to either side of him, to either side of the surgical tables, and run as fast as we can. His feet sound like jackhammers against the tiled floor just behind, and I can sense him right at my heels, chasing me down.

My eyes dart to the corridor through the window, my brain starting up with ideas coming of finding the security guard and creating a delay …

But with time advancing so slowly, my thoughts are like storm-tossed waves upon the vast ocean that is my mind. And deeper down, I know we have no chance. This guy's faster, stronger. The world beyond the veil is just not enough. Even so, I continue the count.

My legs whip back and forth, my breath like fire in my chest. I glance to the side, glimpsing the guy in the reflective metal doors. He's practically on top of me. The door to the theatre still sits fifty feet away.

More thoughts come … *I'm not going to make it … Natasha might, so put up a fight, buy her some time, but she'll most likely be dead before she reaches the lobby.*

I concentrate even harder on stilling my mind as I reach again for the shimmering world and focus everything on prying open the veil. Deep within, I notice the strange compulsion again, only a faint impulse. I sense my eyes drawn to the other side, to the surgical tables I'm sprinting past.

An object glints on the second one from the door – only a glimpse. But with my enhanced awareness, the flash of silver is so clear in my mind.

I barrel along the side of the table and reach for it with hungry fingers, fumbling among the tools laid out there. Grabbing an instrument without looking, I find a thin metal against my palm.

Then powerful hands seize my neck from behind. Icy. Choking.

I focus my mind and fight the rising panic, concentrating hard on remaining anchored in the calm. I spin my body as I run. My legs tangle with my assailant's. And in slowed time, we start to fall together, chest to chest, me underneath.

The guy's hands squeeze, crushing my throat. I tense my fingers around the metal tool and bring its base to my sternum. The guy lands on me with all his weight, smashing me into the stonelike floor, and my breath is driven out of me. The blunt end of the instrument digs hard into my chest, but still I grip it with all my strength.

I choke. Can't breathe. My skin burns with the cold. My heart pulsates. Spots of white cloud my vision. I fight to hold on to the calm but sense it swirling away.

My arms remain trapped underneath the hulk's body. I jerk, strain to move, to breathe. A warm liquid pools around my hands, and images swarm behind my closed eyes. Memories. My mother. I feel her gaze on me, her fingers running through my hair. Sunlight. Pain … more distant now. Growing shadows.

Darkness.

———

SOUNDS. Muffled, like I'm underwater. Then images flare. Sparks of brightness against the black. The sound again, insistent.

"Jake!"

I feel my body being pulled, rolled – one way and then the other. Pain blossoms through my awareness as an immense weight presses down on every inch of me. I can barely breathe.

"Come on, help me!" Natasha's voice again. "*Push!*"

My eyes flutter open. Our assailant's face … only inches from mine. The guy's hands … still around my neck but no longer squeezing. The guy's not moving at all.

My hands remain trapped to my chest, the scalpel warm and sticky in my grip. I shove with my elbow, shoulder, and legs, roaring with the effort till, finally, the guy's body rolls off me and onto the ground.

The scalpel sticks out of his chest, wedged deeply between his ribs.

I take a trembling breath and stagger to my feet, almost

falling. Natasha grabs my arm. I glance down at the guy's unmoving body and remember staring into his eyes, seeing the face of Death. Then a shudder rolls through me from head to foot.

Natasha gazes at me, relief in her face but tightness as well. "We have to get out of here," she says.

I spin from the pursuer – the guy's corpse lying in full view of the corridor – and stagger to the theatre door. I lurch through it and away from the freezers.

Yet a chill slithers back into my stomach as an image flashes through my mind … a building. And stumbling on toward the stairs, a new weight begins to grow.

I know where we need to go next.

# 45

"THEY'VE CREATED ... A DISEASE?" Father Thomas asks, his mouth hanging open. He looks at us dumbstruck across his battered kitchen table, his hands shaking on the walking stick between his knees.

Natasha nods. She insisted we go and see the old man, to work out our next move. And now she sits at my side, the same determined look on her features that she's worn ever since leaving the morgue. I hunch down further in my chair, my shoulders twitching, the discomfort pressing down on me like a flea-ridden blanket.

For the hundredth time, I glance toward the far wall, the office building just on the other side. The fucking vision of it won't leave me alone – first in the stone circle and then when we fled the morgue. And the giant's words revolve around my head. *You have already seen your destination.* Then the vision morphs into the face of Death, and the echo of its strange chill slides deep into my bones.

Natasha glances at me, and I avert my gaze, keeping my trap firmly shut.

"And this scientist," the old man continues, "the one that was infected. Why would Gabriel kill him if he wants the disease to spread?"

"It would not have spread," says Natasha. "I checked the man's throat. It was not yet airborne." She takes the crumpled graphs from her jacket and dumps them on the table. "But now they have perfected it."

The papers sit there like radioactive material.

"It will be a global pandemic," she says.

The priest blinks down at the graphs, the single bulb above us doing little to shake the gloom.

"The train crash was partly to kill this man?" Father Thomas asks again, disbelief in his tone.

"So it seems," Natasha says.

Then she stares in my direction, her arms crossed. Again, I feel an urge to glance at the far wall, a pressure building inside, and a growing hum in my ears. Natasha raises an eyebrow at me.

I swallow. "A con, a diversion, a cover-up. Two birds with one well-aimed stone," I say quickly and then glance between them. "Gabriel gets another failure of modernity, one the government would want hushed up and buried fast. So, there'd be few better ways to cover a killing, the death of an important scientist."

The priest's blank gaze remains somewhere over my shoulder. "This goddess said that Gabriel is real, that all the angels are *real*," he says, his voice trembling with awe or fear; I'm not sure. "Maybe Gabriel wants things concealed because the others don't necessarily approve of his intercessions. Yet …"

He trails off, the inference obvious … *How many angels would complain about the results?* So similar to what Qetesh told us. There's no way they'll get involved.

The old man glances from me to Natasha, his brow furrowed. "But after leaving the stone circle … this dead scientist. How *did* you find him?"

Natasha pauses. "We had help." She tilts her chin up. "Just when it was needed."

Then she describes the janitor in the morgue, though she

278

leaves out her own developing abilities, her masterclass in persuasion getting us into the building.

The priest sits that bit taller. "Maybe we're not entirely alone in fighting them," he says.

"*Please*," I scoff. "He was a janitor, a normal guy."

Though the memory comes of the man standing statuesque in the corridor, those dark eyes, that odd sensation of timelessness.

Natasha frowns at me and then swivels back to the priest. "But, Father, this disease will kill millions, maybe *billions*," she says. "Would Gabriel really do this? Religion is *already* strong. The Puritans are growing, organising. There may even be a Puritan prime minister ..."

The priest shrugs. "Perhaps it is not enough," he says, pausing. "The battle between the old and the new is an eternal struggle. Gabriel must be concerned about the march of modernity – that, one day, angels will wake to find their power gone, with the entire world worshipping only money and fame." The old man sighs. "He's lost his faith. He's worried that, eventually, modernity will win."

The priest sinks lower in his chair again, his eyes duller. "Puritans are the context, the fertile ground," he says. "Gabriel is clearly looking to cleanse the unfaithful."

"Maybe," I mutter.

Natasha whips her gaze around to meet mine. But I keep my eyes on the priest, as the vision invades my brain again of the office building next door.

*But not only.*

I remember the excitement in Gabriel's tone in the station, the sense of surety in his unfolding plan. He's a master conman. He doesn't want this airborne strain simply released. No. He's got something much grander in store. Somehow, I know it.

I swallow. "And, so Qetesh says, he's done this before," I say. "Many times."

The priest takes a rattling breath and shrugs weakly. "So it seems," he says, his tone heavy. "It will be another Dark Ages, another swing in civilisation." He clasps his trembling hands together. "Half the world dead. I can't imagine it matters much to these beings." He shakes his head. "Those people remaining would be purer, their devotion brighter. The angels restored to their rightful place, ready to shepherd humankind into a new age."

I swivel away from the table and try again to order my cascading thoughts …

The genius of the thing. Already, poverty's driving people away from modernity and toward religion. But a pandemic? The impact would be on an entirely different scale. They'll release it from London – a financial pantheon, connected to the world – and it'll spread first to every other urban area. So, modernists and atheists will contract it first, and more of the religious will be saved, at least initially, those in smaller towns and villages. A clear sign of God's hand. And when the disease strikes, there'll be mass panic, and in their fear, people will turn to God, saints, and angels. Anything for salvation. With their powers, the angels are undoubtedly immune. And for the truly devoted, they might even intercede. The odd miracle in the face of death will only help spread devotion. I shake my head. A perfect plan.

"This is the great tragedy," the priest says, gazing vaguely upward. "Faith is man's birthright. Our divine spark."

I grunt, the heat rising, scratchy in my chest.

"It's the aspect of us that truly means we were made in God's image," the old man goes on, turning his gaze toward Natasha. "And they've stolen this from us." His fingers clench the top of his walking stick. "We are kept in bondage."

The heat continues to build. "How can you speak like that?" I snap, the words pressing up my throat. "This is *your* religion, the shit you've been peddling for decades!"

"Yet I believe it is still all God's will," he says, calmly.

"*What?*" I say, eyes wide. "The scheming, the control? You can't believe—"

"I do," he says, staring back at me. "Just as I believe there's a reason you're sitting there." He raises his arms toward us. "How could it be otherwise?"

I feel the pressure in my head again, the hum building in my ears. "But these are *your* gods!" I say.

The priest nods and says, "And you need to trust, to have—"

"Stop it!" Natasha slams her palm down on the table. "We cannot waste time arguing." She shifts her narrowed gaze between Father Thomas and me. "We must work out how to stop them!"

Again, the image of the office building next door forms in my mind, the pressure squeezing down into my chest. I sit forward. "Can't we just bail?"

Natasha glances at me, her eyes wide, and opens her mouth.

"Get out of the city," I blurt. "Into the sticks."

And so quickly my heart thuds with the prospect of freedom, *finally*, the dream I've been saving for since forever.

More silence. Natasha slumps back down in her chair, and both she and the priest stare back at me, their shared vow so apparent in their stunned expressions. Distant words sound in my head, Qetesh's voice … *You're pure of heart … Anger like white fire.*

I push the words away and lean further over the table. "We've got evidence," I say, pointing to the papers. "We could go to the authorities first and leave them to deal with it."

Natasha crosses her arms. "They would never believe us," she says and fixes me with a stare. "These people are too well organised, they will have removed all traces."

She raises a knowing eyebrow. And my ribs contract. Those were my words to her in the diner and city centre.

"We—" I start.

"You want to escape?" she says, her tone hardening. "Where will you go?"

My mouth opens.

"It's pointless," she continues. "You cannot be safe without knowing the dispersal mechanism. They could drop it from the air, put it into the water supply, or a dozen other things."

I screw my eyes shut and dig my nails into my palms. She's fucking right. Where would be safe? Deep underground, in a shack in the middle of nowhere, on a boat on the ocean—

"We must move *now*," Natasha says. "They killed the scientist to silence him. It means they are ready."

My eyes open to find Natasha grabbing the papers off the table.

"It will spread quickly, but they will still need to infect a number of people," she says.

"How many?" the priest says.

"Hundreds to be certain it catches," Natasha says. "Maybe thousands. We have seen how deadly the previous strain was."

Images swim of the contorted bodies, the clenched teeth. And the pressure keeps building in my chest, the hum rising in my ears.

"We could track down the scientist," she says. "Find out where he worked."

Again, I hear the giant's words – *you already know what to do … you have already seen your destination.* I grip my head and squeeze.

"If we find him," Natasha continues, "we could find his associates. They might even have made a cure. If we get that to the authorities, we—"

"I know where we've got to go next," I say softly, the words tumbling out.

Natasha sits still and then swivels her gaze on me. The priest turns as well.

I nod and take a deep breath. "I know where we've got to go," I say again. "And sadly, it's not far."

## 46

INTO THE SILENCE of Father Thomas's kitchen, I roll my idea – the possibility of breaking into the office building next door, Gabriel's likely headquarters. The proposal feels like a primed grenade.

Natasha blinks at me, her lips parted. The priest shakes his head, his brow a network of furrows. I gaze between them, ready for something to explode.

Natasha leans forward and grips the kitchen table, opening her mouth, when Father Thomas cuts across her.

"How can you be so sure?" he demands.

Again, I remember the giant's words, the images of the office building they conjured in my head – its religious statues and glowing surfaces. I pull the white-haired guy's wallet from my pocket and pluck out the pile of receipts. I rifle through them, find the one that caught my eye in the morgue, and then lay it on the table.

Natasha leans in closer and picks it up. "What is this?"

"Some delivery slip," I say.

"For what?" she says.

"Research, equipment," I say, shrugging. "Something that helps their plan. But it's not the *what* that matters."

Natasha glances at it again. "It's the address," she says.

I nod. "The building next door," I say, eyeing the priest. "They've been taking deliveries there. You tracked guards from the place. It's got to be important. Will have info on the disease."

And my mind scrambles for possibilities ... *the dispersal mechanism, how to get safe, and maybe even a cure.*

Father Thomas gazes between us, his features slowly hardening. Natasha stares straight at me, the resolve shining so clearly in her eyes. My gaze flicks back to the priest. He's attempting to sit straighter, his shoulders back. A strange smile tilts his lips.

"I'm coming with you," he says.

I almost choke. "*You?*" I ask.

"Yes, Jacob. Me," he says.

"But ..." I splutter. "You're ancient, close to blind, can barely walk!"

And with every word, the smile spreads across the priest's face, each worry line growing thinner. I shoot a gaze at Natasha.

"Father," she says and reaches for his hand. "That is very kind of you, but I think we should—"

The priest raises a single finger. "Don't patronise me, my child," he says. "I am old enough to know when I'm being fobbed off, and I won't have it." He sits back in his chair and wraps his hands around his walking stick.

I throw up my arms. "You're going to get us killed!"

The priest simply shakes his head, resolved, and I lapse into silence, thoughts frothing about the task at hand, the likely disaster, and how to keep the old man occupied without messing things up.

I grit my teeth and force a deep breath. *Time.* At least we have that – a few hours, for sure. If Gabriel releases the disease imminently, it's all over anyway. Plus, we've got another job to do first. I eye Natasha in her jacket and club dress.

A change of clothes.

LATE AFTERNOON. We leave the church by the side exit like last time, the streets of the city centre full of evening commuters. Natasha and I stride forward to lose ourselves in the masses and head toward the nearest department store.

"So what are you thinking about the office building?" Natasha says. "How will we do this? How are we going to get in?"

She babbles on nervously as we walk. I keep silent, the same questions running around my brain. After a few minutes, Natasha ceases her interrogation and falls into step at my side, seemingly content to be patient.

Half an hour later, we're standing facing an oblong monster – five floors of shops, restaurants, and bars. A couple of security guards eye my scruffy clothes. I smooth out the jacket, staying behind Natasha, and they let us inside just fine.

Fourth floor. We find a different shop from where I stole Natasha's dress. This one's the size of three football fields, with every type of clothing spread across every type of room – shopping as an art form. Clothing displays mingle with sculptures and water features. Posing mannequins stand in themed areas – office, home, bar, club … And hefty shoplifting gates line every exit, each of the clothes pinned with high-sensitivity security tags. I tap my pocket subconsciously. No cash. No card.

I go to search out another shop when Natasha's eyes widen at the boundless racks of clothes. She hurries inside, and I follow behind as she eagerly fingers through an endless range of tops and skirts, all her prior nervousness gone. I shake my head at her excitement – her shining face, her brisk movements – yet I find my shoulders starting to relax.

I watch two female clerks bustle over from their square island of tills with offers of help while really extricating the many clothes Natasha's already carrying. She dips her head and blushes.

Then our task hits me.

I shake myself and scan the space out of the corner of my eye. Three more clerks in the room, a dozen customers, and no one's looking in my direction.

As a clerk's pointing Natasha to the changing rooms, I dart over to the island, reach into the packaging materials, and snatch one of the larger store plastic bags before slipping it under my jacket. No one shouts. And I slink away, watching for any surprised glances.

Natasha turns to me, empty-handed. And I quickly angle my head at a wide passageway in the far wall. She nods. And I meander between the rails, focusing on keeping my posture relaxed as we pick our way toward the next room.

It's split into lingerie and women's casual wear, and I begin scanning the space for clerks. The half-dozen of them are helping customers or tending to displays. No one is looking for us. At least so far.

I'm about to search for the men's section when I glimpse another smile forming on Natasha's lips.

"Having fun?" I ask.

Her face flushes again, though she doesn't look down. "Maybe," she says and then raises an eyebrow as her smile grows mischievous. "You should try it sometime."

I snort. "We've got a job to do," I reply. "I'll meet you back here in a couple." Then I attempt my best stern expression. "And remember, this is *serious*. Don't be causing *too* much of a scene."

She holds my gaze, grinning. "I will do my best," she says with a wink.

I shake my head again and pad off toward another passageway. Yet her grin doesn't leave me, and among the racks of men's clothes, I experiment with browsing, trying to imitate Natasha's fun. I just end up feeling ridiculous and grab stuff that looks the right size. Jeans, T-shirt, and hooded top. Everything in black.

Walking back between rooms, I fold the clothes tightly and carry the bundle down at my side under the flap of my jacket. When I finally find Natasha, she's standing by yet another display, holding up a high-necked top in black with what looks like a pair of jeans over her arm.

She meets my eye and then heads over to the changing rooms. I follow. She slips beyond a curtain into the cubicle, and I lean against a wall just outside, making sure to stay hidden behind the leaves of a towering fern. And there I wait.

My fingers tap rhythms against my legs, and my thoughts return to infiltrating Gabriel's headquarters. The muscles in my back knit up, and I breathe, trying to focus on this con instead. But it's so hard. My concerns spiral ever faster – the impossibility of the bigger task and the need to do it as soon as possible before Gabriel releases the disease … As in, this very evening.

I force myself to scan the shoppers, searching for a likely mark. Around twenty mill about this room, some perusing while others talk with attendants. And most of them women. Except …

A rich guy sporting a cashmere sweater is browsing through the lingerie section for someone. His wife, his mistress? It doesn't matter. What does is the guy's obvious nerves, his flitting gaze, his forehead shiny with sweat. I tap my leg and watch his fumbling hands, his—

Then suddenly I'm back in the train station, staring at the mark with his phone, rows of glittering outfits in between us, Liam as my partner. I can hear Natasha humming in the cubicle to my side, and I brace myself for the customary sense of distrust, the tightness in my chest.

It doesn't come.

"I think this works," Natasha says from behind the curtain, her voice whimsical as if half talking to herself.

I drive my mind back and then lean toward her cubicle and hiss, "*Hurry up.*"

"I'm working on it," she says, that same edge of teasing in her tone. "And anyway, you do *your* job. I will do mine."

I snort. "Mine's done," I say, my eyes fixed on the mark. He's shuffling down the lingerie aisles, his eyes darting between the various collections, with a large pile of clothes over one arm. "But we've got to move soon."

Natasha exits the cubicle and slinks over to my side.

"Ready?" I say, all too aware that I'm one of two people hiding behind a bloody fern. I hold out my arm for her clothes.

She doesn't give them to me. Instead she simply nods and remains still. "May I ask you a question?" she says.

I feel a sinking sensation in my gut, and I keep my gaze forward, my eyes trained on the mark, my mouth shut. I can sense what's coming.

Bloody clever of her. I'm stuck. Can't move.

She clears her throat. "The first time we met," she continues. "In the hospital. You had a dream. You started to talk to me. You believed I was somebody else."

I wince, the customary contraction inside me, like a drawstring, the need to close down.

"Who?" she says, looking up at me, her tone soft.

I don't meet her gaze and don't reply.

"Jake?" she says.

I turn on her. "*Why?*" I say, unable to keep the bite from my tone.

She shrinks a little and then shrugs. "I don't know," she says. "It feels important that you get to speak about it. I remember such softness in your voice. It was so … I don't know … so different to how you …"

I swivel and stare out across the room again, feeling her gaze on my cheek while my mind yells at me to push her away. It'd be so much fucking easier.

I watch the mark grab two sets of underwear and hide

them between his folded clothes. Then he starts toward one of the payment islands. My brain urges me into action while my shoulders feel like rock.

I take a deep breath and let it out.

Natasha tries again, "Was it—"

"My mother," I say, feeling the rawness in my heart. "I saw her sitting on the bed."

Natasha takes a breath and leans back against the wall at my side. "She must have been an amazing woman," she says.

My chest clenches, my ribs tightening. She abandoned me for the drugs, and pain spears me with every memory – her indifferent gaze as I stood on the doorstep, the turn of her head before I left. She was all I ever had. I have no memory of my father. She never spoke of him.

"Amazing … and not," I say. And again, I focus on my breath, on steadying my heartbeat. Gradually, my insides relax. "But it wasn't her fault. They got her addicted."

"The gangs?" she says.

I blink across at her. "How'd you know?"

She shrugs. "Your life," she says. "It is a product of it. You have tried to get away from them, but at some level, it is all you've ever known."

Memories come of the groups I fell in with after leaving home – the errand boys that quickly became gang members with me, drug couriers, thieves …

I swivel back to face the mark. He's reached the front of the queue to pay, and the clerks are beginning to bag his items.

"It's why you hate the powerful. Isn't it?" Natasha says. "You distrust everyone and everything because of the gangs … they stripped your mother from you."

I bite my cheek. The love, the pain, the rage – it all bubbles up inside me. I keep my gaze trained on the mark, trying to breathe again, to find some calm.

"And so you hide your goodness deep down," she says. "I can see it. It's just infuriating that you cannot."

The mark's finished paying, and the clerk hands over his bags.

"Have you forgotten what I'm doing here?" I say and grab Natasha's clothes from her. "Stealing. Just like when we first met." I pile her clothes and mine into the plastic bag that I pilfered, my gaze still on the mark.

"Ah, but this is different," she says, her tone suddenly light again. "You are doing it for a higher goal."

And I can't help picturing the smile on her lips.

"I will see you outside," she continues. And with that, I turn and watch her swan off toward another room of clothes, shoulders relaxed, gait easy. Totally crazy.

I grip the bag tighter. The mark's already hurrying for the exit with his purchases. I push off the wall and head in the same direction. He glances left and right as he walks, his bags clutched tightly in his hands. And I quicken my steps along parallel aisles, avoiding the clerks as I go.

Twenty feet from the exit, I position my bag in front of my legs, those electronic tags still attached inside. We draw abreast, and I angle my walk in the mark's direction, speeding up a little.

The guy approaches the shoplifting gates, and I close in, timing my stride to pass them at exactly the same time as him. He glances at me, and I feign a look behind. I bump the man's shoulder just as the beeping starts.

Its shrill noise turns heads, and a dozen sets of eyes scan the wide exit for the perpetrator. The guy spins back immediately – on automatic – his features colouring with guilt.

Apologising, I peel off to the side and pace away from the store, down an avenue with countless accessory shops.

I find Natasha leaning against a wall by the escalators, that mischievous grin pulling at her lips.

"Not so hard on my actions now?" I say.

She nods. "Perhaps," she says and then tiptoes closer and peers into the bag. "But only when it comes to clothes for me."

I find myself smiling. "Come on."

We leave the store and walk back toward the church in the dying sunlight, the sky above a deepening blue.

Again, I see a vision of Gabriel's headquarters, and my doubts start to jabber. But walking alongside Natasha, I feel a new sense of ease in my body, the questions that bit more distant – how we're going to break in, involve the priest, find the disease's distribution mechanism and possibly even a cure.

My pace slows. That's what's strange. It's a *we*. Somehow, we've got to do this *together*. I blink. Probably for the first time in my life, that feels okay.

## 47

GABRIEL'S HEADQUARTERS towers above me. I press my back into the outer church wall, my heel bouncing up and down, the corner of the archangel's building only a few feet to my side. Natasha and I are standing facing another office across the courtyard, the entire reception area of Gabriel's headquarters visible in its mirrored glass front.

Three people sit behind a desk, all men, and all in identical dark robes. They're Puritans and not pursuers, yet still a shiver goes through me.

I take a breath and scan all fifty storeys of Gabriel's building. It's early evening and there's still no movement.

The information on the disease. Is it even in there?

The tapping of a walking stick makes me swivel. The priest shuffles toward Gabriel's office building – a blind, frail old man in a shabby habit, hobbling between smartly dressed office workers toward the epitome of corporate majesty. His stick taps the ground in front, a square-shaped package held under his other arm, wrapped in brown paper. All from the church supplies. My eyes dart back to the reception area, my doubts starting to squawk.

I squeeze the burner phone and pretend to speak into it as several evening commuters still stroll around. In my other hand, I'm holding a different package. Same brown paper, but this one's larger – just over a foot long – and heavier, too. My shoulder aches with the weight.

"Remember … misdirection," I whisper to Natasha.

She elbows me in the ribs.

But I prattle on, "Closeness, speed—"

"I know. I know," she says with mock seriousness. Then she angles her chin at the reflection in the mirrored glass opposite. "Shh. I want to watch."

I grunt back but can't help the faintest smile. And standing side by side, we watch the priest stumble toward the building's revolving door. The closer he gets, the more my smile falters.

I briefed the old man repeatedly. Hammered on and on about how to deal with resistance from the guards. But it felt like wasted words. And now, the most he can do is manage his decrepitude – leaning on his stick and lurching forward to maintain momentum.

"He's going to ruin it all," I say and go to stride toward the entrance.

Natasha grabs my hand. "Jake, it will be fine," she says softly.

"Really?" I say.

She smiles. I try to breathe, and a subtle warmth buds in my chest. I force myself to settle back, to watch as Father Thomas taps his stick against the revolving door and pushes through it. Then he shuffles toward reception.

One security guard jumps up, raises a hand, and barks something. The old man presses forward and reaches the desk. It's twenty feet wide and sits right in the middle of the reception area, facing the street. Not much else is in there, just a few sofas positioned around the edge and a darkened space at the rear.

The priest carefully leans his stick against the polished white surface of the desk, staring vaguely upward. Then he places his package on top of it. The standing guard shakes his head, his hands clasped in front of his dark robes – one religious brother appealing to another.

I can't hear the priest's words, though my lips mutter the lines we practised over and over … *This package has been delivered to the wrong address, to the church next door. It's addressed to this building and seems important.*

We put all the details we could on the label to make it seem familiar. The address of the headquarters, along with one of the senders' addresses frequently mentioned in the white-haired guy's receipts. Even the name we got from his briefcase – A. Lydon.

The standing Puritan stares down at the package. Then he turns to exchange words with his colleagues. A tense moment passes, and I grip the phone tighter, staring into the mirrored glass opposite.

Finally, the guard bows and swivels away from the desk. He pads toward the back of the ground floor, toward the darkened area, and disappears out of sight. Hopefully he's on his way to bring the priest's package to the same place as previous deliveries, to where details about the disease might be kept.

I pocket the phone and spin toward the entrance, the larger package gripped in my other hand. Natasha's already moving, dressed in the brown jacket and cap of a parcel company, a fake ID pinned to her lapel, and a clipboard in her hand. All bought from a local deliveryman with the little cash the priest had in the church.

She strides toward the revolving door, and I shove my own cap on and fall in right behind her. We've got only seconds if the next phase is going to work.

Father Thomas trundles away from the reception desk. And I follow Natasha through the doors. She sweeps toward the remaining guards while I keep out of sight behind her.

"Hi!" she says, her tone warm and open. I can almost see her beaming. "Has a package been dropped off here?"

Both guards gaze at her, mouths gaping. Visitors are

clearly unusual. The second guard stands up at his colleague's side.

"Brown paper, with a label like this?" Natasha says, pointing at her cap.

First rule of misdirection – control the attention.

Both guards peer at Natasha's cap. One of them nods. I pass my package forward into Natasha's arms. It's so heavy she has to grip it with both hands, the clipboard underneath.

Reaching the reception desk, she heaves the package toward the top. Its shiny surface is about three and a half feet off the ground and comes up to the guards' navels. She slides the package in their direction. And I can't help but watch the placement intently. The bulk pointing toward them, the thinner end hanging several inches over our side of the desk.

"There was a mistake," she says, her hands now on her hips.

Rule two – keep things urgent, keep talking.

"A parcel got switched, I'm afraid," she continues, her tone still warm and disarming. "This is the correct one." She pats the package in front of her.

I hover behind her shoulder, out of the way, my head down. The parcel sits between the guards, each one standing two feet to either side of it along the polished surface of the desk.

My mind rehearses her next lines, my heartbeat quickening. I have to stop myself from jumping forward and taking over the con.

"They are both from this sender," she says and points at a specific part of the label. "Do you recall the address?"

Both guards glance down to read the sender's address – we made the writing almost illegible. Though after several seconds, neither moves any nearer to the package. They remain peering at it from a couple of feet away, like the bloody thing's going to bite them.

Gazing at the guards over Natasha's shoulder, my adrenaline builds, and I start willing them closer to the parcel with my mind. But of course they don't move a fucking inch.

"Is the address different?" Natasha says, her voice tightening. "Can you make it out?"

I grit my teeth and risk stepping to her side. I stare intently down at the package also, trying to direct their attention.

And it works … in part. Both guards lean down further to decipher the writing. The first shuffles several inches closer to the parcel, but the second keeps his feet bloody rooted. He raises his head and glances at Natasha, then at me.

Then his features harden as if he's clocked me for the first time. Natasha gazes at me also, her face paling. And the second guard narrows his eyes, opening his mouth to shout.

I dart toward the desk and grab the end of the package with both hands, tensing my shoulders and arms. The package is seriously heavy – a solid stone crucifix. And the first guard is further away from it than expected – maybe a foot and a half. But he's still leaning down over the thing, his attention fixed. I yank the package upward and to the side. The guard shoots his head up and tries to pull back.

Too slow.

I smash the crucifix up into his jaw. His head snaps right back. Then his muscles slacken, his knees buckle, and he collapses.

My eyes whip to the second guard. The guy's frozen with lips parted, standing a whole two feet further along the desk. I clench my teeth and swing the crucifix at him with everything I have. But he jerks his head backward in time, and the edge of the stone misses his chin by inches.

The fucking crucifix. It's so heavy that having missed, its momentum pulls my entire body around like it's some kind of Olympic hammer. And I end up facing away from the guard, a desk between us, the worst weapon in the world in my hands. And instead of dropping it or throwing it, I stare dumbly back at the guy as he opens his mouth even wider to yell, to alert everyone in the bloody building—

Natasha moves like lightning. She darts for the desk and rams her clipboard straight into the guy's throat. He stumbles back a step, chin to his chest, choking. And finally, my mind snaps into focus. I lurch toward the guy, grab his robes, and yank his head down, clonking it into the top of the desk. The guy slides, unconscious, to the ground.

Natasha turns to me, her hands trembling.

I grip her wrist. "You did great," I say, holding her gaze. "He's only knocked out. He'll be fine."

She still leans over the desk and stares down at the body. The priest is already shuffling around to look. He hunches over to examine the guards.

"They're both breathing," he says.

I tighten my grip on Natasha's arm. "Come on. Clothes, *now*," I say.

She pauses and then nods. We both sprint around the desk and start yanking off the guards' habits.

Twenty seconds later, we're holding two sets of robes, both bodies hidden from the courtyard behind the desk.

"Let's go," I say, slipping the robes over my clothes, and I hasten toward the rear of the building.

Natasha follows, leaving Father Thomas behind to keep our escape route clear and our two friendly receptionists unconscious.

I picture the guard with the package, probably already far up ahead of us by now, and quicken my pace, my pulse beating faster.

The guards only just went on duty, which means we have a bit under ninety minutes before the next rotation. Only ninety fucking minutes. To get right inside Gabriel's building – the heart of the beast – and back out again.

# 48

I HURRY beyond the reception area, Natasha just behind, our feet clicking on the limestone floor. We pass sparkling mirrors and framed prints on the walls, banks of leather sofas with shiny glass tables in between. Like our pursuers' clothes, most of the stuff looks new, as if it's just for show, the spaces never used.

A wide staircase opens up before us, and it's made of … *yes* … uncovered stone, near impossible to keep silent on. I lean over it and listen for the first guard's footsteps, off to deliver our package …

There. Distant, but just barely audible. The faint clack of soles on stone above me. Our guide to discovering the disease's dispersal mechanism, perhaps even a cure.

My heart thumps, and I climb, taking two steps at a time. The stairwell winds in a square up into what's got to be the centre of the building. There's an open space between the sets of steps, thirty feet across, and walls around the edge.

We reach the first-floor landing. An office corridor extends beyond the stairwell in both directions with white walls, glass doors, and strip lights in the ceiling. The guard's footsteps sound louder above us, maybe a couple of floors above, their tempo slackening.

I push myself faster up the next staircase while trying to keep my focus on my own footsteps, on placing my feet as noiselessly as I can. But it's tough. My concentration keeps slipping.

The furnishings are shifting around me – corporate agency morphing into baroque cathedral. Reaching the second-floor landing, the stone floor has become a rich red carpet. By the third floor, the white walls of the stairwell and corridors have become dark wood covered with carved relief depicting wreaths. And the lights – they're spots on the walls one moment and flickering candles the next, the brightness dying as the shadows creep in.

I take a breath and try to concentrate on something steady, fixing my eyes on the stairwell railing. But the woodgrain shifts under my gaze, and my chin shoots up. None of our surroundings are stable. If I look closely at anything, the feature morphs. I stare at a wall tapestry depicting clouds and sunbeams, and the rays shift into tree branches, the clouds into a thousand leaves. My head starts to spin, and the veil feels thinner before my senses.

I sniff the air. The burnt metal odour's present and growing stronger. And something else is there too. Undeniable. An imprint of that strange chill, the icy fingers creeping beneath my skin.

A shiver runs through me as I climb. The familiar thrill of the con is dying down – the excitement of getting us past reception – and my doubts start yelling at me. Searching an archangel's building, in terrible disguises. *This is fucking insane.*

I take a breath and begin the count. Focus on stilling my mind, on ignoring the cold. I try to spark some kind of belief as I ascend, Natasha just behind me. The guard's footsteps have quieted, maybe muffled by the new carpet, their tempo even slower now.

Fourth floor. I stare down the landing and do a double take. The corridor's longer, far longer, as if it's somehow stretching well beyond the bounds of the building. The end of it lies over a hundred yards distant. And the guard's footsteps grow ever closer above.

I push myself upward, but reaching the fifth-floor landing, the chill grips my lungs, sears my insides, and causes me to stumble to a stop.

Natasha goes to step past me, but I put out my arm and then swallow.

*"Wait here,"* I rasp and pad across the landing to the next set of steps before glancing up the square stairwell.

No sign of the guard, though his footsteps are even slower above me. And the chill continues to grow in my bones.

"What is—" Natasha starts.

I put my finger to my lips and begin to ascend the stairs in a crouch, peering up to glimpse the staircase above and opposite.

Finally, I see him, trudging up to the landing above with the parcel, his head bowed, almost facing me directly. I freeze, my pulse a fucking drum.

But he keeps climbing, and I don't scramble out of sight. Instead, I lean forward, peering closer through the bannisters. The man's hands tremble, his posture shrinks, and his gait becomes tentative – terror obvious in his movements.

And with every step he takes, the icy fingers delve ever deeper under my skin.

He reaches the landing above and stops moving. A new silence presses in at my ears, and I listen hard.

But there's nothing.

I jerk out of my crouch, my brain finally clicking into gear, the revelation hitting like a smack to my forehead. My adrenaline fires, and I leap back down the steps.

Natasha stares up at me from the far side of the landing.

"He's handed it over to a fucking pursuer!" I blurt, desperately trying to keep the volume low.

Her frown deepens. "So?" she says.

But I'm already whirling my head left and right, desperately searching for hiding places. The corridor has columns along one side of it and doors along the other, with tables and decorative objects in between them.

And still Natasha hasn't moved a damn muscle. She's standing on the opposite side of the landing, in full bloody view of the stairwell.

"The guard!" I hiss. "He's not allowed any further up, which means—"

And there they are, footsteps, coming down the steps. I swivel. The awful chill ebbs a fraction, the pursuer undoubtedly heading further up the stairs with the parcel.

I start waving my hands frantically at Natasha, but she's already darting away from me down the landing. She slips behind the far corner wall of the stairwell, and I retreat behind my corner wall as well.

The guard's footsteps speed up, hastening down to the safety of reception. Images swamp me of the unconscious bodies lying there, and every muscle in my back tightens up.

I dash over to a table and grab up a statue of a golden cherub. It's only seven or eight inches tall but still nice and heavy. I back up against the corner wall again with the statue in my hand.

Natasha continues to stare at me from across the landing, hood up, eyes wide, ten feet further down the corridor from the descending steps.

"*Distract him,*" I mouth at her.

She shakes her head at me and begins unconsciously fingering her crucifix necklace beneath her robe.

"*You've got to,*" I mouth.

She steps behind a column. I hold my breath and keep still.

The guard appears in front of me, half facing the other direction, his hood pulled low over his face. He pads away across the landing toward the next staircase down and Natasha. The silence in the building feels almost absolute. I find myself starting to pray.

Natasha clears her throat and slips out from behind the column. "Brother?" she says, her voice so quiet.

The guard stutters in his step for an instant. Then keeps on striding.

"Brother," she says again, louder now, trying to deepen her voice.

The guy gives an urgent shake of his head, his gaze still fixed on the floor. He approaches the other side of the landing, the steps down.

"Your help has been requested," Natasha says.

Finally, the guy halts. And there he waits, his back to me. I steal a few steps toward him, placing my feet as quietly as I can, the statue held tightly by my side.

Natasha says nothing further. And the guard begins to turn for the staircase down.

Natasha steps toward him. "There is an impostor," she says and pulls back her own hood, revealing her very obviously female face plus the plait of long hair.

The guy stumbles rearward, his hood falling back to expose a bald head, and simply stares at her without moving.

I dart across the landing toward him. Eight feet, five feet. All too aware of the sound of my footsteps. The guard comes to and starts to whirl around. I bring my hand up with the cherub and swing it hard at his head. The guy ends up spinning directly into the strike. The statue smashes into his temple, and he goes down instantly.

And there I wait, breathing hard, my fingers quivering. I strain to listen but only hear silence. No sound below us. No sound above.

"Jake!" Natasha says.

She's pointing at the unconscious guard, another body. This one lying in full view of the stairwell.

"Grab his legs!" I say.

Together, we drag the guard to the side of the corridor, behind a column, and barely out of sight.

I have to force myself back toward the stairwell, toward

the pursuer climbing somewhere above us. The chill grows, stealing further into my bones, and it becomes my new guide as we climb.

We reach the next landing, and then the next, my heart beating ever faster. The luxury's increasing, the carved wood becoming gilded panels, the tapestries spun from threaded silver and gold. And the landing corridors now stretching endlessly, staircases extending from multiple junctions. Suddenly, it's as if we're back in the infinite palace realm, the risk of the nobility figures behind every corner. And, as with that place, there are no windows. No way to see outside. No sign we're even in a damn office building any more. My head spins faster, our only anchor the chill of a pursuer climbing above us. And following him up feels like slipping ever deeper into a nightmare.

As I reach the top of one of the staircases, the face of Death appears in my mind, the skull-like form made of writhing shapes. I try to maintain the count, to still my mind. But my doubts just yell louder, stronger. I end up concentrating only on my feet, on placing one foot on a step … and then the next.

We reach the eighth landing, and I hear the sound of a door closing. Maybe two storeys up? I stop moving, waiting for the chill to grow or diminish.

It does neither.

After a while, I creep more slowly upward, peering up the stairwell, constantly expecting a pursuer to descend on us. The charge in the air builds with every step, static energy tingling the skin across my back and shoulders.

Tenth floor. I scan the landing. It's empty, with three doors facing the stairwell. I'm about to step forward to try the first door but then stop.

"*What is it?*" Natasha hisses.

"What if I mess this up?" I say. "We've got no bloody idea what or who's behind them."

Natasha grips my hand. "We have left three unconscious

bodies down there," she says. "They may already be searching!"

I bite my lip and stare at the three doors. Each one's intricately carved with polished golden handles, the middle one the shiniest of all. I picture what's behind the correct door – hopefully our package along with others, and so details of the disease, things of science … of humans, not angels.

I check the handles and find the tiniest smears on the underside of the middle one. Any normal person climbing this high would have been terrified, would have sweated all over it.

I risk touching the tip with my finger. Cold. I feel into the strange chill in my bones. It remains, but it's not been increasing. Yet I don't move. I simply stand there, rooted.

Natasha squeezes my wrist tighter, opening her mouth, and I grab the handle and twist. There's a click, and I push. The door swings inward. I stand stock-still on the threshold, poised for the flaring chill, to be smashed backward.

Nothing happens.

I peer around the door and catch a glimpse of wooden shelves along with the edge of a rich patterned carpet. I still hear no sound from within, no movement. I jump inside and yank Natasha after me, closing the door quietly behind us. Then I spin.

The room's empty. I let out a long breath. The strange chill *is* weaker in here, the cordite smell as well.

I scan the room, which resembles a library, with wooden shelves along both side walls and glass cabinets full of parchments. The decor's ornate, every inch of the wood panelling carved into rolling scrolls and patterns, and the domed ceiling exhibits a huge painting of a divine scene with dazzling clouds, rays of sunlight, and flying cherubim. Opaque windows line the far wall, only shades of the night outside visible. And in the middle of the room stands a large varnished table.

Natasha hurries over. Several piles of paper and a couple

of large binders lie on top. Modern, plastic, and glossy. Completely out of place among the room's ornamental design.

And sitting by the papers is a parcel. *Our* parcel. Though I find my attention drawn to what's covering the rest of the table.

A map. The outline depicts the southeast of the country, several sites marked with red crosses. Major hospitals, maybe? Places to release the disease from? I peer closer at their locations. No. The crosses *are* by main roads, but they're all in rural areas, located around but not within the major cities. Not the most efficient way to spread a disease.

"What could they be?" I mutter.

Natasha grabs up the larger of the two binders and flicks through it, stopping on one of the first pages. Then she glances back down at the map.

"They are marked here," she says.

I move over to scan the page. There are six typed addresses.

"Distribution centres, apparently," she continues, pointing at the page title.

I glance back at the map. There are seven crosses marked here, not six. All spread out across the region except two that lie pretty close together, which is odd.

"Distribution of what?" I say.

Natasha shrugs. I leaf back to the beginning of the binder and then inspect the cover. It's some kind of technical manual with only a logo on the front. A double helix. The symbol's familiar.

I clench my fingers around the hard plastic, warnings jabbering, pursuers probably on their way. My eyes dart to the other glossy binder, the same logo on its spine.

And then the connection forms – the same image plastered all over the city.

I whip the binder up and start shuffling through it. The pristine white pages are covered in pictures of Petri dishes and syringes, images of happy patients in hospital beds. And the text describes the new cancer treatment, the one advertised outside the hospital, outside the morgue … everywhere. Now finally ready. About to be launched.

I lower the binder and stare vacantly at the opaque windows. It makes no sense. This is a pharmaceutical company. The enemy of the Puritan movement. A prickling sensation climbs my spine.

I dart back to Natasha. She continues to flick through the technical manual. There are no stock images, no wonderful claims, only a few pictures of vials and cardboard boxes. Then page after page of batch numbers.

"Look," she says and shoves a page in my direction. "They have highlighted one delivery." She jabs her finger at a series of numbers circled in red. "It corresponds with one of the centres."

I glance back at the map, my chest growing cold.

"It's one of these. Right?" I say and point at the two crosses lying closer together.

Natasha follows my finger and then rechecks the binder. "How did you know?" she says and glances up at me.

I close my eyes. "Because you found it," I say, my stomach plunging, "and I know what they're going to do."

## 49

WITH SHAKING HANDS, I grab the binder with the distribution lists and place it down flat on the library tabletop. "You said we had to find the disease's dispersal mechanism?" I say.

Natasha nods.

"This is it," I say and point at the ringed times for the deliveries. "They've got to infect hundreds of people, maybe thousands. Right?"

"To be sure it spreads, yes," she says. "But this is only an estimate—"

"Well, what better way than to switch up vials of the disease with some hot drug that every clinic's going to be screaming for?"

She just looks at me.

"I'm thinking the extra cross on the map is where they're holding the disease, maybe even where it was made," I say. "It's close to one of the distribution centres, the one with the marked shipment." I move over to the map. "And they want to switch this shipment of cancer drug with vials of the disease. That way it'll look like the new drug is causing the pandemic – the perfect attack on science, on modernity. The Puritans will lap it up."

Natasha's mouth hangs open.

"The ones who survive," I add.

Again, images of the contorted bodies flash through my brain, and I spin in place, my eyes raking the piles of papers – printouts of graphs, tables, and chemical equations. I dart toward them. Natasha grabs my arm.

I whirl. "But the cure!" I say. "They've got to have made one to save the devoted. If we can find the specs, get our hands on them—"

"We don't have *time*," she says. "There's far too much to search. They could find us any second. Take photos of all this." She waves at the binders. "We *must* get this evidence to the authorities."

I stare back at her, visions coming of my body writhing on one of Qetesh's stone plinths … and Natasha's.

"But …" I start.

She continues to stare up at me with that determined look, the single line etching her forehead. And the words die on my lips. She squeezes my arm tighter.

"*Damn it!*" I whip out my burner phone.

I begin snapping images of the ringed times for the deliveries, the dates and batch numbers, along with the crosses on the map. I focus on keeping my hand steady while my stomach wedges itself up my throat.

"Done, we've got what we need," I say, while my mind scrambles to track time. How much of the ninety-minute window remains?

"Okay, I will make this look right," Natasha says, grabbing up the binders to place them back in their original positions.

I swivel and hurry to the door. The knob feels like ice against my palm, colder than before. I press an ear to the wood to listen and can't hear a bloody thing. Yet my brain's conjuring images of a hundred pursuers out there, all homing in on us.

My eyes find the windows opposite, and I picture us opening them, trying to climb down. My head spins at just the idea. Are we on the tenth floor or the hundredth? The memory of our climb's a fucking haze in my brain.

Natasha runs over and stares at me.

I take a breath. "Here we go," I say and turn to pull the handle, my fingers slippery with sweat.

The door swings open soundlessly. I lean forward and peer out into the corridor, limbs poised.

No one there. Only the same balustrade along the edge of the landing, the same golden relief running down the stairs.

I allow myself a slow breath and step out to stare along the passageway. Empty, aside from flickering candles and closed doors.

Natasha pushes past me toward the stairwell down while I find my gaze drawn to the corridor ends, to the staircases disappearing up and down in the distance like the branches of an enormous tree.

She spins back. "What are you *doing?*" she asks.

My mind babbles. "We could find another way down, one they don't see coming," I say. "Or cook up a diversion, maybe?"

Natasha tenses her arms, her neck. "Let's just get back down to reception, *now*," she snaps. "The priest's all alone. He may need our help."

I nod, yanking my thoughts back, and then hurry toward the stairwell. Upon reaching it, it takes every effort not to jump the steps, to avoid bolting straight down to the lobby. I tiptoe down the inside of the stairwell instead, my body crouched to get a better view of the winding staircase. I try to take calm, slow breaths as we descend.

One set of steps. Another. And another—

Then the cold grips my insides, and my foot slips. I lurch down a couple of steps.

The strange chill is unmistakable, growing within my bones. I scan the staircase up and down with wild eyes, the next landing just below. No movement. Not yet. I try to feel into the sensation. Is it coming from above, from below? It's impossible to bloody tell.

My adrenaline surges, and I gamble. I throw myself down the remaining stairs to the landing, Natasha just behind, our footsteps like damn drumbeats in the silence. Then I spin away from the stairwell and sprint several feet down the corridor before darting behind one of the cream pillars that abuts the wall.

Natasha hurries past. And I yank her into the relative darkness at my side. She squeezes up against the wall, and I stand there, my pulse surging, and stare at the carved panelling opposite.

Images come of our pursuer turning the corner, stalking in our direction, and my mind starts running mitigation strategies, contingencies. The chill grows, and I start the count in my head, focusing on damming my thoughts.

Once again, the veil's there before me, the subtle screen in front of my senses. Fewer candles line this corridor. And I imagine drawing the darkness to me. I fight to believe we're invisible in the gloom. All the while a part of my brain screams insanity.

The cold sidles deeper inside, and my legs go numb. I clench my teeth, close my eyes, and focus even harder on *feeling* the shadows, on pulling them closer. The seconds crawl by.

Finally, the chill thaws a fraction, and sensation returns to my limbs. I open my eyes. Natasha's staring past me, past the pillar toward the central stairwell. No sign of our pursuers. And we've still got seven bloody floors to get down. Maybe more.

I slip from our hiding place and hurry back toward the stairs. We start downward, scrambling faster now.

Six floors.

Five.

My heart hammers in my chest. I go to look over the bannisters of the central stairwell, desperate to catch a glimpse of the ground floor. But my head spins, my vision woozy, and I veer backward from the railing. It's as if I've got some strange case of vertigo, the sense of teetering off the edge of the world.

I settle myself, plant a foot on the next staircase, and stop. The strange chill again. Fiercer this time. Icy talons grip my chest. I swivel my head, my eyes searching for another hiding place … corridors, doorways. But no pools of darkness line this landing corridor, no convenient corners. Just two chairs and a carved wooden table.

I hesitate, my eyes still scanning. Natasha yanks at my arm and then I'm hurrying down the corridor toward the chairs, pulling her with me. I drop to my knees and slide under the table. Natasha does the same. We crouch side by side, our backs to the wall.

And wait.

The chill grows savagely. Again, I glimpse the face of Death hovering before me. Skull-like, its mouth cavernous, the dark eyes searching, searching …

I squeeze my eyes shut, focusing desperately on blanking my mind. The frost-like chill creeps up my legs, my back. It's as if I'm being frozen to the wall. I take a shallow breath and grope for calm.

And still the chill builds … and my eyes fly open. I can't help it. From under the table, the red carpet shines like blood, and the religious paintings shift on the facing wall – peasants reaching up toward angelic figures, rays of sunshine dancing among silver-lined clouds.

And then brown shoes appear, cream trousers, and the air freezes in my lungs. My pulse roars as legs sweep past us in a flowing gait, entirely silent. No sounds, no reverberation. It's as if my senses are failing in the growing chill. And as before in the priest's pulpit, I feel a strange force tugging at my limbs, pulling me out of our hiding place.

Yanking my knees tighter to my chest and scrunching my eyes shut again, I try to imagine it all away, to focus on the sensation of hope – an impossible spark, flitting somewhere in the darkness …

Fingers touch my chest. I open my eyes.

Natasha's staring at me, her face deathly pale, her jaw set. I grind the heels of my palms into my eye sockets. Natasha squeezes my wrist, swivels, and silently creeps out from under the table.

The corridor's empty again. The winding staircase lies just ten feet away down the corridor. I take a slow breath, stand, and keep my back to the wall as I move. A part of me can't believe we survived two pursuers. No way could we endure a third.

I approach the edge of the stairwell. A faint sound comes from beyond it, a tapping muffled by soft fabric but growing louder. And strangely familiar. I set my feet, tense my arms, and peer around the corner.

A flash of black fabric, of white skin, right in front of me. My chest constricts, and I leap backward.

The priest's grey hair stands up, wild, on top of his head. His face is ashen, his eyes wide. I blink back at him. Natasha grabs his hand and helps him around the corner, out of sight of the stairwell.

"It's us, Father," she whispers in his ear.

The old man nods, staring between us, and the tension flares into heat at my core, my shoulders tightening.

"What the hell are you *doing* here?" I hiss.

"I came to find you," the priest says, gazing blankly over my shoulder. "You were a long time. I got scared for you."

The heat rises and scorches my insides, my brain railing at the impossibility of getting *three* people out of the building now, one of whom is decrepit and partially blind.

"But how'd you get here?" I snap.

"I took the stairs," he says.

I open my mouth, but Natasha silences me with a look.

The priest's features set. "I go where I'm directed," he says firmly, some of the colour returning to his cheeks. He lifts his walking stick. "It is God's will."

My fingers curl.

Natasha grips my arm. "*Jake,*" she says and shakes me, staring into my eyes. "It means that the stairs *are* the way out."

I try a deep breath and force my gaze from the priest onto her.

"We have to get down there," she says. "*Now.*"

I swallow and nod. "Okay," I say. "Let's—"

The sensation flares anew – the awful chill at the very centre of my being. The strange humming sound drifts up the stairwell. I whirl around to face the corridor behind and eye the table. Too damn small for us all. No fucking place to hide. Again, the heat blazes inside me.

I shove the priest down the corridor. "You bloody led them here," I snap and sprint past him away from the stairs, the sound of my footsteps so loud in my ears. My eyes scour the corridor as I go, searching for some kind of nook to hide three people.

Natasha's hurried footsteps and the old man's tapping stick follow behind. And the corridor darkens with every step. Closed doors grow out of the blackness along both sides, the few flickering candles failing to illuminate the growing gloom.

Then more footsteps impinge on my awareness. This time from straight ahead, coming down a stairwell at the far end of the corridor.

I skid to a halt.

The shadows deepen; the footsteps grow louder from up ahead, the humming sound from behind. And the chill continues to build inside me. I spin, my eyes darting from side to side, from the central stairwell to the steps at the end of the corridor, visions coming of our pursuers closing in from both directions. I back up against the wall.

Something digs into my spine. A handle, the contours of a

door around it. I whirl and glance down at the floor. Little or no light leaks from above the sill, the room most likely dark beyond. And empty, too?

My mind stampedes. My gut constricts. And for an instant, I try to still my thoughts, to peel back the veil, to wait for any revelations. But it's impossible, all calm, all insight trampled by my galloping dread.

I grip the handle and turn, believing it will open, believing there's a way out of the corridor. The lock clicks, the door swings inward, and I stumble into the room.

Natasha drags the priest after her. And I ease the door closed behind us as silently as I can. Then I start to back away from it.

Perspiration coats my sides, and I can't help picturing the handle swivelling and figures barrelling in through the door.

The priest and Natasha retreat at my side. The edges of the door stand out in the darkness, flanked by plain wood panels, and the shadows sway slightly.

I feel myself frowning and peer closer at the shifting areas of shade. They dance in the subtle illumination. I spin around, my insides plummeting, and my eyes scan the space for the source of the flickering light.

A fire. It burns in a grand fireplace to our side, broad and majestic, the only source of light in the room. Facing it stands a scarlet armchair.

I stop dead.

The figure looks ridiculous sitting there. His knees reach his head, and his matted hair dangles down the upholstered back of the chair. He remains entirely still, as if unaware of our presence, merely intent on the book he holds between his massive hands.

My body trembles, an awful understanding beginning to grow inside me. My gaze shoots to the door behind.

"It's locked," the giant says, not even looking up. He turns a page with his enormous fingers.

The possibilities race around my head, visions coming of forcing the door.

"There are three others behind it." The giant's voice is deep, like a landslide. Unrecognisable from the high, soft tones he used in the stone circle. "You'd never get through."

I feel a knife carving a cold, hollow ache in my chest as I realise the trap I've delivered us into.

## 50

"COME IN," the giant's voice rumbles. He turns the corner of a page in his book with a gigantic thumb.

My legs move. Natasha's and Father Thomas's too. We shuffle across the wooden floorboards toward the centre of the room, the hollow in my chest deepening with every step. The metallic scent hangs thick in the air, the static charge building again.

My head swivels. The room's seventy feet broad and longer still. Aside from the fireplace and the giant's chair, there's no other furniture, none of the rest of the building's opulence.

The floorboards are bare and unvarnished, and plain wood panels cover three of the walls. There's another closed door to the side of the fireplace, and crosshatched windows span the length of the wall opposite the corridor, the glass opaque, the glow of night barely visible behind.

Are we still on the fifth floor? Maybe higher? Again, my vision swims with just the thoughts, the same strange sense of vertigo making my head spin.

I try to breathe to keep my chest from shaking. But the awful chill bites at my flesh, scouring ever deeper under my skin. Something's approaching. I can feel it.

Natasha presses herself into my back, the priest shivers at her side, and my own thoughts run rampant. We've been played, enticed into this building, and then funnelled into this room. Flies in a web. And now the monster approaches.

Again, my eyes rake the space. No fixtures, no furnishings, no weapons of any sort. And the giant sits there, calmly in his chair.

Qetesh sent us to him, and the idea that she might have betrayed us pierces me like a shard in my heart.

I reach behind and feel for Natasha's fingers, pushing the phone directly into her hand. "Maybe they'll just take me," I whisper over my shoulder.

Her fingers go rigid around the phone, and she tries to shove it back. But I whip my hand away and then spin my head back around.

The giant gives a growl-like sigh and rises slowly to his feet. It's like watching a mountain emerge from the ground. His head almost touches the ceiling as it turns, and his hair and beard tumble down his huge shoulders and chest, small bones matted among the strands.

The childlike fascination, the kindness he showed in the highlands, are all gone. He stares at each of us, his eyes shining with a malicious joy. The cold deepens further. Frost coats the walls, extracting every drop of moisture from the air. Another shudder rolls through me.

The side door swings open, and two figures enter. Our pursuers – a woman and man, each sporting the same bland expressions, the same bizarre clothes: a floral print dress on the woman and a polo shirt on the man. She glides to the main door while he positions himself at the giant's side by the fireplace. And their eyes pull at my attention, the same fathomless dark.

I bite down on my lip, fixing my gaze on the floor before me, and concentrate fiercely on keeping it there.

An icy wind blows. It sweeps the room, courses around and through my body, biting at my skin and bones. I grit my teeth to stop them rattling. And a third figure enters, the fire dying, the light being sucked away, the few colours in the room replaced by darkening greys. With trembling limbs, I focus harder on keeping my gaze averted. Yet still, I feel it being drawn upward.

A web of flickering shadow hovers there – Death. Somehow I know it – a giant void to the side of the fireplace, as if that part of the room has been rubbed out. It resembles a nest of black snakes smothering a human body; feet, hands and head occasionally visible around the thrashing oval of darkness. And that face – the cave-like eyes, the yawning mouth, all made of the writhing shapes. It sears deep into my brain.

Natasha presses herself ever closer, huddling into my back, while I see the same wall of wind from my dream in the hospital, the same inevitable end drawing ever nearer. The faintest heat flares inside, sparks in a blizzard. I tense my neck and manage to rip my gaze aside.

The giant stares down at me and raises his massive arms at his sides. "So, this truly is *it*?" he says, his deep voice a mixture of mocking and disbelief. "Your whole band, your entire ensemble?"

I find myself shaking my head, my mind fantasising images of fucking armies on their way. But in the next instant, memories assail me of my first day with Mandem – being bullied, beaten, all alone.

No one else is ever coming for me.

The giant barks a laugh. "Oh, how simple you make it," he says, an edge of disappointment in his tone. "Building your trust, playing upon your petty emotions. For our esteemed scientists, it was their *pride*."

The giant's dark eyes glow as he turns his head and gazes through the window.

"All that was needed was to furnish them up with the best equipment," he goes on. "While whispering tales of global terrorist threats, inviting them to splice abominable diseases, and to fabricate cures too, and all for the promise of great riches, for the sake of king and country." He pauses and smiles. "Of course, they never did get around to that cure."

That's it. No cure. No hope. My throat goes bone dry.

"And you, little thief," the giant says, gazing back down at me, "even easier than expected. *One* clue was all it took." He lifts a single finger. "And you did all our work, rallied what scant allies you possessed, and went to chase it down."

*Fuck.* My mouth falls open. They didn't know the location of the white-haired guy's body. They followed us there and then disposed of the bodies, the guy's briefcase, all the evidence.

The giant grins. "And fortuitously, you survived," he says. "For it appears there *are* more of you." He flicks his gaze over my shoulder toward the priest. "But ultimately, I knew you'd come."

His grin widens into a vicious smile and again, the vision he gave me in the circle of stones flashes through my mind – this building with its saints and angels, its glowing entrance. My whole body stiffens.

The giant sighs again and then stretches his huge arms to the ceiling.

"And now I believe we've indulged your visit long enough," he says. "Because there really *is* no one else coming. Is there?" He pauses, eyebrow raised. Then his eyes glint. "For it's vital we root out *all* of you."

My gut constricts as the giant walks toward the side door while the implications of his final words are like metal bands around my neck, gagging, choking. The giant ducks his shoulder under the jamb and extends his arm through the door. I find myself leaning toward him, my pulse racing.

The giant nods at me and yanks a woman into the room. I feel a blade pass through my heart. He grips her by her hair and hauls her maliciously across the floor. The giant holds my gaze the entire way. That same cruel grin on his lips.

Qetesh, her long, flowing dress tattered and torn. Her

hands claw at the giant's wrists. She struggles to keep her feet. He slams her against the chair and she collapses. Then he drags her the rest of the way and dumps her, head bowed, on the wooden floor before us, ten yards away.

A shiver runs over her bare shoulders. She glances up, lip cut, body battered. And in that bleak place, her beauty still shines.

Warmth and love swell inside me. And before I know it, I'm stumbling toward her, my eyes brimming with tears. I feel ready to give up my life in that moment, no question, to surrender it all so that she might live.

A sound like thunder stops me in my tracks. The giant laughs, on and on, enormous hands holding a bigger chest.

The absurdity of it all, a worm loving a queen.

The giant stares at me again. "See what you've *done?*" he says, his hand raised toward the goddess at his feet.

I can barely look. The truth spears me. She spoke to us, helped us, gave us information. And she'll probably die for it.

The giant lowers his gaze at Qetesh. "*You,*" he hisses.

She glares back at him, her eyes as narrow as knives.

"You sent them to *me?*" he almost shouts. "Of all of us, in all the realms, you really thought I'd betray *him?*" A mixture of wild rage and incredulity shine in his eyes. "*Are you insane?*"

Gabriel. The master architect. I feel glacial winds claiming my chest.

Qetesh snarls, her lips drawn back over gleaming teeth. "Do *you* think I didn't know?" she says.

He frowns at that and takes a tiny step back.

Qetesh pushes herself to her knees and stares defiantly up at him. "I knew you were complicit, that you'd gift them what they needed," she says.

Then she glances at me. I brace myself for a look full of fear, of anger. But there's none of that. Simple tenderness shines in her eyes. Beauty, as always. And love. All mixed with a knowing determination, a steely grit. My knees quiver.

"They will overcome," she continues, her gaze still fixed on me.

Currents battle inside – warmth and ice – my body shaking more, the weakness growing in my limbs, desperate questions coming … *What the hell can I do?*

The giant glances at us. "They are insects!" he says and flicks his hand. "Simple-minded, naive."

I find myself nodding and scrunch my eyes shut, a weight yanking me down to the floor, the guilt for prompting *all* of this.

I sense heat, a burning stare. My eyes fly open. Qetesh is still gazing at me, confidence shining in her gaze.

"Yet Gabriel picked him out," she says, addressing the giant. "I do not think that was a random act. No." She shakes her head. "A change is coming. This is *all* intended."

I shiver.

Qetesh glances up at the giant. "You cannot prevent this," she says. "None of you can."

The giant's massive hand blurs as he slaps her, hard. The impact reverberates like a gunshot, and Qetesh is flung backward onto her hands.

I leap toward her. And the giant fixes me with a glare, eyebrow raised, daring me to take another step.

Qetesh thrusts herself back up to face him. Blood drips from her mouth.

"After thousands of years of rule," he spits back at her, "these will be your *last* moments."

"Yes." Qetesh nods, her eyes burning. "Perhaps. But it will be worth it. You will see in the end."

I stare at her, my mind yelling at the madness. And then, for a moment, I'm transported … back to the club, the glimpse she gifted me of her pain, an ocean of grief and despair. Wrenched from her homeland, turned into a plaything, forced to beg for scraps of devotion. A lifetime of torture. Lifetimes of it. Yet she's willing to sacrifice herself.

The weight crushes my chest and grips my mind. My

arms shake, the same questions screaming about what to do, ideas coming around using the shimmering world, the power behind the veil. But my doubts shriek like a cacophony of crows.

Death bears down on her. A six-foot black hole, sucking away existence, its surface writhing with millions of the angry snakes. Flashes of the inhabited pursuer emerge again around the edges – a foot, a hand, fingers gripping a vicious-looking knife.

The blade sweeps toward Qetesh, and it's as if the darkness is holding it, steering it. I can sense Death's excitement, can almost smell it. The light dims once more, and the giant seizes Qetesh under the arms, lifting her up like she's livestock.

My breath comes hard, fast. I picture myself darting forward, getting in the way, giving up my life … But I feel chained to the spot.

And in that instant, I'm back in my childhood home – the gang invading it, my mother stripped from me – that feeling of numbing impotence building at my core.

"Immortality won't save you here," I hear the giant growling at Qetesh. But the words barely register. I can only stare on.

Qetesh gazes directly back at me. Calm in her eyes, radiance against the growing shadow. A single tear winds its way down the curve of her jaw.

I gaze back, my whole body shaking. Tears pool at the corners of my eyes.

Qetesh opens her mouth. But the knife is too quick. The darkness slashes it across her throat. Blood sprays. Her eyes dull and roll backward. Her body goes limp.

And she's truly gone.

# 51

My legs crumple. The pain eats away at my insides, gouging me out. I stagger forward one step, another, my eyes fixed on Qetesh. One pursuer glides over – the woman. She reaches down and hauls Qetesh's beautiful body toward the side door.

I feel only devastation, any heat within me now ash, the cold of the room even fiercer as her glow's been stripped away. Qetesh – the manifestation of radiance, of vitality, of love – now being dragged like a slab of meat toward the door.

As she vanishes, the giant fixes his eyes on me again and smiles widely. "I expect we need a replacement," he says, cocking his head. "Do you not think?"

Then he shifts his gaze to Natasha. He looks her up and down and nods. That awful smile animates his lips. "Want to become an angel, my dear?"

My gaze darts to the side. Natasha's eyes are huge. Her face bone-white. Her worst nightmare. The fate she fled her home to escape.

"No, no, *no.*"

She mumbles the words like some kind of warding spell. A slave, not just for one lifetime but for a thousand years. She backs away.

The giant smiles once more and then gives a tiny nod. The male pursuer sweeps silently toward us. Again, the man moves so effortlessly – total fluidity, total power.

I push forward to get in between them. And the man shoves me back, sending me stumbling, his touch burning cold.

I can only watch as the guy grabs Natasha by her robes and pulls her to the giant's side. She fumbles the phone from her pocket, grips it with shaking hands, and hides it in front of her.

The giant glances at the priest. "And you. We've spied you, little man of God, nosing around," he spits. "We didn't know where you'd scuttled off to hide, but we do now." He leans toward us. "Your *arrogance*." His voice trembles with rage. "Your death will not be so quick."

He smirks, and Death glides toward us. Arctic winds tear around the room, pulling at my limbs. I start to turn, but the priest's already shuffling out from behind me, his tapping stick echoing on the wooden floorboards. He stumbles toward the agitating darkness. Ancient and feeble, yet still he holds his head high.

Though he probably can't see the windows, the old man seems to sense them. He stops ten feet from Death and turns to face the opaque, crosshatched glass, as if feeling God's presence beyond in those last moments.

"He will *enjoy* you," the giant says, his grin growing wider.

Death circles the priest, the writhing void moving ever closer to him.

The awful chill seizes my core, the same questions shrieking now ... *What the fuck to do?* I try to kick-start my thoughts, to plan, but my mind's a stuttering wreck.

The shadows in the room deepen, as if its walls have become the limits of the world. No space for anything but darkness. The old man's body visibly quakes. Death spirals closer, the pursuer's hands and feet barely visible, the shadows twisting more wildly around them.

The priest dips his head and lowers his sightless eyes to the floor. He brings his hands together in prayer, his walking stick between them. Still facing the windows, his lips move in a silent invocation. *Is this all still God's will?*

Death halts and hovers in front of him. The air hums with the static charge, and my hair stands on end. Dark shapes stretch toward the old man. My pulse hammers, and I glance across at Natasha. I spy the horror in her eyes, her trembling lips.

The chill deepens. Death's tendrils writhe faster – magnetic, mesmerising – and I feel the veil peeling back from my senses, the shimmering world asserting itself. Time slows and stretches. And while I'm desperate to look away, I feel my gaze drawn, as if I'm being forced to witness everything – every fucking moment.

There's no knife this time. Instead, the possessed figure's hands reach out. And beyond the veil, I can make out every detail of the pursuer's thumbs as they creep toward the priest's head, toward his dull eyes.

Natasha strains to avert her gaze. The giant stares on and smiles.

The mass of darkness thrashes ever more fiercely as it closes in on the priest's bowed head. Shadows. Hands. Fingers. Eyes.

With his head still down, Father Thomas clasps his walking stick tighter in his hands, the only thing keeping him upright. The thumbs hover over the old man's eye sockets, poised, tongues of shadow licking hungrily behind.

*No. No.* Still, time stretches. Again, I fight to look away.

A flash of movement. The priest grips his stick and rams it upward, into the mass of the writhing darkness.

I hear a sickening crunch, and the black tendrils shoot back, revealing the possessed pursuer's head – a man – the thin wooden end of the priest's stick having smashed into the guy's throat.

Father Thomas jerks the stick back down. The pursuer's chin rockets forward, a gurgling escaping from his lips. And the priest thrusts his bowed head forward like a battering ram, smashing it into the pursuer's nose.

There's an explosion of blood and bone, and the possessed figure staggers backward toward the crosshatched glass, the dark shadows teeming around his lower body like a swarm of angry bees.

I just stare. It all took less than a second. The images ran together. Even with my mind blank, with time slowed, the priest's movements were so quick they were barely discernible.

The black forms fight to regain possession of the pursuer's body. And the priest keeps moving. He seems different … taller? Somehow straight and lean, his stick abandoned on the floor. The images register too fast for understanding. As the pursuer tries to regroup, Father Thomas swivels his hip and kicks out with enormous force, catching the guy with his foot full in the chest, and the impact sends the pursuer crashing through the opaque window.

Glass shatters. The body soars out of the building and into the night air. Gravity takes hold. He starts to plummet, the writhing void thrashing madly around him. His hands claw vainly at the air as he disappears from view.

Then comes a roar. Wind gusts around me like arrows of ice. The nest of black snakes hurtles back through the window and into the room. It speeds by my arm, almost sending me sprawling, while the smell of cordite assails my throat.

The fingers of Death take possession of the female pursuer by the fireplace, entering her mouth like a dark river and coalescing around her body. She becomes a sphere of writhing darkness and sweeps toward the priest and me.

The giant growls at her side and bears down on us as well,

thirty feet away. Natasha strains against the male pursuer holding her.

And I just stare on at it all.

The priest stands poised in between, ten feet from me. He leaps in my direction.

"Go!" Natasha screams, the sound stretched behind the veil. Her fingers arc upward, and I watch every movement in slowed time. She throws something black and small.

The phone.

It soars toward me over the giant's head. And all the while our enemies sweep in our direction like thundering waves. I tear my gaze from them, glance upward, raise an arm, and open my hand.

In the corner of my vision, I spy the priest's whirling body, his arm rotating at speed like some kind of windmill, aimed right at my torso. Even so, I keep all my attention on the phone.

I reach and catch it. My fingers grip the plastic casing just as the priest's arm smashes into my chest. The force flings me backward, and the priest wrenches me toward the broken window behind, his arm still across my torso, pushing hard.

I find my gaze fixed over the priest's shoulder while my legs stagger rearward. I spy Death and the giant still advancing on me. Plus Natasha, standing in the male pursuer's grip by the fireplace, her face like snow. Trapped. And behind me … the wind whips at my back, the drop beckoning beyond.

"No!"

A strange sound. My own voice.

The priest grips my arm with his opposite hand. I plant my feet to resist but still feel my body yanked around, toward the window, away from Natasha.

"No!" I yell louder.

And now in front of me, emptiness pulls – the open night sky – the splintered window only a few feet away, its ledge a foot or so off the floor.

"*Jump!*" the priest yells at my side.

The idea flares and dies in my mind. I simply try to find my balance at his side, but my feet slip on broken glass, causing me to stumble. I reach instinctively for the window frame with both hands, striving to prevent myself from sprawling forward.

Fingers grasp my shoulder – the grip like iron – and I feel myself being lifted and hurled through the gaping hole in the glass. Out into the night.

## 52

FLOATING. Falling. The wind howls in my ears as I tumble down, feet first, time still slowed. My brain scrambles to fathom the sight of the nightscape ahead, the blurred shapes of office buildings and twinkling lights. I feel vaguely aware of the priest plummeting several feet above me.

*He threw us out of a fucking window.*

My mind churns. I can't compute. My limbs flail wildly at the air, my balance pitching forward as my body plunges ever more parallel with the ground. The wind presses hard against my eyes, but it can't stop me gawking at everything below.

The ground. It's bloody hundreds of feet down. The sense of vertigo makes my head swirl, and the bottom drops out of my stomach. Thoughts scream in my mind, notions that it should be the fourth floor, not the damn fortieth, as the matchstick streetlights hurtle toward me.

*I'm going to die. I'm going to die …*

I feel something in my hand. The phone. *Natasha.* My fingers grip the casing, and I focus on the sensation like it's some kind of tether in the madness.

I spy a neighbouring rooftop eighty feet below, the horizontal gap ten feet. I picture myself throwing the phone up onto it as I plummet past, conserving the evidence for someone to find. I reach out, ready to launch the phone, when a hand seizes my shoulder.

The priest is beside me, somehow tugging me upward. Up and across. Toward the neighbouring rooftop. The wind begins rushing faster upward, cradling my body. The air is viscous, like I'm swimming not falling.

Then the memories of the shimmering world strike me so hard that my brain hurts – my experiences behind the veil, the solidity of the air, Natasha and me jumping off the marble railing, the air holding us up, gravity somehow shifting.

I fight to clear my mind, to remember the experiences, to *believe*. And I cling to the possibility like a tree root atop a crumbling cliff.

The priest continues to tug me up and to the side. The wind presses up against every inch of my body. The roof of the neighbouring building barrels upward – fifty feet away – the horizontal gap now only five feet, getting smaller …

Plunging down, I focus hard on drawing back the veil, on slowing our fall. But my doubts are legion, stabbing at my mind. And I still feel myself plummeting fast through the air.

Forty feet. Thirty.

I battle to shut out the thoughts, to concentrate on my memory of the cradling air, on believing I can float with every fibre of my being. The wind pushes up a little harder, and my momentum slows just a fraction.

Twenty. Fifteen.

The neighbouring rooftop angles away from us, shiny metal plates extending across its surface with small ridges visible in between. Solid, hard, and still approaching way too damn fast.

I grit my teeth and count on as I grasp onto each number and focus madly on feeling the thickness of the air. Try so fucking hard to believe—

The priest's grip on my shoulder tightens like a vice, and I feel my fall almost slowed to a halt. The sky wheels as I'm thrown upward and toward the neighbouring building. I spin through the air.

The sound of a collision happens somewhere behind me. Then the rooftop smashes into my side, scattering my breath.

I bounce off one of the shiny plates and land again on my stomach. Then I slip across the roof's slick surface, my lungs taking in wild breaths. Three feet from the edge, I manage to grip the slick metal and barely halt myself.

Lying there, my back screams, my lungs fight against weights. I experiment with moving my legs, my arms. I go to roll over but then stop.

The priest. Images come of the inevitable devastation behind me. The old man threw me upward to soften my landing and then took what remained of the impact, crashing himself into the roof. Nausea seizes my stomach, and while my back tenses to lift my head, I don't move.

A hand grips my collar. "Come," a voice says, firm and clipped. And I'm heaved effortlessly to my feet.

I try to glance over my shoulder, but the priest pushes me toward the roof's edge.

"Clear your mind," Father Thomas orders gently. "Focus on the solidity of the air. *Have faith.*"

"Wait—" I start.

And the bottom drops out of my world again. The priest shoves me off the sloping roof, and we swim in open space.

I glance down. Another rooftop, flat this time, and only ten feet below. As before, time slows, and though the priest tempers our fall, the impact still sends shooting pain up my legs.

I straighten and blink.

The new rooftop's twenty yards square with a fire exit located right in the middle. And there's no pause. Limping slightly, the priest stalks to the door, kicks it in, and leads me down a set of stairs.

We descend the remaining storeys of the building via a

stairwell and emerge through an alarmed fire door at street level.

The priest turns his back on the shrill beeping and strides away down a narrow pathway between two office blocks. I hurry to catch up with the man as he flows along side streets and meanders between towering buildings, out into the night and away.

He doesn't let up for a second.

## 53

THE PRIEST USHERS me into a cramped attic room. The ceiling slopes from an inch above my head down to the floor. Remnants of insulation droop from the occasional beam, their outlines just visible in the light that filters in through cracks in the roof. The room's a mere ten feet wide but much deeper, the far end invisible in the darkness.

The priest shuts the door behind me. And I stagger to a halt, stopping for the first time since leaving Gabriel's headquarters. My legs sway, and I almost tumble forward.

"This is one of my places," he says. "We should be safe here."

My thoughts immediately dart back to Qetesh. Dead. And Natasha. Gone. Taken. The sensation's a stabbing pain in my chest, and I take a shaky breath, shoving the thoughts away.

The priest pads over to rummage through a large cardboard box. I slump down against the wall, ignoring the cracked bricks digging into my spine.

He yanks out a water bottle from the box. "Here, Jacob," he says, offering the bottle to me. "Drink. You'll feel better."

I don't move, instead just staring blindly ahead.

The priest swivels back to the box and then tosses the bottle over his shoulder. It arcs down perfectly toward me.

I'm forced to grab it out of the air a few inches from my face. The visible side of his mouth widens in a faint smile.

The pain inside morphs into rising heat. "Who *are* you?" I snap.

The priest straightens up. "You mean this?" he says, indicating his face and body.

Then his eyes dull, and his mouth falls slack. He stares blankly over my shoulder, and the familiar image of the old Father Thomas emerges. His shoulders curve, his entire body stooping, and his hands shake. He frowns, and the lines on his face multiply. The man gains forty years in a matter of seconds.

"It is not so difficult to alter your appearance," he says in his old slow and trembling voice. "You change your facial expressions … your posture … your movements … and people will fill in the blanks." He raises a shaking finger. "We see what we expect to see."

Then he straightens, and the image of the new priest returns – younger-looking and stronger. He pulls out a wooden crate from the side, lays a blanket from the box on top and sits down on it, his injured leg extended in front.

I swallow. "You're an angel?"

He barks a laugh. "No, no," he says and shakes his head. "Simply an ordinary man."

The heat flares. "*An ordinary man?*" I say.

Father Thomas lets out a deep sigh. "The last in a long line of an order," he says. "One that's almost as old as the angels themselves."

I just stare back at him.

"Let me explain," he says, settling back on his crate. "In ancient times, there were those who wanted to democratise the power of belief, to unleash it in every man and woman." The carved lines deepen across his cheeks. "But the angels took it, stole humanity's divine essence. And so we fought. But, of course, my lineage couldn't compete. The more devotion the angels built, the more powerful they became." His voice softens. "They worked to wipe us out, to obliterate any chance that faith could empower the masses."

"Yet you survived," I say. "How?"

"Sacrifice, pragmatism, and luck," the priest says. "Many centuries ago, my order made survival our key concern so we could pass along our knowledge, our mission. And so they decreed that there could be only one mentor and one student. Any more would attract too much attention from the angels. Each mentor was tasked with identifying an apprentice, to whom they'd pass on their abilities and the sacred task of survival. The angels were simply too powerful for anything else."

"And their power comes from devotion?" I say.

He nods.

"Then how'd you throw us out of a fucking building?" I snap. Sensations sear my mind of our fall, of the air somehow viscous around me, pushing me upward. "If you're no angel, nobody believes in you."

He smiles at me. "Jacob," he says, "I've tried to tell you – the only thing that controls your abilities is your *own* beliefs."

"*What?*" I ask. "But you said power comes from the belief of others."

"*It does*," the priest says, his eyes gleaming. "The things we believe to be true are hugely *influenced* by others. Look at society." He raises both arms as if to contain the world. "Our beliefs are moulded by what the people around us believe, by the beliefs of our families, communities, nations. The angels *use* this. They've anchored their faith about themselves to the faith of others. Many millions of people believe in their powers, and that becomes their reality because they choose it to, because it serves them, and has for millennia."

"That doesn't explain what you can do," I say. "You don't have these cultural beliefs."

"You're right," the priest says. "On the contrary, being mere mortals, almost everything anyone tells us enforces normality, determines all the things that are and aren't possible for us. It's society's glue." He sits up straighter. "The strength of mind that we need to move beyond these thoughts is immense. And then we have to stretch our self-belief so we might be more than others make us. We cultivate our faith." He grins at me. "You've been doing this since we first met."

I shake my head. I can't stop myself.

"Jacob, you've witnessed *first-hand* what's possible," he says. "We can even bend a law like gravity … with enough preparation and practice. My order considers it the ultimate accomplishment. The leap of faith."

The leap of faith. Qetesh's words down by the starry pool. Memories stir, the pain augments. And again, I focus intently on the broken brickwork digging into my back.

"I learned it from my mentor," the priest goes on. "Built my faith by observing him bend physical laws – speed, strength, time – day in and day out, for what felt like life-times. Whereas you were gifted an experience of the angelic realm in a *single moment* …" He raises a finger. "And somehow it seems to have taken hold in you."

He shakes his head as if amazed.

"And now *you* know the potential, the possibility, how much richer life could be," he says. "Can you imagine what would happen if people everywhere could reclaim this birthright? Can you imagine what would be possible? All angels stripped of their power, leaving the masses to claim theirs."

He sits there, his eyes shining. The same passion I saw back in his kitchen, Natasha at my side.

"Why did you not tell us the truth?" I ask, my voice barely a whisper.

"Think back to when we met," he says. "Would you have believed me if I had?"

I shut my eyes for an instant and lean further back against the wall behind. "Maybe not," I breathe.

"The truth is that I didn't know about the disease, about Gabriel's plan," the priest says.

"But you knew Qetesh," I say.

Father Thomas nods. "I knew *of* her … of her situation, her despair," he says. "And I believed she'd be moved by you, that she would try to help."

The pain pierces my heart. And I can't banish the image of her bruised and broken body, of her being dragged up by her hair, her throat cut.

The priest fixes me with his gaze. "You have to believe me, Jacob," he says. "I did what I did because I believed it was my role. Remember, there's a power greater than these angels, a reason for all that's happening." He clasps his hands together. "It's not overt and controlling but subtle and guiding. I believe this is *all* God's hand. That eventually we will all be connected with the divine spark that exists in us … with the power of our faith and what it makes us capable of. To become *true* reflections of God. To realise that divinity isn't outside us."

He leans forward on his crate.

"This is why you're here, why God delivered you to me," he continues. "I shunned the vow of my order. I took no apprentice, for I believe God spoke to me, instructed me to follow the angels and wait. I believe it's been my role to place you on the path. This has been the task I've been waiting for my entire life."

I sense a growing weight on my shoulders, my chest, a building pressure, the skin of my arms and neck scratchy. I shift against the attic wall and grind my back into the fractured bricks, my body desperate to move, to get out.

"I led us into that trap," I say. "*Me.*"

And with the thought, a crushing ache swells at my core, the feeling so familiar. I see myself again in my childhood home. Desperately fighting to make the gang leave. Persuading my mother. Pleading with her. And failing.

Constantly failing. The ache grows. I can't banish it. And I let my head fall forward and close my eyes.

"Qetesh believed in you," the priest says. "Don't belittle her memory."

My eyes fly open, and I shoot my head back up, trying to focus on his image sitting there.

"Qetesh is – *was* – an angel," he says, his gaze stern. "She was moved by what she saw in you, was willing to give up everything for it. Don't think she made the decision lightly."

The words cut like razors, Qetesh's legacy my responsibility.

"What the hell am I supposed to *do?*" I ask, the words tumbling out.

The priest takes a deep breath, and his gaze softens. "That's for you to discover," he says. "But know that it's no accident you're sitting there. None of it is."

"You keep saying that!" I slam my palm on the floorboards beside me. "These beings are fucking *angels.*"

The priest keeps his voice level. "There was a time, not long ago, when you didn't even *believe* in angels. *Now* look at you." He raises a hand. "Just as the Bible describes the angels, there are *countless* stories of the tyrannical being overthrown by the virtuous, of the weak overcoming the strong. You are David. They are Goliath."

I open my mouth. But the priest keeps going.

"There's *power* in these stories, immense power." He wags a finger. "Do you think Gabriel's disease is an accidental plot?" He raises an eyebrow. "It'll leave a world of the pious saved from the deluge of sin, just like the biblical story of the flood. Do you think the Puritans won't make the connection?"

He continues to gaze at me as if he's waiting for a response. I keep quiet.

"They'll see divine intervention," he goes on. "It'll *double* its impact on devotion, at least! Gabriel knows the power of story, of belief. He's a master."

"And what the hell am I?" I say. "A fucking thief. An insect. A *nothing*."

"Gabriel doesn't believe that," the priest says. "He might never admit it, but he fears your importance, that you might upset his plans. Otherwise, why seek to trap you, why spend the energy? At some level, Gabriel *believes*." He nods. "And we can *use* this."

I shake my head again and press my palms hard into my temples.

Then Father Thomas leans toward me, almost uncomfortably close. "Faith is *power*, Jacob," he says. "You have to decide what to believe." His eyes blaze even brighter. "Have faith, build it, cultivate it. And incredible things become possible."

Still he holds my gaze. And I feel the pressure building inside me, the weight growing, the hum intensifying. Then the memories flare again – Qetesh held in the giant's grip, the words she spoke … *They will overcome*. And I can hear Natasha's voice in my ear, over and over … *Do the right thing*.

My ribs constrict, and I squeeze my eyes shut, focusing instead on Gabriel in the station. His blinding radiance. His effortless power. Impossible to beat.

Then a new memory creeps in – the nun, shoving me to safety, saving my life. Why?

It feels as if the pressure's going to split my head apart. The weight bears down on my shoulders, squashes me into the floorboards. I scramble up on numb feet and shove myself away from the crumbling brick wall. I stumble past the priest and deeper into the attic space, under the eaves and into darkness.

And there I stop. The smell of damp, of dust, and of old, forgotten things permeates my nose. I grip a rafter and scrunch my eyes shut again, trying to force my planning brain into action.

The cancer drug as dispersal mechanism. So clever. A high

price means the rich will become infected first, will infect more of their own.

I take a quick breath. Get out of the city. Maybe back up to the highlands? The prospect of freedom makes my pulse race. And Mandem won't track me there, not with the disease on the rampage. Maybe Gabriel, too.

I picture Natasha and Father Thomas around the kitchen table and imagine leaving them. That's okay. There have been so many lies. She doesn't care for me. For her, all that matters is her mission, her divine role. She won't …

My thoughts ebb and die. And a new stillness creeps in among the swirling motes of dust. I exhale slowly.

Natasha. Hell, it stings. The pain of her loss is like a barb in my heart, a needling in my brain. Again, I try to push away the sensations, to focus on what's next, my escape plan. But the image of her face keeps returning, the diner, that conversation. Her words play over in my mind …

*You think everyone is selfish, so you are selfish first, and so everyone becomes selfish, too. People can be generous, but you will never experience it.*

Then the memories shift, and I glimpse a figure sitting on my hospital bed … the dream … sunlight, the feeling of fingers through my hair. My mother.

*Shit.* All those years before. Me standing on the doorstep, my mother's eyes glassy and unseeing. Her turning away. Not pain in my chest then but agony … cutting, shredding. Worse than death. And then me leaving her. Never coming back.

The story I told myself back then, over and over – she abandoned you, craves only drugs, no longer cares – words I've repeated to myself ever since.

And Natasha. I picture her held prisoner by the giant's fireplace. It's the same belief again, the same words revolving around my head. *She doesn't care.*

And in that moment, the two sets of memories fuse in my

mind – my mother and Natasha – and for the first time, I glimpse it, the cycle I'm trapped in …

I never believe others care and so don't care for others.

I don't trust and so don't expect to be trusted.

And so it goes on.

I swivel back toward the priest, a strange tingling in my chest.

The cycle. It's got to end.

Now.

## 54

I coast the front tyres to the kerb and crank the handbrake. Through the windscreen, the darkness remains unbroken, all the lights in the housing estate windows still off.

I grab up my burner phone, jab the quick dial, and scramble between the seats into the back. Father Thomas picks up even before the first ring.

"I'm here," I whisper. "Got the van."

"Good, you're going to need it," the priest replies, his words quiet but distinct. "Give me a moment." Then the sound dies. The call on mute.

I scan the tools that I got with the stolen van, snatch up a screwdriver and pliers, and dump them in my pocket. Then I ease open the van's rear door, climb out, and shut it behind me.

A chill in the night air makes my skin tingle, and I hurry toward the edge of the estate.

The priest unmutes his call, a background crackle audible.

"You inside the centre?" I ask.

"Yes, and the cancer medication's here, already packed up and ready to go," the priest says. "And I've seen the batches. They're on crates, far too large to carry by hand. If Gabriel's going to replace a batch with the disease, he's going to need it replicated exactly. So you'll need the van to get the crate out."

My pulse starts to thump behind my ear. I reach the final corner and peer around it down the road I've driven by, the forlorn buildings stretching out on both sides, the city and wider world beyond. No one following.

I breathe deeply, swivel, and take in our target building, the location of the extra cross we found on the map in Gabriel's headquarters, the one right next to the priest's distribution centre.

It's fucking huge. Three storeys, the size and shape of a football field, and totally dark. No lights at all. In the obscured moonlight, it resembles a behemoth, ready to roll straight over me.

"Any sign?" Father Thomas asks.

I settle myself. "Can't be sure," I say, peering more closely at the building and trying to scan it for movement. But I can only make out its dark outline. "Not from this distance. You?"

"Puritan guards," the priest says.

My pulse speeds up.

"But they're just waiting around the edge of the centre," he continues. "I don't think they've made the switch yet. The cancer medication only arrived a couple of hours ago."

Images come of the photographs we took of the binder, the cancer treatment due to be shipped out to hospitals tomorrow or the next day. The window is *now*.

"Okay," I say. "Give me a sec."

I slink along the edge of the estate blocks toward the massive building, a hundred yards away.

All too soon, the cover of the apartments falls behind me, and I'm darting past old cars, many of them abandoned by the road. I keep my head low. But I'm still entirely visible from the front and side.

Eventually, the working streetlights fall away as well, and slowly my eyes adjust to the darkness. I pick out a massive fence around the building, built to keep people out, and a row of windows across the top floor. The reflection is dull, as if someone's painted them over. Plus, some kind of chimney sits above the lip of the roof – maybe an extractor flue.

Exactly what you'd expect on a laboratory.

I bring the phone to my lips and go to speak. But then I glimpse black shapes shifting, right at the fence line, and right at the edge of my vision. I whip my eyes to follow, but the image disappears.

Just like in the station.

I take a step forward and peer closer at the fence. Three figures turn the corner of the building, directly ahead of me. My spine goes rigid. They begin padding along its side, and they're each wearing the same monk-like uniform from Gabriel's headquarters, with long objects slung over their far shoulders. Guns. Large guns.

I scramble behind the nearest parked car, put my back to the bumper, and shrink down out of sight. Yet the familiar chill slinks beneath my skin. And there it is, the metallic scent.

"They're here," I whisper into the phone, my voice shaking and my thoughts automatically stilling as the veil starts to peel back.

And from nowhere, the image of Death materialises in the darkness before me, the skull-like face formed of the thrashing shapes. And a new level of chill grips my insides. I shudder.

"*Come,*" a disembodied voice sounds in my ears.

"Are you okay?" the priest asks.

I focus on his voice as I shake my head to clear it. The veil slips back into place, and the face disappears.

"Fine," I say.

Yet my thoughts jabber. Death. According to Father Thomas, an unembodied spirit, a being that possesses minions to exist – our pursuers, members of a centuries-old sect. Possessed or not, they have inhuman strength and can communicate with each other telepathically.

And somehow I've got to get inside the building, find the disease, and then drive the van in and out.

The breath leaks from my lungs.

"Are you sure you want to go through with this?" the priest asks.

And the idiocy of my plan yells loudly within me. I sent Father Thomas away. Insisted on splitting up. My logic seemed so damn foolproof in that attic room. I figure if this *is* intended, I've been chosen because of the entirety of who I am. Not only because of the veil, but because I'm a thief, too. And so this means working a con. The biggest of my life.

I squeeze my shoulders, flex my fingers, and then force conviction into my tone. "Yes," I say.

"Don't worry," the priest says. "Gabriel and his retinue – I'll get them out of there, just like you planned it. Your looka-like is here." The thief we recruited to act as my double. "But well out of harm's way. And I'll make just enough noise to make sure we're both noticed."

"Okay," I say, feeling the strength flowing into me with his words.

"This can work. You can do this," the priest says. "Give me two minutes."

I nod and force myself to spin and face the building. The Puritan guards have continued on their circuit, almost at the far corner, padding along the inside of the giant fence. There's no bloody way over that.

My gaze falls on the access road between the left-hand side of the building, invisible from where I am, and a massive gate – their way out and my way in. A huge padlock hangs from it. Easily lockable after they leave. And the priest's last words sound in my head ... *Give me two minutes.*

My adrenaline fires, and I abandon my cover to scurry toward the building. I try desperately to keep my feet light, being entirely out in the open, and with the guards still visible, ten feet from the corner.

I skid to a stop in front of the padlock and wait for the

345

guards to finally disappear. Then I grab the screwdriver from my pocket, jam it into the slot, and twist till it connects with the tumblers inside. I go to yank out the pliers when I hear a faint creaking noise from the building.

I glance up. The left-hand and shorter side of the building's visible now, along with a couple of shipping containers beyond. A wide set of bay doors spans almost the side's entire length. I strain to listen.

The bay doors start to lift, an inch at a time, engines growling behind them.

My heart gallops and questions scream … *Is this the crate of disease, or the force going after the priest?* Whichever, images bombard my mind of guards or pursuers barrelling down the road toward me.

I grab the pliers and clamp them on the end of the screwdriver, in full fucking view of the rising doors. I clench my teeth and wrench the screwdriver tip among the tumblers to break them, and a few seconds later the padlock's ruined.

The doors continue to lift, almost halfway up now.

My heads whips to and fro, my eyes scanning wildly for cover. A line of spindly trees starts twenty yards from the nearby corner of the fence. I throw myself toward them, both tools in hand.

Light from the opening bay doors bathes the concrete around me, and adrenaline's coursing through my veins now, my footsteps so fucking loud in my ears.

I dive under the spindly branches of the nearest tree and then swivel among the strewn rubbish to get my back against the narrow trunk.

A door on the nearside of the bay doors is already open, a figure emerging through it. Dark robes. Gun in hand. The guard hurries down the access road that curves through ninety degrees in front of me, running from the loading bay entrance to the gate in the fence.

The moon breaks the clouds and shines through the leaves above my head like a damn searchlight. I grab a nearby piece of ripped tarpaulin and begin tugging it over my body, but the scraping sound's so bloody loud.

The guard bustles closer, only thirty yards away. And I stop pulling, the tarpaulin only half covering me. Gusts of wind flutter it around my ears.

The guard reaches the gate and jabs a key into the padlock to undo it. The bay doors are two-thirds of the way up now while the low roar builds from underneath. Two vehicles approach the threshold, engines revving. I peer closer at the headlights. Definitely cars. The lights are too close to the ground to be anything big enough to transport the disease.

And while the guard continues to struggle with the lock, I peer past the cars to glimpse the building's insides, attempting to spy any sign of where they're keeping the disease. But it's nigh on impossible. My tree's diagonally away from the corner of the building. Hence, I'm staring into the loading bay from an angle. I can only make out the far wall and what looks like a series of scrawled symbols.

The guard abandons his efforts and dashes back into the building, returning with a set of bolt clippers to begin cutting feverishly at the lock. But his arms are shaking. He can't get a proper grip, can't break the chain. The car engines rev louder. And the guy's entire body trembles.

My own limbs shake. The awful chill is climbing my body now, crawling deeper under my skin. And my gut starts to twist.

Another figure materialises around the near corner of the building. One of Death's minions – a woman. She approaches with the same flowing movements, gliding right up to the open door to make way for …

The moonlight vanishes behind the clouds, the air suddenly still. And Death itself emerges through the open bay doors – a hovering void, an oval of absolute nothingness, dark snakes coiling angrily around its edge.

The chill seeps along the bones of my pelvis, my ribs, exuding toward my navel. And while every part of me yearns to scramble away, I concentrate fiercely on calming my thoughts while tensing every muscle in my body to remain still. Despite the chill, I can feel the sweat trickling down my sides.

The guard hunkers down over the lock, trembling more intensely and twisting ever more madly with the bolt cutters, making it even harder for himself. The black void glides toward him through the air, the female pursuer and another male in its wake. I can sense Death's hunger, its impatience.

It approaches the guard's shoulder. The guy's hands shake so badly he drops the bolt cutters. He leans over to grab them while the writhing shapes follow him down. The guard straightens as a hand darts out of the void and grabs his neck – which shatters on contact, bones surely crumbling to dust. The guard collapses like a puppet being dumped by his master, all the strings slack.

The cold scales my ribs, ice filling my chest. And I feel myself pressing backward into the tree.

The void moves forward to subsume the padlock, and the thick metal chain falls too. Like slicing butter. The male pursuer grabs the dead guard's leg and drags him out of the way of the gate while the woman yanks it open.

Engines growl like lions. And then one ... two ... and three sleek cars accelerate out of the building and speed along the curved road toward me. My pulse races, and I crouch there, waiting to be torn apart, eaten alive.

Tyres screech, and the cars race out of the gate and down the road toward the city, undoubtedly heading for the nearby distribution centre and Father Thomas.

My plan was to lure away Death, his minions, the giant, even Gabriel. But my eyes shoot back to the fence.

Death remains there, hovering by the gate, flanked by a pursuer on either side. And for an instant, the writhing face hovers in the air before me again, the cavernous eyes burning into mine. The strange chill burns my chest, and a numbness clouds my senses. Like in the church, I feel the entity pulling on my limbs and dragging me out of my hiding place.

I clamp my hands around my head – I can't help it – and the tarpaulin crinkles, the sound like gunshots to my ears. I scrunch my eyes shut and squeeze the sides of my head, my heart thumping hard. And I hold myself like that for what feels like an age.

Finally, the sense of cold ebbs a fraction, and I risk opening my eyes. The hovering void's gliding back toward the building, the female pursuer at its side. The male follows behind, the bolt cutters held in one hand, the dead guard's leg in the other. He drags the body all the way to the bay doors, and all three disappear beyond.

Then the doors inch down, a diminishing sliver of the loading bay visible through them as they close. The gate remains open, only twenty yards away.

I blink at it, my brain shouting at me ... This is my moment. My only opportunity to glimpse inside the loading bay and locate the disease. Nevertheless, I don't move. It's like I've been frozen to the tree, my doubts shrieking ... *Death is still inside the fucking building, along with at least two pursuers, and what about Gabriel?*

And then the image of Father Thomas flashes through my mind – in the distribution centre, doing his part.

I take a faltering breath and push myself to stand. I shake the tarpaulin off, thrust the spindly branches aside, and lurch out from under their cover. And I stumble toward the open gate.

# 55

I scurry through the gate and along the shadow of the fence, my gaze raking the short and long sides of the building that I can see. No sign of the guards on their circuit. Yet.

The corner of the building's before me, and my eyes flick to the closing bay doors, only three feet from the ground now. The disease lies somewhere beyond, my chance to spy it disappearing fast … with the damn side door between the opening and me, Death and two pursuers beyond it.

I sprint toward the bay doors on shaking legs, the smell of cordite growing with every step, and the awful chill creeping down my throat. The side door remains shut. And reaching the corner, I dive to the ground in front of it, my palms scraping on the cracked asphalt.

The bay doors continue to rattle down only inches from my nose, while the cold seeps into my bones. I scoot forward on my stomach and peer around the corner. I get a two-second glimpse of the loading bay before the doors clank to the ground.

It's huge, taking up the entire width of the building, probably half its depth, and reaching right to the roof, forty feet in the air. Across the top of the back wall, a row of windows runs all the way from one side of the building to the other, looking into a corridor on the upper floor. And below them, two closed doors have been set into the far wall. One of them is metallic, surely some kind of refrigerated room. Maybe storage for the disease? And there, parked across the width of the loading bays, stand four white vans.

With the bay doors closed, I scramble to my feet. My body shivers as I swivel away from the building, back toward my stolen van.

Then I stop.

Visions of the loading bay continue to revolve around my head. The four vans. Just sitting there. The disease within easy reach. A much simpler transport.

Yet the visions morph into images of Death and the two pursuers, just beyond the bloody door. Plus more damn guards, for sure. I force myself to breathe, to calm, to focus only on the next step ...

Just get inside.

I find my eyes drawn upward, a memory nagging at me.

The roof. The chimney I spied from the road. Might it be an extractor flue? A way in? And there'd be fewer people upstairs if the disease is down.

I spin on the spot and fix my gaze on the shipping containers beyond the far corner of the building, one on top of the other. Then I throw myself into a run toward them.

Sprinting along the front of the bay doors, the three storeys of the behemoth loom ever higher above me, like they're staring down. Finally, I reach the far corner and skid to a halt before peering around it to stare down the side of the building that faces away from the road.

No sign of the guards. Only a couple of doors with no obvious handles and the two rusted shipping containers, eight feet from the corner of the building. The top container stands closed, the bottom one open with all sorts of things poking out – cardboard boxes, packing materials. Obviously the rubbish pile.

I dash toward the lower container with doors at both ends

and start to scale its far side. I reach, swing, and heave, grabbing the ridges in the doors, the locking bars. The upper container stinks – chemicals mingling with the scent of burnt metal. Clearly a laboratory, after all.

I grit my teeth and concentrate only on the climb. My arms and legs burn with the effort. And finally, I clamber onto the top container, breathing hard, and then push myself forward on hands and knees to peer over the edge.

And freeze. Both guards are rounding the corner. One of them glances up in my direction. I wheel backward and out of sight beyond the lip of the container. Then I hold my breath and listen, my heart pounding against my ribs.

No shouts, no hurried footsteps.

I make myself count to fifty before peeking over the edge of the container again. There they are – both guards, continuing their circuit around the building, their backs to me. I let out a slow exhalation, the tension in my chest easing a fraction.

I haul myself to standing. The wind blows stronger up here, gusting out of the darkness from my side. My eyes take in the laboratory rooftop.

A brand-new-looking extractor flue stands gleaming in the moonlight. Plus there's a line of skylights. My heart beats faster, and for some reason, images come to me of Natasha. I see her somewhere inside, safe and close by. Gabriel would want his fresh captive in the thick of things. Possibly as leverage—

I smack my temple and bring my focus back again, training my gaze on the rooftop and the gap from its edge to my container. Eight bloody feet. With a forty-foot drop to the hard concrete floor in between. A metal gutter runs along the top lip of the building, now just a faint outline in the moonlight.

My eyes find the two guards again, disappearing around the far corner of the building. I retreat two steps, set myself, and start to run. The wind jostles me, as if trying to push me aside, and the strange chill seeps through my skin, stealing into my joints. I drive myself faster, plant my feet on the edge of the container, and jump.

I thrust upward with all my strength and sail through the air. The gutter thunders toward me, the void below. I whip my arms forward, legs too, and reach out with grasping fingers. The metal edge slams into my palms, my feet thump against the wall, and I clench the gutter hard, my jaw tight.

But the sweat on my fingers is like grease, and one hand slips right off. I flail backward with that arm and barely get my toes onto a thin ledge, four feet from the top. I teeter, only one hand holding on. The damn gutter creaks with my weight, clearly about to fall off, the sound all too loud in the night.

My mind conjures images of the guards reappearing around the corner, and every instinct screams at me to yank hard with my remaining hand, to pull myself up and out of sight. But I force myself to stop, to go still, and begin the count in my head.

My thoughts slowly quieten, and I inch my weight forward, tugging as gently as I can. The gutter shakes more, and I keep my gaze off the massive drop below as I continue pulling. I finally get my other hand onto the slick metal again and then risk heaving myself upward. The gutter creaks louder but holds.

Eventually, I get one hand over the flat lip of the building and haul myself the remaining way. Then I roll onto the rooftop and stagger to my feet.

Lactic acid gnaws at my limbs. The wind chills the sweat on my back. But I focus on the skylights. Three of them in a line along the entire width of the rooftop, parallel to the loading bay doors and exactly halfway along the building.

I pad over to the first one – blacked-out glass, cracked wood, flaking paint, old. Clearly not replaced when the chimney was installed.

I run my fingers around it, inch by inch, moving in an

entire circle to feel for a weakness or leverage point. It's ponderously slow and takes me two full circuits till I notice the faintest indentation. The locking mechanism. I prise my fingers under the edge and tug, first softly and then harder.

The window doesn't give. Locked or painted shut.

I reposition myself and begin to rock the skylight from side to side, gently pressuring the old lock. It could crunch open and alert people inside—

I hear a click. I pull a bit harder, and the skylight creaks open an inch. I hold my breath and peer inside.

A corridor directly below, six feet by eight – the same one I saw from the loading bay. It stretches the width of the building, the skylights dotted along it. And only a third of the corridor's visible through the gap. A strange graffiti decorates each wall, the same scrawled symbols I glimpsed on the wall of the loading bay. I clock two doors on one side of the corridor while windows line the other. The loading bay is visible through them, forty feet below, the four vans down there along with a couple of pallet trucks.

I shift around the skylight and peer at the corridor wall opposite the loading bay, at the nearest door. It's half-metal, half-glass, sturdy-looking. The handle's large and grey. I stare through the glass into the room beyond, and my gaze falls on two unmoving figures.

I stumble back away from the skylight, the shock physical like I've been struck full in the chest. I scrunch my eyes shut, and still the images flit before my mind. Two bodies. Limbs contorted terribly – legs splayed out, arms bent at impossible angles, fingers curled over like claws.

Memories burn of a candlelit room. Bodies on stone plinths. The awful scars, the agonised expressions, the bleached white faces.

Again, I see Natasha in my mind, and I force my eyes open. I scramble forward, my stomach in my throat, and stare back down through the glass in the door.

No. Both bodies wear lab coats. Can't be her.

There's equipment all around them – microscopes, refrigeration units, fume hoods. Some kind of laboratory.

And these *were* scientists – like the white-haired man, disposable. Their job was already done, the disease ready for dispersal and most likely still in the building. Death and its pursuers have remained here, after all.

I shift even further around the skylight till I'm facing the way I came. The corridor continues right up to the exterior wall I climbed. And … *there*. I spy the first few steps of a staircase that must link this top corridor with the loading bay.

A way down.

I rotate around the skylight till I'm back where I started and then lift the wood a little further, risking the creaking sound. I glance toward the far end of the corridor, and more of it comes into view. More windows, another closed door, a simple silver handle, and … a kneeling figure.

My ribs squeeze. Another Puritan guard. Halfway down the corridor, outside one of the rooms. The door's open, the guy poised in front of it facing the loading bay, a sizeable gun by his side.

The sense of impossibility grips me like clenching fingers. *What the hell's a guard doing up here? How the fuck am I supposed to get in* now?

The heat flares inside, tightening every muscle. It forces me to my feet. I swing my leg back to kick a stone, when a thought flashes through my mind. My foot stops dead as a tingling sensation climbs the back of my neck.

I spin back to face the skylight, crouch down, and peer along the corridor again, my heart racing.

The middle room. A guard outside. The door's open, unlike the others. And once more, an image forms of Natasha. Is she in there? I have no real clue, just the tiniest sense, the faintest feeling of her.

My fingers tighten around the window frame, my heartbeat speeding up. And I take a breath as I circle my mind through everything I need to do …

Avoid however many guards there are, at least two pursuers, and Death; find the disease and somehow get it into a van and out of the building; all without being seen or followed.

My doubts wail, my thoughts flitting ever more wildly.

I close my eyes and breathe deeper, concentrating on the feeling of the roof under my feet, the wind against my skin. And I start the count again in my head, fighting to quiet my mind and block the trampling doubt.

Memories hit me of going behind the veil, all the extra insights, the new details that bombarded my senses. I continue the count and focus on my memory of the shimmering world, of accessing it before. Gradually, my thoughts calm, and the veil peels back a fraction. Time slows.

Against the blankness of my mind, I circle through everything I've glimpsed. Fence, forecourt, loading bay, vans below, rooftop, corridor, windows, doors … That's my profession, my expertise – observe everything, forget nothing.

Beyond the veil, more features appear. Just as they did in the circle of stones, when remembering the white-haired guy in the station, it seems as if the resolution's been turned up on my memories. And instead of engaging my thinking brain, I let my attention wander over all I've observed here, *feeling* for a possibility.

It's the integration of two worlds – the power of the angelic realm and my learned awareness as a thief. I try to focus on the intersection between the two, and trust.

I notice a strange impulse. My eyes fly open, my gaze drawn to the edge of the rooftop, to some broken bricks lying by the lip, cracked and heavy.

An idea starts to form, just the rudiments of one, a feeling more than a set of thoughts. And instead of forcing it, I breathe easily and allow the threads to weave together, my nerves joined by that customary thrill of exhilaration from conceiving a con.

I let my mind run through all the necessary ingredients – a

guarded room, an open door, a simple handle, a corridor, a gun, windows to the loading bay, several vans below, my stolen van parked around the corner. Along with Natasha in the middle room, probably restrained. *If* she's even there.

My stomach tightens. So many assumptions. The whole notion's fucking crazy, still half-formed. My doubts start up again, my mind flitting, and the veil slips back into place.

And while a part of me yearns to think, to assess, I stop my thoughts and stare back at the line of skylights. I go to grab my burner phone from my pocket.

*Just believe.*

## 56

SQUATTING ON THE ROOFTOP, I start jabbing out a text message to the enforcers. We're close to Mandem's turf. But with every typed word, my insides plunge, a weight building inside with just the thought of involving them.

I delay for a second more and then finish the message, press send, and lower my phone. I then compose another message to Father Thomas, outlining the change of plan. I'm about to pocket the phone when it buzzes.

Message already back from Mandem.

*Bout bloody time. Don't you fucking run. We'll be there in ten to fifteen.*

My fingers tighten around the casing, and I shove the ballooning weight down inside.

I whip off my top, tear off the hood, and rip it in half, each piece big enough to cover one hand. With a broken roof tile, I make a small hole near the top of each one for a single finger, to hold them in place. Then I stuff them into my pockets.

Next, I creep over to the second skylight, the one directly over the guard, and use the same rocking motion though much more quietly. Eventually, this lock clicks open too. I listen hard, but there's no sound from below.

I leave the window unlocked but closed and back softly

away. Then I hurry over to the pile of broken bricks, grab up two smaller ones along with one larger, and carry them to the first skylight.

Five minutes gone since sending my text.

I take another deep breath and pull open the skylight. I weigh the smaller bricks in my hand and choose the bigger of the two. It's got to attract the guard's attention, but not the pursuers below …

And through it all, my doubts fire. Somehow, I've got to get them and Death out of the loading bay to buy me enough time to get the disease into one of the vans.

And while my thoughts blather, I force the medium-sized brick through the opening and let it fall.

A moment of silence. I hold my breath till finally it thumps against the corridor's vinyl flooring.

My mind conjures images of the guard setting off to investigate, and I dash across to the second skylight, above the guy's prior position, directly over the middle room. I yank the skylight open.

No guard below.

I lean over and thrust my head through, one hand on the edge, the other gripped around the second small brick.

The door's in the corner of the middle room, and I peer through it. Most of the room is invisible behind the corridor wall to the side. And there's no sign of Natasha, either.

My chest constricts as images bombard me of the guard down the corridor turning around and spying me.

I force myself further down. Blood rushes to my head, and I draw back my arm, steel myself, and yell, "Natasha!"

My yell splits the silence. And hanging down through the skylight, I glimpse the guard – still facing away, though he's starting to wheel in my direction.

I raise the second brick behind my ear and hurl it through the door, into the section of the middle room that I can see. It clatters against the floor and side wall while I'm already grasping the hatch and yanking myself back up onto the rooftop. I train my ears.

The guard's footsteps stomp down the corridor toward me, toward the middle room.

I grab the largest brick and swivel around. I slip my feet through the open skylight while praying the guard doesn't look up. He reaches the open door and storms inside the room, gun raised, tension obvious in every jerky movement.

I exhale and calm myself with the count. Then I drop, fixing my mind on the solidity of the air, on the sensation of it holding me up, while trying to remember my experience of falling from the building with the priest. But it feels near impossible.

The ground rushes up fast. My doubts yell, and I land hard on the corridor floor. Pain shoots up my calves. I stagger, almost fall.

The guard's already spinning to face me from inside the room, bringing his massive gun around. I leap toward the door. Get to see the rest of the room.

Natasha. She *is* there, tied to a chair, fifteen feet away, and to one side of the guard.

I grab the doorknob and yank it closed, shutting them both inside. Then I crash the larger brick down onto the handle. One blow. Two. The handle holds firm.

I picture the guard raising his gun on the other side of the solid door, taking aim, and my adrenaline stampedes. I bring the brick down a third time, hard, all my weight behind it, and the handle breaks off. Panting, I grab the lock's spindle and yank it out of the central mechanism, rendering the handle useless. The door can't be opened.

The guard starts shooting. I throw myself to the side, my ears ringing. Bullets fly all over the place as I scramble several feet down the corridor on my hands and knees, getting out of range of the gun.

I swivel around. The shots keep coming, obliterating the door, the strange graffiti in the corridor, and the opposite window that overlooks the loading bay. And probably attracting everyone in the building.

That's the plan.

Finally, everything's quiet. I pull my hands from my ears. My mind spins images of the guard reloading in the room, of Death and our pursuers below moving with superhuman speed to find me, any remaining guards in their wake.

I scramble to my feet and dart back up the corridor. With the larger brick, I clear the lingering glass from the exploded window opposite the door. Then I yank the fabric patches from my pockets, slip my index fingers through the holes, and grab the bottom edge of the open window. I swing myself out over the side.

I hang in mid-air, the loading bay a good twenty feet below and one of the vans off a few feet to my side. I shuffle my hands toward it, moving an inch at a time along the window frame, the material just barely covering my palms.

Visions come of my enemies teeming toward the stairs to the top floor. It's a massive building. Lots of places to search up here. Hopefully, it'll take a while.

I grip the frame tighter, the sweat building on my palms again. Then the image comes of Death, the black nest hovering directly below my feet. A shiver rocks my body. My arms start to ache.

And Natasha. I picture her still tied to that chair. She'll have heard my voice and will be wondering where I am. The weight grows in my stomach, yanking me further downward.

I squeeze my fingers. My forearms quiver. And the strange chill seeps down my arms into my shoulders.

Death and its pursuers – I imagine them gliding up the stairs, maybe even already flowing down the corridor toward me. The air's spiced with cordite, charged with static. My arms burn. And still, I hold on.

Finally, the sound of pounding feet on metal rings out, the guards barrelling up the stairs as well. I hang on a few more seconds and then drop. Again, the fall's heavy. I land on the van's distended roof with a muffled clang and scrabble down to the ground.

I glance around the massive loading bay. No one there. Only the four vans side by side, two pallet trucks, and the two doors set into the wall behind the vans.

I fix my gaze on the metal one, my heartbeat rising. The door's chunky, new-looking, with a rubber seal around the edge and a long handle fastened to the wall by a chain.

Cold storage for vials of airborne agony. It has to be.

Plus, each of the four vans have raised roofs, undoubtedly temperature controlled. And one of them stands parked in front of the refrigerator door, facing away. Perfectly lined up.

I run to the driver's window and peer inside. The key already sits in the ignition.

My ticket out. *If* I can get the disease.

My eyes dart back to the refrigerator handle and the heavy metal chain locking it closed. I sprint toward it, my gaze fixed on the padlock, ideas for opening it flashing through my mind.

Then I stumble to a halt.

The strange impulse from the rooftop is back. I sense more of the plan hovering just beyond the edges of my awareness. I glimpsed the chain from outside – while peering under the loading bay door – along with something else, something missing.

Again, I don't force it. Just blank my mind and focus on staving off the sense of urgency.

*Believe.*

And I wait for the image to come.

It does. The fence outside … the gate. The bolt cutters. The male pursuer brought them back inside.

My head whirls from side to side. I scour every corner of the loading bay, every wall. The strange graffiti covers the place – a single symbol drawn thousands of times, a capital *A* with a circle around it. Other than that … nothing.

I glance back toward the locked fridge and then, just to the side, the second door. Another storeroom? I barrel toward it, wrench the door open, and blink into darkness.

The space extends the rest of the width of the loading bay, twenty-five yards in total, and the back wall is illuminated by a faint green glow, the only light in the room.

I search both sides of the door and find the bolt cutters propped up against the wall alongside a few other tools. I grab up the cutters and a crowbar, too. While my brain shouts at me to go, I remain still, a niggling sensation between my shoulder blades.

I peer deeper into the room, into the darkness. I can pick out the outline of discarded pallets, of chemical drums, and … the source of the pale green light.

It's coming from a barrel. Two of them … no, three. Set at intervals along the far wall of the storage room. I take a step into the room. Each barrel has a rectangular box attached to the front. Wires. Antennae. Glowing electronic displays.

Bombs. No countdown timers visible, so the detonators must be connected to a trigger. Gabriel or one of his minions is probably holding the button.

I quickly search the room. More circled *A*s graffitied on the walls – the markings of the atheists, the group attacking religious sites, seeking to counter modernity's accidents.

*Why are* they *here?*

My thoughts start to ramble. And I stop them dead, darting back into the loading bay toward the refrigerator door. I prop the crowbar against the wall, my mind on the pursuers and guards, hopefully still searching the rooms upstairs. *Hopefully.*

I clasp the cutter jaws on the padlock link and bring to mind the trembling guard at the gate. Then I breathe, focus on holding myself steady, and squeeze with all my strength.

The chain crunches open.

I pull it with shaking hands from the handle and lower it quietly to the floor. Then I stare at the metal door and try to swallow. I wrap my fingers around the handle and haul the door wide.

The air freezes the breath in my lungs, and my head starts to pound. There it is. Gabriel's disease. Several cardboard boxes sitting on a pallet, all wrapped in plastic, right in the middle of the room.

No way it's the cancer treatment. Because if they've already made the switch, there'd be no reason to keep it here, on ice.

A shudder rolls through me. They're on a pallet truck but still a fair way from the van behind. The pursuers and guards may have already realised I'm not upstairs and may already be on the way down.

I force myself on toward the boxes, sweat climbing my back. And the closer I get, the more my head pounds, and the more my vision begins to haze.

The next minute's a blur. Pushing and pulling the pallet while images bombard my brain – the vials full of liquid death; the contorted bodies upstairs; the pursuers gliding back down the stairs toward me, moving so quietly, I'll have no warning.

Finally, I manage to shove the boxes into the van – fast, not elegant – and retract the pallet truck.

Ready. And my doubts don't stop churning ... So many things that could still go wrong. I roll the pallet truck away and slam the rear doors. Then I go rigid.

The sound of feet on metal. Guards scrabbling back down the stairs at the edge of the loading bay. And the pursuers? They're undoubtedly out in front of the baying pack. I sprint back to the fridge door, my mind still jabbering at me.

Four vans all lined up, each with the double helix logo on the side, each with keys in the ignition. I'll be so easy to follow.

I grasp the bolt cutters and sprint toward the van nearest the stairs. I open the metal arms and swing the blade at the back tyre. It blows with the first hit.

The footsteps grow louder – rubber on concrete now – running across the loading bay, only forty feet away.

My whole body tightens. Out of time, I fling away the bolt cutters and dart toward the next van, the one in front of the fridge door. I leap into the cab, my heart like a piston in my chest, and slam the door.

The footsteps keep coming – six or seven people. And the awful chill ... it grips my insides, like I've been dropped into a well of icy water. Visions come of dark hands grasping the door handle, yanking it open, and dragging me out.

I clutch the ignition key and twist it. The engine fires into life. I thrust it into first gear, floor the accelerator, and jump my foot off the clutch.

The van shoots forward, the bay doors still closed. I crunch the gearstick into second and gun the accelerator. The doors barrel toward me. I grip the steering wheel with one hand and shield my face with the other. The van smashes through.

The outline of threadbare bushes appears ahead, the razor-wire fence, and the dark night beyond. I yank the wheel to steer the van for the open gate, my arms juddering as I fight to keep control. The van skids out onto the main road, the engine shrieking in protest. I narrowly miss a car and receive a couple of sharp blasts from a horn.

I wrestle the van straight and glance to my side, toward the loading bay doors. No movement. Not yet.

I accelerate again, the first turning to the housing estate barrelling toward me.

Twenty feet away. Ten.

I slam on the brakes. The tires squeal. I spin the wheel and shoot the van into the side street, hopefully well out of sight.

Then I kill the engine and coast onward, trying to get my breath back. My whole body trembles. I lean forward and peer through the windscreen. All the apartment lights remain off. And the stolen van sits in the bay, exactly where I left it.

I scan the road ahead again, the pavement, my heartbeat refusing to calm. It's deserted. No one there.

I inch the van closer to the parked one. Then two figures step out from behind it. I can't help squirming. It's Mandem's enforcers. Don and Maddox. Two of the three that came to the train station. Only Twist's absent. They stand in the middle of the road, blocking my route, their hands in the pockets of long coats. Weapons. Probably shotguns.

They stare at me. I bring the van to a halt. Then they order me out of the cab.

## 57

My palms smash into the guttering, harder this time. And pain knifes up my forearms. I grit my teeth against it, grip hard, and find the same lower ledge with my toes.

Then I glance along the building wall below me. Still no pursuers or guards. There's been no sign of them on my entire run back from the housing estate, nor on my circuit of the building.

I clench my stomach, squeeze the gutter, and pull. I swing my leg up and over the rim of the laboratory building with one last heave, and roll my body back onto the rooftop.

This time I lie there panting for a moment, staring up at the sky, dark clouds billowing across me. And the weight's back in my chest.

Don and Maddox. Poor guys. They came. My offer to pay off the bond again too big a temptation, plus a couple of vans as compensation for the lost phone. I picture both vans racing for the city. The angels might think I switched the disease from one to the other. It matters little. They'll be found quickly enough. Found and surely …

I shake my head to clear it and force myself to stand. The wind lashes at my clothes while doubts continue to raze my mind. The boxed disease. My idiotic plan. Will it work? Such a slim fucking chance.

I turn to the skylights, Natasha just beyond, still tied up in the middle room. My muscles flex. There's no sound aside from the wind, the van engines still a memory. I hurry over to the first skylight, lever the window open again, and scan the corridor.

Empty.

I slip through the gap in the skylight, lower myself toward the ground, and drop. Again, the impact's heavy. Feet stinging, I back away from the side of the corridor with the windows and strain my ears as I stare both ways. Nothing. Only the doors stretching out in front of me.

I start toward the middle room and halt, tension flashing up my spine. At the end of the corridor, something's attached to a vertical beam. A black barrel: wires, antenna, and an electronic display.

Another bomb.

I swivel my gaze and spot one at this end of the corridor, too. Surely dozens across the building, all wired to detonate with a single trigger.

My stomach plunges. Again, I picture the vans hurtling away from the building, the angels giving chase, intent on getting their disease back. For Gabriel, there'd be no reason to preserve this place. He could blow it any second.

I hurry forward, trying to move as quietly as I can, my thoughts rambling on. Natasha. In the next room. Only twenty feet away. My heart beats faster. Bullet holes dot the walls and the corridor opposite. Shards of glass and plaster litter the floor. It's like a war zone. The smashed-up door's fully open now, jutting into the room.

I turn the corner, hold my breath, and blink.

Gagged and tied to a chair in the middle of the room sits Natasha, wide-eyed, neck tense, and staring right at me.

Warmth floods my chest. I step over the threshold and scan the rest of the room. Empty. Only a few packing boxes in the corners, a couple of filing cabinets, and the door to my side with its splintered front and heavy handle hanging down, held in place by a single screw.

I smile and glance back at Natasha, the tension in my shoulders uncoiling. Then I falter. My gut twists. Her face. It's ashen. Her eyes wide with warning, not surprise. They flick to one side.

My breath congeals in my throat. It's as if the walls are toppling around me. She's not alone. My brain rages at my idiocy. The door. Someone's behind it. They've seen the open skylights, assumed someone would be back for her. Is it a pursuer? I can't feel the strange chill …

Then my mind begins to still, the count starting up, the veil peeling back – more automatic now. I contract my stomach and spin toward the door, letting my body take over and trusting that I've glimpsed what I need to, that a plan will come.

The shimmering world unfolds around me, time stretches, and I begin to feel everything – the floor, the walls, the door. I find myself raising a knee and reaching for the handle with grasping fingers.

The door hurtles toward me – shoved from the other side – straight into my raised foot. I grab the hanging door handle and kick back hard at the pitted wood.

The door slams into something. I hear a grunt of pain, and the handle comes off in my hand. It's heavy, and I swing it behind me to build up momentum. Then I dodge around the door and come face to face with a figure, only a few feet away.

A Puritan guard. One of the pair who patrolled outside. He stands short and squat in his dark robes, his cheeks ruddy, eyes burning, and teeth clenched. Time still advances at fractional speed as he grips his rifle in both hands and raises it toward me.

I swing my arm forward and let the handle fly. The metal arcs at the guard's head. He dodges and puts up a hand to shield his face. The handle catches his shoulder, spins him around, and smashes into the wall behind.

I leap toward him and reach for the gun, but my right foot slips on broken glass and shards of plaster. I flail with both arms, stretch out, and feel the cold barrel between my fingers. I grab at it and try to yank the weapon to one side but teeter off-balance. The guard holds on tightly.

He sidesteps my fall and kicks out at my chest, sending me crashing backward. Then he seizes the gun with both hands again and wrenches the barrel from my grip.

I scramble to my knees. The guard's already advancing on me, gun raised at my head. I register the entire scene in slow motion – the guard's half grin, the righteous zeal in his eyes, the darkness of the barrel inching toward my face.

The impulse grabs me to turn away, to close my eyes. Yet I stare straight back at him. His finger tightens around the trigger. I brace myself.

A flash of movement behind him. The guard yelps, his eyes wide, and the gun barrel jerks up in the air. He thrusts one hand behind his back as if to shield himself from something.

Natasha, still strapped to the chair and right behind the guy now. Her eyes gleam with fire, her lips a thin line.

She bit him.

I explode off the ground, my knees catapulting forward, and reach for the gun with both hands. The guard pulls it back down. I curl my fingers around the barrel and then smash it into the guy's nose.

The guard's grip weakens. I yank the gun toward me and ram it into his temple. The guy's eyes roll backward, his legs go slack, and he tumbles to the ground.

Natasha gazes at me. And with adrenaline still running hot, I dart into the corridor. I grab a shard of glass from the floor and hurry back toward her.

I go to work on her binding, the sharp edge of the glass

slicing my palm in the process. Finally, I manage to cut her free.

She stands slowly, her legs unsteady, and looks into my eyes. I open my mouth, and Natasha flings her arms around me. She buries her face in my neck and squeezes.

## 58

THE HUG LASTS a couple of seconds. I don't move a muscle. Natasha untangles herself and looks down at the ground, cheeks flushed.

Then she steps back and glances up at me. "What are you doing here?" she asks, her voice soft.

I continue staring over her shoulder, my thoughts sparking and dying. I can still feel the imprint of her arms around me. Can still smell the scent of her hair.

A jolt goes through my body. "More guards, *shit!*" I say and whirl to face the corridor. I go still and listen.

The faintest scuffing sounds from outside, barely audible. My stomach cramps. I can't sense the strange chill, but are they here? Do we fight or hide?

I take a breath to quiet my thoughts and then dart my gaze around the room and the corridor outside, taking in everything … Natasha, the gun, the dented door standing ajar. I feel the sting in my palm, the wet blood against my fingers.

Natasha's still staring up at me, and an idea coalesces in my mind.

I jab my finger at the unconscious guard and hiss, "Crouch

down, *quick.*" Then I grab the gun from the floor and scuttle over to the body itself.

"*What?*" Natasha says, not moving.

"Trust me," I say and wipe my cut palm over the guy's face, smearing blood over his temples, his forehead, his chin. Then I snatch up a piece of chipped plaster from the ground.

"What are you …" Natasha starts.

I dart behind the door, gun in hand, my back to the wall. There I go entirely still.

Again, the sound of a near-silent tread just outside the door. A tremor runs across my neck and shoulders. Natasha swivels her head away from me and then drops beside the body.

I tense my legs to stop them shaking, my mind conjuring images of our attacker's view – his colleague covered in blood, their captive at his side. Is she trying to save him or strangle him? It doesn't matter. Shock – one of the best diversions going. *If* you can create it.

The padded footsteps cease, right at the threshold to the room, just on the other side of the door.

Silence.

I swallow, the sound all too loud in my ears.

The guard takes another two steps forward. The gun barrel extends past the door. I lift my arm and toss the plaster over the top of it, over the guard. It clatters against the far wall. Shoes swivel on broken plaster.

I leap out from behind the door, the stock of the gun raised, both hands gripping the barrel. The guy tenses and starts spinning back to face me. I bring the gun down and crack the butt against the side of his head. The guy collapses in a heap.

I stand still, close my eyes, and strain my attention for more of them, but there's no sound. Only my own heartbeat, Natasha's shallow breathing, and a deathly silence beyond.

"Jake?" she says.

I open my eyes.

"Where is the disease?" she says, her voice tight.

An engine growls, distant but growing steadily louder. I freeze, my mind spinning. I crouch low and leap into the corridor. I take up position underneath the broken corridor window, the loading bay below. Natasha darts to my side and grips my hand. I force my head upward and peer over the edge, hope and dread swirling inside me.

A van shoots through the busted bay door, circles around and stops on one side of the loading bay. White. Larger than the other vans. The same double helix logo on the side.

"Who is it?" Natasha says.

"Not sure," I say, staring down, every muscle taut.

And there he is. Father Thomas jumps out of the van and runs across the loading bay, the slight limp clear. He's dumped his habit but still wears black trousers and top, the dog collar around his neck.

My eyes whip back to the bay doors, just waiting for a van of pursuers to be following behind. Nothing comes. I let my breath out slowly.

The priest stops and lifts his head to stare straight toward me. I push myself up and into view above the window frame.

"How did it go?" Father Thomas says, his voice level. He stands at least fifty feet away, and still the sound carries perfectly.

I nod. Natasha leaps up to my side. She stares down at the man who hardly resembles the old priest, her lips parted.

"It's him," I say.

Natasha runs toward the end of the corridor. I follow behind. She stops dead at the top of the stairs and gives a quick intake of breath, her gaze fixed on the black barrel positioned by the girder.

"A bomb," I say, stepping to her side. "They're everywhere. All over the building."

I give her a gentle nudge, and we scuttle down the stairs. We reach the loading bay and hurry on toward the priest, toward the fridge door.

"So?" he says, his gaze flicking between us. "The angels?"

"I can't say for sure," I say, speaking between snatched breaths. "Three cars rolled out with a first group … maybe looking for you. But two pursuers stayed back, along with Death." I can't help but shiver. "Plus lots of guards. They all drove out of here ten minutes ago. Tracking two vans heading for the city. They left a couple of guards. Both knocked out upstairs."

"Okay," Father Thomas says. His shoulders drop a fraction. "Good."

I nod toward the priest's van. "You couldn't have brought a smaller one?" I say.

The priest shrugs. "It's all there was," he says.

"Well, at least it's different-looking," I say.

Natasha glances from me to the priest, eyes wide, jawline tight.

"*I don't get it!*" The words explode out of her. "The disease – I *heard* you drive it out of here. Everyone followed. And now you're back. *Where is it?*"

The priest strides toward the only remaining van of the initial four. He gazes down at the slashed tyre, at the bolt cutters lying a few feet away.

"Best I could do," I say with a shrug. "No other way to disable it."

The priest paces to the back of the van and yanks open the doors. Natasha steps across behind him to peer inside.

There. The pallet. The cardboard boxes, plastic-wrapped. The disease.

Her eyes widen. She stares at it and blinks.

"You left it … *here?*" she says.

"With the back doors shut, I was gambling they'd have no reason to look," I say.

Father Thomas smiles. "Misdirection," he says.

"*You didn't take it?*" Natasha says.

"I couldn't," I say. "Our pursuers – I'd never have outrun them."

375

"They communicate with each other telepathically," the priest says. He nods toward me. "Even if he'd managed to get the disease out of here, they'd have known the van they were following. Tracking him would have been all too easy."

"This was the only way to shake them," I say. "The Mandem enforcers drove both vans off. Probably looking to sell them, to make some cash. Hopefully, the pursuers are still chasing them." I bite my lip, the same weight in my chest again. "But they may already be dead."

I feel the priest's eyes on me. He takes a deep breath and then pivots back to face the packaged disease.

"Which means we have little time," he says. "We can transport it out of here in my van. There are batches of the real cancer treatment in there. It was already loaded up to be driven to the clinics. But there's still space."

I eye the priest's van. It stands over twenty feet long with the same bloated roof, refrigerated just like the original four. But it does look different.

"They won't know what they're looking for," Father Thomas says. "It means we can get the disease out of here without them ever knowing."

Natasha glances at the priest. Then at me.

"So what's the plan?" she says.

"Incinerator," I say.

"Local hospital, it's close by," the priest says. "Only viable place we can be sure we'll be able to destroy the disease."

Natasha nods, and I find my gaze drifting back up toward the corridor above, a niggling heaviness growing in my chest once more. I try to push it aside. To focus on something else.

"And there's just one batch, of the disease," I say. "I *think*."

Again, the reasons scamper through my mind …

First, the virulence of the disease means they'd only need one batch. Second, leaving only two guards means there's nothing precious left in the building. Third, I remember Qetesh's words – whereas other angels would appreciate more devotion, few would sanction Gabriel's methods. And when the pandemic broke, they might come looking for explanations. It'd be risky to have another batch lying around.

It's the logic I've been repeating to myself, trying to make it true.

Natasha stares again at the boxed disease in the back of the van. And I can't help picturing the tiny vials of death, the laboratory upstairs with its contorted limbs like twisted tree branches, as if the victims thrashed so wildly they broke their own bones.

The priest hurries toward the pallet truck while the heaviness swells in my chest. I feel my neck tensing, the words bubbling up. I glance across at him and clear my throat.

Father Thomas swivels back to face me.

"There's a problem," I hear myself say.

The priest holds my gaze.

I sigh. "Look for yourself."

And I run toward the storage room at the back of the loading bay and open the door. The priest steps into the darkened room. I point at the nearest green glow, the dim light from the electronic display.

"A bomb," Father Thomas says, hands on hips.

"Building's littered with them," I say.

The priest goes quiet. Natasha gazes at him from the side.

"Gabriel's got plans to blow the place sky high," I continue. "Might do it any second. And anyone still alive who finds it will spot only scraps of the equipment and the atheist tags. That's why they're here. So the atheists will be blamed."

The priest closes his eyes. "The unconscious guards," he says.

"I knew you'd say that," I say. "I wanted to give you the choice."

"We need to move their bodies," he says.

It's exactly what I expected, and still my throat tightens further.

"It'll eat up more time," I say. "And if the pursuers circle back, if they spot the new van, all our efforts will be for nothing."

"We have to move them," the priest says, his tone insistent. "They'd be killed in the blast."

"Look—" I say.

"Trust this. We'll be quick!" the priest says, already spinning away from me. "You get the disease into my van." He jabs a finger at his stolen vehicle and then sprints toward the stairs. "I'll deal with the guards. Natasha will show me where they are."

She moves that very instant and runs after him.

I shake my head but still reach for the pallet truck and clench my fingers around the handle.

*Shit.*

# 59

I PUSH my hips against the inside of the van's cargo area and haul at the boxed disease, strain to get it back on the raised pallet truck. I maintain the count in my head, my attention fixed on the escalating numbers. They circle my mind like vultures.

No sign of Father Thomas or Natasha. I imagine them dragging the unconscious guards out of the side door and try to will their movements faster with my mind.

I shove again at the pallet till it clunks onto the truck's forks. Then I scramble out of the van, yank the pallet truck's handle, and start lugging it toward the priest's vehicle.

My thoughts scoot back to Don and Maddox. The angels know the vans they're tracking. They must have found the enforcers by now.

I swallow and focus my attention on the pallet, on keeping it straight across the loading bay, on moving as fast as I can.

"We're done!"

Father Thomas's voice echoes from high above. And I whip my head up.

Then a distant sound snags my attention. An engine. Like before, but higher – a rampant whine. My feet slow, and the sweat turns cold up my back.

"*Keep going!*" the priest yells again, his voice as tense as I've ever heard it.

I clench my teeth and shove again. The boxes lie suspended two feet from the ground on the pallet truck. A lurch to either side and they're loose, vials tumbling. Broken glass. Airborne disease. We'd become its bearer – a bringer of death to millions ... maybe billions.

My hands tremble. And the engine howls louder. The vibrations climb my calves, reverberate in my hips, while my mind jabbers ... *They're coming. They're coming.*

I lurch to a halt. My head turns, and I find myself staring at the shattered bay doors, at the night beyond.

An approaching shadow. A van. Identical to the ones that were parked here only twenty bloody minutes ago. The van shoots through the gap, and the roar of its engine explodes across the bay. I glimpse it not as a vehicle, but as a void hurtling in my direction, a million dark fingers reaching for me. And I feel the awful chill coating my feet and legs, freezing me to the spot.

Tyres screech, and the van swerves to a halt in the middle of the loading bay, thirty yards away from where I'm standing. The doors open, and the cordite smell bites at my nose. Two figures climb out.

Our pursuers. The woman wears tight jeans and a blouse. The man in cream trousers, dark blue jacket, and brown boating shoes. Everything looks brand new. The strange chill thickens the very air in my lungs, and a deep shudder rolls up my back.

The man blocks our route to the broken bay doors while the woman pads toward me like a tigress, her eyes searching for mine. I rip my gaze away and stare down at her stalking feet instead. Still I don't move. My fingers grip the pallet truck as if it's some kind of anchor.

Because it's over. *Over.* The pursuers. They're telepathic. They've now seen we have the boxed disease, the priest's van. And they now know our plan. I feel my insides sink through the floor.

From nowhere, Father Thomas is at my side. He grips my shoulder and squeezes, leaning in to whisper in my ear. "*Keep going.*"

His words slice through my stupor. I shake myself and angle my body into the pallet truck. The boxes shift. And I drive them toward the priest's van. Drive them hard.

The chill's a constant in my bones, and the further I get, the heavier the pallet truck becomes, like pushing a boulder up a mountain. I can't help glancing over my shoulder.

The male pursuer's abandoned his position in front of the doors and is now creeping in the direction of the priest; the woman, too. The priest retreats, drawing them toward the other side of the loading bay.

My mind spins. This isn't like in the room with the giant. The priest's not got the element of surprise here. And now there are two of them.

"*Don't stop!*"

The priest's voice hits me like a fierce wind, and I find myself swept along toward his van. I keep pushing.

Natasha presses in at my side and grabs the truck handle next to me. I feel a glow of heat in my chest, the chill driven back a fraction.

We shove together, heaving the pallet faster across the loading bay. I pour every ounce of focus into our destination – the priest's van, just up ahead – willing myself forward, not to turn around.

We reach the van's back doors. Natasha yanks them open. Inside sits the real cancer treatment in identical-looking boxes to the disease. Gabriel's people did a superb job of copying the packaging. The boxes lie stacked against the far end of the cabin, leaving enough space for another pallet. Just enough.

I press on, fiercely working the hand pump on the pallet truck, the priest's words running over and over in my mind ... *Keep going. Don't stop.*

The boxes continue to rise toward the height of the cabin bed.

Only a foot to go.

The blood thunders through my veins. Natasha bounces up and down at my side.

Seven inches …

Images flash through my mind, my focus broken, memories stealing in – the priest, Father Thomas. I remember sitting by his side in the attic room, creating our plan together, those warm eyes, that wide smile.

My hands slow with the hand pump, and my head edges around.

The priest continues his retreat toward the far side of the loading bay. The pursuers have flanked him and are creeping forward, cornering him against the disabled van, so close now. The priest watches them come, his stance ready, gaze flicking between them.

"I'll slow them down!" he yells to us. "Go, go, *go!*"

The bottom drops fully out of my stomach. Natasha yanks me around, her eyes wide.

But I spin back toward the priest. The male pursuer lunges, a blue and cream blur. His fist flies, and Father Thomas darts back to avoid it. Then the woman leaps into the space he retreated into. He swivels away and parries her strike, scarcely remaining out of reach.

My heart beats harder. They're so bloody fast, their blows barely visible as they fly at him. It'll be a fucking massacre. The pursuers attack and attack, keeping the priest between them, like an animal leashed by two masters.

My fingers squeeze the truck handle. *Get out of here.* It should be so damn easy. I reach for my customary thoughts, my familiar judgements … *The priest will let you down. Leave him first, get free—*

My mind stutters to a halt, and staring at Father Thomas, the count starts up in my head. I take a slow breath, remember the shimmering world, and the veil starts to peel back.

Surfaces glitter. Time slows. And I can see so much more, the pursuers' blurred shapes becoming distinct attacks.

The male pursuer strikes out once more. The priest leans back to avoid it. A second fist careens at his chest, and the priest grabs the guy's wrist out of the air. Then he yanks the pursuer off-balance and follows up with an elbow to the back of the head.

Father Thomas continues to fight hard, his defence wasp-like. He darts out of the way of the heavy strikes and retaliates with lighter blows to the ribs, stomach, temple ... over and over. He engages the male pursuer while trying to keep the woman off-balance.

I swivel back toward the van and the pallet just sitting there, already halfway through the rear doors. My thoughts start up again ... *One more push, then jump in the cab, race away, hospital, incinerator, destroy the disease ... the plan!*

"Go!" the priest yells.

A part of my brain screams to comply. Yet still I don't move, my thoughts slowing, the veil peeling back further. I find myself swivelling back to face Father Thomas, a strange pull growing in my chest, something drawing me across the loading bay. My fingertips buzz.

Perspiration glints on the priest's neck. The pursuers draw closer. Strike faster. And my legs start toward them, one step after another.

*What the hell am I doing?*

The priest's giving up everything to buy us time. And here I am, fucking squandering it.

As quickly as the thoughts spark, they die again, my mind dropping into stillness.

I stumble on toward Father Thomas, toward the pursuers. Thirty yards away. My gaze remains fixed on the fight while time drifts by, the ascending numbers like wave crests with fathoms in between them. And still, I sense the maddening intuition drawing me on. Like in the morgue, it's unclear, unresolved. And still, I follow the pull.

The priest's tiring, slowing down. And it's as if the pursuers sense his vulnerability and attack even harder.

The male pursuer leans into one of Father Thomas's punches and sends a crushing blow toward the old man's chest. The priest tries to spin out of the way, but the attack catches him on the side of the ribs. Pain carves itself into his face, yet still he uses the spinning impact to lash out with his other hand and connect with the pursuer's jaw.

The guy staggers forward. The priest pauses, just a fraction of a second, and then brings his other arm up to grab the guy under his chin. And while my fleeting thoughts scream impossibility, Father Thomas flips over the pursuer's head, his arm still locked under the guy's chin. He lands behind his assailant and uses the momentum to jerk the guy off his feet. The pursuer crashes backward toward the ground. The priest lets go of his lock and drops onto the guy's throat, knee under his chin, to deliver a harrowing crack. Broken neck.

My gaze snaps to the female pursuer. She's closing in and doesn't hesitate. While the priest's crouching down and facing away. It's as if this is the moment she's been waiting for.

I continue running toward them, still anchored in the strange calm, everything still advancing at half speed. I find myself almost at the metallic fridge door, only ten feet from the priest, Natasha sprinting at my shoulder.

*Where the hell am I going?*

A part of my brain's desperate to take control, to think, to plan. But the thoughts rise and fall, spark and die. I continue following the strange pull in my chest, an image forming in my mind – just flashes of Father Thomas, the female pursuer, Natasha, and me, in some kind of configuration. Still hazy. But again, I don't force it.

The priest's arms tremble, and his forehead drips with

sweat. The woman bears down on him from behind. He starts to swivel, to rise, to lift his hands. And she kicks his forearm aside, spinning him back around. Only a step away now, she raises a hand and lines up a killer blow to the back of his neck.

I don't alter my course, don't run faster or slower. The sense of trust remains, the strange pull, and I *believe*.

I run up behind the female pursuer's arm – almost side on – and find my hands sweeping upward and to the side. I glance over my shoulder, half expecting what I'm going to see.

Something's flying in my direction – a crowbar, Natasha having scooped it up from beside the fridge door.

Beyond the veil, I can feel the metal bar arcing toward me, and in one fluid movement, I step forward into its trajectory, catch it in mid-air, and swing its tip toward the female pursuer. The woman's attention remains fixed on the priest, so she doesn't see me coming. Father Thomas dips his head as I smash the bar into her temple.

A sickening sound. The impact vibrates up my arm, and I fight to maintain my grip. The woman's body goes limp and crumples to the ground.

I stagger to a halt before her and stare down. Matted hair and blood. She doesn't move. My heart pounds. My mind starts up and then falters, my insides a hollow ache. I open my hand, and the crowbar falls from my fingers. The clang echoes around the empty loading bay.

The priest stands, inhales deeply, and lets the breath out. A huge shiver rolls from his feet to his neck. The old man glances down at both bodies and then lifts his head to stare across at the loading bay doors. He goes still, and his eyes dull. Is that sadness?

His entire lineage is at an end. His life wasted. Thousands of years of effort against the angels … gone.

Natasha steps toward us. "Why are we waiting?" she asks, her voice tense. She glances from me to the priest. "Come on."

She grabs my arm. "The boxes, the van. Let's get them inside."

I glance down at her hand. "Won't work," I breathe.

She shakes her head. "But we have to—"

"It won't work!" I say, whirling on her. "They've spotted the van, and they're telepathic. Death already knows our plan. And so Gabriel will. If we drive off in that thing" – I jab my finger at the priest's van – "they'll be able to track us. That was the whole point of the switch!" I clutch at the air. "They found Mandem's vans and then doubled back." I motion to the pursuers on the ground. "They'll find us in an instant."

Natasha sets herself and steps toward me. "The hospital, the incinerator," she says. "We can still get there—"

"Forget it, we have no time!" I snap back. "Fifteen minutes to the hospital, five to get the disease inside. Best case. Then there's getting it to the incinerator, destroying every box. All this and surviving!"

The heat blazes in my ribs while my brain runs on. Would we have had a chance if we'd done as the priest said? Just driven the disease out of here?

Natasha's mouth opens.

"Gabriel's going to be so fucking angry," I say. "He's going to find us, *soon*. And when he does, our deaths won't be quick." I glance from Natasha to Father Thomas, the sense of weight growing inside me. "I failed. I'm sorry."

The priest stares at me, his expression unreadable. I close my eyes and swivel away from Natasha. Anything to avoid her gaze.

Again, I feel her hand on my arm. "It's okay," she says, resolution in her tone. "It's going to work." Her fingers squeeze. "We can do this."

I spin back to face her.

"This is God's will," she says. "There is a reason this happened." She stands up straighter. "There's a solution."

I blink and then stare at the earnestness in her eyes, just waiting for the heat to broil inside me again.

It doesn't.

Instead, I feel her words as strangely calming. Deluded or not, it's her faith. And the weight in my stomach begins to lift.

"We can destroy the disease," she says with a nod. "Trust me."

## 60
---

THE VAN HURTLES toward the hospital, Father Thomas at the wheel. He swerves it around the night-time vehicles and into gaps that seem to appear magically between them.

"Not long now," he says.

Natasha nods and leans forward next to me. I notice a kindling warmth at my core. So fucking weird. I've worked alone for most of my life. Yet here I am, sitting in the cab between Father Thomas and Natasha, feeling a strange sense of togetherness. And we're not following my plan. We're following *hers*.

Again, my thoughts flit back to the loading bay – talking things through, readying the boxed disease, placing it where it needed to go. It was still on the pallet truck, almost inside the priest's van. We pulled, pushed, got the placement just right. Fucking crazy to think we can pull this off. Then we jumped into Father Thomas's van and sped out of there.

It was only fifteen minutes ago. Yet with my rambling brain, it feels like fifteen seconds.

I shake my head to try to clear it and then swivel to face the plastic-wrapped cardboard boxes in the storage area behind, juddering along with the priest's revving engine. And the image comes of our large van barrelling down streets with its double helix on the side. Known to the pursuers, which means they're tracking us right bloody now. The memory of the strange chill's still so strong in my bones, and my nerves jangle.

The priest skids the van around a corner and accelerates again.

"There it is!" Natasha says, pointing through the windscreen.

I spin back around.

"The incinerator will be on its ground floor," Natasha says, her other fingers gripping the crucifix on her necklace. "Look for a chimney!"

My eyes take in the building. It resembles a massive pile of rectangular blocks crammed between ancient sets of apartments. And suddenly, they morph into office buildings of mirror and steel towering above us, and I'm back in the station, his blinding light crippling my vision, his disembodied voice ripping through my head. And I feel pressed into my chair, squeezed by gigantic weights. My gut constricts horribly.

"He's coming," I whisper, barely audible even to myself.

Natasha whirls her head to face me.

"Gabriel," I say more loudly, fighting against the weight. "*He's coming!*"

And staring down the street past the hospital, my mind conjures images of desolate highlands, and then forests, and beaches. Fantasies dance of us escaping, of freedom.

The priest angles the van toward the entrance road. And my hips pivot forward, my arms tense, and I only just stop myself from reaching out and grabbing the wheel, from forcing us to continue.

"Jake!" Natasha calls.

The priest swings the van into the entrance road, and I shove myself back in the chair.

"I'm sorry, Nat ... This is Gabriel. You have *no idea*," I say, the memories bombarding me becoming ever stronger, ever more vivid. I feel again how he froze me in place, how he effortlessly controlled my body. "And now he's close ... I can *feel* it."

Crumbling walls pass us faster on both sides. And my heart's pounding, my gut's twisting ever tighter.

"So we have to get there first," Father Thomas says and guns the engine. He throws the van down a ramp and across some kind of parking lot, past several bays of delivery trucks.

I grab the dashboard as he brings the van to a screeching halt by the back doors.

He jumps out of the cab and runs to the rear. Natasha swivels toward me, her body poised, waiting for me to leap out. Yet I remain still in the seat like I've been cast in ice.

"What are you *doing?*" Natasha yells and shoves at my chest.

Again, the visions of escape swirl through my mind, and the words tumble from my lips. "We could get away," I say.

"*What?*" she says. "After everything you did in the warehouse, all the effort ... *why stop now?*"

I stare back at her, the warmth there at my core, and a single thought swirls ... *Because now, there's so much more to lose.*

Natasha only gapes at me and gives me one final shove. Then she gives up and scrambles the other way out of the cab before racing to the rear of the van to help the priest. He's got a trolley already and is wrestling the pallet out of the back.

And I sit there, the weight pressing me down ever harder into my seat. My eyes find the exit road. And the moment comes when the van bounces up on its springs, the pallet safely out and on the trolley, my way clear to drive away from all this. Yet I take a deep breath and slide out of the van, down to the ground.

Father Thomas is smiling at me from beside the trolley. And Natasha's bouncing on her toes at his side. "Come on!" she calls.

I run toward them and grab the handle, side by side with

the priest. Natasha gives me a sharp look and then sprints ahead to the hospital's rear entrance. Together, the priest and I spin the trolley around and drive it up the ramp after her.

"The incinerator is off to the right," Natasha shouts, opening the double doors for us. "I spotted the chimney."

We rattle past her into the building, and I feel a sudden sense of timelessness, like the world outside has been suspended. I push faster down a rubber-floored corridor, the walls covered in a million scars and scrapes.

We approach a crossroads. The priest starts to rotate the trolley to get it around the corner while my eyes fall on a lone figure beyond the junction. I anchor my feet and yank the trolley to a halt, my shoulders tight.

The priest spins on me. "What—"

I raise a finger. The man stands only twenty feet away. Dark mottled skin, woollen hat, and overalls. He's staring directly at us, his eyes deep and inscrutable, and he has a kind of knowing smile on his lips, like he's been waiting for this very moment.

He lifts his hand and points down the corridor to his side.

I blink at him. Then the connection forms, and gooseflesh prickles up my back. Blue uniform. Coloured beads around his neck and wrists.

It's the janitor from the morgue.

# 61

NATASHA STEPS toward the janitor and raises a hand in greeting. I recognise the same strange sense of timelessness from the morgue, the silence palpable, like a presence in and of itself. It's as if the entire hospital's been deserted. No one for a hundred miles.

"Is that ...?" Father Thomas starts, his voice ebbing away into the quiet.

I cock my head. *Another angel?* The thought was my own; yet the janitor glances at me and nods once. My mouth falls open.

The guy continues to point down the corridor to his side.

"*Shit,*" I say, the priest's words in the kitchen chiming in my head ... *We're not alone in fighting them.*

Father Thomas swivels to face me.

"I reckon you were right," I say to him and spin the trolley in the direction the janitor is indicating.

The janitor wags his finger insistently down the branching corridor. A shimmering haze surrounds his head, a great majesty, while his features tighten, a new alarm kindling in his expression.

The memories of Gabriel keep intensifying, and I shove at

the trolley, following the janitor's direction. Father Thomas and I drive it hard between the grey walls. Somehow, the janitor reappears at the end of the corridor and points down another walkway. The guy's eyes look ancient. Hundreds of years old? Thousands?

A new lightness forms in my chest. We have help, a guide. We're a team. Still so fucking strange. I squeeze my hands around the trolley handle.

*Believe. Believe …*

The janitor's posture continues to tense as we travel further, concern animating his eyes. He jabs his finger down the next corridor with even greater urgency.

Natasha shoves open another set of double doors, and I charge through at the priest's side, visions coming of Gabriel descending on us in his fury and ripping us limb from limb. My doubts start to bellow, and my heart beats as if it's trying to break out of my chest.

I grit my teeth and force myself on, concentrating hard on keeping the trolley straight, on squeezing every inch of speed out of my legs. And there it is, a faint warmth on my forehead. My head darts up, and my eyes fix on a set of double doors on one side of the corridor up ahead, covered in scrapes.

"This is it!" I yell and lurch the trolley toward the doors, the sensation of shadows clawing at my heels. I burst through and run straight into a wall of heat.

A massive room, over fifty yards square, the door situated right in the corner. It's nearly empty aside from the incinerator – a huge metal structure halfway along and ten feet from the middle of the side wall. A face without eyes, its enormous mouth gaping, flames licking hungrily inside.

Some guy stands in front of it, throwing sacks down a chute that extends into the opening like a massive tongue. Then he grabs up a metal bar with a hook and spears a tiny loop in the incinerator door to shove it closed.

"This is a restricted area!" he yells, swivelling to face us.

His words are like insects to a speeding train. The priest thrusts the trolley along the side wall toward him, and I run out into the centre of the room, my eyes scanning the entire space.

It's over half the size of a football field and at least half as high, with a few lights hanging up above. The incinerator chimney is a large chrome cylinder that disappears into one side of the ceiling.

And my thoughts keep darting back to the task. Destroying the disease will be one thing. Getting out alive, quite another.

"No one's supposed to be here," the guy says, unhooking his bar from the incinerator door. He steps toward us.

The priest ignores him and slams the trolley into the side of the incinerator chute. The metal ramp is fifteen feet long and extends out at waist height – flat first, before sliding down toward the inferno. I hurry around it to get a better look.

And stop dead, my stomach in my throat. The incinerator mouth's too narrow for the pallet.

The attendant drops his bar, letting it clang to the ground, and barges past Natasha. He runs from the room.

"Leave him," Father Thomas says, his hands ripping at the plastic coating, starting to tear it off the twenty or so boxes. "He'll be safer away from here."

The priest throws the first box onto the flat of the chute. Natasha helps him strip the remaining plastic. And I just stand there, staring on, new images of Gabriel flashing before my eyes, like he's already reaching into my mind. As if he's already here.

I hear a creak behind me, and I spin around.

The janitor steps hesitantly through the door. He stares at us and then creeps along the edge of the neighbouring wall.

"The *door*, Jacob!" the priest yells.

I whirl back around to face him.

"The incinerator door!" he says again and stabs his finger at the hatch. "We need it open!"

I tighten my shoulders and stumble toward the heat. I scan the ground surrounding the chute for the metal bar. It's not here. There's only six inches of space under the bottom of the chute. I drop to my knees and begin groping at the floor underneath with trembling fingers.

Perspiration breaks out across my back, and the smell of cordite creeps in around the burning stench. I stretch, fumble. And eventually find the bar right by the incinerator wall. I grab it up and lurch to my feet.

Natasha stands poised over the chute. The priest lifts the remaining boxes onto it. Just one final push and they'll slide down the chute, through the opening, and into the raging flames.

If I can get the fucking door open.

The priest screams, *"Come on!"*

I slam the bar toward the door. The bloody loop's only a half- inch across, fixed to its top right-hand corner. I try to spear it with the hook on the end of the bar, but it slips. And then slips again.

*Shit, shit, shit.*

My arms shake. I go to grab the bar nearer to the hook, to make it easier, but it's so close to the incinerator door, the heat singes the skin on my hands. I shift back to holding the bar by the end.

Father Thomas keeps urging me on, and sweat's now trickling down my cheeks and arms, my palms becoming more slippery, my internal alarm clamouring.

I start the count, and my thoughts splurge, my pulse throbbing in my ears, my insides in knots. I clench my jaw and train my attention on the shimmering world, trying so hard to believe. And finally, my thoughts start to slow as I move my arm, guide it toward the loop. Closer … closer.

My heart and lungs work in tandem. Time stretches, and I let my body take over, my mind focused fiercely on the count.

I *feel* for the loop. And eventually, the hook slips into it with a click.

I glance across at the priest, at Natasha, the lightness sparking. I prepare to pull, to open the door.

And the wall explodes behind me.

## 62

THE FORCE of the explosion's like a smack to the shoulders and sends me wheeling. I grip the connected bar hard and only just stop myself from being thrown against the incinerator's searing hot surface.

I right myself, my adrenaline firing and my thoughts jabbering. I try to cling to the metal bar, but my hands start to shake, my grip loosening. And just like at the station, the sensation of immeasurable power permeates my muscles and seizes control of my body. The bar drops from my hand, landing on the metal chute with a clang.

I fight so hard not to turn, but I'm compelled. My body swivels away from the incinerator and spins to face the far wall, thirty yards away. Natasha stumbles forward a step at my side, and the priest stands rigidly behind her, the chute at his back.

Gabriel.

Framed by the hole torn in the wall, by the night beyond, his radiance is blinding. It's as if the archangel's sucking all the light from the room, the darkness spreading toward us like a cancer. And in the brightness, his image keeps slipping, as if I'm watching a movie of two frames – man and colossus, the normal world and the one behind the veil. The man stands normal height, the colossus much taller, broader … his head reaching two feet above mine.

I find my gaze drawn upward, the shadows deepening above, coalescing into two huge black wings that spread far across the ceiling above us.

My doubts stampede. To challenge such a thing. So futile. A part of me laughs at my insolence. The archangel has come alone. He needs no one else. The giant and Death are nothing compared to him.

Gabriel claps. Slowly. Painstakingly. Just like he did in the station. He stands thirty yards away but every impact's still like thunder, a gong clanging inside my skull.

"Valiant … attempt," he says, his voice ringing with layered symphonies, horribly distorted.

I concentrate hard to make out the words.

"It's been an exceedingly long time since I have been so … diverted," he says, stepping closer.

He's so difficult to look at – his radiance, his flitting image – and with every attempt I make, pain sears behind my temples.

"It evokes memories of bygone days," he says wistfully and angles his head, glancing up at the ceiling. "Of a time when my retribution was more often required."

Then he sighs and turns back toward me. "But you …" he says, the amusement in his tone falling away. "I do not think you comprehend what you're attempting."

A shiver rolls through my body, and he raises a massive arm toward the boxes of vials on the chute behind me.

"Did you believe this would end things?" he asks, his gaze scouring into the three of us. "That you all could best *me?*" His radiance burns, and the archangel towers even higher, his shadow wings stealing all the way down the wall behind us.

I fight to keep still, not to strain, and it takes almost every ounce of focus not to try to flee.

"Your life is but a *blink* compared to mine," he bellows, the words pounding me like flying hammers. "I have been mankind's shepherd for *thousands of years*."

Shepherd? Images come of the contorted figures on Qetesh's stone plinths, of the ruined bodies in the train crash.

He glances off to the side as if addressing an unseen audience. "Yet I have been patient, I have shown mercy," he says, his words softer. "I have afforded mankind every chance to embrace the light." He gives a subtle shake of the head. "Yet there remains such vanity."

And while his words trill with a strange softness, the anger mounting beneath is so clear – the air vibrating, his muscles tensing. It's as if the wall of wind is consuming the horizon, sweeping toward us. I can't help tightening my own legs and arms.

"So *many* have forgotten," he says, clenching a giant fist at his side. "You see, to live without the sacred, without reverence, is to squander life's greatest gift."

He swivels back to me, his features morphing into a thin smile, barely discernible. "And I gave it to *you* … child," he says, his voice even softer, its tone trembling with fury. "I gifted you a glimpse of the ultimate, and this is how you repay me?"

I strain against his hold while his gaze flicks to the boxes on the chute behind me, only a push away from sliding toward the incinerator door. His eyes burn, and I feel the torrent of wind looming ever larger, the pressure building in my chest.

I find myself starting up the count, my thoughts slowing. He shifts his gaze back to me, and I can't help struggling to look away, to resist his hold. My head turns.

"*How dare you?*" he snarls.

And the archangel throws himself at me.

The movement's too fast to see, just a blur, and the barrelling dread claws at my insides like jackals. I screw my eyes shut and feel myself grabbed by the neck, lifted off the floor. Natasha yells, the sound strangely remote. I flail at Gabriel's hands, his grip burning hot around my throat.

"You were supposed to *die*," Gabriel rasps at me, the sound resembling a million tortured violins.

He squeezes tighter, and I strain for breath, my neck ready to snap.

Then the sound comes of metal buckling. My eyes flash open. The archangel's focused on one of the incinerator pipes instead, and he's squeezing and wrenching it. The pipe crumples. Then he opens his giant fingers, and I fall to the ground.

I roll onto my front and gulp in breath, my blistered neck stinging.

Gabriel gives a deep sigh and steps away from me. "You test me," he says, quietly. "Yes, you test me."

I blink, and Gabriel vanishes. He moves so fast that he's already standing by the broken wall.

"I'm moved to end you now," he says and then lowers his voice. "But there is a profound role you can still play."

I focus on getting my breathing back under control and then struggle to my feet.

"In many respects, I should be grateful to you," Gabriel says and offers me a mocking bow. "If there was ever just cause to bring humanity to its proper place, it is your arrogance."

He waves a hand toward the cardboard boxes again. "Do you have any notion how virulent this disease is?" he asks. "It is airborne and any contact will claim your respiratory and nervous systems." He speaks so lightly as his gaze dances over the three of us. "Your lives will be agony, an agony that your merry band will spread to so many more unbelievers." He smiles. "For the greater the despair, the more the heathens will seek the light."

Gabriel reaches out his fingers toward the boxes on the chute. And my heart vibrates like a mad bird behind my ribs, images coming of him crossing the room in an instant and smashing the vials. It'd be so fucking easy. I force a strangled breath and focus on finding an inch of calm.

Destroy the disease. Survive.

I tense my stomach and start the count. I feel Natasha's and the priest's eyes on me from the side, both further along the chute. And it's as if I can hear their voices in my head … *It's up to you now.*

And while my doubts cascade, I let go of my rational brain and simply breathe and count.

*Believe.*

As my thoughts still, I find myself more able to move. My fingers creep toward the chute, toward the metal bar that I dropped onto it.

Gabriel takes a step toward me. "So," he says, raising an eyebrow, his voice still discordant. "Are you ready to die?"

Again, the dread grips me. And while every part of my brain screams lunacy, I concentrate harder on the count, on quietening my mind. And slowly, painfully, my thoughts slow further and time stretches. Surfaces glimmer, partially at first, and then the shimmering world unfurls around me.

As before, solid objects become fluid, the floor undulating like tiny waves, the sharp edges of the hole in the wall rippling up and down. And I force my gaze onto Gabriel.

He stands there only as the colossus now, eight feet tall. His boulder-like arms and torso are covered in plate armour of brilliant gold, shining so brightly it resembles the sun itself. His face glows also, every feature harrowing perfection.

I shift my weight and force a slow breath, searching again for the warmth inside, for the sense of togetherness nestled at my core.

*Save Natasha. Save the priest.*

I try to stand tall.

"I called them, you know?" My voice sounds so feeble. "The police."

The archangel lowers his head toward me. "Oh, my word," he says, such amusement and steel in his tone. And now in the shimmering world, every awful syllable's clear. "The insect speaks."

I try to silence the baying voices inside, to hold on to the trust.

"The terrorist unit, the chemical weapons people …" I say and close my eyes for a moment. My throat's so raw. "I called them … on the way here, told them about your laboratory. Gave them the address."

I glance back at him.

Gabriel raises a glittering eyebrow. "Why would I care?" he says. "They won't save you."

In the shimmering world, I feel Gabriel's power radiating off him like a blazing heat. And while a part of me is desperate to stop talking, to melt into the floor, I fight to keep going.

"But they'll find your equipment, your guards in their uniforms," I say. "It'll be clear it wasn't the atheists who did this."

Gabriel laughs, the sound echoing around the cavernous space, cold and haunting. "It matters little," he says. "They could never conceive of the great hand behind all this, would have no conception who we even *are*." He towers even higher above me. "We are gods, you little insect … or do I need to prove it to you again?"

The heat burns icy cold inside me. I clear my throat. "That might be, but your fellow angels will find out." I wince at my own words. "How many will be pleased to know that an archangel did this?"

I point a shaking finger at the boxes and then glance back up at Gabriel. I tense every muscle to prevent myself from bolting.

His jawline tightens like rock, and his brightness builds, the heat scorching my face. And still he stands there, fists clenched, staring at me, as if working to contain himself.

"They'll find out it was you," I say, my voice shaking.

"The teams are probably already there. It's too late to stop them. No one will blame modernity for this."

Gabriel takes a deep breath. Something appears in his hand.

"But they won't," the archangel says, turning the object over in his fingers. "For I can destroy the laboratory in a moment."

I stiffen.

A phone. The detonator.

"I can destroy the evidence and everyone will blame those idiot atheists," he continues. "No one will know anything different – not God, nor man."

The sweat streams down my back, the incinerator door only feet behind me, my heartbeat a fierce companion to the numbers still escalating in my mind. And still I focus on the calm, on keeping the veil peeled back. And every moment sears itself into my awareness, every detail …

I glance across. Natasha, only a few feet away, her hand gripping the chute as if it's ballast in the face of the coming storm. Father Thomas beyond her, poised by the boxes, every muscle in his body taut. The janitor, standing by the wall, is almost invisible in the unfurling maelstrom. His eyes flash between Gabriel and me, over and over. Gabriel is still playing with the phone, a piece of technology, something so far beneath him. He brings it to his face as if he's examining the buttons.

I cease breathing. Natasha tenses beside me. The boxes to her side, the incinerator entrance just down the chute, the closed door at the end. It only requires me to open it.

While Gabriel's thirty feet away. He could stop us before we've even blinked.

The pressure builds, squeezing my chest and pressing down on my shoulders. I feel my gaze drawn to the side once more. The priest's staring back at me, and a lifetime of waiting shines in his eyes, the legacy of a thousand-year lineage.

I swallow and swivel back to face the archangel, Father Thomas's words in my head ... *This can work. Have faith.*

I tense my arm, my fingers, and focus again on the shimmering world, ready myself.

With a sigh, Gabriel presses a button on the phone. Behind the veil, the movement registers a millisecond before it happens. I spin toward the incinerator door.

Then all hell breaks loose.

# 63

A DISTANT RUMBLE makes my heart jump. The bombs in the warehouse – a colossal explosion to be heard this far away. And the thoughts die as quickly as they form, my attention drawn to the side.

The janitor's thrown himself at Gabriel. The old man moves like lightning, arms and legs striking, but he gets no closer. The archangel blocks every attack, but the janitor keeps battling, positions himself between Gabriel and us.

"*Now!*" Father Thomas screams.

I'm already grasping for the incinerator chute, for the metal bar I dropped there. Natasha and the priest start shoving at the pile of twenty boxes, sliding them down toward the door.

Fighting to calm my doubts, to stay anchored beyond the veil, I grab up the metal bar and jab it toward the loop above the door. All in one movement. Of course, we'll never make it, never get the boxes into the incinerator – Gabriel's too fast, his rage too powerful. And while my mind chatters and splutters, I feel the currents of trust propelling me on, the warmth, the togetherness still cradled in my chest.

I hear a dull thud behind me, something hitting the far wall. The janitor. Is he dead?

Time creeps by, slow and steady. And I focus on shutting everything else out, on *feeling* the loop at the corner of the door, just as I did before.

I guide the metal bar toward it, making minute adjustments as I go. A click resounds as the hook hits home. I wrench the door open, and the wave of heat slaps me in the face. The first box disappears inside, the second on its way. Eighteen still on the chute behind.

My pulse rampages. The third box heads down the chute. And a wild roar erupts at our backs, the sound shredding my nerves. I whirl, and behind the veil, the scene unfolds in awful slow motion.

Natasha shoves another box down the chute while the priest plants his feet and grabs her around her waist, yanking her away from the incinerator.

I bend my knees and fling myself in the opposite direction.

Gabriel smashes into the incinerator chute, right where we were standing. It crumples like paper. My body spins around as I flail backward.

The archangel stands there. A flaming sun. The shadows deepen behind him as he reaches for the remaining boxes on the chute. He lifts two up in his massive hands, a terrible smile playing across his face. For a moment our eyes meet, triumph in his gaze. Then he crushes the boxes together, pulverising them.

Careening backward, my heels strike something, and I trip as the shattered vials fly into the air, releasing the serum in a billion tiny droplets. They fall over us like fine rain.

I hit the ground, elbows first, and the impact drives the air from my lungs.

Gabriel roars again. And I lie there watching the archangel tear the incinerator apart while the drops of serum cover my hands and face.

Lungs quivering, I roll over. Then I get my knees beneath

me and scamper for the far wall, my feet slipping on broken glass.

Another explosion leaves my ears ringing. Flames leap in all directions from the smashed incinerator behind, igniting the gas from the pipes that have been sheared like grass stems. The space becomes a ball of fire. Flames lick at my arms and back. And I dive for cover before landing hard again.

Blinking back the dust, I glance to my side. The priest's there, helping Natasha toward the far wall, toward the gaping hole.

I stagger to my feet, sway, and stumble after them. Then I gaze over my shoulder.

Gabriel stands amid the chaos of metal and glass. Piling up the intact boxes on the chute, gleefully collecting all the unbroken vials, intent on amassing his gift to humanity, making sure the rest of it can be delivered.

He resembles a devil, a demon, some kind of crazed child.

I swivel away and try to blank out the memory of the archangel's eyes burning into mine.

I stagger to the hole in the far wall, barely able to put one foot in front of the other. Then on through the gap into the concrete of the parking lot, every part of me burnt or aching.

The priest stalks up ahead of me with Natasha, pressing on between the crumbling walls, heading for the main street. I scrabble to catch up, the serum clinging to my skin and hair.

A faint glow illuminates the horizon, the night finally giving way to day. We walk in silence, side by side, the ringing in my ears gradually ebbing. I strain to listen.

The sounds of others, hurrying down the side road in our direction, attracted by the incinerator exploding. They're staring, yelling, and pointing over my shoulder.

It feels like I'm in another world. Memories flash through my mind. The papers in the white-haired guy's briefcase, the descriptions of the agonised symptoms. And the graphs depicting the horrific infection rates of the disease, the devastation of a civilisation.

Natasha. So close at my side. She smiles and reaches for my hand. Our fingers touch and coil together. I feel the dampness of the serum, the fire of my burns, and the warmth of her palm against mine.

I take a deep breath and squeeze.

# 64

OUR FINGERS TOUCH. Just a moment. Natasha passes over the broom, and I take it, still gazing at her. She's already let go, has sat back on the crate, her attention on the clothes in her lap.

And while my mind's cataloguing the bits of the safe house that still need cleaning, I don't move. I simply lean on the broom and watch her and her movements, each one neat and precise. She tears a T-shirt into strips, preparing patches to sew onto other garments. We can't leave the room, so she's keeping active, repairing what she can. The blast shredded most of our clothes. And my thoughts flit back in time ...

Twelve days.

Twelve days since the hospital basement, since facing Gabriel.

It feels like a bloody lifetime.

Venturing out in the daytime is still unsafe, so we've kept to the darkness of the city's derelict areas. Under broken streetlights, our tattered clothing matters little. In fact, it makes it easier to hide among the undesirables – the migrants, the homeless, the drudge workers.

I sigh and shift my gaze around the safe house. The room's twenty feet wide, up in the eaves of an old warehouse.

And the space feels a bit narrower than an hour earlier, the air that bit thicker too, more stifling. I sense the customary itch in my chest while the whispers in the back of my head grow louder … *Just get out of here, run, be free.*

I squeeze the broom handle and force myself to sweep. We've only been in this place forty-eight hours and still signs of our habitation linger on almost every surface – footprints, fingerprints.

My movements take me past the room's solitary window. I can feel a trickle of air on my back and stop to straighten up. A fresh breeze steals between the narrow boards, and I find myself moving my head closer, staring through the gaps.

Evening's descending on the city, the light bleeding out from above the rooftops – a ramshackle collection of tiles and corrugated-iron sheets – while smoke plumes rise from refuse fires in between the abandoned factories. Everything looks strangely calm under the cover of dusk, and still I can sense the river of life flowing just below, with all its sweat, its stink, its chaos.

Staring out, my chest tightens, the vertical boards like prison bars.

And Gabriel. I can't help picturing the archangel out there, scouring the land and sky for us right now.

I step away from the window, and my gaze falls on Natasha again. My mouth feels so dry, and inside me, warm and cold currents swirl.

"He knows," I say eventually.

She ceases tearing the T-shirt, her hands stopping in mid-movement. Then she drops the scraps in her lap and glances up at me.

"It was only a matter of time," she says.

I nod. There have been no infections, no warnings, no alarms. We've been watching the hospitals, looking out for obvious signs.

Twelve days. There should have been symptoms by now.

"There was no way to keep it hidden," she says, smiling.

The arc of her mouth draws me in, the brightness in her eyes. A part of my brain rails at me to look away, to busy myself elsewhere. It'd be so much easier.

And still I hold her gaze. The feeling of warmth pulls at the edges of my lips, and I find myself smiling back. The sense of constriction abates, the itch in my chest lifts a little, and the walls inch back outward.

Sitting there, she seems to glow. I can see the confidence in her eyes, the trust, just like in the laboratory. I remember her standing there in the loading bay, outlining her crazy plan – to pull the disease *out* of the priest's van, to put it into the storage room, right beside the barrel bombs.

All those times I went on and on at her about the principles of the con, of misdirection. I assumed she was ignoring it, humouring me. But no. It was her idea. *Hers*. To leave the disease in the warehouse again, just as I did before. The double con. Those times she chastised me for it – the estate, Qetesh's club – fooling people by pulling the same trick twice. Yet she used it to perfection.

Natasha. This is the nurse I met in the hospital only days before that, so earnest, so straight. I shake my head. Unrecognisable.

Knees together, she clasps her hands in front of her. "Do you think he's worked out what happened?" she says.

"That he blew up his own disease?" I say.

And my thoughts flit back twelve days again.

That conversation, the incinerator room … Gabriel. I sometimes wake up with nightmares about it. It was like walking a razor wire – conning an archangel, convincing him to press the detonator; goading his anger, his desire for vengeance. Gabriel had to believe the disease was on the incinerator chute. Had to. I can still see the priest's frenzied attempts to get the boxed vials onto the metal ramp. But of course it was a pallet of the real cancer treatment that we'd taken from the back of his van. And then – clearly immune himself – Gabriel pulverised those boxes, spread the serum everywhere, thinking he was infecting us, that we'd become his carriers. It was the only way he'd ever let us leave alive.

Crazy.

"He's an archangel," I say. "He's worked it out."

Natasha nods, and a shiver rolls through her body. Then her gaze drops, and she picks up the T-shirt in her lap while my insides tighten again.

"And now he'll be after us forever," I mutter, images swirling of Mandem still out there looking for me, and now a fucking archangel, too.

Yet Natasha continues with her repairs, a single line of determination creasing her forehead. For her and the priest, this is all intended. And what's coming next will present itself in good time, all exactly as it should be.

The memory comes of the nun in the station, sacrificing herself that I might live. Was it a random act of kindness, or was she an agent of God's will, enabling my role in all this?

The priest's words continue to parade through my mind. *It's all God's will if we choose to see it that way. Just trust. What other choice do we have?*

"Almost ready?"

The voice makes me jump. I spin around to face the door.

Father Thomas stands there on the threshold. The quietness of the man's approach is still unnerving. He smiles back at me, lines creasing his temples, and I can feel the tension at my core melt a little.

Natasha's on her feet, fingers gripping the T-shirt.

The priest smiles at her also and shakes his head. He still wears that same disguise – the senile old man – grey hair unkempt, shoulders hunched. Gradually, he unfolds his body, and the glint returns to his eyes. He shuts the door carefully behind him.

"No sign," he says. "Gabriel's bombs left nothing but rubble, and the police have the building cordoned off, but there's no active interest, nothing untoward that they've discovered." His gaze finds Natasha. "Also, there's still no sign of infection elsewhere, clearly no second batch."

The momentary relief in my chest quickly morphs into sparking heat. No infections means we've got nothing to do. Nothing but bloody skulk and hide. I find a coin in my pocket and begin revolving it between my fingers.

Natasha nods. "And the janitor – did you discover anything?" she says.

The priest sighs. "I'm not sure. He may be an Orisha, a Haitian deity. They're truly ancient. My teacher used to speak of them." He steps further into the room. "He could be one of the oldest, a figure prayed to as a saviour from slavery. Maybe over the centuries he moved his focus onto humanity's ultimate bondage – angel over man. Maybe he's been trailing Gabriel as I have."

"Did he survive the archangel's attack, the fight?" Natasha says.

Father Thomas shrugs. "Who knows?" he says. "We can't go back to the incinerator. It's too dangerous. And even if he *is* dead, we wouldn't find a body. Angels rarely exist alone. Others will be taking care of things."

"Others?" I say.

The priest ignores me and strides toward a duffel bag in the corner. "We need to get going," he says and hoists it onto his shoulders. "We've already been here too long. I found another place, on the east side. It's a little smaller but we should be able to remain there a few days."

Natasha heads toward the window. "But it is still dusk," she says. "It's not late enough."

"It's okay, though," the priest says. "It's already getting dark outside. Plus, it's good to vary our routines."

I heave another sigh and go back to sweeping.

Packing up takes only minutes. We're well rehearsed. I grab a bag and swivel to face the open door, my mind already conjuring images of the next safe house we'll be stuck in. Just one more move in a lifetime of damn practice.

Natasha approaches. I step to the side to make way and bump the back of my head on the brickwork behind. She glances up at me as she passes and wraps her fingers around my forearm. I remain rooted to the spot.

She lets her fingers drop, and I watch her pad out of the door and off down the top-floor corridor. Holes line the brickwork, and the walls stand covered in soot from the fires below around which vagrants huddle. I follow her, the priest at my back. And an echo of the warmth stirs again at my core.

We descend the building. The going's slow, most of the stairwells having been pulled up for firewood. And by the time we reach the first storey, I feel a scratching desire to go faster, to get the hell out of this place.

Natasha climbs down the final rafters and then slinks toward the open doorway, a slice of sky visible under the head jamb. I jump the last few feet. Pain lances up my ankles, and I stare out at the cobbled alleyway between the old storehouses. It's crammed with broken crates and barrels, a maze of passageways in between, perfect to run and get lost among.

I teeter on the threshold, an image forming of Gabriel on the incinerator, the crazed fury in his eyes.

The priest leans in. "God will be there when we face him," he says.

I can't help taking a step back, glancing across. "*When* we face him?" I say.

There's a knowing expression on his face. His eyes twinkle.

"In the meantime, there's much for us to do together," he says. "Preparation, practice."

I find myself staring over the top of the neighbouring storehouse, the setting sun barely visible above the slanted roof. My fingers go back to revolving the coin in my pocket.

"Yes, the tricks are useful," Father Thomas says. "But there's a great deal more you can learn."

He grips my shoulder, and I step through the door at his side.

"This has been but one act of a millennia-old play, one turning of the wheel that will now spin ever faster," he says with a pat on my back. "We'll need to be ready."

———

THE FAITH TRILOGY continues in Book Two – **Wrath** – which is currently available on Amazon. For updates on the series and to get your free ebook, join my reader list today by visiting:

https://www.thefaithtrilogy.com/free

# FACTION - YOUR FREE EBOOK IS WAITING

**Destroying Gabriel's disease was just the beginning**. Now Natasha and Jake are on the run, hiding from an irate archangel, and being urged by Father Thomas to develop the abilities they'll need for the coming fight. Natasha's desperate to discover Gabriel's plan, to identify angelic activity, while Jake's working hard just to keep them safe.

Yet perhaps he's looking in the wrong place.

When the gang that enslaved him for six years re-emerge, they aren't merely seeking their best thief; it turns out a growing Mandem army want Jake for a specific job, and one that bears all the hallmarks of the angelic activity he's trying so desperately to avoid.

Jake soon realises that what's at stake isn't just his own freedom and Natasha's safety, but the freedom and safety of a growing army of the downtrodden – young grunts just like him. And as Mandem's plan unfolds, it becomes clear that there won't be a corner of London unaffected.

In this heart-pounding tale of survival and rebellion, Jake must confront his past, harness his powers, and lead a revolution against forces both human and divine. The fate of a city hangs in the balance.

———

Get a free ebook copy of the immediate sequel in the series – **Faction** – the short story between Faith and Wrath, by visiting:

https://www.thefaithtrilogy.com/free

# SPREADING THE FAITH?

Thank you so much for joining Natasha and Jake on the adventure. If you enjoyed the book and have a moment to spare, I would greatly appreciate a short review on Amazon. Even just a sentence is wonderful, and reviews make a big difference in helping new readers find the series. Thank you!

————

As a reminder, receive a free ebook copy of the immediate sequel in the series, **Faction** – the short story between Faith and Wrath – when you sign up for my reader's list. You'll also be notified about upcoming releases and additional features in the series. Just visit:

https://www.thefaithtrilogy.com/free

# ABOUT NICK NIELSEN

Nick loves reading clever, fast-paced, and engaging fantasy stories which say something about the real world we live in. So much so that he decided to write them. Professionally, he's an award-winning entrepreneur, the director of the social change agency Osca, and the founder of Envision – a Guardian Charity Award winner. He's also a winner of the Shackleton Leadership Award. In his fantasy stories he leans heavily not only on his professional background working in the area of behavioural psychology, but on his twenty-year experience learning from real magicians – practitioners of the mystical arts – from Eastern, Western, and African lineages. Nick lives in London with his wife, two overly chilled teenage children, and one neurotic bunny rabbit.

# ACKNOWLEDGMENTS

First to you, the reader, for not only investing your valuable time in this book but also for continuing through the scrubland of the back matter to find out who I might be humbly thanking. And first of all ... this is you. Your care and attention are the reason we authors write – to entertain, enliven, and bring you joy. But this is only possible because of your curiosity and commitment, without which there would be fewer stories, and the world would be a considerably poorer place.

So thank you. I sincerely hope you found the investment worthwhile.

Continuing on, there are a great many people to thank. Foremost is Leslie Watts, this trilogy's amazing editor. When I first came to her five years ago with the story idea, she showed nothing but enthusiasm for the project, despite the roughness of my writing. I am so thankful for her kindness and enduring patience in helping me to improve my craft over the innumerable drafts, for her dedication to the project over the five years it took to complete, and her absolute commitment to the craft in not letting me run ahead and publish before the books were as good as we could make them.

In finishing the final versions, thank you so much to Amanda Brown for her love of the words, and to Alison Birch for her eagle eye. Thank you also to Stuart Bache for the wonderful cover designs.

And then there's my amazing tribe. Thank you Eva and Luke for your love, patience, and impatience with this project, and for understanding the stupid thing their dad does every single morning at five am. Thank you, Beth for always being there, for being my biggest supporter and most demanding critic, and for more than I can ever say. Thank you to a mother whose heart and home are always open, and to a father for whom it all became too much in the end. We miss you, we honour your choice, and we thank you for everything you gave us. Thank you, brothers and sisters – Thomas, Trine, Sach, and last but definitely not least, Steph. Thank you, fellow story craft lover, both for the ongoing support with this project and for walking alongside me on this crazy journey.

Thank you to my own Father Thomas – Colin, Saniel, and Krishna. My debt of gratitude to you, your care, and your work is also more than I can express.

Thank you to my readers over the years – to Ian, Mark, Chris, Thomas, Debs, Ray, and Dave – and to my teachers of the craft, Danielle and Rachel and the many others. Thank you also to Shawn Coyne without whom these books would have been published five years ago, and yet so much of the richness in both them and me would have been lacking.

Thank you to Ian Craig, who was there near the beginning. And thank you to Jean who encouraged me right from the start. It's almost fifteen years ago now, and I don't know if I'd have gotten here without you.

Thank you all.

Made in the USA
Middletown, DE
04 June 2024

55255529R00255